MUTE

BRAD STEEL

GRAPHOS
BOOKS

graphosbooks.com

MUTE

1. noun

Carcass displaying unusual and inexplicable features such as burns, excisions, incisions, and the absence of blood or organs.
[abbr: mutilation]

2. transitive verb

To silence; render unable to speak.

Library and Archives Canada Cataloguing in Publication

Steel, Brad, 1969–
Mute: a novel / Brad Steel; edited by Monique Kovithavongs.

ISBN 0-97 36421-0-6

I. Title.

PS8637.T44M88 2005   C813'.6   C2004-905310-8

This is a work of fiction. Names, characters, places, and incidents
are either the products of the author's imagination, or are used fictitiously,
and any resemblance to persons living or dead, business establishments, institutions,
events, or locales is entirely coincidental.

This book contains an excerpt from the forthcoming novel *CRUDE* by Brad Steel. This excerpt has
been set for this edition only and may not reflect the final content of the forthcoming book.

The lyrics on page 36 are from "Origami" by Ani DiFranco. Copyright © 2004
by Righteous Babe Records. All rights reserved. Used by permission.

GRAPHOS

BOOKS

graphosbooks.com

PRINTED AND BOUND IN CANADA

10 9 8 7 6 5 4 3 2 1

For Tia,
my everything.

PROLOGUE

Ten months ago
The Canadian Midwest

THE FALLING SNOW was Dr. Duncan Henderson's second rude surprise of the very early morning.

First had been the phone call.

At three-twenty—the latter bit of Henderson's critical fourth sleep stage, and the onset of REM. In his early years as a neurologist, he'd studied the sleep patterns of many subjects under widely varying circumstances. He'd also learned to sleep with electrodes plastered to his own skin while computers logged his polysomnographic data. If that still held true, the phone had begun its warbling assault precisely when his pons—a structure in the brainstem—was in the midst of switching off motor neurons in his spinal cord, causing temporary paralysis.

Despite the typical age-related changes in Henderson's body since he'd done the testing—not to mention that seven-time-zone differential—it seemed his sleep patterns were more or less unchanged. He'd had a hard time responding to the call, which he might attribute equally to exhaustion. But REM was also the stage when his dreams were at their most vivid—and the blasted phone had shattered a delightful image of his childhood home in Glasgow, tonight distorted Seussville-style and painted up in impossibly vivid primary colours. Better still, a talking giraffe had moved in and was serving up pancake-like crumpets better than a foot thick, slathered in day-glo Scots *blaeberry* jam.

A marvellous dream. Bloody shame to have interrupted it—especially considering the nightmares that had beset him these past several nights.

And snow in June, for pity's sake! They'd told Henderson the stuff could come any month of the year in these parts, and though he hadn't doubted it was *possible*, he'd hoped such a thing to be an extreme rarity: like an epochal flood or a plague of gnats. *Perhaps the gnats would be next...*

It was still incomprehensible that the weather here could be so extreme, and that he'd found his first Canadian winter so utterly unbearable. After all, he was a hardy *Glaswegian*. Even the southernmost tip of Scotland sat farther north than here, and Glasgow was at the very same latitude as Moscow. Unlike the Russian capital, however, with its legendary winters that defeated the likes of Napoleon and Hitler, Glasgow benefited from warm winds off the Atlantic, and was hunkered between great hills to the north and southeast. Back home, the moist air's chill went right through your clothes and into your pores, yet even in January the temperature seldom dipped much below freezing. It could be highly unpleasant, but he couldn't recall it ever killing anyone. Forty below could do the job in *minutes*. The low humidity would probably leave you freeze-dried, he thought with a grin, so that in the spring all they'd find would be a shrivelled husk which could be reconstituted with hot water to present nicely in a casket.

Not only was the snow still coming, but it was damned cold out—and the mercury continued to plummet.

Not good. The first snowflakes to fall would have melted on contact with the blacktop. If that were to freeze, a slushy build-up over it would make for utter treachery.

But it was urgent, Regional Director Frank Weissmann had said. The subject—a sixty-four-year-old male—had died of respiratory failure just after midnight, and the post-mortem was to begin immediately. Two other pathologists worked at the facility and both would be present tonight, each of them capable of handling the entire procedure alone if necessary. But Weissmann had demanded Henderson get over there *immediately*. It was he—by far—who had the most experience.

And in spite of the timing and road conditions, Henderson actually wanted to go. Since coming to Canada fourteen months ago, he had already examined nearly fifty dead subjects, but this was a rare *human* one.

Human beings were what Henderson was trained for, as a neurologist and clinical neuropathologist. Even among his Edinburgh peers—themselves considered the word's finest—he'd been without question the foremost expert, having conducted more post-mortems on cases of this kind than anyone alive.

Then he'd done the disappearing act. Retired, officially, due to a make-believe heart condition. At forty-four, if anyone believed it.

It had been unexpectedly pleasurable relocating his family on an acreage a half-hour north of the town of St. Paul, to pose as a hobby farmer and in-house animal nutritionist at a pet food plant located another fifty kilometres into nowhere. Mairi, his wife, had adapted well to life on the little alpaca ranch they'd been provided—fully furnished and loaded with wonderful new possessions from pro-quality kitchen appliances to his-and-hers Sea-Doos and four-wheeled sport ATVs. And the money Henderson was earning made it possible for Mairi to quit working as a physiotherapist and focus at last on her art. She was an exceptional portraiture artist in many media—charcoal, pencil, gouache, watercolours—but she had an incomparable mastery of oil paint. Her paintings were always, as anyone able to make the comparison was certain to attest, more lifelike than the model. Mairi had a rare gift for creating ultra-realistic depth through some inexplicable synthesis of shadow and light via her palette of pigments. Even better, she possessed an uncanny ability to observe and play up the subtle details wherein dwelled every person's essence—without ever going just a wee bit too far and turning the rendition into a caricature. By restoring the dim twinkle of girlhood mischief in an old woman's eye, or augmenting a whimsical smirk in a gentleman's lips that was in reality all but imperceptible—she created *life*. It was wondrous to observe. Since moving here, she had taken advantage of the tranquillity and produced an impressive number of works. She seemed to thrive on the bloody isolation.

Yes, Mairi was getting on just fine here.

It was not so easy an adjustment for young Glenn and Fiona. With their polished manners and rolling Scottish brogues, they spoke and behaved quite differently from the other kids at the school in town, and both had been demure enough to begin with. Especially the laddy—but he too was holding his own. It would get easier. He'd promised them that. Kids were remarkably adaptable.

Henderson peeked into the room where the *wains* slept. The house had five large bedrooms, yet the children had insisted on bunking together here just as they had back home. Light from the bright security bulb outside reflected off the new snow on the ground, and was then diffused by millions of fluffy white orbs that continued to tumble down from heaven like puffs of goose down. It created an unearthly effulgence in the sky and bathed the children in an artificial pink glow. As always, Glenn slept covered in a fetal self-embrace, thumb in his mouth just as the ultrasound had first shown him inside Mairi's womb. Fiona was atop her blankets, spread out like a red-haired starfish. Little furnace, that one.

Henderson smiled, and padded back to his own bed to give Mairi a peck on the forehead. Her blue eyes flicked open momentarily and she mumbled a goodbye, one he did not expect she would remember in the morning. She would understand he had to go, though. Mairi always understood.

Inside his salsa-red Toyota Tundra, Henderson immediately hit the elliptical H2/H4 button to activate four-wheel-drive. He'd need all the help he could get to keep it between the ditches tonight. One of the best things about Canada was the lorries. You never called them that here, of course. They were *trucks*. It was still a thrill to drive a full-sized pickup on the broad, mostly empty Alberta highways. You could easily put a hundred miles behind you in an hour, with little chance of getting stopped.

Not that being pulled over was ever a concern. Immunity to civil laws was another of the job's perks. Still, he'd been advised not to flash the black passport too often. The police in rural Alberta were federal, thus quite easy to control from the Commissioner down, but there were far too many individual officers to entrust with such important secrets. Here, everyone but the staff sergeant—the chief-of-police and detachment commander—was kept completely in the dark about what really went on at NutraPet Foods.

That was the theory, anyway.

Henderson had been pulled over just once in more than a year of frequent speeding. "Jesus, is *everyone* at NutraPet a diplomat?" the constable had said with a smirk, shaking her bonnie head. That was Jessica Bolduc, a dark-haired beauty he'd heard jocosely referred to by men in town as *Officer Bulldike*.

No legal immunity would be called for tonight. You'd be taking your life in your hands even to drive the posted limit.

He wondered what he would see very soon on the slab. They'd do a complete post-mortem, of course. He'd help another pathologist, either Jean Letendre or Carol Benson, to cut a Y-incision from shoulders to midchest and down to the pubic region. All the internal organs would be removed, then measured, weighed and examined using the method of Virchow.

While the bodily organs were being looked at and the data noted on a blackboard, Henderson would occupy himself with the most important part—the brain. He fully expected to find countless vacuoles in the cerebellum and astrocytosis in the cerebral cortex. But would there be cerebellar amyloid plaques, like in the New Guinea cases? Or necrotising lesions throughout the white matter as he'd seen in several of his Edinburgh subjects? One never knew until the skull vault was sawed open and the dyed tissue slides went under the microscope.

Henderson trembled, though the heater embedded in his bucket seat was functioning well and the air in the cab was now better than room temperature. He gripped the wheel tighter to steady himself. The Director had seemed especially uptight on the phone tonight. Perhaps that had rubbed off.

Things were not going well at work, for certain. Carol Benson, one of the other two pathologists, had told him some disturbing things, and he'd decided two days ago to personally talk to the Director about them— without betraying his source, naturally. While pacing the corridor outside the closed door of Weissmann's office, he'd overheard Charles Busby, the American Director-General, blow his top. From the voices, Henderson recognised Weissmann and a weasel-eyed man named Paul Warburton, the Pennsylvania-based Chief of Biotechnical Research. Punctuated by booms of a meaty fist on Weissmann's mahogany desktop, Busby had roared that the project—maybe the entire operation—had been compromised by an *information leak*. Carol Benson's name was also mentioned, though the context was obscure.

At that point, Henderson had absconded, knowing that being spotted anywhere in the area might prove fatal. Most of all, he feared what Busby's words probably meant.

More human specimens...

BOOK **I**

CHAPTER 1

The present day
Vancouver Island

DISCIPLINE—MAHATMA GANDHI SAID—is learned in the school of adversity.
I suppose if there's any truth to this, the past seven months ought to leave me with the discipline of a *kunoichi*, the female Ninja.

Kat Francis: Ninja Veterinarian.

I can handle that.

The first disaster came in late January: the sudden death of my brother Steve in a no-limits freediving accident. Steve had turned thirty-three only a week earlier, fourteen months behind me. He'd tried his hand at pretty well every extreme sport you can name, from street luge to ice climbing. I used to tease him that *extreme* was a euphemism for *stupid*, but no amount of badgering or pleading could have deterred Steve. More likely, every acknowledgement of the dangers he faced even heightened the thrill. Discovering new ways to imperil his own life—then pushing these to the limit—had become as fundamental to him as food, water, and air. A bona fide adrenaline junkie, psychologically dependent on the hormone as a stimulant.

Eventually realising this, Mom and I gave up trying to discourage Steve's appetite for endangerment and did our best to be supportive of his efforts. She and I arranged to meet that terrible afternoon in a downtown Victoria sports bar, along with a ragtag crew of Steve's thoroughly pierced and tattooed friends, to watch him dive in Guadeloupe on TV. I got there late, just as he began his descent.

I'd spent the early part of that day battling what I believed to be a stomach virus. Mom thought otherwise. She assured me it was purely psychological, that she often made herself physically sick worrying about Steve. As I nodded in resignation, people began to stand and gasp, all eyes locked on the TV.

It felt like the air had been sucked from the room. The sportscaster's voice seemed to now be coming from within my own skull: *Folks, this isn't good. It looks like Steve Francis is unconscious. He keeps spiralling deeper and deeper. Good God, what a terrible turn of events...*

I can tell you those are his exact words. They've resounded in my mind a million times.

Next, as the longest minutes of my life dragged by, we shared the horror of watching Steve die in real-time, courtesy of the satellite video feed.

His descent to a hundred and eighty metres below the surface of the Caribbean Sea on a weighted "sled" would have been a world record. But two or three metres shy, he lost motor control. *Samba* is the funky word they've got for it.

Then he blacked out. By the time the rescue divers got him back to the surface, his heart had stopped. It was too late for the lone French doctor—who wasn't equipped with a defibrillator—to revive him. I shrieked, and threw myself at the big TV screen, pleading for the little man to thrust harder, to continue the chest compressions a bit longer.

To no avail. My brother was gone.

There's now talk in the freediving community of awarding Steve the record posthumously, since the underwater footage clearly shows he had one hand on the sled when it reached the marker. It wouldn't be the first time a freediving record stood when the athlete didn't survive to exercise bragging rights. It's how deep you get that counts; making it back up alive is not amid the criteria. I hope they toss the record out, for the sake of all the other nutbars like my brother out there.

The shock and grief of losing her only son must have done a number on Mom's immune system, because her breast cancer exploded out of its eight-year remission like a lion from a Roman pen. It spread fast, metastasising through her lymph nodes into her liver, lungs and brain. Then, nine weeks after finding myself an only child, I was also an orphan.

I've been fatherless most of my life. My dad passed away two weeks before my fourth birthday from complications due to miner's pneumoconiosis, better known as *black lung*. He'd survived more than two decades in a career replete with earthquake-like "bumps" and methane blowouts, then died within weeks of the last remaining BC shaft mine being shut down in favour of open-pit operations that don't expose workers to deadly coal dust.

My life is like that. A tapestry of ironies.

I was still floundering in the details of Steve's estate when Mom succumbed.

Named by both as sole heiress and executrix (the latter being unquestionably the most burdensome honour with which a person can be bestowed), I fulfilled my obligations in a haze of grief. I took the easy route in disposing of their worldly possessions, hiring a liquidation company to sell off most of the collective assets in a single offsite auction. A room in my house contains the rest, stacked to the ceiling in uniform brown mover's boxes. When the time comes to open them, I will surely curse my impulsive decisions about which items to keep and which to let go to auction. I think I'll put that day off for as long as I can.

After mom passed away, the next crisis was my own doing. Bad things happen in threes, they say, and perhaps I was unwilling to simply sit back and wait for the final one. With the anguish of suddenly losing my family unit, I no longer had the strength to carry on the charade that was my marriage. I'd known for some time that Jack and I were not meant to be, and it seemed I might as well perform all the surgeries while the cavity was wide open.

Bad idea.

The divorce proceedings wrapped up only three weeks ago. Jack claimed my decision caught him by surprise—shows you how much attention he'd been paying. He came back at me with more vigour and intensity than I had seen him show in ages. The battle was far worse than I was up for, and I'm not even sure how I escaped with my sanity.

*   *   *

FOR SIX years, I've been running my current veterinary practice on the ground floor of a Greater Victoria office building. After earning my DVM, I stayed in Saskatoon a further four years, doing research in the Small Animal Clinical Sciences Department of the University of Saskatchewan's College of Veterinary Medicine, on back-to-back postdoctoral fellowships. It was during my final year of research that I met Jack. We married eight months later, immediately after he finished his business degree, and moved together to my hometown on Vancouver Island. The move was quite a shock for him. Having lived in landlocked Saskatchewan all his life, Jack had never even *seen* an ocean before. And suddenly, he found himself living on a ribbon of land completely encompassed by the biggest body of water in the world.

I lost myself in building my new practice, while Jack became focused on satisfying his addiction to painkillers—selling the odd piece of commercial real estate on the side. Back in college, as running back for the Huskies, he'd suffered a stress fracture to his fourth lumbar vertebra that led to spondylolysis. (That's when your vertebrae and intervertebral discs go all to mush.) In Jack's case, the bones continued slipping further and further out of alignment, until anti-inflammatories and even epidural steroid injections were of no use. After years of suffering, he finally went through with a decompressive laminectomy to remove the part of the bone that put pressure on the nerves, followed by spinal fusion to compensate for the lost stability. But the pain persisted, and a narcotic similar to morphine called oxycodone became Jack's best friend. He managed to continue working a little—barely earning enough in commissions to pay for his drugs. As the addiction worsened, he devoted an increasing amount of his time and energy to building a network of illicit sources for the tablets. Jack was so out of it most of the time, I still wonder how he managed *that*.

He promised repeatedly to get help, but never took the first step on his own. The handful of times I booked him in with an addictions counsellor, something urgent always came up at the last minute . No surprise. He didn't want to quit, to beat the addiction and go back to the pain. He tried cold turkey once, but it was predictably short-lived.

Even if I had truly loved Jack, it would have been hard to stay with him. But I never did.

* * *

I'VE JUST completed an ovariohysterectomy on Perla—a stray cat adopted by a sweet old widow named Lucia Perez after a family down the block moved out and abandoned the poor animal. Lucia took the gorgeous, long-haired silver cat home, unaware it came with plenty of excess baggage: ear mites, roundworms, a tapeworm, and a tummy full of kittens. She hit up all her friends and neighbours, but found not a single taker for Perla's unborn babies. I hate doing pregnant spays. It's more than just the added danger to the mother as a result of the increased blood and tissue loss. Kittens are among the sweetest of all baby animals, and it rips at my heart to snuff the life out of the tiny fetuses. I remind myself that the alternative fates for unwanted felines can be far worse—but weep nonetheless.

Perla is a scrapper, but once I wrestle the little mask over her snout and the isoflurane starts to flow, her pupils dilate and she soon surrenders, descending quickly into stage three anesthesia.

I get a bit of a hemorrhaging scare removing the cat's engorged uterus, but once I have the bleeding under control, the surgery goes as well as can be expected. I move Perla into a quiet kennel to recover, and have gone on to an emergency case—Ziegenbock the weimaraner's abraded footpads—when my stomach begins to churn and I feel slightly vertiginous.

Zieg is thunderphobic, which means that almost any loud, sudden noise can hurl him into an out-of-control frenzy. Last night brought a spectacular electrical storm—a rare occurrence on this island—and Zieg freaked. He leapt clear over a two-metre fence, then zipped amid vehicles on the Pat Bay Highway like a slalom skier dodging flags. It's a miracle he escaped with only fairly minor injuries: a few contusions, a partial axillary laceration, and deep abrasions to the pads of both hind feet. Zieg's master is Klaus Schuler, a Volkswagen mechanic who recently emigrated here from a village near Wolfsburg. I met Klaus when I took my Passat in for an oil change and spotted Zieg curled up near a vehicle he was working on. We connected instantly—and it turned out I got on well with his master, too.

Zieg is one lucky dog, though he probably doesn't feel like it. After getting him home, Klaus immediately wrapped the wounded feet in fresh rags, but didn't dare attempt to clean the still-frantic dog's wounds first. Zieg instinctively gnawed the fabric away to lick out the embedded dirt. A dog's footpads are filled with blood vessels, so he bled significantly during the night, at the same time making the beige carpet in Klaus's spare bedroom into a wall-to-wall pointillage of bloody paw prints.

I tell Klaus he waited too long to come to me—well past the eight-hour *golden period*, but luckily no infection appears to have set in yet. With his shiny bald head, rosy cheeks, and heavily stubbled face, the little man looks more like a frightened forest gnome than a mechanic. A tuft of white hair peeks out from his navy blue coveralls, zipped only to the middle of his chest, and his feet are in fuzzy brown slippers with rubber soles. His face and scalp are deeply suntanned, and his bulging grey eyes are encircled by permanent dark rings, more likely *allergic shiners* than a manifestation of fatigue. He watches as I work, grunting occasionally out of either approval or revulsion, though from his face it's impossible to tell which.

Zieg growls softly to let me know what I'm doing hurts a lot, but his amber eyes submit morose consent as I dab at the abrasions with chlorhexidine. He will probably leave these new bandages alone, sparing himself the humiliation of an Elizabethan collar, but I tell Klaus to come back immediately if that changes.

"Hear zat, Zieg? You chew on zese banditches, ve come bek and *die Veterinär* dress you up like a *wiebchen*," he warns, then continues to punch his PIN into the debit pad. Even with my very limited German, I recognise the word and smile. The dog squeezes his eyes shut, as if to block out the thought of looking like a *bitch*.

"You'll want to change the dressings every two to three days," says Pam, my pretty, raven-haired animal health technician. "A dog's feet perspire the same as yours do."

"Diz-*gooz*ting," Klaus says, wrinkling the bridge of his potato-dumpling nose.

"Worse than disgusting if he gets an infection and we have to remove a footpad," I say in a firm voice. "A dog his size *needs* those large ones for weight bearing."

"*Ja. Verstanden.*" Klaus says softly. *Understood.* He continues to nod sombrely as he nudges Zieg towards the door, the little mechanic's jaw bouncing like an open glove box as his handsome silver hound tries out his feet. Zieg struggles initially in his slippery socks, spinning out on the clinic's ceramic tiles. Then, at once, he lunges ahead, towing Klaus toward the exit with surprising inattention to his injuries. Klaus stops before opening the door and looks back wide-eyed at me, as if hoping for one final scrap of advice.

"He'll be fine," I offer. "If it looks like there's another thunderstorm coming, get Zieg into a quiet room with nothing he can break, and stay with him if you can. Stroke his fur and talk in a gentle voice," I say as I absent-mindedly scoop the morning's mail from the counter.

Klaus and Zieg leave, and the door bangs shut behind them. I use the front counter to steady myself. The slight nausea I initially felt while cleaning Zieg's wounds is much more severe now. My stomach tumbles end-over-end like a Slinky making its way down a long flight of stairs. *Something I ate?*

The mail carrier came by hours ago, and I tried to get to the stack more than once, each time distracted by some greater urgency. On top of the bills and flyers is a new addition that's impossible to miss. The oversized, once-white envelope is conspicuously grimy, not like any of the typical mailings an urban veterinarian receives, yet my name (or a variation thereof) is on the front. The packet's thinness tells me there isn't much inside. I am intrigued.

I retrieve my brass letter opener from the reception desk. My thoughts are diverted by another unexpected rebellion of my GI system as I slice open the sealed end of the big nine-by-twelve inch envelope, taking care not to sully my hands on its exterior.

I hold my breath and peek inside. No suspicious powder.

Still not breathing, I slide the contents out from their sheath, and look at one print, then the other.

What on earth? Such terrible images...

The clinic walls around me begin to spin independently, each on its own axis. My old sun-bleached poster of Favourite Cat Breeds and the bulletin board plastered with photos of lost pets crumble inward on one another like the crystals in a kaleidoscope.

Then it all blurs to nothing.

* * *

I AM down on the cold floor, whirling and shivering in the blackness. When I open my eyes, the ceiling tiles and reception desk come at me in violent thrusts, again and again and again and again. Then—just as abruptly—it all holds still. Something else slides into the scene, too close for me to focus on. I recognise the blurry tones as an abstract rendering of Pam's delicate features, framed in the soft descending rays of her plumb-straight black hair. When she draws back, I can see that her lips are parted and bowed in the shape of an upside-down jellybean.

"You... okay? Kat? I think you fainted. You—you fell."

"And I can't get up," I croak, trying to smile but not sure if it's working.

"Omigod, Kat. I hurried to catch you, but you went straight down. So suddenly—"

Head still spinning, I arch my back to elevate my butt from the floor, and shuffle my feet backwards until they are directly beneath me. Then I lunge upward.

A bit too quickly, I realize, and reach for the countertop. Gripping the laminate with my fingertips like a spider-woman on a wall, I suck in a few good breaths.

Better. I stand freely and smooth my knee-length khaki skirt, then tug the lapel of my white lab coat to re-centre it. I wobble a bit on my almost-sensible heels, and set my shoulders back in an effort to look unruffled. Pam grips my arms just above the elbows, and hits me with a glare of discord. My act is apparently a little weak.

"Easy," she says. "Let's sit you down, Casper."

"I'm fine." My voice, still frail and shaky, makes me feel like a liar exposed. "Did Klaus see *that*?"

She smiles a little, but her jaw remains clamped. "Doubt it. Zieg was flying him like a kite before you went down."

"That's a bit of a relief, though probably better for him to see it than you. Klaus doesn't have to work with me every day. God, I'm sorry about this."

Pam doesn't seem to be listening to me anymore. She drops into a crouch near my feet, and stares at the images on the floor. "What the *hell* are these?" It's the first time I've ever heard Pam use a remotely profane word. She is shaking her head quickly from side to side. "Oh! What happened to these poor cows?"

"I have no idea."

"Omigod. This is *sick*."

She scoops up the two contact sheets and the envelope, and sets them on the countertop, then draws her hands away and shudders as if she's accidentally handled rotten meat instead of mere images of it. Her fingerprints are plainly visible alongside the ones I made in handling the eight-by-tens. There seem to be no other prints—which doesn't truly reveal anything aside from that the sender knows how to properly handle a photograph.

The envelope, on the other hand, looks like it has been dragged along on a combat mission. Along with smears of dirt and who-knows-what, a coffee-cup ring bleeds off one edge. A white label is imprinted with spattery characters from a bad inkjet:

KATHERINE COLMAN
VICTORIA VETERINARY CLINIC

No postage stamp, and no return address. Hand delivered, then—and not by clean hands. In harsh contrast to the care someone has taken to keep the contact sheets clean, the rumpled envelope is a mess. Someone must have carried it around for a while before it got here.

The sender used my married name, which is not particularly strange in itself. Only a few friends and clients know that I've reverted to Francis, my maiden name. It'll take a while for the directories to be updated.

They also got the clinic's name wrong. The *West Saanich Animal Hospital* is what it's called. Technically, Saanich is not actually part of metro Victoria but a municipality unto itself. It's a distinction only a local would make, however.

I thank Pam for gathering up the items and offer another weak apology for my collapse. The girl has already been worrying too much about me. She is truly an angel—a reliable support and sounding board through my recent ordeals. Numerous times, when I was unable to make it in because of issues with the divorce or the estates, she shuffled my appointments and smoothed things over with frustrated clients, keeping the overall impact on the business remarkably small. I feel ashamed of myself for cranking up her stress level yet another notch. The boss getting sent dead cow photos then doing a jellyfish on the floor can't be easy to take in stride, even for a Steady Eddie like Pam.

"This didn't come in with the mail," I say to her. "Did you see who left it?"

She purses her lips and twists them to one side, something Pam does habitually when she is unnerved. "Not really," she says, looking confused. "I mean I found it in the mail slot, but I didn't see it actually get dropped in. There was a man standing outside the door about an hour ago. Strange old guy, in a green baseball cap."

"Just a hat? That *is* strange."

She smiles. "I'm glad you're feeling better. He was wearing a faded jean jacket and dirty black sweatpants. Caked up with dried mud or something." She thinks some more, then continues, "He had a beard, mostly white, and a big paunch."

"A slumming Santa," I say, scanning my mental database for a match. The description doesn't sound like any of my clients—and Pam knows them all as well as I do. "But you didn't actually *see* him drop it in?"

She shakes her head. "Sorry. I was updating our pet food inventory and managing animal relations, not paying a lot of attention to what was going on in the outside world. I noticed the guy hanging around, then looked up again when he almost knocked over the newspaper box. See how it's out of place now? He gave it a boot, as if it was the box's fault, then stumbled into a little blue car and drove away. An old Honda Civic. My girlfriend Patty had one in high school, except hers was in better shape."

"Did you catch the license plate number?"

"That's a funny thing. There *was* none. I actually checked for the plate, since the guy might have been drunk and I thought maybe I ought to report him if he's getting into a car. But the bracket on his front bumper was empty. *Good*, I figured. Might get the police's attention."

"None in the back either?"

"Didn't see. That's when Mr. Ork over here started harassing the bull-terrier-bite shih tzu again, so I had to get up and move the dog to the back. Pam walks over to the fluffy white mixed-breed cat dozing atop several eight-kilo bags of low-calorie dog food, and gingerly strokes his back. Mr. Ork can't be bothered to move.

With his dazzling white hair and black throat patch, most people presume the cat to be named after the white-suited Mr. Roarke from the seventies TV series *Fantasy Island*. That is unless they happen to hear the cat working on a hairball, with his distinctive *Ork-ork! O-ork!*

I let out a sigh. Mr. Ork has been a ward of the clinic since his former owners' baby girl developed a severe cat allergy. They replaced him with a hypoallergenic curly-haired rex kitten they named Perm-Elia. "I've pretty well surrendered that Mr. Ork doesn't have the right stuff to be a clinic cat," I say. "Have you come up with any prospects?"

"If Zoé's kidneys get any worse, Jen Smart might need a replacement cat. I've just got to make sure Jen doesn't see Mr. Ork's dark side in the meantime."

"Right. Maybe we should put him on acepromazine until we find a good candidate."

Pam laughs. "I think we might need to start sedating you too, Kat. I'm so glad you decided to take next week off. You really need it."

I rub at my temples with my thumb and forefingers. It's been such a crazy day, I've forgotten that I'm supposed to be preparing the clinic for a week of my absence.

She squints, and her jaw protrudes comically, bringing to mind an image of an irate old woman. "You *are* still going kayaking on Sunday. *Right?*"

"You're really okay looking after everything?"

"I've been booking around it for weeks. Talked to Doc Gurney at Central Vic, and he said they'd be happy to take care of our emergency cases. They've always been great whenever I've run into a snag. That's where I've been sending clients when you're unavailable and after hours, and I've never heard anything but praise for the service they get. Yet they always come back here."

"That's because we're cheaper."

"No. They love us, that's why. One week won't change that. So what does that leave me to do? Sell cat food and remove a few sutures? If I'm lucky maybe do some x-rays and refill the odd prescription. I think I'll manage."

I know she's right. The Central Victoria Veterinary Hospital is a good place, and it's true that they don't tend to steal our clients. It was founded about thirty years ago as the island's only twenty-four-hour vet clinic, and it still handles most of the city's after-hours emergencies. I have a lot of respect for docs who can pull night shifts. I'm a day person, and don't think I could handle shiftwork on an ongoing basis. It *would* be nice to have a clinic with other vets and a team of animal health technicians, not to mention ward nurses and a dedicated receptionist like Central Vic has.

One day.

"Make sure to bring a few books to read at the desk," I say. "It'll be a little dull around here."

Some part of me has been hoping Pam would plead with me *not* to go. This is to be the first real vacation I've taken since opening the clinic. Like most business owners, I've turned into something of a control freak. Entrepreneurial Disease, I think it's called.

No question, though, I am in dire need of a vacation.

A few photos of carved-up cows really ought to be nothing. The images *are* grim, but should hardly faze me, much less make me faint outright. I've *never* fainted in my life, and I've witnessed a lot of hideous sights in my years as a vet. What's really bizarre is that even before I saw the pictures, I had already begun to feel woozy. Perhaps it was a premonition of some sort, like the way I felt ill right before Steve died. Many things in my life have caused me to wonder if I have some kind of extrasensory perception, though I have yet to identify one of my mini-premonitions early enough. Perhaps it's my own stubbornness that keeps me from acting on them. I have a hard time with anyone—or any*thing*—telling me what to do.

And that's why I'll probably ignore the voice screaming at me not to go on this trip.

CHAPTER 2

FROM WHERE I SIT, there is a spectacular view of Patricia Bay and, beyond that, Saanich Inlet. The stone patio was originally built eighty years ago on one of several natural rocky terraces that are now the backyard of my house. Not long ago, it was *our* house. Jack's and mine.

It's a monstrous place, and I at times questioned why I was fighting so hard to keep it. *He* would surely have sold it off. But from up here tonight, witnessing alchemy as the setting sun turns seawater into gold, there's no doubt I made the right choice.

The right choices.

Ironically, if Mom hadn't died, I might have been forced to give the house up. Meagre as Jack's financial contributions were, they helped us squeak by our monthly mortgage payments and keep from completely drowning in debt. Mom didn't have much money of her own, but she *had* inherited her parents' home in the posh Uplands of Oak Bay, where I grew up. After my father died we left Fernie, a mining town near the Alberta border, and moved in with my grandparents. The municipality of Oak Bay—the *Tweed Curtain*—is the most prestigious, not to mention the most English part of Greater Victoria. Grandpa made a good living from the two lumber mills he established up-island near Qualicum Beach after the war. He sold the mills in the late seventies for what was in those days very big money, but his investments tanked. A few years after he died, when Grandma was in her final days, Mom got her first look at the finances—and was shocked at how little was left. She returned to her former métier as a dressmaker to cover expenses—the biggest being property taxes on the house and its sprawling lot, replete with orchards and fountains. Fortunately, Mom hadn't lost her touch. Her beautifully detailed dresses and blouses sold at the island's most prestigious boutiques as fast as she could sew them.

Mom loved her work. Even as the ambulance took her away for what turned out to be the last time, she told the EMTs that she needed to get back soon to finish a gown she'd been working on. She spoke about that dress so many times in the auxiliary hospital that I knew exactly what it looked like—a two-piece number in beige silk, with small pearls sewn in around a delicate fern pattern. After she died, I found the dress in her sewing room.

It was *fabulous*.

It was also size five. *My* size—and it will need only a small amount of attention to be wearable. Perhaps I'll find the time to finish it myself.

Selling the place in Oak Bay was excruciating, but it enabled me to pay off my own mortgage and some other debts, including my old student loans. Of course, Jack sauntered off with a fairly handsome allotment. Not that Mom would have been displeased, I'm sure. It made me ill to watch the way he could woo her. I learned not to speak to Mom of our quarrels, not *purely* because she would always take Jack's side, but also because it distressed her terribly to know we weren't getting along. Our divorce would have devastated her.

So as long as Mom lived, I don't know if I could have left Jack. But the freedom I've obtained as a by-product of losing my mother has not made the loss remotely easier to bear. I'd slam-dunk my pride down the garborator and be begging at Jack's door in a blink if that could somehow buy me just one more day with Mom.

* * *

I LEAN back in my chair and take a sip of Merlot de Carsac. Normally, I'm a green tea girl—decaf in the evenings—but today calls for something stronger. Not that it's helping any. My thoughts continue to be unwillingly drawn back to the cow photos. I want nothing more than to forget all about them, but the mystery of their arrival and their sheer peculiarity keep drawing me back. I can't fathom why anyone would send such a thing to me.

And who?

Jack?

No question he is still harbouring a lot of rage. I know the man well enough to predict he will stay that way for a very long time. And though passive-aggressive is more Jack's style, psychological warfare is probably not beyond his limits. Has he invented the most convoluted way conceivable of calling someone a *cow?*

At the clinic, I was too startled, flustered, and dizzy to examine the animals in the pictures very closely. I peeked at them a couple of times afterwards— once before leaving for the day and again shortly after I got home—and made a few mental notes.

There were distinct sequences of several different animals—three of them herefords, two that were limousin, and one each of black angus, charolais, and simmental—surrounded by various types of flora. One of the carcasses was surrounded by numerous tiny yellow blossoms. A canola field. Another lay on harrowed black earth that had been lightly dusted with snow. All of the dead animals had been adroitly photographed to medium format film, on a 6x6 camera probably not all that different from my own fifteen-year-old Hasselblad 501. Decently composed pictures, with sharp focus throughout. Jack could certainly not do *that*. The photos he took with his silly point-and-click thirty-five-millimetre were consistently abysmal. He wouldn't know how to *load* a Hasselblad, much less focus one or adjust the aperture and shutter speed for the right exposure under the varying conditions on the contact sheets.

I contemplate this for a moment, then set my Merlot on the glass tabletop. Sasha, my intuitive five-year-old calico, senses I'm getting set to make a move, and rubs the pheromone glands of her face and flanks against my bare leg. I reach down and sink my fingertips into her luxuriant multihued fur, scratching behind her ears and in her favourite place—at the base of her back, where her body ends and her billowy tail begins.

It's like pushing the starter button for her purring engine. The velocity of a low-range cat purr is in fact the same as that of an idling diesel engine: twenty-six cycles per second. Sasha paces side-to-side, rubbing against my shins each way. I heave a sigh, calmed by Sasha's rumbling and the soft touch of her coat on my skin. Felines have that effect on people; it's known that cat owners tend to have lower blood pressure than the general population.

By that token, I should have hypotension. I've been a cat lover all my life. As a young girl, I was trailed by four purring companions everywhere I went (thus earning my nickname), but I have now been reduced to one warm-blooded dependant for the first time that I can recall. This excludes, naturally, the slippery denizens of my two indoor koi ponds. They came with the house. Nor can I count the gentle bull terrier that I brought home but Jack immediately named Arnie and claimed as his own. When he took Arnie away, I forced myself to resist the immediate compulsion to throw a new animal into the void. Let's see how long that lasts.

"I'll be right back, pretty girl," I tell Sasha.

She stares up at me, her huge yellow eyes narrowing to slits. *You'd better.*

Back in the house, I cross the walkway spanning the sunken koi ponds and navigate the dim rooms to my roll-top desk in the study. I touch the base of the capacitance-sensing lamp, and squint in its harsh light as I pull the top drawer out. Removing the *Canadian Veterinary Journal* that I placed on top of the envelope to hide it from view, I catch myself looking at the cover photo.

How *young* I seem in the picture, ramrod straight blonde hair nearly to my waist. Hard to believe that was just five years ago! I might have passed for nineteen, though I was actually all of ten years older at the time. Not long after the photo was taken, I cut my hair to shoulder length, then shorter still three weeks ago, the day my divorce was finalised.

It's made me appear more mature, people say. No more disbelieving chuckles when I tell someone I've been a doctor for ten years.

I don't really miss the hair. It wasn't me anymore.

When my friend Zaina first saw me after the big chop-job, she said I was a dead ringer for Anne Heche when she wore her hair short. Zaina read my blank look and chuckled at my ignorance. Although the name sounded vaguely familiar, I couldn't put a face to it. To educate me, Zane rented the *Psycho* remake the actress had starred in. I had to admit she was right. (Based on what I saw through the gaps between my fingers.) Both of us have blue eyes set far apart on a small face, with a not-so-small nose, thin lips, and a pointed chin. Even our body types are quite similar. I hope my mental situation is a little steadier than Anne's, from what Zane said. Perhaps in Beverly Hills, the recent happenings in my life might be considered normal.

The dog I'm holding in the photo is a caramel-coloured cocker spaniel named Daisy, for whom I performed cranial cruciate ligament repair under epidural morphine, adding an experimental blend of meloxicam and mepivacaine. My theory was that this would lessen the likelihood of her needing rescue analgesia. It worked. So did similar trials I reported, hence my moment of fame in the national vet community. Daisy and four others with similar problems responded beautifully to the experimental mixture, all with decreased pain scores over every time period.

I haven't done *any* research lately, and barely managed to keep my fingers in it before Steve's death. I just don't have the focus to balance it on top of my day job as solo veterinarian-*cum*-manager of a clinic. I keep pledging to spend some time in my little basement lab, but it's not happening yet.

I will. There is a lot of room for improvement in the care we give our animals. While treating them one at a time can be highly rewarding, you can't beat the feeling of making a discovery that may help many.

* * *

FROM INSIDE the drawer, the dirty envelope taunts me. Something about its mere presence is menacing, and I'm inclined to cover it back up and close the drawer. I've promised myself to leave the filthy thing and its repulsive contents there at least until after my kayaking trip, but I can't hold out that long. I need to take a better look. Maybe *this* time, the answer will be right in front of me. I take the envelope and close the drawer.

The desk also has two large box drawers on one side. In the upper one, I find my ancient magnifying glass, and palm it. I touch the lamp again to turn it off.

I flip a switch by the sliding doors, turning on the outside floodlights nearest my chair. With the last sliver of sun now sliding behind a small mountain across the inlet, I'll need them in a few minutes.

Another sip of Merlot and I'm ready to take a look. Sasha saunters over and curls up by my feet.

Even before opening the envelope, I notice something I missed earlier. On the bottom side of it, there's a U-shaped indentation. Something was once paper-clipped to it. A written explanation, perhaps, of what the fuck the photos were about? I squeeze the end of the envelope I slit open at the clinic, popping agape a toothless mouth. I peer inside, then turn it over and give a gentle shake. As the eight-by-tens emerge, I grasp them by the edges to avoid adding to the fingerprints Pam and I made on their glossy emulsions. Sasha arches her back like a Halloween cat and darts away between the trees.

"Thanks, chick. Abandon me in my hour of need," I mutter into the shrubbery. An eerie yowl is Sasha's unsettling reply.

The magnifying glass is a big, antique one with a lathe-turned wooden handle that retains only a few flakes of its original black lacquer. It belonged to my paternal grandmother. She and my dad's father spent practically their entire lives in Ware—a small town now on the north-west outskirts of London—and were both dead by the time I was in secondary school. I only met them once—when they came for Dad's funeral. I barely remember the day, having been only four, and have no recollection of anyone who was there.

This glass is the only heirloom my father had. Most people would probably keep it in a cabinet, where it could gather dust safe and untouched, but I'm a bit too practical for that. I tell myself not to get dizzy again, and risk smashing the precious antique on the stone patio. Just to be sure, I draw my thighs together and position the heavy lens nice and low over them, elbow over hip joint, so if my hand *did* happen to go slack, the glass would come down gently on my lap.

There are twenty-four images in all, twelve per sheet. A contact print is made by overlaying sleeves filled with negatives atop photographic paper (hence the *contact*), then exposing it briefly to light from an enlarger before developing and fixing the print like any photograph. These two were done with care, nicely centred on the photo paper.

Although I haven't used my own cameras much in recent years, my fascination with photography is undiminished. A long time ago, picture-taking was my immersion into the arts. I was always a doodler, but never became adept at expressing myself that way. The attraction of photography was natural—a perfect fusion of art with the sciences. A photographer starts out by artistically selecting, manipulating, composing, and cropping wonders of geological, biological, and architectural magnificence, bending light to create a precise but invisible negative replication of the subject on a substrate of silver-halide crystals. The latent images are made permanently visible by darkening the silver with chemical reducing agents. Finally, the procedure is repeated, bending light a second time to create a positive image on paper, once again chemically reduced and fixed. All that trouble to create a simple snapshot—or preserve an historic moment.

I can't help but feel something is being lost in the sudden shift to digital imaging. It seems a shame to replace the delightful uncertainty, surprise, and veracity of the traditional celluloid-based processes with an instantaneous conversion of photons to readily viewable, editable pixels.

* * *

I NOTICE a difference between the two sheets. Both were printed on Kodak Supra Endura, a pro paper often used by commercial photographers. But the filmstrips on one sheet are imprinted FUJI NPH400 while the other read KODAK PJ400.

The PJ400 is a Kodak Ektapress variety, no longer available. It was my personal favourite for shooting colour negs. I presume these Fuji photos are newer, the photographer having switched brands when the Ektapress line was discontinued. Or possibly a different shooter altogether.

I realize I am forestalling looking at the subject matter. It's not that the photos are horribly revolting in themselves. I see wounded and incised animals every day, and although some of the ones in the pictures have been decomposing a while, they're really not much worse. At least none of *these* animals are suffering.

What *is* it, then?

They're just cow carcasses, lying in a variety of unlikely poses. There seems to be a consistent sequence to the shots. The first image is invariably a full-frame photo of the entire animal, showing its position relative to the surrounding environment. The next two in each series are close-ups—detail shots of wounds.

Most of the carcasses are sternally recumbent—chest to the ground—which makes sense. Cows always stay upright, so long as they have any say in the matter. But a few of these didn't, it seems. Five—almost half of them—are lying belly-up. One of these is a black angus calf. It's on its back, or what little remains of the back, all four legs splayed away from the body in an X shape. Field stubble the calf had been feeding on still protrudes from its mouth in a tight bundle. This little guy died *suddenly*. All the entrails and internal organs have been removed, so there's little more than the spine and narrow strips of black-and-white hide connecting the hind quarters to the shoulders. The remaining meat of the carcass looks as clean as a Safeway T-bone, and my magnifying glass reveals not so much as a smear of blood on the yellow grain stalks around it.

The next frame is a close-up of the topmost part of the calf's head, where the ear and eye used to be. Even without the magnifying glass, it's clear that a sharp instrument has been used to cut away the skin, cartilage, and connective tissue. These incisions are inexplicably clean and bloodless—certainly not like what you'd ever see in an operating theatre.

It's a bizarre consistency in all the photos: no visible blood in any of them. Whomever killed the animals appears to have completely exsanguinated every one of them before beginning to cut.

The next set of frames I take the glass to is *really* freaky. A bloated hereford cow, also lying on its back. What gets me is the way it's lying: all four legs skyward, and the hind end partly suspended from the ground by the trunks of six aspens. The trees are all about the thickness of a wine bottle, and bowed outward near their bases under the big animal's weight. In order to get the cow into such a position, you'd have to lift her above the height of the trees—a good six metres—and drop her *straight* down. And it looks like that's exactly what has happened. The inner branches above the carcass have been sheared off, a single remaining twig bent sharply downward where it meets the trunk.

The first close-up photo of this cow shows that her jaw tissue has been cleanly excised to the bone, removed along with the flesh of the nape. The ears and eyes have also been sliced away. The incision around the eye is perfectly round, as if whoever did the cutting used a template of some sort. The tissue is a sickening brown, with a row of gas-filled bubbles emerging from one side of the cut. This one sat awhile before the photographer arrived. Clearly, someone with either a long lens or a very strong stomach took these close-ups.

The next frame shows three dark chasms in the same cow's hide, all flawlessly circular. There's a dinner-plate-sized hole where the cow's udder was, and between hind quarters parted by massive bloating, two smaller cores have been excised where the cow's vulva and anus belonged.

The remaining images are all variations on the same ghastly theme. The uniformity and cleanness of the cuts is consistently remarkable. Three of the sequences on the second sheet include close-ups of jawbones stripped of their tissues and cleanly removed vertebrae. For each of these particular animals, there is a crisply focused frame of a perfect round hole bored through the top of its skull, a secondary light source probably used to illuminate the vacant braincases.

And then there are more missing eyes, ears, anuses and udders. The organ thief clearly has a hang-up with certain parts.

"Who the hell would do this?" I whisper to myself.

Only now do I notice that two of the carcasses on the second sheet are shrouded in a faint blue haze. *What is it that's so familiar about that effect?* I wonder momentarily if it's a flaw in the processing. Then I am jolted by a recollection—a series of pictures I once took of leading-edge cancer therapies for pets, in the misguided hope of selling them for publication. Among several other treatments, I photographed dogs undergoing electron radiotherapy to destroy the malignant cells. Those particular images came back from the lab showing blue clouds just like the ones here.

These cows are radioactive!

I'm always leery of any theory or supposition that hasn't been authenticated enough to show up in textbooks and journals—yet here I am wondering if I'm looking at the work of extraterrestrial beings. Cattle mutilations are not a new phenomenon. I've heard a little bit about this stuff on radio talk shows, and have even chatted about the subject with friends and colleagues—usually amid tongue-in-cheek discussions encompassing the latest cover story of the *Weekly World News* and such characters as Ogopogo and the Abominable Snowman.

This is my first look at forensic evidence of any one of those things. On cattle mutilations themselves, I was more than a little sceptical. I flat-out believed the cases to be hoaxes, perpetrated by half-crazed hillbillies with enough time on their hands to do a somewhat convincing job of it—and given credence only by the gullible sorts who buy into anything that might diminish the harsh realities of real life.

Of course, *these* pictures may be fakes. Am *I* being gullible now?

Perhaps—yet not a thing about the photos gives me cause to believe they've been staged. With all the similarities between them, there is also a peculiar, unsettling randomness.

Moreover, few hillbillies would have the wherewithal to set these things up. In order to fake the blue-haze scene, someone would require not only surgical skills and equipment, but a means of acquiring and dispensing radioactive material. *And* the use of either a hoist powerful enough to lift a thousand-kilogram animal—or a slow-moving aircraft like a helicopter. In other words, the prerequisites would be not only a warped sense of humour and a steady scalpel hand, but a big budget.

And who *took* the pictures?

The most haunting question remains *why send them to Kat Francis?*

Sure, I am an animal doctor. But there are hundreds of veterinarians in western Canada who *specialise* in large animals. My patients are dogs, cats, rabbits, pocket pets, and the occasional domesticated ferret or pot-bellied pig. I haven't examined a bovine in years.

As I slide the contact sheets back into the envelope, a shudder ripples up through my body. It's followed by a powerful compulsion to get rid of the whole package, and to do it right now.

Throw the damned stuff in the fireplace and burn it!

I hear a soft but unmistakable rustling sound, and climb instantly to my feet, clutching the magnifying glass and envelope tightly to my breasts. I scan the property, watching my fruit trees, shrubs and hydrangea plants for the subtlest movement.

The queasiness of earlier in the day has returned to me.

Up here it can get windy, but the air is still now.

Could the sender be watching, making sure I'm appropriately frightened by his package? Surely it was sent to me for a reason.

My name is on it.

Will there be some kind of a follow-up?

I take my wineglass and go inside. I latch the patio doors, and automatically begin to check the locks on the other doors and windows. For the first time since Jack left, I wish that I did not live alone.

Sleep will not come easily tonight.

I pour myself a little more wine.

CHAPTER 3

IT'S A LONG-STANDING tradition for me to hook up with Zaina Marikar on Saturday mornings at Mount Royal Bagel. Years ahead of the nineties bagel craze, before I went off to college and Zane to Kenya, we would rendezvous at the original factory location on Park Street. We'd slather cream cheese onto our steaming whole-wheat cinnamon bagels at the sales counter, then jump in my car and smuggle our snack into a nearby café. Whenever the sweet aroma didn't compel us to devour everything en route, that is. About five years ago, a new Mount Royal location opened on Fairfield Road—complete with cappuccino machine and seating area—and eliminated the most stressful part of our Saturday. We now *nosh out* at once, sipping our lattés and trash-talking the men who seek to destroy our lives. The bagels may not always be *quite* as fresh as before because they're still made at the Park Street factory, but we agree it's an acceptable trade-off.

Meeting with Zaina to eat a food that was once exclusive to New York Jews—on the Jewish Sabbath—is a bit paradoxical. She grew up in a devout Muslim family, headed up by a fiercely anti-Semitic father. *They worship Moolah, not Allah* was one of his favourite rants. I'm glad Zane has not taken up many of her old man's fundamentalist ways. She likes to tell inquisitive people that Islam, Judaism, and Christianity are all religions of the same family.

The Koran, Torah and Bible would concur. Ishmael, the father of the Arab Nation, was half-brother to Isaac, who founded the Jewish Nation—both were sons of Abraham. The Prophet Mohammed, who of course gave rise to Islam, was a direct descendant of Ishmael, while Moses and Jesus descended from Isaac. So the three faiths truly do have common family roots.

And despite the violent battles that have raged between their followers through the ages, they share many congruent—sometimes identical—ideals and beliefs. Enough to help Zane and me to philosophically relate to one another most of the time, in spite of our family cultures being as different as the colours of our hair. I was raised an Anglican, and though it's been years since I sat in a pew, those beliefs have helped me through my most trying times. Many times it's been Zaina who reminded me of them.

I can't fathom why the world's embattled spiritual leaders can't put aside their egos and differences and focus on the abundant common ground, for all that's riding on the outcome. It's a nice luxury to be so simplistic, I suppose.

* * *

THE SWEET aroma of warm cinnamon bagels makes me remember I haven't eaten yet today. A fresh batch must have just arrived.

Zane's got her long, brown legs crossed at the knees, midway between ten Smarties-coloured toenails and one outrageously short skirt. A simple white tank top shows off her lean, muscular arms and a bit more of her perky little breasts than I am comfortable seeing here. Her wide, brilliant smile and wicked black-coffee eyes melt away the top layer of my panic.

"You're late, date," Zaina says with a few playful taps on her clunky black watch, which is also a heart rate monitor.

"By what, five minutes? That's only about half as late as the last three or four times."

"What—so you're telling me you are actually five minutes early, on *Kat Standard Time*?"

Her watch beeps as she fiddles with its settings. "I'm coming into your time zone, Kat. Right now. There... we... *go*. All done." Big Zaina smile.

"Now you'll be late for everything too."

"That's alright. Just as long as you don't start to compensate. My work commitments go by days and hours, not minutes. Those don't matter much aside from meeting you."

"Must be nice to be a freelance writer. Operative word being *free*."

"The hell it is. Sucks the big fat one, as always. *Free*loading and *free*falling is what it's about more often than not. Those are some bitchin' shoes, by the way. Where from?"

I glance down. I'm wearing a pair of open-toed Couture Vogs, with thick wooden wedge soles and a white dove hand-painted on the side of each upper. "Thanks. Picked 'em up at the John Fluevog on Granville Street when I was in Vancouver for that god-awful antibiotics seminar."

She squeals with delight, the fingertips of both hands to her cheeks. "I *knew* it. I'd die for a pair of Vogs. Well, maybe not *die*, but I'd hurt myself bad."

I smile, embarrassed, and look back at the shoes. "They're a little too hippie for me, but the salesman was a master of his craft. Truth is the damned things *kill* my feet, and I've had them on less than an hour."

"You just need to break them in."

"Shoes don't break in, girlfriend. Feet are a lot more malleable than leather and wood."

"That's what I mean. You've got to build calluses in the right places. Those babies are worth it. How much?"

"I don't remember," I say, not wanting to tell Zaina I dropped three hundred dollars on a pair of shoes I don't think I'll wear a second time.

She giggles. "Oh, you do so, you wench. You're just not telling me. That means they cost a mint. I envy you *so* much, Kat. I don't even dare go into Fluevog. My credit cards start to vibrate a block away."

"You don't want my life. I'm jealous of *you*, Zaina."

"I'll bet," she says, kicking an open-toed sandal up where I can see it. "Check these suckers out. Twelve million Turkish liras."

"Wow." I examine her feet more closely. The sandals appear to be very well made of dark brown leather, intricately braided and embossed in an ornate pattern. "What's that in Canadian money?"

"You *should* be impressed, Kat-Girl," she says blankly. "We're talking damn near eleven bucks here."

A grin spreads across her face, then she breaks into her unique, highly communicable giggle. It start out soft, and escalates, never failing to infect me, no matter how rotten a mood I've started out in. It feels especially good to laugh with Zaina today.

"Give me the Vogs and I'll bring you enough of these to fill a drawer next time I'm there," she finally says, teary-eyed.

"Deal."

"And then, when you're towing them all in a U-Haul behind your Passat to your hilltop mansion, think about me. A sardine in a bus, with my nose stuck in some drunken vagrant's armpit. Or else whacking red ants with a wooden shoe as they seize command of my miserable little basement suite."

"Right, Zane. And when the plane lifts off to take you to Albania, and you haven't got a care in the world, I hope you're thinking about me with my finger up a vicious samoyed's ass."

"I'm stuck here for a while yet. But how are *your* vacation preps going, Kat? One more sleep, right?"

I focus on Zaina's sandals again. "I think I'm going to cancel. I have a bad feeling."

"Oh, *no*. You're going, babe. That feeling is fear. It's a symptom of Getting-a-Life Syndrome. The only known cure is a thing called *fun*."

"I know. You're probably right. I'd be more excited if you were coming."

"Nope. Greece left me broke flatter than piss on a plate. Should've stayed in Turkey where I had free accommodations and the food was cheap. But Love went to Corfu and I followed."

"*Lust*, you mean. A person tends to remember *Love's* name two weeks after the fact."

"What*ever*. Even if I found two grand on the sidewalk, I wouldn't blow it on a week of paddling a boat the width of my butt over ice-cold water. I'd use it to pay bills, or to fly somewhere."

"Two thousand dollars is for regular customers. We get the high school buddies' special. And we could go tandem. I pay, and I paddle." I flex a bicep, and she indulges me by giving it a squeeze.

"Looks like all that Body Pump is doing you good. But I've got to decline, Kat. It's humiliating enough I'm going to ask you to pick up my bagel and coffee. I'm two weeks late on rent, and still a couple twenties short. I may still end up doing Love for Loot on Blanshard Street if I can't talk one of my publishers into advancing me on an assignment I've yet to start. Still feeling envious?"

"Always. You never let little things like rent cause you a fraction of the stress I go through over all my expenses at home and at the clinic. You're not going to get evicted, and it wouldn't even matter if you did. You've got a fool friend who lives in a half-empty house."

She glares at me briefly for the uninvited charity, then smiles. "I'll keep that in mind. The landlady isn't as easy-going as she used to be. I keep expecting to see all my stuff piled up by the curb whenever I come home."

It's harder than one might think to feel sorry for Zaina. She had it all at twenty-one, but walked away. A giant house in a quaint Ontario neighbourhood, a cute Alpha Romeo convertible, and a handsome and doting husband. She woke up one day certain she'd married too young, and fled. Left D'arcy and the house and the car behind. A week later, she filed for divorce. Then it was off to New Zealand, where she spent most of a year lying on beaches and staying with a different man every night. By the time Zaina checked back in, D'arcy was happily remarried with the first of a half-dozen rugrats in the oven. Funny thing is, I'm quite sure Zaina has never regretted her decision.

"You need me to take care of Sasha while you're away?" she asks.

"Pam offered to come by once or twice a day. My place isn't far out of her way, so I took her up on it."

"That's still a lot of trips for her. Are you sure?"

"It's probably better this way. Pam likes my cat, and Sasha gives Muezza stress. They don't seem to remember each other from one visit to the next."

"Oh, they always hiss and give each other the cold shoulder at first. But after two or three days, they're best buds all over again. That gives them at least ninety-six hours of nuzzling up and licking one another from nose to tail until you come home. Wish I could have that kind of happiness-to-hostility ratio in my love life."

"Please. I'd rather not think of you doing that with some icky backpacker." She giggles. "You like it."

"More than you want to know." We share another loud burst of laughter. "I guess it wouldn't have been a bad idea for our cats to get re-acquainted. You'll need me to look after Muezza when you go to Albania."

"I'm thinking Afghanistan now."

"*Zane*! You're nuts."

She smiles. "A little. I would *definitely* have been crazy to go during the war with Russia or under Taliban rule. It'll be safer now. I won't have to worry so much about being stoned to death for fornication. Speaking of which, I know a yummy Reuters journalist stationed in Kabul. He promised if I made it there, he would take me to Kandahar to visit the Forty Steps and Prophet's Sacred Cloak, then down to Nuristan to see the pink cliffs at the Dam of the King."

"Damn the whole crazy idea, Zaina. That country's covered in land mines. Even military vehicles can't stay clear of them. I don't think I approve of a guy who would put you in that kind of danger. Don't forget that most of those people who would have had you stoned before are still around."

"Hey. You're talking to Airplane Zane the Islamic Itinerant, remember? You think I don't know how to take care of myself in a Muslim country? Besides, you're jumping the gun. The whole thing is still at the planning stage. I'm broke, remember?"

"Right. And you *are* the globetrotting goddess," I admit with a playful hands-forward bow. "But I still hope you go somewhere safer, *Birdbrain Zane.*"

"*Airplane,*" she says with a crooked smirk that makes me laugh again.

I really want to tell Zaina about yesterday's strange package, but I know her well enough to expect she would only harangue me for getting so distressed over them. This is a woman who was stalked by a drug lord in Sicily, then had her identity stolen by an organised crime ring that rang up nearly a hundred thousand dollars of debt—amassing thirty-some credit cards and a dozen lines of credit in her name. The fraud police suspected the Sicilian kingpin was at the bottom of it, partly because the job was so pro they couldn't piece together enough evidence to prove *anything*. It didn't help that Zaina has a habit of discarding unopened envelopes. By the time the banks started to call and she alerted the police, the perpetrators had already had their fun. They'd exhausted the usefulness of her ID and moved on to the next victim.

I don't mention my cow conundrum. She'd only tell me to forget about it and focus on having a good time. Which would probably be good advice.

Well, I'll do my darnedest.

CHAPTER 4

DRIVING PRETTY WELL ANYWHERE on Vancouver Island is invigorating, and few parts more so than the two-hour trip from Victoria to Port Alberni. A panorama of rich greenery streaks by in the mist, broken periodically by rocky grey cliffs popping up along the inland side of the Trans-Canada. To my right is the deep indigo of the Georgia Strait, dappled from time to time with one or more of its four hundred and fifty-odd verdant islands.

How incredible it is to be out here. I am overcome by an inner lightness, a sensation that seems all but alien to me. Yet so refreshing. I understand what it is.

I feel *free*.

It's been a long time. I crank up the volume on the car's CD player and wail happily along with my beloved Ani DiFranco:

> *i know men are delicate*
> *origami creatures*
> *who need women to unfold them*
> *hold them when they cry*
> *but I am tired of being your saviour...*

* * *

A LOOK at the dashboard clock, and my old familiar tension makes a comeback. All my clothing was packed and set to go by bedtime last night, and I was up before dawn. But I blew it. I spent too much time this morning hugging Sasha and making advance apologies for the coming week of abandonment. She's an independent sort, though—even by feline standards—and Pam will be by twice a day to make sure she's adequately fed, watered, and caressed.

In the two years since I adopted Sasha, I've never been away longer than overnight, yet she seemed to understand the implication of my clothing getting stuffed into bags. Perhaps she was worried that I was leaving forever like Jack did. She followed me from room to room last night, mewing pitifully and often rolling uncharacteristically onto her back in the middle of the hallway for a tummy rub.

Even as I was chugging my morning cup of double-strength green tea, I still expected to get away early. Perhaps have time to stop and gaze up at the eight-hundred-year-old Douglas firs of Cathedral Grove. Or even drive a little out of my way up-island, I thought, to take in some of those breathtaking murals in Chemainus.

Perhaps on the way back. Somehow, I found a way to end up behind schedule. Zaina would get a kick out of this.

At the turn-off to Highway 4, it occurs to me that I'm not far from Qualicum Beach, where my grandfather ran his lumber mills. Another place I'd love to visit, but this too will have to wait. While reminiscing, I glance down at the clock again—and panic. It's twenty minutes to eight.

Damn.

The ferry leaves at eight, and I'm still *at least* a half-hour away if I keep doing the speed limit.

I pin it.

I round the next curve with the speedo needle at one-eighty and climbing. My heart vaults up into my throat when a full-grown cougar springs onto the road, right in front of me. It arches its back. I nail the brakes and crank hard to the right.

Tires screaming, I fight to manoeuvre around the big cat. It decides to retreat back to the bushes it came from—until it sees I'm now going the *same* way.

I get a close-up look at its hind end and long, tawny tail as my tires grind against the rough edge of the road's shoulder, then drop off sharply. With the brakes gripping properly on only one side, my car spins an instantaneous half turn, coming to a stop with the front wheels on the road and the rear ones in the ditch. It all takes about half a second.

"Bad kitty," I mutter. The cougar disappears into the foliage.

It's only the second one I've ever seen on the island, and the other had been anesthetised after showing up in a local schoolyard. Black-tailed deer are a staple of cougars' diet here, but a surge in the number of wolves has cut the deer population to a quarter of what it was a mere two decades ago. This, along with the loss of traditional hunting grounds, has driven the cougars to explore and hunt areas where they were previously seldom seen.

Like on this highway.

I look nervously to my left, and realize that if another vehicle comes flying around the blind curve like I did, my door will be right in its path—just as the cougar was in mine a moment ago.

My tires spin on the slick asphalt. I shift the automatic transmission into low gear and touch the accelerator lightly, taking another nervous glance down the road. I inch forward, the car's rear end clinging heavily to the ditch. Just as the rubber grabs, I see converging beams of light coming at me in the mist.

A bus!

I flash back to yesterday's unwell feeling, and recognise that I have been forewarned.

CHAPTER 5

I TROMP THE GAS and steer hard to the right, somehow remembering to shift back out of low gear. A long, throaty horn blast resonates through my skull— now pinned against the leather-wrapped headrest as I lurch ahead in a crazy turn. When the car is headed more or less in the proper direction, I check the mirror and see only an illustration of a sleek racedog centred between laser-bright headlights. I let out a little scream.

I barely correct my path in time to avoid leaving the pavement again, and immediately question if the road is *really* where I want to be. In the ditch, I'd have surely crashed into boulders and trees—but would no longer be in a ten-tonne bus's path.

The Passat upshifts, its engine roaring louder as I surge forward again. I hear a *whonk-whonk!* from the bus's horn. This time it sounds more like an irate reprimand than a panicked alert. I continue to pick up speed, and feel relief in watching the bus fall behind. It wouldn't be pleasant to face a career driver after endangering the lives of his patrons. I imagine about forty people are bad-mouthing me right now, and rightly so. Driving too fast got me in that bind—and here I am, back near the same speed again.

"You're one *stupid* chick, Katherine," I mumble, getting a glimpse of my eyes in my next check of the rear-view mirror. I expect to see repentance or residual fear, but they mostly just look tired.

* * *

AT TWO minutes to eight, a sign welcomes me to Port Alberni, *Salmon Capital of the World*. I feel exhilarated to have arrived here, and I don't even care for salmon.

I check my map and find the best way to the ferry terminal on the Alberni Inlet. I squeal into the lot, and leap out, pausing as I yank my bags from the trunk to call out to Nate Alison. Nate is rushing past the front of my car carrying two colourful gear bags. He is trailed by Sylvia, his slender, ponytailed wife, who lugs a third. Both stop in their tracks and offer big, warm-looking grins.

Nate sets down his load and runs over to shake my hand. His bare skin is very warm, probably a combination of healthy circulation and strenuous activity. "Got your email yesterday," he says. "But we were starting to think you changed your mind on us. We'd better hustle. The *Frances Barkley* is ready to sail."

Nate gathers in one hand the two bags he was previously carrying, and uses the other to grab my backpack, leaving me the duffel bag. "You brought a lot. I *did* tell you we supply all the gear and food, didn't I?" He leads me to the craft—which looks to me like an oversized white fishing boat—and calls out to the ferryman, "*Yo*, Jimmy! Got room for one more?"

"One passenger with two people's worth of gear!" Jimmy says with a laugh.

Bad enough I've overpacked, but people must think the other bags are mine as well. Typical city-slicking girlie girl. "I always pack too much," I say to Nate. "For an over-nighter, I take two of everything, and three changes of underwear."

"Good thing our kayaks have lots of cargo space," he says with a laugh. "We're just razzin' you, Kat. What you've got here won't be a problem. You wouldn't believe how much *some* beginners bring. It all has to be stuffed into my dry bags, but there's three hours to do that on the ferry."

"You coming too, Sylvia?" I ask.

"In my dreams. Someone's got to stay here and run the business. We run four trips at a time in high season. It's pretty unusual for Nate to get away too these days, but he told me it was the only way he could convince you to go. I had my doubts, of course."

"It's the honest-to-God truth. I was a pretty tough sell."

I am saddened to hear that Sylvia and Nate spend most of their summers operating the company instead of getting out in the islands. Sylvia gave up a prestigious and high-paying job as marketing director at a big petrochemical corporation in Calgary so the couple could go into the adventure tour business—a lifelong aspiration for Nate. He'd taken on a number of business ventures over the years, starting not long after we first met in grade school, most of them centred in one way or another around outdoor activities.

At least Nate and Sylvia are living a dream, if often only in their dreams...

"I can help you with that," says a man on the boat, snatching the duffel bag from my hands. "Ho-*lee*, you've got a lot in here, lady!" He carries it to a pile where Nate has placed my backpack, and reunites the two items. Then he's back in my face.

"Thomas Austin," he says, sticking out a leathery hand. I reach for it, just as the boat's big diesel engine kicks in and we lurch away from the pier. I am pitched off balance, and one of Thomas Austin's large hands grips my waist, while the other squeezes my right breast.

He releases me as soon as I regain balance, and holds his hands up in a surrender pose.

"I'm sorry," he says. His cheeks have reddened, and I sense he really is.

I give him a hard look anyway.

I can tell by the warmth in my face that I'm blushing too. My eyes zoom down to his hiking boots. "Thanks for catching me, Thomas. That water looks really cold. I'm Katherine Francis. I go by Kat."

"Glad to meet you, Kat. They call me Stompin' Tom," he says. "You know, after the goofy singer." I think I detect a slight French accent that doesn't seem to go with the name Thomas Austin, but don't ask. It's not like I've heard him speak a lot, and I'm no dialect expert.

"You sing?" I ask.

He smiles. "You don't want me to. But I can stomp." He demonstrates, booming the hard Vibram sole of his hiking boot on the wooden deck. I have to smile back.

Stompin' Tom's face is handsome, I suppose, in a rugged, Marlboro Man way. Or rugged in a handsome way. Yes, definitely more rugged than handsome. His eyes, though, are something else: the profound turquoise of an icy Rocky Mountain lake. I'd put him at about forty-five, factoring in plenty of weathering. He wears a moss-coloured fleece vest over a red-and-blue checked shirt, unbuttoned to reveal hairless skin in the low V of a white undershirt. He has a neatly trimmed goatee, and wavy brown hair cascades down to his shoulders, streaked with blond peroxide highlights— to camouflage some grey, I suspect.

"You one of Nate's guides?" I ask.

He erupts in laughter as if I've just delivered a kick-ass punchline. "No. I sell life insurance in *Hong-couver*, actually. But I like to get out now and then to do outdoorsy shit like this."

"You've done this tour before?"

"Nope. Never even touched a kayak. First time for everything, right?"

"Guess so," I say, distracted because I'm scoping out the boat for a place to sit down and transfer my gear into the dry bags. Hopefully one with less Stompin' Tom around.

Nate comes to my rescue. I step back, allowing him room to get between Thomas and me. He does just that.

"How're you liking it so far, Kat?" he asks.

"I nearly fell off the boat when we pulled away from the pier, but other than that it's great. The ferry is sort of *different* from what I envisioned."

"Older?"

"That too. Smaller, I meant. When you said we'd ride out on a ferry, I envisioned something more like the *Spirit of British Columbia* that you take to the mainland. You know, along with about two thousand other people, plus five hundred cars and buses."

He laughs. "The *Frances Barkley* does the job just fine. Built in 1958 in Norway, where she sailed 'til they shipped her here about fifteen years ago. She's rated for two hundred passengers and a hundred tons of cargo, you know. No cars, though." He rubs a hand lovingly over the many layers of paint on the light blue handrail. "A good vessel."

"Oh, I didn't mean to insult the boat. I've never been in anything like it is all. She does look great for her age."

"If you were from Bangladesh, you would think this is the nicest ferry in the world," he says with a crooked smile. He's alluding, I think, to the ancient South Asian boats that make the news here every time one goes down with tremendous loss of life. "She's very seaworthy, though she never sees much rough water on her route up the inlet and across Barkley Sound. It's nicely sheltered in here, so you just don't get any big swells. Unless you were here in 1964, I guess."

"What happened *then*?"

"The Great Alaskan Earthquake," he says, giving me a funny look. "Second worst quake in history, at nine-point-two on the Richter Scale. Kicked the ocean floor forty-five feet straight up. Biggest underwater upshift ever recorded. The *tsunami* it made was clocked at seven hundred and twenty clicks in the open sea. Came sixty kilometres up the inlet in ten minutes."

"A *tsunami* hit *here*?" I've lived on the island long enough to have heard more than enough talk about possible future killer quakes and so-called tidal waves, but was completely ignorant that one had hit so close to home. It was before I was born, but only by a few years.

Thomas steps forward, wide-eyed. "I remember it," he says. "I was *very* young," he assures me. "Did some pretty good damage around here, then?"

Nate nods. "Locals still talk about it a lot. The same *tsunami* also hit the West Coast and Hawaii, but aside from Anchorage, they say Port Alberni got the worst of it. It's at the head of the inlet, so right where all the incoming water piled up. There were actually two big waves, almost an hour apart. First one was the smaller of them, but it drained the entire inlet on its way back out. Left ships laying on their sides in the silt. Luckily the RCMP managed to clear most people out of town before the really big one hit. Entire log booms were swept into streets. One family came back to find their house sitting by the pumps at the gas station. Others never knew where their home went, but found someone's fishing boat in their basement. The church ended up on a tennis court, right on top of the net."

"That's horrible," I say. "Doesn't it scare you then, living here? Nature tends to run in cycles. A spot in the seafloor that's seismically flawed doesn't usually heal itself."

"Oh, I know. They say we're *overdue* for another big one in this area, whatever that exactly means. As if disasters run on a schedule or something. But if we had another one the same size today, it would be a lot worse. They've set up dykes and tried to rezone the worst-hit spots as flood plains, but there are more people living all around the inlet now than there were forty years ago. Folks love to be close to the water."

"What was the body count in sixty-four?" Thomas asks with a twisted smile.

Nate takes a few seconds to answer. "About a hundred and thirty, if I remember right. Mostly in Alaska."

Stompin' Tom smiles. "That's nothing,"

"Yeah, *right*," I say. I want to walk away, but stay for Nate's sake.

"No, Thomas is absolutely right," Nate says. "For the magnitude of the quake and size of the waves, that's really not bad. The Boxing Day *tsunami* in the Indian Ocean basin killed tens of thousands—and the quake that caused it was smaller, an even nine points.

"It was closer to *two hundred* thousand," I say. "Zaina is from Sri Lanka, remember? What I meant was a hundred and thirty lives is still a whole lot of vanished dreams and shattered hearts."

His cheeks flush, eyes flitting faraway for a moment. "I recall, and I'm sorry. Still, no denying we were fortunate here. Partly thanks to the low population density in this part of the world at the time, plus the quake hit at suppertime on Good Friday, so businesses and schools were empty. But around here, not a single person was even hurt badly. Anyone who lived through it will tell you that's nothing short of miraculous. Some people couldn't get their front door open when the wall of water hit and floated them away. Yet everyone came out of it okay."

"*Crazy*," Thomas says. "So I'll bet you got your place up on stilts, eh, Nate."

Nate wrinkles his brow in a pained expression. "Nope. Sylvia and I could hardly be in a worse spot, actually. We live out of the back of our office. We haven't had you there yet, have we, Kat?"

I shake my head.

"It's a converted warehouse close to the wharf. Not zoned for residential use for that very reason, so please don't mention it to anyone on town council. It came cheap, though, and made it possible for us to start out here. Guess if a big earthquake hit, we'd just have to hope for a quick evacuation notice from the Tsunamic Warning Centre, and that the epicentre is nice and far away. They say a quake closer to home could have a twenty-metre wave on top of us in minutes. And there's a very nasty ridge just a hundred kilometres offshore that's been primed for a nine-pointer—*minimum*—for three hundred years, just building pressure. At least it'd all be over fast. Something to be said for being at ground zero."

Thomas smiles. "This might be a stupid question, but if you're not supposed to be living where you are, how are the authorities going to give you the warning?" It seems a good point. I've always known Nate to be extraordinarily prudent—he must have wanted desperately to get into this business.

Nate flashes pain. "We keep the radio on a lot. And the town's got speakers mounted on top of wooden poles. In a sense we're sort of wagering it doesn't come to that. For now. We're keeping our eyes open for a place higher up."

"Maybe I'll drop by *after* you and Sylvia move," I say, and shiver as a chill slides over me.

He laughs. "Okay, but then you have to bring Zaina. How is our girl?"

"Was wondering when you'd ask. Great. She's Zane. Always great, no matter what. Tried to get her to come, but she had a bag of excuses and threw me one after another."

Nate seems surprised at this. He and Zaina dated in high school, but only briefly. I think she was too much of a wild child for him. Some things don't change. "I can't believe Zaina Marikar turned down a shot at adventure."

"Came down to budget. She's trying to save up to go to Afghanistan."

He shakes his head, but smiles. "She's off her bean. I'll take my chances living at the end of *Tsunami* Inlet, but you couldn't pay me enough to spend five minutes *there*."

"How about we don't talk about killer waves anymore."

Stompin' Tom grins at me. "Why not? That shit is *fascinating*."

"Put it out of your mind, Kat," Nate says, casting a scowl at Thomas. "The good news is waves like that don't come along very often. Every year that goes by with the seismologists still chanting how we're past due, I doubt more and more I'll see it in my lifetime. And the waves have far less impact on a cluster of islands like we'll be on or at sea than on the shore of an inlet. They say you could be sitting on the deck of a boat out here and not even feel one passing under you."

I immediately think about how the Indian Ocean's islands were ravaged by waves that hit there, but don't bother to mention it. "I'm actually hoping there isn't much wave action at all where we'll be paddling," I say, quite comfortable in revealing straight away what a wussy I am.

"The Broken Group is more than a hundred islands, and they buffer the water and wind real nice. The reason I recommended this tour for your first outing is that even if it *does* get a little choppy, you never need to go far from shore to tour around. We essentially just take you from the shelter of one island to another."

"Bummer," Thomas says, still the tough guy. Nate winks at me.

* * *

FOR AN activity that archeologists say to be at least four thousand years old, there sure is a lot to learn about kayaking. As our Trip Leader, Nate takes no shortcuts, beginning our training even before we get off the ferry. He calls us all astern and runs us through every component of the kayaks, showing how to work the rudder and attach the spray skirt that keeps the ocean out of the boat if things get rough. Then he goes through the four basic strokes, which he promises each of us will fully master over the course of the week. First, the planting-and-pulling power stroke, the one he says we'll use ninety percent of the time. Then the forward and reverse sweep, and the stern rudder (which, he demonstrates, is actually not a stroke but a drag), followed by the draw and pry. The draw consists of pulling the blade of the paddle inward, and the pry is the opposite.

Even with a blade on both sides, my paddle is astonishingly lightweight. It's nothing like what the Inuit used, to be sure. Each of the plastic blades is set at a different angle than the other, and the shaft is ergonomically curved and made of honeycombed black carbon fibre, like a pro-quality fishing rod or bicycle frame. Similarly expensive, I presume.

Once on the beach, Nate teaches us a few basic recovery techniques—including how to perform a T-rescue and paddle-float self-rescue—then helps some of the others pack their gear in dry bags with precision most people might reserve for stuffing parachutes. Back on the ferry, I crammed mine in like meat into sausage casings—uncomfortable about the thought of Thomas leering at my personal effects—and now I have the urge to re-pack it. But that can wait until I'm in the privacy of my tent. Everything I brought is quite wrinkleproof.

There are six other paddlers on this trip, which is one "man" short of an optimum group according to Nate. So if Zaina had come, it'd be perfect.

I'd be happier, anyway.

Four of my six new friends are a family: a fit-looking yuppie couple and their perfect pre-teen twins, named Jennie and Jerry for maximal cutesy-ness. Then there's Stompin' Tom, of course, and a guy called Blur, a scrawny fifty-something time-warp-victim hippie who seems to move very slowly considering his name. I wonder if Blur is the only one he's got, like Sting or Bono, minus the fame.

I don't sense a bond, nor do I feel terribly comfortable around any of the others, but that will probably change. It takes a while for a group's dynamics to evolve.

Nate gives what he warns will be the "first and worst of several" safety lectures. It starts out with things I can well imagine happening, like one of our kayaks being overturned—and moves on to less likely eventualities, such as a grey whale or orca deciding to surface beneath someone. Since Nate's got no *obvious* motivation to terrify us, I presume he is merely covering his butt legally. I call him on it.

"Kat's right," he admits. "That one's a pretty rare occurrence. But I can't be too emphatic about being prepared and staying safe out here. You need to know that no matter what, we always stay in sight of a buddy, and avoid panicking if anything does go wrong. The ocean doesn't make allowances for unskilled newcomers—or for old fools like me. It's easy to get overconfident once you're comfortable and forget that all the rules still apply. Never, ever get caught too far out or by yourself. The ocean eats what it catches."

* * *

THE FIRST day of paddling goes smoothly, with Nate being sure to provide plenty of rest stops thinly camouflaged as beach walks and bladder breaks. A benefit of the Broken Group being within the Pacific Rim National Park is that many of the islands are outfitted with solar toilets. If only there were solar showers, it would be ideal.

I am glad I'll have a tent to myself. On the ferry ride, somebody mentioned we were to sleep two to a tent, and I noticed in my peripheral vision that Stompin' Tom turned to face me. I felt like a child who, upon arriving at summer camp, would suddenly do anything to be back at home—even spend the week washing dishes or cleaning her bedroom. Luckily, Nate stepped in and made it clear that Thomas and Blur were to bunk together, and I'd be solo.

When we arrive on the island Nate has selected for our first night, I see Thomas carrying the tent he is to share with Blur, and wait for him to pick a spot to pitch it. A chess game, as he's clearly biding his time for me to do the same. I pretend I've found an ideal area—as indeed I may have—and slowly clear away a few stones and fallen branches. Stompin' Tom has apparently also discovered the ultimate spot, though it's easy for me to see that it is on top of a nasty hump and at an intersection of protruding tree roots—because it's hardly ten paces away. When he gets started, I shake my head with feigned disgust at some invisible site-flaw, grab my gear, and move as far away as I feel safe going, compromising my toilet and cooking area access. Thankfully, Thomas does not follow, but ultimately does claim my abandoned location.

* * *

I AM pleased to discover I am a better kayaker than Thomas, and do not have a hard time staying out of flirting range. He's persistent, though, and it makes for a more intense workout on every outing.

* * *

BY THE second night, I decide it's time to try and upgrade my standing in the eyes of my fellow kayakers from *antisocial* to *extreme introvert*. I've been so reclusive on this trip, I can hardly blame people if they think I'm a little weird.

Even Blur seems to intentionally steer clear of me.

Everyone seems duly surprised when I appear at the fire. It's a small pit, dug below the high-tide mark of the beach without a stone fire ring. Nate is very particular about such things. No-trace camping, he calls it.

Nate smiles, then silently pulls a small folding chair from behind a pile of driftwood and sets it up for me. It is the kind of ultra-compact and low-slung portable seat people use at outdoor concerts because it allows you to keep below other show-goers' sightlines. This one is also remarkably comfortable, I discover.

Harco and Valerie, the yuppie couple, also give me welcoming smile. Jennie and Jerry sit silently near them, Jennie immersed in a thick Harry Potter book. Jerry fiercely works the buttons of an electronic game that resembles a miniature notebook computer.

Blur continues to lean back in his chair, oblivious to me as he gazes slack-jawed at the glittering starscape.

"How would you like your marshmallow?" Harco says to me as he pulls a fireball-on-a-stick out of the little campfire. "Black on the outside only, or black all the way through?"

With a mighty puff, he extinguishes the little torch. I've never enjoyed marshmallows, incinerated or not. Still, I think it best to accept his offer. "That's *perfect*. Thank you."

He turns the willow stick and hands me the end opposite the burned offering. I take it and cautiously slide the carbon hull away from the sticky white mass of aerated corn syrup.

"*Aw*, that was the best part," he says after I toss the crispy pocket into the fire.

"It could be carcinogenic, and I've got a scary history of cancer on both sides of my family." I don't actually know the first part to be true, but it sounds good to me. Although acrylamide produced by burning some starches has been linked to the disease, I've never read anything about burned sugar posing a danger. Regardless, Harco seems to consider it an acceptable excuse for my wastefulness. His next marshmallow comes out of the fire golden-brown.

Blur takes a break from his stargazing, but still doesn't seem to notice me. "Tommy," he says quietly, and makes a gesture with the tips of his thumb and index finger together at his lips. Stompin' Tom smiles, and the two trundle off into the bushes.

Nate smiles and leans over to me. "Nature walk," he whispers.

I quietly laugh. "Yes. Caught the ASL."

"It's bizarre," he says, "Tom told me he hates drugs, because his brother's an addict."

"Maybe pot doesn't count."

Nate lowers his voice even more. "Personally, I think Stompin' Tom is full of shit." Then he resumes speaking at full volume. "I'm really glad you decided to give the rest of us a chance and come sit out here. We can actually be quite amusing at times, and the stars are magnificent tonight. Sad to think how many city people go to their graves never having seen the night sky without light pollution. Most of the world's population, you know."

I look up at the dazzling display, and the depth of such a tragedy stirs me. Something so significant and elementary, yet it lies beyond the reach of billions of people—and not just those stuck in the never-ending shantytowns surrounding Calcutta or São Paulo, but in cities throughout the world.

I was an adult before I first experienced the sky at night in all its glory. Our first summer together, when we visited Jack's family farm near the Saskatchewan town of Melville, he took me to a clover field he sometimes visited as a boy. His parents made us sleep in separate rooms, which by the third night was unbearable to him. After we made love, the sky was immense and cloudless. We wrapped ourselves in a blanket and spent hours counting satellites and shooting stars together. Jack surprised me with his ability to identify constellations by their Latin names and spout facts about the planets. "Pluto shouldn't count," he told me, apparently miffed. "It's a chunk of ice like a comet, and it orbits at a different angle than the eight *real* planets. And it's not even as big as the goddam moon."

Before that night, I'd had no idea how many stars could actually be seen with the naked eye, or how crammed together they all appeared, though in reality unfathomable distances apart.

That night was completely lost to my memory for years, and—suddenly—here it is. It's no coincidence, but simply because this is the only view I've ever had of the heavens to rival it...

Nate cuts short my reverie. "Hard to believe that some of those stars might have burned out millions of years ago, but they're so far away no one alive will ever know it."

"We *are* looking back in time, aren't we? Nothing we're seeing right now is truly the way it looks to us, but only as each body was when the light left it eons ago. Every one of those stars is sending us a view of a different point in antiquity."

"Closest thing there is to a time machine."

"That's pretty deep," Harco interjects. "Way too heavy for me. Well there, Val, I think it's time you and I got these kids down, or we'll have to squeeze them out of their bags like toothpaste in the morning."

Valerie stands up, and Jennie closes her book without further prompting. Jerry's eyes remain locked on the little video screen, his thumbs a frenzy of motion. Valerie snatches the Game Boy away and claps the screen down on its hinges.

"*Hey!*" Jerry shouts, making a face. "You just trashed my new high score."

"That's really tragic, Jerry. But Mario and the Mushroom Kingdom are done for the day. Your father told you that if this thing becomes an obsession, It's going to disappear."

Jerry grumbles, but doesn't argue. I get the feeling he knows from experience that Harco would be happy to deep-six the Game Boy. The four meander off, Harco and Val going to their tent and the children to the one next to it.

Soon, Thomas and Blur return, with a chuckle they shared in the bushes still reverberating back and forth between them. They sit down and both stare up at the sky to see what a little THC does for it. I sort of wish I could look at it through their eyes for a few minutes.

"So, how are you doing, Kat?" Nate asks at a volume clearly intended to limit his audience to me.

"I have to apologise, Nate. Guess you know I'm going through a dark period. I'm not much fun to be around, and don't want to spoil everyone else's trip."

Thomas puts his hand on the side of my chair. I recoil, and the hand goes back to cradling his plastic mug. His eyes are soft. "I've been through a lot of crap myself," he says. "The Triple D—Deaths, Divorce, and Drug addiction. Go ahead and unload on me if you want. Talking is the best therapy."

"Well, I don't have a narcotic addiction. You've got that on me," I say, not wanting to let on what Nate said about Thomas's brother.

"I should qualify that one. Not *my* addictions, but those of friends and relatives. Not that I'd be ashamed if *I* beat heroin. That's something to brag about, and I'm damn proud of my kid brother. Shit does a lot more kicking than getting kicked, but he's been clean eighteen months now."

"Good for him," I say. I think my discomfort may have made my tone come off as a little sarcastic, so I bite my lip and add, "I mean it, Thomas."

"So divorce and death, eh? Recent?"

"Three weeks on the divorce. And I've lost my mom and brother since January." If I'd known I would be telling Thomas this, I would never have come to the fire. Yet somehow I feel nothing but relief.

"*Who-oa*," Blur says, but it quickly becomes clear from his expression that he's simply moved by something the sky is doing inside his mind.

Thomas blinks repeatedly and wipes his eyes, but I don't see any tears. "Shit, Kat. Pardon my French. Anyone could see you were shouldering something, but I swear to God I had *no* idea. I'm sorry for being so aggressive."

"Hey, don't apologise. You've been friendly, that's all."

"No, he's been a total jerk, baby," Blur says. He launches into a throaty *ha-huh–ha-huh* laugh like a sputtering boat motor, still looking at the sky.

"You knew all this, Nate?" Thomas curls a corner of his upper lip, apparently perturbed that Nate has held out—and this evidence of confidentiality impresses me. I figured he would surely have said something as an explanation for my behaviour by now. No question my story would have made for interesting fireside fodder.

"Dr. Francis is an amazing woman," Nate says. "But her privacy has always been important to her. Which I respect. And with that, I think I'm going to excuse myself and head off to bed. The rest of you make sure the fire is doused with water before you call it a night. I want to see a hand print in those ashes."

"We will, Nate," I say. He is already out of his chair and heading for his tent.

"I'm gonna crash too, man," Blur says. "These dudes get up way too fucking early." He picks himself out of the chair and stammers off.

I wonder for a moment if it's my presence here that has cleared the fireside. Probably not, I tell myself. Blur is not exaggerating about the mornings here. This is an early-to-bed and early-to-rise trip.

Surprisingly, I'm feeling more comfortable with Thomas now that he knows a little about my situation. I doubt he will be insensitive enough to try anything. And if I yelp, Nate's tent is within earshot.

"So you're a doctor." Thomas says. "I knew you were bright. What's your specialty?"

"Veterinary medicine."

"That's *awesome*." His lips spread to a huge grin, and he rubs at his little goatee. My cynical side warns that I've just elevated my standing as an insurance sales prospect. "I've got a dog," he announces.

"Let me guess. Akita? Or is it a rottweiler?"

"What's that supposed to mean?" His brow knits deeply, then he laughs. "Chuck is a Tibetan mastiff."

"A guard dog. So I wasn't far off."

"Bred to guard monasteries and sheep, not attack people. Chuck is *very* gentle."

"I acquiesce. A very loyal breed. And I *was* being judgmental. I suppose I had you down as being sort of a warrior type."

"Got me pegged. Spent some time in the Forces."

"No kidding?"

"Did tours as a peacekeeper in El Salvador, Cambodia and Rwanda between ninety-one and ninety-six. That was it for me. Got myself enough nightmares to last several lifetimes."

"My best friend's brother was in Bosnia-Herzegovina, and he's a complete mess now. I've heard a few horrendous stories from him."

"No offence, but *stories* don't cut it. No one, not me or anyone else, can give you the slightest concept of the reek of burned and rotting flesh, how it crawls so deep into your sinuses you swear you can still smell it years later. No words can make someone perceive the hollow look in the eyes of a little girl who just watched her family killed by soldiers, then was gang-raped and had her arms hacked off with a fucking machete. Same shit at every house you went to in Rwanda. Doubt I'll ever tell anyone the worst stuff. What sucks most is not being able to do a damned thing to really *help* the people you see. By the time you show up, the damage is done. You can't fix those things. Can't do shit. You can only hope to be a speed bump to the violence. Maybe narrow its swath just a tiny bit." Thomas's eyes look profoundly melancholy now. I feel an impulse to take his hand, to nurture him somehow. But I don't dare. I'm terrified, though of precisely what I'm not sure.

"You're right, Thomas. I *can't* imagine."

"Thank your lucky stars, Kat. Thank your *fucking* lucky stars. We say war is hell, but I bet down in hell they make a parallel comparison. I'd do damn near anything to stop a war from happening. Make any goddam sacrifice. Would *you*?"

"Tough question. What could *I* do to stop a war?"

"Hypothetically. Would you be able to give your life? Or the life of someone dear to you, to save countless others?"

"I don't know—"

"I would. In a fucking heartbeat, babe."

"Maybe, because of your experience—"

"But you wouldn't, huh?"

"My life, yes. I think I probably could. But others... You mean kill them, or betray them to be killed?"

"I suppose. I didn't mean *anything* specifically. But let's say a relatively small number of people—real people like the ones you care the most about—have to die to save a great number of others and prevent the kind of atrocities I've seen. Wouldn't you have to step up?"

"I do agree in principle. But I could never turn in my best friend to a murderous regime or pull the trigger on someone I love. Not even if it would stop another Rwanda. So I guess that's a no. Sorry."

He shakes his head. "And therein lies the problem with this world. Ergo, terrible regimes succeed. You can call it mercy, but to me it's damned selfishness. Plain and simple."

We stare into the fire together until nothing is left but embers.

"Go to bed, Kat," Thomas finally says without looking up. "I'll douse the damned ashes."

*   *   *

Tuesday begins with a residual coolness between Thomas and me. At breakfast, I'm sitting alone when he comes over, carrying a small bowl and a plastic mug. "This spot taken?" he asks, pointing to a boulder near the stump I'm using for a chair.

"A squirrel was there a minute ago," I say, probably sounding more acerbic than I intend to. "Care to join me?" I add.

His head bobs slightly, and he works to swallow a big spoonful of hot cereal, holding the bowl and spoon together in one hand and a mug in the other. "Thanks," he says when he manages to get the oatmeal down. "I made you a cup of Stompin' Tom's special hot cocoa. Best in the world."

I take the mug and have a big sip. It's too sweet and minty, and leaves a bitter aftertaste. Probably not the best cocoa on the island, forget the world. "It *is* very good," I tell him, already looking for a place to dump the rest of it first chance I get.

Thomas is wearing a T-shirt with its sleeves torn off, and I'm impressed with the musculature of his arms. No wonder he kayaks so well. His biceps are certainly better developed than those of most men his age, but it's his triceps that are truly impressive. They're large and exceptionally well-defined, chiselled horseshoes of sinew. On the hump of his shoulder, he has a blurry tattoo that looks like four tiles of a checkerboard, rotated at forty-five degrees.

"That's old," he says, catching me staring. "Got it long before tattoos were in vogue. What a hell of a stupid thing for a fad, huh? I'm just glad acid-washed jeans weren't permanent."

"Did that start out as what I think it was?" I ask. I wonder immediately if it was a wise thing to say, but he grins and shakes his head as if in inward frustration.

"Yes, it did," he says. "Not too many people think of that, you know. You're astute. Guess I was a little insurgent in my youth, but I've mellowed, you'll be glad to know. Maybe too much. Bottoms up, and let's hit some waves." He shovels another bite of oatmeal into his mouth.

I can't help but be struck by the irony of this, especially in light of our conversation last night.

Thomas used to have a swastika tattoo.

CHAPTER 6

THOMAS'S KAYAKING SKILLS HAVE improved speedily, and I now find myself always trailing behind him, struggling more and more to keep up. He obviously has more muscle, but I'm lighter, so my boat sits higher up and creates less drag in the water. I also know I'm quite strong for a girl—and better than ten years younger than he is. Our strength-to-weight ratios are probably similar, so it seems we should be more closely matched on the water. Perhaps the difference comes down to technique.

There is indeed a supple effortlessness in the way Thomas moves, and it seems that unlike me with my meandering course, he seldom needs to correct his kayak's direction. I decide to study him closely to find out what it is he does to make his boat move so fast and track so straight.

I notice he uses long strokes and keeps the paddle in much closer to the kayak's gunwale than I do. I imitate him, and quickly feel the difference. Stroking closer to the boat seems to exert less turning force, and also allows me to keep the paddle in the water longer—adding length to my draw. It even seems to give better leverage.

It becomes significantly easier to keep up. Thomas seems to notice and take exception, because his cadence increases. When you watch someone paddle for hours at a time, it's easy to tell when he or she makes any kind of change, and this evidently works both ways. I laugh out loud and pick up mine too.

The faster paddling is not all bad. It helps me to see how Thomas applies power, often letting out a soft *euh!* as he digs hard at the beginning, and finishing easy. I've been doing essentially the opposite, concentrating most of my effort on the finish. Doing it Thomas's way, it seems I'm exerting even less turning force on the kayak. I pull up alongside him, and can't help but grin.

He takes his paddle from the water and squints at me. "Well, look who's Little Miss Happy Pants this morning."

I continue to smile, and paddle a bit harder. He's right. This is the best I've felt in months.

"Are you copying my technique, you brat?"

"Course not."

"You sure as hell are *so.*"

"Alright, maybe just a *little*. Where'd you learn?"

"Out here on the water. Just thought out the mechanics of it. Energy transfer physics."

"I didn't know they taught that stuff in the army. Must have been your insurance training then. You could have at least told me what I was doing wrong. Didn't want to have me on even footing, did you? So I've had to work twice as hard just to keep you in sight."

He laughs. "I'm not here to train people. Besides, a guy's got to have *some* advantage. When you learn to work smarter, you shouldn't have to give that up. Natural selection would fail."

"We're not in competition for survival, Thomas. And you said *I* was selfish." I take off, scooping a paddle of seawater right in his face.

* * *

THOMAS SEEMS to have a knack for finding pockets of exceptional beauty between the islands. We have spoken little in the short time we've been out today, so when he calls my name—pulling me away from my own little fantasy world—it's a sure bet he's found something fantastic. I paddle out to where he sits motionless, his kayak rising and falling with the waves, and I'm not disappointed. It's an undersea rock garden—more spectacular than any I've seen. Countless orange and purple starfish and brilliant yellow sunfish wallpaper the rocks and coral reefs. Enormous flower-like anemones of violet and powder blue undulate slowly with the currents, atop their long and phallic stems. I paddle on, utterly enthralled by what I'm seeing below me.

The blustery breeze speeds my outward progress, and when I glance up to the sound of a splash, I expect to catch a retaliatory face-full of water from Thomas's paddle.

I am ecstatic to instead see a trio of Pacific white-sided dolphins playing in the royal blue water ahead of me. The waves are rolling higher, but I'm seduced by the mystic beauty of the two-tone grey cetaceans, and it seems almost as if they are putting on a special show for me. They breach, bounding high over the waves, then begin to flip one over another, over another.

We've already encountered many other animals on this trip. Bald eagles are ubiquitous. We spent nearly an hour yesterday watching a large group of sea lions lounge and frolic from about a hundred metres away. (They might have allowed us nearer, but the stink held us back—Nate says it's the way their feces become from eating the squid abundant here.) We observed a pair of tiny black-tailed deer swimming between islands, and even saw the dorsal fin and tail of a grey whale that our guide said was one of the biggest he'd ever seen. Nate declared it to weigh between twenty-five and thirty tonnes, and no one had reason to question the precision of his blubber-o-meter.

But the dolphins weave magic like no animals I've seen. I can't bear to let them leave me. My chest flutters with a delightfully blissful, tranquil feeling—like being in love, it occurs to me.

I completely lose track of the distance between Thomas and me. Spacing out goes against one of Nate's many rules, but I hardly give it any more than a fleeting thought. *Who cares?* I'm on autopilot, in the open sea. There's plenty of daylight, and I've got a compass. I'm propelled by this strange and delightful curiosity, baited by the chimeral allure of the dolphins.

Everything is so vivid, so colourful. All of my senses seem to be heightened. The air itself has taken on a deliciously fresh taste and smell. I want to drink deeply of it.

I'm euphoric.

I don't know what happens next, but it feels like I've been struck in the back of the neck with a baseball bat. It takes a few seconds to comprehend that I am underwater. In an instant, my incredible delight has been replaced by shock and terror. A wave must have come up behind me like a cougar, without a sound. The heaviness of the water drives me downward like a tent peg, my lungs—unprepared—taking in a solid, choking shot of raw brine.

The bow of my kayak rockets out from the waves. I'm gasping and coughing violently, crazy with hysteria, when the next wave hits. I think it's even bigger than the first, and as the icy water blasts my eyes and ears, Nate's *tsunami* story flashes through my mind. *This is what it must be like to die that way.*

I am underwater once more, but this time I do not shoot out again.

I'm wearing a life vest. Why am I not coming back up?

I suddenly understand I'm upside down, and flat out of oxygen. Panic explodes inside of me, and it's nearly impossible to think. I remember the *wet exit* procedure Nate showed us, and fumble for my sprayskirt cord. Yanking it, I thrust myself out of the seat.

Just as I find air, another wave hits. I kick hard until I break the surface again, lungs exploding in a fit of wretched, agonising spurts with precious little air to clear the passage. As I hack, my body convulses and my legs kick involuntarily at the endless ocean beneath me.

This time I anticipate the next stray wave, looking everywhere for it, but only a few smaller ones wash over me. I survey the water for my kayak, but can't see it anywhere. *Those stupid things don't sink, do they?* It must have surfed away on a whitecap.

I won't drown out here. Not with the vest on.

No, instead I'll die of hypothermia in this fucking cold water that hammers on my bones with the forgiveness of an iron rod. In eight-degree ocean water, ten minutes is probably all I've got to contemplate my life. Maybe as much as thirty, if I'm really unlucky.

The ocean eats what it catches.

And it's caught me.

CHAPTER 7

"I'M GOING TO TEACH you all to *grok* the sea," Nate told us at the introductory lesson. He explained for the ignorant in the group (a category apparently limited to me and young Jennie) that the word *grok* came from Robert A. Heinlein's novel *Stranger in a Strange Land*, a Martian term meaning *to be one with*.

Now I'm *grokking* this water in the most literal way.

I paddle with my hands to rotate myself, scanning the waves for nearby land. In the distance, a few green clumps of treetops are visible from time to time. *How did I get out so freaking far?* None of the islands are anywhere near close enough to try swimming for.

My shivering becomes more intense, culminating in seizure-like spasms that rumble up and down inside my torso. I try in spite of the wild tremors to keep my arms folded and ankles crossed. My hope is to minimise heat loss to whatever extent can be expected by someone bobbing like a cork in ice-cold seawater.

I'm not worrying so much any more, or even thinking very much about anything. My fingertips are wrinkled and cyanotic, the tissues being denied circulation as my body automatically sacrifices its extremities in desperation to preserve the core.

"Ish not gun a-work," I slur like a drunkard to the shutdown mechanism, then let out a delirious laugh that disintegrates into a sharp, stabbing cough. The shivering has stopped. I'm glad, though I know this is not a good thing. I feel strangely detached from the water now, and even my own body seems foreign and insignificant. All I have left out here is my own fear.

Though I may lack the brain power to properly fret, I *am* scared. I don't want to die. Not out here, all alone.

A few verses come to mind, from an old Anglican prayer Mom taught me to say at bedtime as a child. I'm not able to get my lips and tongue around even the simplest words, but I mumble to myself as it plays through my mind:

Four corners are on my bed,
Four angels around my head,
One to watch, one to pray,
And two to bear my soul away.

I go by sea, I go by land,
The Lord made me with his right hand,
If any danger comes to be,
Sweet Jesus please deliver me.

* * *

In my dream-state, strong hands pull me from the sucking ocean like a foot from a water-filled boot, hauling me upward onto a hard surface.

After a moment of heavy breathing that seems to come from all around my body but not within it, my lifeless legs and torso are directed into a tubular chamber. I visualise myself entering a body bag, right before the icy morgue drawer gets around over me. A voice murmurs, like Charlie Brown's teacher. *"Wah wor wah wa-ah. Waor?"* I can't process the ridiculous noises.

I manage to open my eyes to see the pointed nose of a kayak, parting endless black waves. I want to turn to see who is piloting it in the seat behind me, but moving takes far more strength than I've got. The boat seems to be made of the same water as the sea, its shape transforming along with the moving ripples beneath it. A Thule hunter is taking me to his snow house on his sealskin kayak, where he will feed me to his family. I find this strangely amusing. Perhaps I am already dead.

Good. Then being eaten will not hurt.

The reverie drifts in and out, replaced in periods of absence with perfect nothingness. There is no tunnel of light, and although perhaps this should concern me, it does not.

* * *

I'm in a snug cocoon, a hot body snug against my own, yet I continue to shiver spasmodically. At least I'm out of the water. A soft mouth presses against my lips, but what it does bears no resemblance to a kiss. Warm air puffs into my lungs, and it feels bizarrely nice.

I'm lost, but what's stranger is that this seems completely impertinent. I force my eyes open, and find only further blackness. *Where am I?*

I recall the kayak trip, and wonder if I am inside a house, or a tent. Who is here with me? Another gentle puff of air enters my lungs.

Stompin' Tom?

I try to pull away, but there is nowhere near enough room. I must be in a sleeping bag, my bag-mate and I apparently bound together from head to toe.

"Shhh. Relax," a feminine voice says. "You're going to be okay, Kat."

I open my eyes and strain to focus on the face in front of mine. It's not easy. I wait for my pupils to dilate, and somewhere a light comes on. It accelerates the savage pounding inside my head. It feels like I've got a terrible hangover.

I recognise the face. It's Valerie.

With my hands pinned to my chest, I can feel that I'm wearing something dry. The fabric is thick and itchy like a felt insole.

"My clothes—"

"Don't try to talk. Just rest. *I* changed you."

"Oh, good. I thought maybe…"

She laughs. "Thomas? Don't think he didn't volunteer," she says with a warm smile. "Nate gave me hot packs to put in your armpits and groin. The guy knows his stuff. I don't know how he ever found you out there. All that water, and no one knew where you went. Thomas came back alone and said the two of you had a fight, so you took off by yourself. Nate flipped. He shook Tom up, asking where he last saw you, then told us all to stay together here. He shoved off in the two-seater Harco and I were using, and paddled away like a demon. Not a chance of any of us keeping up with him if our *own* lives depended on it. We all started freaking, feeling helpless and thinking we should be out searching too. But Nate told us to stay. After a while, everyone went quiet. No one said it, but we all started to think you were both gone."

* * *

VALERIE STAYS with me through the night, climbing out just once for a bathroom break. It's not until after dawn that I'm beginning to feel warm for the first time.

"I'm ready to try and get up," I say. "Thirsty."

"I wanted to give you something hot to drink, but Nate said it was a bad idea."

"He was right. Hot liquid drives body heat away from the vital organs. But I'm warm enough now."

"That makes sense, I guess. I thought it was stupid you couldn't have a bit of cocoa. I forgot you're a doctor."

"An animal doctor. I just have a photographic memory that hangs on to all kinds of useless factoids. A lot of them are more *toid* than *fact*." I bring my hand up, wanting to check my wristwatch for the time and day, having no clue how long I've been here.

It's gone. "Did someone take my watch?" I ask.

"I don't think so. Must have come off in the water. Was it expensive?"

"Not at all. It was a fashion watch, and the clasp liked to let go every time I wrestled with a big dog or pulled off a sweater. No big deal."

*   *   *

MY EXIT from the tent triggers scattered applause. Nate walks over and hands me a tin mug full of water. I guzzle it all down. "Thanks, Nate," I gasp. "Thirsty business, recovering from hypothermia. Do you have a Tylenol? I've got a massive headache."

He finds a bottle of generic acetaminophen in his first aid kit, and gives two tablets to me. I wash them down with some more water. Nate can't prevent himself from scolding me just a little. "You probably shouldn't be alive, you know. You're one heck of a lucky girl."

I bow my head like a bad puppy. "I know. And a heck of a stupid one. I got dumped by a couple of rogue waves."

"Haystacks," Nate says.

"No. I'm quite sure they were waves."

He smiles. "*Haystacks* are a series of big waves that get created when multiple currents come together. There's a lot of tidal rips not far from where I found you. What the heck were you doing way out there?"

"I followed some dolphins."

Thomas has been gradually edging nearer with a silly grin on his face, and stops two paces from me. "*I* didn't see any dolphins. Did you, Nate?"

Nate shakes his head. "Not today. But it was hard to see *anything* over the rollers. I was afraid I'd get in trouble myself if I went out much further into open sea. Used up all my strength paddling so hard, and decided to make one big loop before throwing in the towel and coming home, hoping maybe Kat'd already come back up on her own. Half a minute later, I spotted a life vest in the water. That was scary. I didn't know if you'd even still be alive."

"I tried to keep an eye on you, Kat, but you vanished," Thomas says with repentant eyes. "I went back between the islands where we came from, but you weren't there either."

"Of course not. I followed *you* out. And what's this crap about us getting in a fight?"

"I'd say we did. You splashed me, then took off in a huff."

"That was in fun, Thomas. And I didn't go away mad. I was having a great time."

Nate slaps me on the back. "I'm glad you did, Kat. But you broke rules number one *and* two. You left your buddy and abandoned your boat, and now your trip is over. You need to be examined by a doctor."

"I didn't abandon my boat. It disappeared. And I don't need a physician to tell me I'm all right."

I anticipate that Nate is about to issue a reminder that my specialty is animals, or even counsel me against self-diagnosis, but he does neither. "I'm the guide who is responsible for your well-being," he says.

I grin at him. "Are not. I read the waiver before I signed it. You're not responsible for anything except feeding me. Menu items subject to substitution."

He smiles and nods. "On that note, think you can handle some breakfast? I've got some killer blueberry pancakes going."

"They smell delicious." I'm lying. My sinuses are so packed with mucous that I can't smell a blessed thing.

I manage to choke down a few of the fluffy cakes, and then Nate wraps me in a blanket while he takes down my tent. Blur surprises me with a solid goodbye handshake, and I make my way to where Harco is playing with the kids on the beach, managing to circumvent Thomas who wanders aimlessly around the camp.

I'm hugging Valerie near her tent when I see him circling. It's not easy to extricate myself from her life-saving warmth and the now-familiar smell of her skin and hair.

Thomas spreads his arms, ready for his turn. I offer him my right hand. "It was good meeting you, Thomas."

"I was thinking I should probably paddle back with you to the take-out. I can buddy Nate back here. We don't need any more disasters."

"I'll take you up on that," says a voice behind me. It's Nate. "But before we go, pack up your stuff too, Thomas. I've already told Blur and Harco to do a cleanup and be ready for my inspection. I don't want to see the slightest evidence that we camped on this island. No trace."

"Are we *all* going home?" I ask, hoping I haven't prematurely ended the whole trip.

"Yeah," Thomas says. "Wha-sup?"

"Nothing's up," Nate says. "We've been on this island two nights already."

"There's a maximum stay, or what?"

"Actually, yes. Four nights is the park's limit for any one island, but I've never done that. It's too limiting for the guests' experiences. My intention was to break camp yesterday, but as we all know, that didn't work out. There's an island I really like less than an hour's paddle from here. We'll have time to go there after you and I get back."

I am relieved. And there is no denying that Thomas's offer to accompany us is a sound one safety-wise—a realm within which I'm in no position to argue. I grab my bags and start for the beach.

CHAPTER 8

THE WAY I FEEL as I drive the familiar streets of Saanich makes me think of Dorothy in *The Wizard of Oz,* clicking her heels and chanting *there's no place like home.* I didn't think I'd ever be here again.

And no house has ever looked more inviting than mine does as I pull up onto the long concrete driveway and click the middle of three buttons embedded in the sun visor. The garage door instantly glides upward in response. I'm going to put on a pot of green tea and wrap a thick duvet around myself in bed. I can stay there as long as I want: I'm on vacation for four more days.

It'll be much better than spending that time in a little tent or paddling a ridiculously unstable boat with a crew of oddballs. What the hell was I *thinking,* anyway?

But even before I enter the house from the garage, something feels wrong. When I turn the knob and push the door, it opens less than a foot before slamming into something.

I poke my head through the opening, and see terrible things. I'm instantly overcome with a sick numbness of shock and disbelief.

My house, my sanctuary, has been trashed.

Cabinets are toppled over. Bills, photos, and once-dried flowers float in the koi ponds. Things are missing. The stereo. The television and DVD player.

Sasha.

"Sasha!" I call out, digging frantically through tall mounds of books and magazines and documents. She's nowhere. I run into the bedroom, weeping as I call for her again. "Sasha! Sasha-girl! Where are you, baby?"

I curse myself for not leaving her with Zaina.

My bed sits very low to the floor, and I'm not sure if even a very scared cat Sasha's size could squeeze under it. So I'm startled by the two green circles reflecting at me from the darkness. Sasha shimmies forward until my outstretched hands can reach her, and I slide her the rest of the way into my arms. I bury my face in her thick fur.

Still holding Sasha, I pick up the kitchen phone, and cradle it in my shoulder to dial 9-1-1. After blurting a panicked description of what has happened, followed by my address, I go back to the bedroom and find my duvet, then curl up on the bed with the cat until the police arrive.

*　*　*

AN AMICABLE Saanich PD detective with a greying buzzcut seems much more concerned about my mental state than about the house and all my possessions. If I told him about my recent brush with death, he'd probably have a better understanding of why I'm such a mess, but then might forget about the robbery entirely. His young partner, on the other hand, wants nothing but answers to an endless stream of boilerplate questions. *Where was I? When did I leave? Who knew that I was away? Have any tradespeople, missionaries or door-to-door sales types been inside the house recently?*

He asks if anything was taken, other than the living room furniture. I give him a list of the things I've noticed so far, and tell him that I have recently divorced, and my ex-husband got the sofa and loveseat.

"Any reason to believe your former husband might have something to do with this?" the younger officer asks.

"I'm quite sure he didn't," I say, but feel obliged to give him Jack's new address. You never know, I guess.

The interrogation seems to be over, so I ask the two officers to please do their thing while I take a time-out.

I go into the study. It's in worse shape than any of the other rooms. The contents of my large bookcase have been dumped onto the floor, books torn apart at the bindings and the pieces thrown all over. The drawers have been pulled right out of the desk, one of them smashed into splintered planks of wood. The envelope is nowhere to be seen.

I go and curl up on the bed with Sasha again, and wait for the police to finish. My feelings alternate between intense fear and even more intense fury. What did I do to get mixed up in all this shit? I have never felt so victimised, so vulnerable, so stinking *violated!* I wonder if I can ever feel safe in this house again. I grasp my ankles and rock on my buttocks. It even hurts to cry.

"Sorry to bother you again, ma'am." It's the detective, standing in the doorway to my bedroom. "May I have another word with you."

I don't like the look on his face. I try to talk, but have to stop and scrape the heavy phlegm from my throat first. "What is it?"

"I was just talking to the Inspector on my radio. I understand our General Investigation Section was looking for you last night. Calls were placed to your residence, but of course there was no answer."

"*What*? Why were they looking for me *last night*?" I catch myself holding my breath, and my body goes insensate again.

"You own an animal hospital in West Saanich?"

"Yes. Yes, I do. What's going on?"

"I'm sorry to be the bearer of more bad news, ma'am. Someone ransacked the place last night. Pretty much same thing as here."

CHAPTER 9

TEARS BLUR MY VISION as I pound harder on the heavy fir door.

"Who is it?" says a gruff voice from inside. The speaker is Zaina, sounding very much like a woman who means to sound like a man.

"Open up, Zane. It's Kat. And Sasha."

The latch clatters, and the door begins to open, banging to a stop when it hits the end of a short chain.

"What are you two doing here? It's nearly midnight. And I thought you weren't supposed to be back until next Sunday." Zaina undoes the chain and opens the door. She is still wearing the usual intense makeup on her eyes and cheekbones, though she has put on a nightie that looks like it's made out of lacy mosquito netting. The fabric serves only to create a sexy haze over her dark nipples, the large faux gem in her navel, and the narrow landing strip of hair below that. I can see three other piercings and a couple of colourful tattoos that aren't normally visible. She doesn't care that I'm looking. This is Zaina.

I let out a heavy sigh. "Sorry, Zane. I lost Nate's kayak and tried to freeze myself to death in the water, so he sent me home," I say. An unexpected sniffle contributes to my pitiful air. "And while I was gone, someone broke into my house and clinic. Everything is *ruined*." I lose it, and start sobbing. Tears rain from my eyes. I'm able to restrain myself from screaming only because I would *really* hate for Zaina's landlady to show up now.

Zane enfolds me in her slender arms, pulling me in close and squeezing hard, while her fingertips gently knead the flesh around my shoulder blades. "Oh, Kat. Kat-Kat-Kat," she clucks. "You poor girl. Get in here and sit down. You're all right now, dear. Let's break Sasha out of that awful mobile jail and I'll put on some nice green tea," she says. "I've got some of the Japanese stuff you like, with the toasted rice mixed in."

The cat mews ruefully at the sound of her own name, and I set the kennel gently on the floor. "Tell me all about it, Kat. I'm so glad you're okay. What you've been through is terrible, but it's over. Everything's good now."

"Thank you, Zane. I feel much better now that I'm here."

"Good, good. You should have called me right away. I'm going to take care of you. Do you need me to talk to Pam about the clinic?"

"She left me three messages, and I spoke to her on the phone for twenty minutes before I came here. Pam is staying at her mom's place for a few days. She was the one who discovered the clinic had been broken into, when she got there this morning. She called the police, and found out they'd already been by during the night but didn't know who to contact when they couldn't find me. So they went back, and asked a bunch of questions, took a statement, and told her what to do next. After they left, she tidied up a bit and faxed a list to the insurance company of what was gone and broken. She said she locked up, and that when she went by my place to feed Sasha this afternoon, everything was fine. Looks like I didn't miss the house burglars by much."

"Wow."

"I know. It's so scary."

"Yes, that too. What I meant was, wow, Pam has been amazing. See, Kat? You've got good support all around. You're going to be just fine."

"I know. I don't deserve her. Or you."

She smiles. "Yeah, *right*. I deserve a kick in the ass for making you go on that trip against your instincts. Shit."

Another long, despondent mew emanates from Sasha's plastic kennel. I kneel beside it and unlatch the metal door. "Sorry, girl." She casts me an ominous look, pushes the lightweight door open with her face, then slinks out and takes cover under the sofa.

Zaina seats me in her comfy old armchair and wraps me in a ratty quilt of many horrid colours, probably picked up at a second-hand store or flea market somewhere in her travels. A sleek black cat with white paws springs up onto my lap from out of sight beside the chair. I let out a little shriek from the surprise. "Muezza!" Zaina says. "*There* you are, boy." She reaches over to stroke him, but he steps away. I scratch behind his ears, and Muezza closes his eyes and sets into a rumbling good purr. Zaina makes a face. "He loves you better than anyone, including me. The two of you relax together a minute. I'll go get that tea."

I start to sob again, and pull Muezza close to me. His heart-shaped black nose touches a tear that has dribbled down to my chin. He looks puzzled, and licks the moisture from his snout. Then the sandpaper tongue rakes up the side of my face to get more of the salty treat.

Zaina named Muezza after the Prophet Mohammed's favourite feline, for whom The Prophet is said to have reserved a permanent place in heaven. According to the story, one day when Mohammed was called to prayer, the original Muezza was snoozing peacefully on the sleeve of his cloak. Rather than wake the cat, The Prophet snipped off the sleeve. Upon his return, the cat bowed to him in appreciation, earning Mohammed's favour. Unlike dogs, which are to this day shunned by Muslims and considered dirty, cats are actually permitted entry to mosques.

Sasha saunters out from her hiding place, and Muezza turns from me and nearly unhinges his jaw in a possessive hiss. The long hairs on Sasha's back prick up like a porcupine's quills, and she puts a bit more distance between herself and the resident feline.

I stroke Muezza while Zaina crashes and bashes away in the kitchen and Sasha plots against me for my infidelity. Some reality program is playing out with no volume on the small TV: bikini-clad girls screaming at a freaky old man with a blurred midsection. It seems nearly as surreal as my own life.

I'm incredibly grateful that Zaina is here for me. Otherwise, I'm not sure what I would have done. We've been best friends since primary school, despite our incredibly different backgrounds.

In a few minutes, she returns and turns off the television. Her nightie is now more modestly covered by a white robe, embroidered with a Hilton monogram. Acquired while in the company of some long-forgotten suitor, I'm sure. Zaina seldom checks in anywhere that costs more than twenty dollars a night—unless a man is footing the bill.

"So, talk to me, and don't omit a detail," she says as I scorch my fingertips on a ceramic cup of green tea without a handle. "What the hell is going on, girlfriend?"

"I don't know. Swear to God. But that's one of the questions I keep asking myself, over and over again."

Zaina wraps her arms around me again, and holds me for a long moment. "Now listen to me, dear. I want to do everything possible to help you, so you've got to give me the straight goods. When somebody breaks into both your house and your place of business at the same time, it's not a coincidence.

Not even if you live in Miami, which you sure as hell don't. This is a low-crime area."

"That's what the cop said. All of Saanich can go weeks at a time without a B and E."

"There you go. So what did the scumbags take?"

"At the clinic, just a microwave and stuff like syringes and scalpels. None of the big equipment. I guess it's hard to pawn off an x-ray or an autoclave. They're numbered so you'd get caught."

"No. The kind of lowlife who breaks into clinics would have channels. You'd be surprised how many departments the good old black market store has. And at the house?"

"Everything of value that a person could carry away. With no neighbours close by, my house is a robber's dream."

"I'm sure the police are operating on the presumption it was the same culprit for both incidents."

I smile, remembering that there was a time when Zaina wanted to become a police officer. "I guess so. They asked a ton of questions, and I told them almost everything."

"Almost?"

I nod. "Something was taken from my house that I think was the robber's motive."

She raises both hands to the sides of her open mouth, and waits for me to go on.

CHAPTER 10

BECAUSE OF THE HIGH cost of living in Victoria, most of the houses have illegal basement suites like the one Zaina lives in. *Basement* is sort of a misnomer, since it implies *below ground*. A goodly portion of the city is built on rocky slopes, from which a big wedge-shape chunk is often excavated or blasted out prior to construction to accommodate the house's bottommost floor. This way, one wall of the basement is fully below grade, and the opposing side sits at ground level.

Zaina's suite is small and quite barren, especially considering that the landlady allows her to keep her belongings there for a token fee whenever she is abroad. The only living room furniture is an old chest of drawers, a ragged couch, and a matching chair. On the walls hang three hideous wooden masks and a Maasai ostrich-feather headdress. There is a kitchen area with a miniature dining set, and one other near-empty room where Zaina works and sleeps. A few potted plants sit perpetually dying on the wide sill of the south-facing window. She inherited the plants from the previous tenant years ago—an African violet, a Christmas cactus, and some other thing that no one has ever been able to identify, with twisted branches and frizzy foliage. They all somehow manage to sustain a few green leaves as they continue to bravely cling to life. I suspect the plants serve as an inspiration to Zane.

The only other furnishing is Zaina's velvet prayer mat, bearing a colourful if busy pattern, wrapped around the image of a golden mosque. She keeps the dome of the mosque angled to point in precisely the direction of the shrine of Kaaba in Mecca. She prays five times a day, always going through a lengthy cleansing ritual first, and carries in her handbag an annoying little digital alarm that plays the *adhan*—the Muslim call to prayer—to remind her when the sun is nearing the prescribed position for that particular day. Since the prayer times are based on sunrise, noon and sunset, two of the three are different every day of the year. In midsummer, Zane gets out of bed at around three in the morning for the first prayer, and does the last one just before midnight. Even our Saturday bagel ritual is limited to the three or four hour window between the noon and afternoon *salat*. I noticed when she adjusted her watch on Saturday to correspond with my habitual lateness, she left the *salat* timer untouched—but didn't mention it. That's slippery ground.

Although Zane is very lax about many things—including even some Islamic beliefs and traditions—the prayer routine is her one big obsession. Missing a *salat* is a grave sin, so if anything happens to interfere with one, she has to make it up later. Her prayer mat has a little blue compass built into it, which is handy when she is travelling and has to locate al-Kaaba in a hurry. I would have a hard time travelling with Zane, for this among other reasons.

Zaina's family moved to Canada in 1977, forced out of their home in northeastern Sri Lanka as a result of Prime Minister Senanayake's *Gal Oya* colonisation scheme.

They were among the lucky ones—many Tamils and Muslims were killed by Sinhalese mobs that encroached on their homes with full backing of the state.

Zaina is the baby of the Marikar family. Her eldest sibling is a brother named Zoeb. Last I heard, he had been honourably discharged from the Canadian army and was convalescing in Kuala Lumpur, suffering from undiagnosed physical ailments and post-traumatic stress disorder.

She also had a sister back in Sri Lanka. Nadira, six years older than Zane, was among hundreds of youths rounded up by the Sri Lankan government's security forces for "interrogation" and never seen again. Others were found dumped in isolated locations, either dead or badly beaten and sexually assaulted. Any time Zaina speaks of her childhood home, she makes a point of mentioning that rapes and murders of civilians by the country's armed forces have never stopped.

When Zaina was thirteen, her mother, Faiza, woke her up one night and told her to grab only her most precious things. They ran away together from Zane's father, a man whom I seldom saw and only ever knew as *him* or *Mr. Marikar*.

Mr. Marikar believed that the words of the Koran were to be taken literally, including where it says: "Good women are obedient," and, "as for those from whom you fear disobedience, admonish them and send them to beds apart and beat them." Apparently he routinely feared Faiza disobedient, and though I never saw the bruises, I often wondered why Zaina's mom would sometimes wear her veils even at home. It wasn't until they had been safe from Mr. Marikar for months that Zaina dared confirm my suspicions.

Zaina is deeply conflicted about many other things in the Koran, yet finds extraordinary strength in her faith. I admire this about her, though much of it continues to remain outside of my realm of understanding. Her Islam is the Sunni version—the *original and best*, she says, as one might endorse a favourite brand of soft drink. In fact, Zaina feels much more strongly about it than that. When the Prophet Mohammed died in 661, the religion's first and most significant schism began. The Prophet himself is said to have favoured his first cousin and son-in-law Ali to succeed him, but at Mohammed's burial, the leaders of the Medina elected another man named Abu Bakr for the role. Abu, an old man, was the father of the Prophet's favourite wife. His followers, including Zaina and almost ninety percent of today's Muslims, are the Sunni. Sunni Muslims consider themselves the most orthodox sect, as they tend to adhere to more traditional beliefs.

The majority of the other Muslims are Shiite, which literally means "Supporters of Ali." Shiites, the minority sect everywhere except Iraq and Iran, tend to be more militant than the Sunnis. There are several other Islamic sects, though far fewer than in Christianity.

Zaina has always taken the time to explain such things to me, which often means trying to deal with my inane or just plain unanswerable questions. She must know it means a lot to me. When life is in the crapper, advice from someone with such a radically different philosophy can be mind-bending—usually in a good way!

Each of the difficult times we've shared have made our bond more unbreakable. When we were in our teens, Zaina's normally calm and sharp-minded mother started to become disoriented and easily enraged. She would forget the names of people she knew well—including Zaina. As it turned out, these were for her the early signs of Alzheimer's. The symptoms eventually progressed to the point that Faiza had to be put in an extended care facility. Watching the anguish caused by the deterioration of her mother's once-beautiful personality and mind, and the kindness with which Zaina dealt with the many daily challenges, I grew to love my friend profoundly.

Years later, while Zane was on a tropical vacation at twenty-one, she met a well-to-do nickel mine manager from Sudbury who was sixteen years her senior—and moved there almost immediately thereafter to marry him.

I was devastated that my friend was relocating across the country, and apprehensive about her snap decision, but hoped for the best. I took an unpaid leave from my job as a front desk worker at the Victoria Animal Shelter and spent three weeks in the Ontario mining town, helping to make the preparations and set up for her new life. The marriage lasted mere months before Zaina became convinced it was a terrible mistake. She showed up on my doorstep—rain-soaked and crying—with nothing but the clothes she had on. Her own conscience browbeat her so badly for recklessly shattering poor D'arcy's heart that she resisted her divorce lawyer's prompting to pursue half of the guy's ample holdings. In the end, she took back nothing more than what she brought into the relationship—which wasn't much.

George Washington said that True Friendship is a plant of slow growth, and that two people must persevere together through a lot of crap in order to have cultivated one. (I'm paraphrasing a bit). I believe Zaina and I can proudly claim True Friendship.

The emotional support has always gone both ways. Earlier this year, when Zane retrieved my email about Steve's sudden death, she was hanging out on a sleepy Greek island, having a fabulous time. She hopped a boat that very afternoon, and waited all the next day at an airport in Athens for a westbound seat to become available. I was lucky she did. When I lost Mom, Zaina was the only thing that kept me from coming unglued.

CHAPTER 11

I TELL ZAINA EVERYTHING about the cow photos: how they arrived at the clinic, my collapse, all about the strange incisions, the radiation, and the peculiar way that some of the animals appeared to have been dropped from the sky.

"You didn't share *any* of this with the cops? *Why*, Kat?"

"I wasn't positive the pictures were gone until after they had left," I say, which isn't a complete lie. Closer to the truth is that I was embarrassed to mention them, and hoped they would turn up to remove themselves from the equation. "The room they were in was worse than any other part of the house. I went through everything in it at least four times. The envelope wasn't there."

"Kat, you *knew*. I'll bet you knew the damned thing was gone before you even looked. You really should have told them about the photos."

"It's just so crazy, Zane. My life is just like that room now. I'm humiliated. This just makes me look like more of a freak than ever. There's no explanation for any of this bullshit. And if the police are going to catch whoever did the break-ins, they'll do just as well to use other evidence."

"It's always best if they know everything. No one likes doing a jigsaw puzzle after someone's pocketed a few of the pieces. You're right; it is crazy. What I can't get my head around is why someone would take the risk of burglarising two places just for that? I'll grant you those photos sound weird, but really, *who cares?* And why steal all those other things? The stereo, TV, syringes? You said they might have spied on you looking at the pictures on your deck. Then why break into the clinic first?"

"Maybe they were after something else at the clinic. There was a mark on the envelope where something was paper-clipped to it at some point. The office is where the photos were delivered to, and they could have guessed I removed the missing attachment and left it there. I never actually *saw* anyone at my house. Just got the willies. And I happen to think it makes a *lot* of sense that they took the other things, because that's what ordinary burglars do. They steal valuable things. They wanted the police to fill out their reports, and then go off and forget all about the insignificant victim, because that's what cops do. Probably knew taking the other stuff would make it easy for me to forget—or neglect to mention—the photos."

"Give you an *excuse* not to mention them, you mean. I'm sure the police really will be interested in what you've told me. You might have the true motive for them. At least something to start with."

I laugh. "I thought I was the silly one here. You think the Saanich Police are going to assign a special team to find out why someone stole two contact sheets of cow pictures? I'm sure they'll get right on it. Right after they catch the vile degenerate who's been stealing old man Stinson's kiwifruit at night, and the criminal mastermind responsible for kicking in Mary O'Leary's storm door."

She shakes her head, giggling. "Maybe you're right. But why do you think someone might send you mutilated cow photos in the first place?"

"Beats the hell out of me. At first I took it as a personal threat. The envelope was addressed to me by name, so it wasn't just bad luck with a misdirected delivery. Could be a crazy animal rights activist who no one listens to, hoping that I might bring in the media and stir up some publicity."

"Well, you *are* a respected veterinary researcher. *I* happen to admire your work."

"Respected in the field of cocker spaniels with knee ligament injuries, not herefords who've taken bad falls from the sky after little green men carved out their eyes and pink parts. What I'm saying is that I don't believe I was picked out at random. I *wish*, but it doesn't look that way. Someone wanted me to have those photos. And maybe someone else took exception."

"I saw a documentary about cattle mutilations. That's some kind of freaky shit, Katherine. There's never any blood, and scavengers won't go anywhere near the carcasses. They had video footage of a cow slumped over the top of a telephone post. It's got to be aliens."

"I really don't know, Zane. But it wasn't aliens who sent the photos. Or who broke in and stole them from me."

"What about Jack? He grew up on a farm."

"But he hardly ever goes back, and the photos were taken in different seasons. One had snow on harrowed dirt, and another had canola in bloom. This was a long-term project. Not only that, but Jack's the worst photographer on earth. These photos are good—medium format film from a pro camera."

"Someone else could have taken them. Maybe Jack was just the sender. He could have even stumbled upon them on the sidewalk, and thought it would be fun to send them to you."

"I kind of *like* that possibility. It suggests the pictures mean nothing, which is fine by me. But the name of my clinic was wrong, and Jack wouldn't have done that. He *named* it."

"Let's put Jack on our *maybe* list. Now let's think about the people you went to college with. That was a rural school. Anyone who fits the bill there?"

I let out a pained laugh. "About two hundred. The U of S is in the heartland of the Canadian Prairies. Seemed like everyone had a farm background but me."

"Okay. Work with me, Kat. Give me the prime suspect list."

"It's really not so easy. Nobody comes to mind."

"No one? Come *on*."

"Okay, okay. There was a guy named Rudy who had sort of a two-pronged fetish."

"Two-pronged?"

"Cows and me."

She smiles. "That's sounding familiar now. Was he the guy who got caught in a barn, standing on a stool behind a cow?"

I nod. "Not sure if I ever told you that I also found Rudy in the residence laundromat, stealing a pair of my panties out of the washing machine."

"No, I don't think you did. I'd remember *that*. Sounds like a definite A-list suspect to me. Any idea what became of this freakazoid?"

"He was an honours student, in spite of his strange erotic fixations. I'm sure he's working in the field."

"Probably packing beef in a rural vet clinic. Let's look old Rudy up."

CHAPTER 12

ZAINA IS TRULY AMAZING with the Internet. As a freelance writer, she's constantly online, often researching a half dozen stories at any given time. She's also created her own pages on about fifteen travel sites, sharing information on her own globetrotting adventures and gathering juice for upcoming ones. She's met more men through those sites than I care to know about, though the stories always leak—or rather *gush*—out. It's astonishing how many guys will plan their travels around the possibility of getting laid by a complete stranger.

We go into Zaina's tiny and cluttered bedroom-office and she spins a bright red trackball to wake up her PowerBook. She never shuts the machine down, because she's an impulsive sort, and likes to have it ready to tune into a Webcast or to hunt down a story lead as quickly as possible after a flash of inspiration flies from the flint. Sparks die fast in the open air.

Zaina always keeps at least one browser window open, and layered behind that three or four others of Word files—articles in progress.

"What was Two-Prong's last name?"

I have to think about this. "Rudy... God, I don't know. His family was originally from Brazil. Think it started with an R too. Rudy Ramires? No. Rodrigues. Rudy Rodrigues. With an S, not a Z, since it's Portuguese."

Zaina's dark, slender fingers drum on the keys, moving almost too quickly for me to see. In a nanosecond, she's found nearly seven thousand matches.

"Could Rudy be the head of UNICEF's operations in Uzbekistan now?"

I wince. "Jeez, I hope not. That's a *children's* organisation, for God's sakes."

"Doesn't ring right, does it? Let's tighten the net. You veterinarians are DVMs, right? Rudy Rodrigues, DVM. And we'll add his alma mater, but with a pipe symbol first to make it optional."

She types this in and hits the Search button. "Looks like he's living in Sydney."

"No way. Just a few miles from here?"

"That's Sidney with an I. This guy's in Oz."

She clicks the link and a biography page opens up. There's a photo of a much heavier and balder version of the Rudy Rodrigues than the one I knew. "That's him. What's he doing there?"

"Working in an aquatic animal facility. Been there four years now, it says."

"Looks like Rudy's off the list."

"Not necessarily. They have cattle in Australia."

"Not all the breeds I saw. The pictures were taken in Canada. Black dirt, snow, canola, poplar trees."

"Okay. Let's forget about him for now. Who else?"

"I don't know."

"Think," she says, slapping the desk. "Hey!" She stands and grins at me. Her eyes zip around like she's thinking hard.

"Hay is what cows eat. So what?"

"You said the pictures were taken with an expensive camera. What about the guy who gave you that big one you've got? Your hot-looking cowboy sex toy until Jack came along and swept you off your feet. Isn't *he* a farmer?"

Zane likes to embellish the lasciviousness of my relationships, perhaps unable to imagine anything different. Or maybe I'm just fun to tease. "Craig Butler? His father was a cattle breeder, but I have no idea what Craig's been up to the past fifteen years. I doubt he took over the family business, though. He went to Vet School to get away from it."

"But he dropped out at the beginning of fourth year, didn't he? Maybe he fell back on it. You mean you've *never* looked the guy up?"

"No."

"That's weird, Kat. I've tracked down all my early flames. Couldn't be bothered with the recent ones, but the old ones can be interesting. I like to know who they've become—how badly they failed to live up to all their grandiose dreams."

"Not me. I haven't got a clue where Craig Butler is or how many kids he's got. After I met Jack, I guess I never felt a need to look back."

"*Right.* Jack completed you," she says with a laugh. "Come on. Let's find out what old Craig is doing with himself. Maybe he's running a bovine organ co-op."

She begins with a Web search on the name Craig Butler. Even *I* know that a name so common will bring back thousands of matches. Just over three thousand, it turns out.

"What can we use to qualify Craig?" she asks. "He wouldn't be a doctor."

"Try *cattle breeder*."

She goes to a new page for an advanced search, and puts Craig's full name and the word "cattle" in the *all of the words* field. Under *at least one of*, she types in "breeder" and "mutilations."

Four matches.

The top one takes us to a directory of paranormal occurrences, with a first-person account of a rancher's grim discovery that initially appeared to be a mutilated animal, but turned out to be predators feasting on a cow and her calf after a night-time birth went wrong. The name Craig Butler was linked to an article further down on the page, and referred to an eighty-seven-year-old retired infantryman who claimed to have hosted a dinner party for three hungry sasquatches at his Montana ranch.

The other three hits look more promising.

"Craig Butler has personally ... more than sixty **cattle mutilation cases...**" says the summary of the topmost one, truncating the original text and bolding the keywords. I reach for the trackball, and Zaina playfully whacks my hand away.

"Patience," she says with a little smile, and clicks on the hyperlink. Extra slowly, just to aggravate me.

The requested page does not exist on this server.

"Great," I say. "Try the next."

Same thing.

Likewise for the final one.

"They all link to pages on the same site," Zaina says, pointing out how the links originate at the same domain. "It looks like the content about Craig has either been taken down or moved."

She tries a query using the same keywords, but searching newsgroups instead of Web pages. This time, two matches. I'm feeling doubtful.

And as I expected, the first link is dead.

"Look at *this*," Zaina says, after clicking the other.

"I am. But I don't understand newsgroup postings. They're full of low-brow insults and repetitive jibberjabber."

"This is a discussion board, not a newsgroup. What that means is it's posted on a single server rather than being replicated on thousands of different ones all over the world. Looks like it's got all your insults and jibberjabber, though. There are a hundred and forty-eight articles, and Craig's name appears six times, four of those being redundant. Posted only a week ago."

I read the text on the screen:

> I talked to **Craig Butler** from Alberta last summer about the Bluff River cow. He's been a cattle breeder all his life and seen enough of these things to be sure when he's looking at a genuine mute. He said he was positive that one was the real deal. His Geiger counter found ionisation from gamma radiation on the carcass and in the surrounding soil, and there was formaldehyde gel on some of the cuts (he said this keeps predators away) which BTW is all consistent with the theory he was working on. Eyes, tongue, brain, spine, genitals and colon are carved out, the anus taken in a triangular cut that looks like it was cauterised by laser surgery.
>
> > The conspiracy theory stuff is fun. But why would they
> > leave the carcass behind? That makes no sense.
>
> If you can answer that question, grasshopper, maybe you'll have solved tens of thousands of **cattle mutilation** cases. No one knows. Except maybe **Craig Butler**, but he's no help anymore. Oo-ee-ooo. *LOL*

From there, the discussion moves on to animal mutilations in Brazil and Alabama, with no further mention of Craig.

Zaina smiles at me. *"Craig Butler from Alberta.* This has got to be your guy. Wonder why he's *no help anymore."*

"Could be because people are getting ugly with him too. They robbed me twice, and I'm not even involved in this."

"You're *involved*, all right. You have been ever since Craig decided to send you those pictures. You said Pam got a look at whoever did the drop-off. What did he look like?"

"Well, it sure wasn't Craig. Pam said the delivery guy was short, and Craig is six-foot-four. And the guy was fat. Some men put on weight, but I can't see it on Craig's frame. He has an incredible metabolism."

"That'd mean he eats a lot. If his metabolism slowed down like most of ours do, he'd have put on weight. And when someone gets wider, they tend to look shorter. Did Pam notice anything else?"

I shake my head at this, but answer the question. "She said there was no front plate on the car. An older model Honda Civic."

"That's a fit too. Remember when Zoeb was posted to the Canadian Forces Base in eastern Alberta a few years back? He drove over here in a sporty little Acura with a nice clean front bumper. Alberta stopped issuing front plates not long before that to save money. Far as I know, the closest other province that's done the same is Quebec. A man in a beat-up old Civic probably didn't drive three thousand clicks."

"Probably not, particularly considering Pam thought he might have been drinking. Besides, the photos were of cows and bulls, not maple syrup."

"They *do* have cattle in Quebec."

"Kidding. I remember reading during the Mad Cow crisis something like eighty percent of Canadian cattle live in Alberta. So eight in ten odds. I'd look there first, unless I knew someone in Quebec. My aunt Justine lives in Montreal, but her lease agreement doesn't allow pets or steers."

"What about Washington State? Seems to me that a lot of the front bumpers there are clear."

"No. I know a few people in Seattle who don't have front plates, but they're exempt from the law because their bumpers came without the mounting brackets. State law allows people to go without a front plate if adding one would damage the car, and supposedly devalue it. The vehicle has to have been built after 1999 or sometime around then to qualify. I think Kansas is the closest state that issues only a rear plate. Maybe Arizona."

Zaina rolls her eyes. "Okay, Rain Woman. I'm convinced." She's always impressed with my ability to recall such trivial data. "Why don't you call Craig?" Her fingers rumble over the keyboard, and up comes a directory page displaying a telephone number and P.O. box for a Craig Butler in the St. Paul region.

"The absence of a street address tells us it's a rural home," she says.

"I'll give him a try in the morning."

"Better do it first thing if he's a farmer." She writes the telephone number at the bottom of a page in a narrow reporter's notebook filled with indecipherable scribbles. "If he's still single, maybe you can rekindle something," she adds with a nudge.

"Not a chance," I say.

And I mean it.

CHAPTER 13

It's still utterly black outside at three-thirty a.m. when I hear Zaina's prayer alarm sing its annoying tune, followed by running water and the sounds of cleansing. There's a *bump* when she places a chunk of baked clay from Saudi Arabia near the front of her mat and I watch bleary-eyed as she prostrates herself over it. The soft murmur of her voice is soothing, but I'm unable to drift back to sleep.

I'm sitting on the side of the sofa when she finishes. She offers to make me a latté with her little stovetop steam-infusion espresso maker, but I decline. I might try to go back to sleep after we make the call. I wash my face with cold water, which soothes my smouldering eyes.

Zaina toasts rye bread and gives me two big oval slices with plenty of butter and Muslim-friendly mango preserves, made without gelatine. We eat without a word, making no sound other than the crunching of our toast.

When we're finished, Zaina gets up and moves to the flimsy chair by her phone, and places her notebook atop her crossed legs.

"Ready?" she says.

"My God, Zaina. It's not even five. It would be cruel to call Craig now."

"The asshole sent you disgusting photos with no explanation. Don't talk to me about cruel. Besides, it's nearly six where he lives. We don't want to miss him if he's got to go feed the cows or something."

"We still don't even know for sure it was Craig."

"Oh, of course we do, Kat. The guy investigates *alien cattle mutilations* for a hobby. That's not exactly stamp collecting. What are the chances of it being someone else? *Really*? Slim to none, I'd say, and Slim's out of town."

She dials all the numbers but the last one, then stands and offers me the chair—waiting for me to take it before punching the final button.

It rings. And rings. And rings. And rings.

And rings.

Finally, it picks up.

"You've reached Craig Butler," the voice says. He sounds just as I remember, a bit of a prairie drawl and just the slightest lisp. "Please leave me a detailed message at the tone, and rest assured I'll get back to you first chance I get. Take care now."

There's no such tone. After a click, a digital female voice comes on: "This mailbox is full. Please try again later."

I hang up.

"Voice mail," I mutter.

"Why didn't you leave your number?"

"His mailbox was full, thank God. Sounds like he lives alone, too. He said, 'you've reached Craig Butler,' not 'the Butler residence,' or 'Craig and so-and-so.' And then, 'I'll get back to you.'"

"Perfect." She grins mischievously. "Let's try again. Maybe he's sleeping, and someone left him a long-winded message overnight."

"What if it wasn't him who sent the pictures?"

"Then you tell him it was fun talking and have a nice life. But I don't think that's an issue. Craig Butler *is* our man. All clues point to him, and nowhere else. Like OJ Simpson's search for the real killers. All the evidence keeps leading him to one person."

"Yeah. *Himself*. Seriously, though, if Craig lives on an acreage or a farm, you should be able to find out where that is, right?"

"Of course. I think every county and municipal district has maps online, segmented and listed by owner."

With this, she plods over to the computer to begin a new search. In less than a minute, a map of the county of St. Paul is on the screen. She zooms in on an area northwest of the town."

"Right here. Craig Butler. Looks to me like about twenty-five hectares, so I'd say it's a good chance the cattle breeding thing is still what he does. Don't think you can make a living growing anything but weed on an area that small."

"I guess Craig's parents must have moved out or passed on if the property is showing under his name."

"Were they old?"

"Not really. Probably in their seventies by now, though. They might have moved to a condo or something low-maintenance, I suppose. I'm sure they're still alive. Now take us to the WestJet site."

"What?"

"I'm going to visit my old boyfriend."

"Whoa. That's a little extreme, Kat."

"No it isn't. I'm on vacation, and it takes like an hour to fly there. I'll rent a car and be talking to him face-to-face before noon. I need some answers here, Zane, and I'm finished with the games."

"What if he's become... you know, *weird?*"

"We're all weird. Craig is not a danger to me. Come on, Zane. Let me be the one who is a little impulsive for a change."

She just smiles for a moment, not seeming to know what to say to this. "All right. Will you come back tonight?"

"If I can. Otherwise I'll get a cheap motel room and head back first thing in the morning."

"I'm sure Craig will offer to put you up."

"I'd still take the motel."

CHAPTER 14

ZAINA IS HAPPY TO drive me to the airport. In exchange, she gets the use of my car for a few days. She's a remarkably safe driver, considering how adventurous she is in other respects. I know if anything happened to the Passat, it would be harder on her than it would on me. And I feel I owe her for all the emotional support I've needed lately. I've become a high-maintenance friend.

I am anxious to know what the hell Craig is up to with the mutilated cows. What he apparently knows that he isn't telling people. It looks like for some reason he might be waiting to spill the beans to me.

We stop by my house to pick up some clothing and luggage for the trip. Zaina offers to help tidy up while I'm away, but I plead with her to leave things the way they are. I'll get to it in due time.

Zaina parks outside the garage, which is fine. We can enter through the front door. I'd prefer not to go in the same way I did the last time anyway.

A different kind of surprise awaits me now. On the front step stands an enormous bouquet of mixed exotic flowers. Numerous varieties of orchids, mixed with orange and yellow Birds of Paradise, and centred on a big dome-shaped bloom of hot pink ginger.

"Zaina," I stammer. "Are these from you?" I realize even before I finish asking it that this bouquet is *far* out of her price range.

She laughs. "Yeah, right. I don't even know what the hell those things *are*. Maybe from your alien cow mutilators. I'd say the giant pink pine cone looks more Venusian than Martian, what do you think?"

I lift the tag, and almost fall on my face.

Hope you're resting well and staying warm.
Thomas Austin
555-3584

"This is interesting," Zaina says. "Who is Thomas Austin, Kat? Sounds *very* macho. Like Steve Austin, the Six Million Dollar Man."

"Not quite. This is Stompin' Tom, the character I couldn't shake off on the kayaking trip. Looks like he's taken to stalking me now. I'm going to kick Nate's ass for this. He must have told the jerkass where I live."

"Relax, Kat. He just sent you flowers. That's what romantic people do. Stalkers send body parts."

"Now *there's* something to look forward to. Stompin' Tom's pecker, in baby's breath. Thank you, Zane. You want these things?"

"They're weird, but sure, if you don't. What's this guy Thomas like?"

"Me," I say. "That's the problem. He's not my type."

"Mine, then?"

"God, I hope not. He says he sells life insurance in Vancouver, but you'd never know it to look at him. More like Nick Nolte in fleece leggings."

"Hmm. Doesn't sound so bad. Mind if *I* call this number?"

"Please *don't*, Zaina. I mean it. The guy's scary. He had a swastika tattooed on his shoulder." I choose not to mention that it has been converted to a checkerboard. "He came with Nate and me back to the take-out spot, and was supposed to buddy Nate back. Obviously changed his mind."

"But you didn't see him on the ferry back?"

"No. But that hardly means he wasn't on it. I sat in one spot the whole way, watching the inlet go by. Freak must have brought all his gear in the kayak with him. And Nate must have had to paddle back alone."

"You're right, Kat. Tom Austin sounds like too much of an ass even for me."

*   *   *

ON PREVIOUS flights off the island, I've always felt melancholy in leaving my home behind. Now, with my house and office in ruin, I feel guiltily irresponsible. Somehow, this strange relief in escaping even overshadows all my fear and apprehension.

Before leaving home, I telephoned Pam, and she said she would feel better if I let her continue to get the clinic in order, work with the insurance company and lab equipment suppliers to have everything replaced as soon as possible. I might as well even take a few more days, she said with feigned cheer. Not much I can do without my tools.

The same insurance company covers my house, so I've given Pam an initial list of the things I know to be missing so far. There will surely have to be an addendum. I didn't think to check for my camera gear, for one thing. I hope that isn't gone.

Though I asked Zaina not to tidy up my house, I don't feel as bad about letting Pam do the same at the clinic. I'm paying her for it, and it'll be much easier to go back to work with everything restored to some semblance of order.

* * *

THE ONLY baggage I've brought is Mom's weathered brown Louis Vuitton handbag and an overnight tote that met the carry-on restrictions, so I'm spared the gruelling arrivals carousel watch-and-wait. For the first time in my life, I found it easy to pack light. All I've got with me is two changes of underwear (one for tomorrow in case I have to stay, plus the mandatory extra), a pair of stretch-denim jeans, a white crinkled-cotton top (doesn't need ironing), and my light blue windproof fleece jacket. That plus a small stack of Ani DiFranco and Sarah McLaughlan discs (though I managed to forget my Discman), and some basic makeup—lipstick, foundation, eyeliner, mascara, and an all-in-one palette with eyeshadow and blush. Today, I'm wearing blue cotton-spandex Capris and a black-and-white striped T-shirt. I do not wish to look especially attractive for Craig—nor would I want him to think I've let myself go.

I get a rental car as quickly as possible—a cherry-coloured Chrysler Intrepid—and buy a map to plan a course that will get me to Craig's place without going through Edmonton. The city is situated directly between the airport and my destination, but it would probably take an hour longer to make my way through urban streets than to drive an extra thirty kilometres at highway speed.

I take Highway 21, passing to the east of Edmonton and the smaller adjacent city of Sherwood Park. As I crest the summit of a particularly big and broad hill, I glance a couple of times to my left at the faraway clusters of skyscrapers that are downtown Edmonton. Certainly there must be a few new buildings, but it looks to me from out here exactly as I remember it.

I carry on through Fort Saskatchewan, another bedroom community. It's surrounded by tremendous industrial parks where staggering volumes of petrochemicals are processed and refined inside endless monstrous structures of gleaming metal. After that it's typical prairie scenery for the next hundred miles or so, dotted with farmhouses and a handful of French and Ukrainian villages—the kind that seem to grow smaller with time instead of bigger.

* * *

THE BUTLER acreage appears before me far sooner than I'd like it to—just as an Ani D song entitled "Reckoning" begins. I've been envisioning my arrival and our reunion again and again, starting even before the fruitless phone call. I feel nervous as hell.

As I approach on the winding driveway, the home seems somehow different. It's smaller than I remember it—an old two-storey brick farmhouse that belonged to Craig's parents the two times I was here. The online directory listing Zaina found suggested this is no longer the case.

Ivy hangs from the walls and eavestroughs. The lawn is unkempt and has been successfully claimed by legions of dandelions and thistles. Brown bullrushes spray out of a dried-up pond to the left of the house, and a museum of sorts is on display on the right, comprised of an ancient threshing machine, a broken-down windmill and rust-covered water tank. A bright red barn behind the house provides bold contrast to the rest of the tumbledown theme. All of this dilapidation and disorder is unexpected to me, because Craig was always one to take good care of his possessions and keep them orderly.

It makes me wonder if I've made a mistake. Is Craig away, on vacation, perhaps? Or maybe he's sold the property, and the county hasn't updated its map yet.

The joke would sure be on me, wouldn't it?

The driveway splits into a fork, where it becomes a ring road around the house. I go right.

To my relief, a dark green Jeep Cherokee is parked on a gravel pad near the back of the house. I park alongside the Jeep, and climb out. I take a look inside it as I walk by. The interior—glass and all—is covered with fine dust. There is a thinner area within the dust on the windshield where a large patch was wiped away at some point, but enough sediment has since settled there that it would be a challenge to see where one was driving.

I am uneasy about having looked, not knowing if someone in the house is watching from behind any of the curtains drawn over all its windows.

I walk the line of crumbling concrete slabs that lead to Craig's back door. Something doesn't feel right…

CHAPTER 15

THE ANTIQUE PANE OF GLASS on the door rattles loosely within its frame when I rap on it, and I'm able to see just a sliver of the house's interior through a narrow gap between yellowed drapes.

No movement inside. There is an X made from two strips of black tape across the doorbell button, but I try it anyway. A robust Westminster peal rings out, from real carillon-style chimes and not an electronic synthesizer, judging by the rich tonality and impressive resonance. If a deaf man were home, he'd feel the vibrations.

But there is no response. I pound on the wood panel of the door, afraid hitting the glass any harder would shatter it. "Hello?" I shout. "Craig? Anyone home?"

I try the knob. Locked.

The Jeep must belong to Craig. Maybe he is in the barn. As I walk to it on a wide strip of gravel, I make note of something unusual for the ranch of a cattle breeder.

No cattle in sight.

The big red barn has a big mound of earth built up against one side of it, acting as a ramp to give access to elevated double doors. The barn has a second level, presumably so that more of the precious breeding stock can be taken inside when the weather is bad. Near the large front entrance is a human-sized entrance. I try the knob, and it opens.

"Craig?" I call into the darkness.

Nothing. The barn smells only faintly of cow manure. Near the door is a light switch, and I flip it on.

There are no cattle in here either. Only a ghost of their tangy scent remains. Looks like Craig has gotten out of the business. The many wooden stalls are still here, where the animals were once restrained and fed from troughs at one end. Near the big front doors, a rawhide lariat and leather bullwhip hang from spikes on the wooden beams, above a tin bucket still full of oats. An old, teal-coloured Dodge pickup with four flat tires takes up much of the open space, and next to it are many boxes, carelessly packed and piled haphazardly. A couple of them have fallen over and spewed out their contents. Framed photos spill from one like produce from a cornucopia.

I pick up one of the photos, and quickly recognise the boy in it to be Craig—about twenty-five years ago. His million-dollar smile never changed. Another picture is of a couple I don't know, garbed in the worst of seventies clothing. There is a severely faded picture of Craig's parents standing in front of a wood-panelled station wagon, and then more photos of unidentified people. *Why would these be out in the barn?*

The piled boxes are overflowing with all kinds of clothing, from denim overalls to men's briefs. Garments string out from a tear in the side of one carton like the entrails of a deer ripped open by coyotes. Other boxes are stuffed with the kind of things you'd expect to find at a rummage sale: old dishes, records, serving trays and even a blender and toaster oven. If not for all the framed photographs, this is what I would guess Craig to be preparing for. But nobody sells his family photos.

Too bizarre.

I leave the barn and walk back toward my car, but instead of getting in and driving off, I continue to the house, then turn onto a sidewalk that runs parallel to the back wall and follow it around the corner. An elliptical galvanised steel vessel blockades the path, and has been filled almost to the rim with rainwater via a downspout from the eavestroughs. The contents are topped with a frothy layer of rotting algae. The way the tank covers nearly the whole sidewalk, it was probably put here fairly recently, a temporary mitigation to the drought. With its unusually tall trusses, the roof would have much more surface area than most, but I'm nonetheless surprised it has caught enough rain to keep the reservoir so full. An old elm tree and spiky wild rose bushes have grown over what little of the sidewalk the vat doesn't cover. There is a barbed-wire fence on the other side of the big tree, so I can't go around that way—but I think if I squeeze close to the tank and limbo above the green broth, I should have no trouble getting past.

I lean a bit too far, and grab a branch for support—discovering the one I've chosen to originate from a skinny offspring of the elm. Its trunk whips over effortlessly. Somehow, this is enough to keep me from falling in, but I'm still badly off-balance. I kick up a leg to compensate, flailing my hands desperately for anything else to latch onto.

My fingers catch the end of a branch from the big tree. It springs taut just as I'm bracing for the cool sensation of my rump plunging into the festering gumbo—followed immediately thereafter by the rest of me. A dizzying waft of decay assaults my sinuses, and my guts surge into my gullet. Careful not to inhale again, I tow myself forward and manage to swing back onto the path on the other side of the tree.

All that to avoid backtracking and going around the other side of the house. *Very efficient, Kat.*

I try to shake off the thought of how close I was to treading rotten pea soup, and proceed down the walk. DangerGirl I may not be, but I did keep my slacks dry.

I try the front door, and am surprised the knob turns freely. Around and around and around. It doesn't appear to be connected to the mechanism at all. I give the door a push, and it swings open.

"Hello?" I say. How startled I would be at an answer, especially if it were someone other than Craig! Technically I haven't broken in, but getting a package *believed to be* from someone surely doesn't entitle the recipient to trespass on the other's private property.

The front entrance leads into a mudroom, with a pair of clay-encrusted men's rubber boots and tidy white running shoes about the same size on the floor. A wooden coat tree holds a red and black flannel lumberjack's coat, and a green down-filled parka with wolf fur around the collar.

"Anybody home?" I say, managing a singsongy tone.

The air carries a faint chemical smell that's vaguely familiar. A layer of fine dust covers everything, in which numerous boot prints set out from this area into other parts of the house. Mostly from the same boots, I see, with only a few prints that are different. The dust is perceivably heavier in the divergent prints, but their size appears similar enough that the same person may have made them all. I look back at my own footprints and see that I too am leaving a record of my movements.

This place must be a housekeeper's worst nightmare. Ranching can be a gritty business. It seems that every activity a farmer undertakes—clearing land, tilling, seeding, fertilising, harvesting, baling, harrowing—stirs up dust, especially when things get dry. And these have been the driest years since the thirties. It still surprises me that the rain catcher outside was so full, though it is positioned to be out of the afternoon sun and rigged to receive water from the eaves on both sides of the roof. It probably wouldn't take much precipitation to keep it topped up, but Craig can't be using much of the water.

Aside from the dust, the house is remarkably neat and tidy. The furniture is befittingly made from logs and rawhide-coloured upholstery imprinted with wildlife images. Impressive antlers from deer, elk, and moose adorn two of the living room walls. There is only one photo in the room, centred atop the fireplace mantle. It's a large colour print, in an ornate gilded frame. I step over a pine coffee table and go straight for it.

The photo is of a couple, and the man is Craig. He's sporting a pale grey tuxedo, and the long-haired brunette at his side is wearing the kind of elaborate white dress little girls daydream of, complete with puffy sleeves, lacy veil, and a sparkling tiara.

Craig is married!

It doesn't fit with this house. Nothing here seems to belong to—or even suggest the presence of—a woman.

The non-glare glass is badly cracked near the lower right-hand corner, and the white plaster of the frame is visible in two places, where its gilded paint has been chipped away. Looks like the picture has taken a tumble at some point.

I reach out, but stop myself just before my fingers make contact. I shouldn't be in here at all, and that would leave noticeable—potentially incriminating, even—prints in the dust.

Craig's *wife* may not be too forgiving of my presence here.

There is a bathroom just off the living room. I flip the lightswitch, and a big round bulb casts a red luminescence. It's a darkroom safe light. Around the parameter of the doorframe is weather stripping to keep outside light from trickling in, and there is a table next to the sink on which sit empty chemical trays and an enlarger. A small metal cabinet is in the corner, where Craig must hang his film to dry. The cabinet's door is wide open, and inside I see nothing but empty clips. *No projects on the go, Craig? And what kind of a wife would let you convert the main-floor bathroom into a darkroom?*

I peek into the kitchen, and notice there is a laundry room adjacent to that. The washer and dryer are both open, and neither has anything inside.

I want to find the master bedroom. Then I'll know if Craig's wife still lives here. If so, perhaps I should get them a central vac as a belated wedding gift.

I've never been upstairs. The two times Craig brought me here were day trips, and we headed back home by late afternoon on both occasions. Though I believe Craig's parents did their best to be hospitable, they were clearly not comfortable having *The Girlfriend* here, and far from the kind to give household tours.

The doors to the four upstairs rooms are all closed. It occurs to me that Craig may be on the other side of one of them, and that something terrible might have happened to render him unresponsive.

Am I prepared for what I might find inside?

Maybe not. But I've got a keen sense of smell, and it detects no foul odours in this house. But the subtle chemical scent is upstairs too, I notice.

If someone had been dead more than a day in here, it would be unmistakable, even in a closed room.

Right?

I reach for the crystal knob of the nearest door. It's not locked. The door itself is a little sticky, but jerks inward after a bit of coaxing.

It's a room full of junk: piles of cardboard boxes, stacks of old newspapers and periodicals. I walk in and pick through one stack. *Canadian Hereford Digest. Cattleman Magazine. Farm & Ranch. Big Boobs.*

I give my head a shake, and leaf through this last one. The magazine's name is a terrible understatement. Most of these poor women's breasts are larger than watermelons, many taking a kicking in the fight against gravity. A feeling of nervous guilt comes over me as I flip through the pages, checking out the amazing mammaries. Where do they get these mutants? Someone must actually approach top-heavy ladies in public and ask them to pose. What kind of line would that person use? *Excuse me, ma'am. I'm with* Big Boobs, *and couldn't help but notice you've got a freakishly huge rack. How would you like to make the easiest two hundred bucks of your life?*

I look down at my own 34-Bs and wonder what Craig saw in *me*. Then I recall the woman wearing the wedding dress in the photo. *She* appeared to have a normal-sized chest.

It's a silly fetish, that's all. Maybe this is what happens when you spend too much time looking at cow's udders. I hope to God collecting for artificial insemination hasn't also had an effect on him. With this thought, I hold my breath and rummage deeper in the pile, but thankfully the rest of the magazines are typical cattleman's fare. It appears that super-sized breasts may just be a passing interest and not a deep-rooted obsession.

Funny that I questioned my own physical adequacy. After all, I'm the one who broke it off with Craig. I've always been the one to end my relationships. One day, that'll catch up with me, I've often thought, but it hasn't. Yet.

I close the door when I leave the room, and brace myself to try another. It occurs to me that the upper floor of the house is not as dusty as the ground level. Does ranch dust tend to hover that low to the ground? Perhaps the doors and windows up here are kept shut all the time, but the ones on the main floor are normally opened during the day, when farming activity goes on. The windows are all closed now, yet it's found a way in. Where does it come from?

The next room is all but empty, and seems exceptionally large for a house of this vintage. It must have originally been two smaller ones, unified at some point by way of sledgehammer. An expensive bronze light fixture adorns the coven stucco ceiling. This looks like it was meant to be the master bedroom. So where does Craig sleep?

A folding cot sits in one corner, with a cardboard box next to it. That can't be his bed. After my surprise with *Boobs*, I'm not sure if I want to look inside the box. But just a cot and a box, in such a big room? I can't ignore it.

I lift away the flaps covering the top, and am rocked by an emotional shock wave.

It's...

Me.

CHAPTER 16

I REMEMBER CRAIG TAKING the photo now, in the one-person dormitory he shared in third year with an anemic red-haired boy named Tyler Anderson. In an unauthorised but far from uncommon arrangement, Tyler subleased a portion of his space to Craig, who slept there in a folding bed at night. I hated the snapshot, because I was laughing when it was taken and had my head back so you could see up my nostrils. It made me look like Piglet, but for some reason, Craig loved it. I flip the print over, and see the girlish handwriting of my younger days, in slightly smudged blue ink. *To Craig. Glad this makes you smile, but PLEASE hide it! Luv, Kat.* Of course, I made a point of not writing *love*.

Beneath the photo, I find a copy of the veterinary journal with me on the cover. The pages are dog-eared, suggesting it has received a considerable bit of handling. *How did he ever know about this?*

The box is more than half-filled with letters and photos. Letters from *me*, and photos of *me*—some still inside inexpensive metal frames. Our entire relationship, neatly contained in a cardboard box. One note in particular has had its corners worn round. The stationery it's on was my favourite at the time. I unfold it and see the familiar woodcut engraving of a lanky Siamese cat. I have to hold it flat, in the palms of both my hands to prevent it falling apart at the creases as I'm reading it.

Dearest Craig,

Although this is by far the most difficult thing I have ever written, I fear it will be even worse for you. Please, please understand that I am writing it not simply because I am too weak and too childish to say the words to your face. I also feel it is important that you have this in some tangible form, so you know with certainty the feelings I express are sincere and absolutely real. At this point, I probably don't need to say it, do I? You already know. My heart is shredding to tatters as I write these words, fearing what they might do to yours.

I cannot allow myself to continue drawing you in the way that I have, deeper and deeper into something that cannot possibly endure. I see the truest of love in your eyes, and the anguish when you search in vain for reciprocity in mine. I am being horribly unfair to you, Craig. You are far too good a man for such treatment. You deserve the very same amazing love that you so freely give.

You are a generous, compassionate and wonderfully considerate human being. You're also very attractive! Plenty of girls will be glad to see you become available. (One cute redhead with a reputedly excellent brownie recipe comes to mind.)

I know it is not fair of me, but although I dearly wish that you might carry on with relative ease, I also hope that you do not forget me too quickly. I don't know if I will ever find another friend as worthy of my love as you. But I do know with certainty that I cannot force the kind of true-blue love into my heart that two people must share to build a lifelong relationship—the kind that you, more than any other, deserve.

One day, I hope you understand. I can never, ever forget you, Dear Craig.

Kat

I hate myself for leading Craig on, allowing him to fall in love with me, then dropping him flat on his heart. Could I have lived with myself if I knew he would keep the note all this time, probably reading it hundreds of times over the years?

What happened to the pretty wife in the picture downstairs? My God, did she know Craig kept this box? If she left him, I hate to think that I could have been a factor. I look over at the folded cot, and something on it catches my eye. Words scratched in the chestnut-coloured enamel, on an angle that would have them upright to someone lying in the unfolded bed:

KAT + CRAIG.

So this is *that* bed.

I recall him scribing those words in it, with his penknife on a sunny autumn afternoon when we both should have been in a lecture hall instead of between the sheets. But Tyler never let Craig have the room to himself in the evenings. Somehow that afternoon does not feel very far away.

That's why the cot was banished to the Kat Room.

Now where, oh where, is Craig? I fight the temptation to read any more of my own notes. How selfish can I be? These are not mine anymore, haven't been for fifteen years. I try to recreate the way I found the photo, journal, and *Dear Craig* letter.

The next door I try opens to a small bathroom. Though it's not immaculate, it seems almost too clean for a bachelor. On the pedestal sink, however, are a hairbrush and a glass that holds a lone red toothbrush. A tube of Colgate sits on a wall-mounted chrome soap dish, neatly rolled to *Colg*. A smile creases the face in the mirror as I remember how Craig detested the way I like to squeeze from the middle of the tube. Jack was a middle-squeezer too, so this was never an issue with us.

Transparent shower curtain with minimal soap scum, toilet seat down. All very strange for a single man.

One more door to go. I sniff the air again, and detect nothing different. There will be no corpse inside, I promise myself, but hold my breath anyway.

This room is less than half the size of the big empty one. As no one appears to be inside, I allow myself to breathe again.

There is a double bed, a dark-coloured chest of drawers, a small fibreboard desk, a trashcan, and a filing cabinet.

A couple of things are out of place. A drinking glass on the floor looks like it was knocked from the bedside table, and something that might have been orange juice has spilled out and dried there. A small wooden armchair lies on its side in the corner of the room. It seems to me that Craig wouldn't leave these this way. Why are some things here orderly, and others such a mess?

The double bed is made up, but the bedspread is furrowed and wrinkly in the middle, as though one person has slept on top a while, never bothering to climb under the covers.

A chest of drawers has three framed photos on top of it. One is of a pretty girl who wears a tasselled red graduation cap and matching satin gown. I wonder who it is only briefly before I recognise the smile from my two visits here. Craig's cousin Isabel. I'd forgotten all about her. She stayed with the Butler family for a time, accepting refuge from her own mother's self-destructive lifestyle. It's pleasing to see that Isabel graduated from high school. The engaging little girl took a liking to me immediately on my first visit here, and the feeling was mutual. She was a great kid. I wonder how long ago this picture was taken, how Isabel is now, and what she has made with her life.

There is another photo of the woman from the wedding picture, with mountains in the background. It's nicely composed, using the rule of thirds to place the woman in lower left-hand side for optimum interest. Definitely Craig's work. Even the curves of the mountain seem to have been situated to draw attention, then sweep the viewer's eye down toward the subject. The wife looks a little older in this one, though it could be simply because she isn't wearing her bridal makeup.

The third photo is of Craig's parents. I wonder again what became of them. It looks like this picture was taken at a wedding or another big event, judging from the couple's uncharacteristically formal attire and the dark wooden podium in front of them.

I put the photo down and return my attention to the bed. The headboard has a bookcase built into it, with several paperbacks pinned to one side by a single ebony horse-head bookend. Tom Clancy, Ken Follett, Clive Cussler, Jack Higgins, and John LeCarré. Craig is a fan of spy fiction.

The trash can near the barren desk looks like it has recently been emptied, but it stands slightly cockeyed on the carpet. A few extra plastic bags remain folded at the bottom, which suggests that someone took away the full one without bothering to set another up. I pick up the can and find an empty pill bottle nestled beneath one side of its recessed base. The label says:

> Mr. Craig Butler
> Qty: 30
> Aricept (Donepezil HCl) 10 mg.
> Take one capsule daily at bedtime. Refills: 1
> Dr. D. Samuelson

Aricept? That's a cholinesterase inhibitor—used in the treatment of Alzheimer's patients. It works by slowing the breakdown of acetylcholine in the brain, lessening the cognitive decline of dementia. After Zaina's mother was diagnosed, I spent a lot of time helping out with her homecare, and then visited the nursing home regularly until she passed on. Although heart-breaking a thousand times over, that time was precious. Even when she no longer knew who I was, Faiza routinely spoke to me in English—albeit the language, learned in adulthood, had never come easy to her.

In the earlier stages, the daily doses of Aricept helped Faiza a lot, though it could play havoc with her ulcers. It also occasionally brought on a bout of diarrhea, which can be a real problem for someone who has forgotten how to use—never mind where to find—the bathroom.

But Craig doesn't have Alzheimer's. He just *can't.*

Or *can* he? Faiza was sixty-seven when she was diagnosed, but a man named Burt Kramer in the next room at the extended care home died of early onset Alzheimer's just a month short of his fiftieth birthday.

My heart sinks. I've had a lot of dreadful possibilities run through my mind since arriving here, but nothing like this. Perhaps Craig has become disoriented and wandered off, hence his vehicle being left behind. I don't see his wallet anywhere—possibly a good sign, as having it with him would reduce the likelihood of his being listed as a John Doe if he has forgotten who he is.

I feel like I am going to be sick.

Could there be some other reason for the pills? I'm no pharmacist. Perhaps Aricept can be used for treating symptoms other than dementia that I'm not aware of. But ten milligrams is a hefty dose—Faiza needed only five.

No question the drug was Craig's, though. His name is right here on the bottle.

I pocket it and take another look around the room. Not many things here that most people would use to personalise a sleeping space and make it homey. Just a clock radio, three pictures, and the spy novels.

It seems strange to me that there is nothing on top of the desk. I look more closely, and see the footprints of a monitor, keyboard, mouse pad, and something else—a printer?—outlined in the dust. The carpet is still indented where the tower used to stand. Where did the equipment go? The wall above the desk is riddled with pinpricks, as if many small pictures or clippings were once stuck up there with thumbtacks. Near the desk is an empty telephone jack where Craig probably connected to the Internet on a dial-up modem.

I eagerly pull open the top drawer of the filing cabinet, hoping for the breakthrough that will explain everything. It's set up for hanging files, but there is nothing inside except two paper clips, the pointed cap from a blue Bic pen, and dust. The other drawer doesn't even have *that* much in it. Just a pale yellow Post-It with the words *For Len* scrawled on it, in what may or may not be Craig's handwriting. I look at the note. The sticky part of the reverse side is a rectangle of grey where dirt has adhered. Wondering only briefly who Len might be and what item this once tagged as his, I drop the note back where I found it and close the drawer. It could be years old.

Fuck. Something is *so* not right here.

Perhaps the armoire holds something more revelatory.

I slide open the top dresser drawer. There is clothing inside, balled up and carelessly stuffed in. A few T-shirts inside bear creases from proper folding, suggesting that they may have been neatly stacked in here at some point, but were later taken out and rumpled up, then jammed back in.

Next drawer is socks and boxer shorts. It feels odd to be looking at Craig's underwear. The clothes here are in the same kind of messy once-folded state as the ones in the first drawer.

Number three holds a couple of flannel shirts—one red and the other green. Same state of affairs. The bottom drawer is completely empty.

Next, the closet. I feel exasperated already.

The handles are missing from both doors, but I'm able to pop one of them open by applying pressure to an outside edge. Inside, I find a small assortment of pressed western shirts and dark-coloured dress pants, all of which show a hefty layer of dust where they wrap around the hangers. A three-piece suit is at the far end, equally dusty. Cleanest of all are a pair of Wranglers that look like they've never been worn, hard creases ironed-in and ready to go. Honky-tonkin' pants.

I wonder if Craig has been dating since the apparent break-up of his marriage. From the two pictures that are still up, it looks like he remains attached to his wife. Seems he isn't very good at letting go.

I'm feeling antsy, more acutely aware than ever that I have no business here.

There is a dull scraping noise from downstairs, and a few muffled thumps. *Footsteps?* I freeze, and listen.

For minutes, I can detect no other sounds. I leave the closet door open and tiptoe quickly to the stairs, and take a look down them. I descend onto the first step, and just as it makes a squeak, there is another thump from below.

Then, once again, there is nothing but the booming of my heart. I part my lips to call out, but fear—or instinct—stifles my voice. I proceed slowly down the stairs. A few others are a touch squeaky, but there are no further mysterious noises from below.

I cross the living room to the kitchen and take a cursory look around. A coffee mug, percolator, and crumb-covered plate are in the sink. And a chair is lying on its side on the floor. The dust in that area has been disturbed at some point, as if someone might have fallen from the chair and then struggled to get up. One handprint stands out amidst the other marks. That was made a while ago: a newer boot print traverses it in the dust that has since settled. Much newer, I think, quite sure that these prints weren't here before. They lead into an open doorway that gives way to descending wooden stairs—and there are no tracks coming back out.

I tiptoe along the wall, towards the door. Do I dare chance a look downstairs? Perhaps it's Craig. This is *his* house. I wouldn't want to startle him, especially if he is disoriented.

I peek around the frame.

A light is on in the basement. And near the bottom of the stairs, carrying a shiny metallic box, is the strangest thing I have ever seen.

I think it's an alien being.

CHAPTER 17

GET OUT! A VOICE in my head screeches. *Get the fuck out!*

But what is it?

Never mind, dammit. Go NOW!

RUN!

I fly through the kitchen and living room, and out the door. I don't bother to close it behind me.

A black GMC Yukon is parked in the front driveway. *Aliens don't drive SUVs. Come on, Kat. How the hell would you know that? They disguise their landing modules, stupid.*

I run to the side of the house opposite how I came—unprepared to do the limbo over that slime vat again. This is probably the route Craig normally takes from front to back. No trees or obstacles here.

I jump in the car and burn a smoking doughnut from the sandy parking space to the ring road, hurtling around the house and across the grass to get by the parked Yukon.

My mind processes what was in the basement. A yellow-skinned hominid, with a black Darth Vader head and enormous oval eyes. The closest thing in the mental database is a goofy spaceman from a fifties cartoon show.

It could have been a person. Its overall shape was very much that of a human being—perhaps clad in some kind of smooth rubbery suit. Then what was on its head?

More importantly, why was it in Craig's basement? The meter man sure as hell doesn't dress like that. And what was it carrying? The box-like object in its hands looked quite cumbersome—not how I envision a ray gun.

I try to decide what the smart thing is to do at a time like this. Find a phone and call the police? No. It's possible the other intruder was *supposed* to be there—an inspector or technician of some kind—but *I* certainly was not.

Maybe I should turn around and at least get the license number.

Forget *that*. I sensed heavy-duty danger, and I'm afraid to slow down to a reasonable speed, much less go back.

I've got to find out more about Craig and his condition. A neighbouring rancher would probably be able to help, and may even have an explanation for some of the other things I've seen.

There is only one house in sight—and I try to set a land-speed record on the way there.

Still turbocharged with adrenaline, I notice a little late that I'm about to pass the entrance road, and overreact. The tires squeal.

Take it easy, Kat.

I stare out at the home I have stopped before, listening to the *tic-tic-tic-tic* of my turn signal and having serious second thoughts. My jaw clamped like a vice, I turn and enter the property, coming to a stop a short distance from the farmhouse.

It's a small shoebox bungalow—maybe eighty square metres—with faded blue siding and an attached double garage. One of the garage's two big flip-up doors is wedged partway open, and a miscellany of debris—rusty tin cans, part of a lawnmower, and some blackened engine components—trail from the triangular gap at one side.

I thought Craig's yard was bad, but this one makes it look like Stanley Park. What an absolute *dump*! Rusted automobile bodies and a melee of scrap metal litter the entire property. The barn's roof and one of its walls have fallen in— probably years ago—settling on top of an aged farm implement that's still in there. A refrigerator with no door and an old gas range are lawn ornaments.

From there it goes downhill.

How can Craig *stand* having such a disaster area next door—even if that's a mile away? Quite possibly the residents and he are not on good terms.

I've got to give it a try anyway.

Only after the car door has slammed shut behind me do I consider that there might be a guard dog here, like in most junkyards. Very shortly on the heels of this thought comes a booming *Wor-woor-wooorf!*

The hulking animal tears out from behind a pile of scrap metal and onto the driveway, in a beeline for me. I'm a couple of steps too far from the car door to open it again and get safely inside, and it would be unwise to turn my back on this charging beast. I quickly consider the options, and wish I had left myself more of them.

I squat to the ground.

The dog spins his feet in reverse, kicking dirt and pebbles at me. It stops, near enough for me to touch. I offer a hand so that it can sniff my fingers. It does, then drags a wide pink tongue across them.

"Well, I'll be gord-damned," whoops a voice from the house. I look up to the doorway, where a man's face peers at me through a six-inch gap. The door is made of greyed wood, with only the odd strip of blue paint remaining. Its bottom has been eroded thin by decades of scraping claws.

I rub the dog behind its ears, and let it lick my hand a little more.

"How the hell'd you pull *that* off?" the man calls out. His beady eyes dart up and down, studying me through the gap—which he is clearly poised to close in an instant.

"I've got a way with animals. Why didn't you try to call your dog off?"

"What for? You're trespassin' on my property. What do you want?"

"I came to drop in on your neighbour, Craig Butler. He's an old friend of mine, but it doesn't look like he's home. Have you seen him?"

The man casts his eyes downward, and they stay there. "Uh, yuh," he says softly. "Guess I was one of the *last* who did."

"Pardon?" An icy hand tickles my neck and drags its fingers down my spine.

"Mr. Butler passed away Monday, missy. Funeral was only yesterday. And now I'm the poor sucker who's gotta wrap up all his business, being that his ex-wife lives out of province. Not really an ex, I guess, since they never went through with the divorce all the way. So she's gettin' everything. Showed up in a low-cut shirt and batted those eyelashes at me a few times, askin' me to sell off all Craig's things for her. I couldn't say no. *Stupid.*"

I believed I had steeled myself for finding out that something bad had happened to Craig, but maybe nothing can ever prepare you for this kind of thing. There is always some hope, until you know for certain otherwise. I stare at the man blankly, my knees rubbery. "I'm... Oh, God, I'm sorry. This is a terrible shock to me."

"Hate to be the bearer of bad news, ma'am. Hope you didn't come a long ways." His face falls as if under the weight of immense sadness. I'm stunned by the man's sudden shift—one minute indifferent that I might be gobbled up alive by his dog, and the next apparently troubled that I've travelled here for nothing.

It takes a few seconds for my vocal chords to assemble the components of any more words, and when they do, it sounds like somebody's choking a toad. "Uh, a little ways," I say. "So, what... What did he *die* of?" My head is spinning, not at all unlike the way it did in the clinic just a week ago. I hope I don't faint again, right here in the dirt.

The door opens more. I get a better view of the man, and stand staring at him in silence. I'd put him to be a little over sixty. His short, mussed hair is chalk-white—a harsh contrast to the tanned skin of his face. Deep creases run across his forehead and down his cheeks, no doubt carved by many seasons of unprotected UV exposure. Wild white eyebrows float above eyes of the palest blue. He looks like he hasn't shaved in a few days, and the coarse stubble stands out against his leathery skin. Still, something about his way is bizarrely charming. In his flannel shirt and dirty blue jeans, he seems to me rather like a derelict Sean Connery.

"Died of brain disease. Old-timer's."

"He died of *Alzheimer's?*" I'm involuntarily shaking my head, though it's what I was afraid of. "That can't be right. Craig was only thirty-five."

"Doc said he probably had it in his genes, but I think it's the hormones and stuff they put in our food, modifying the genitals to make more money. Always bigger, faster. Feeding animals to plant eaters, playing God like a bunch of crazy Frankensteins. Now all that screwing around is finally catching up. *That's* what I think."

I'm not sure I comprehend what he just said, but don't think it wise to ask for clarification. I'd like to move forward. "Do you know the name of the doctor who treated him?"

"Sure. Dr. Sampson."

"Samuelson?" I ask, remembering the name on the pill bottle.

"No. Dr. *Bob* Sampson. At the hospital in town. Craig stayed there 'til he died. Didn't want to go be just a number in some big city hospital, where they gotta read your toe tag to tell who the hell it was they killed sticking you with the wrong drugs. Craig died right here, where he lived. Where his heart was. I knew him all his life. Gord-damn shame, I tell you."

The dog nudges the fingers of my left hand with his nose, and I give him another scratch behind the ears.

"You know, that there's really something," the man says. He don't ever come up to a stranger like that. You got liver in your pockets, missy?"

I smile. "Animals seem to like me. Something I inherited from my father. He had a gift, my mom said. He died when I was a little girl, but she had a lot of stories about his way with animals."

"Yeah? What kind of stories?" He opens the door a little wider, and seems to relax a bit. A funny smile crosses his lips.

I'm not in the mood to talk about my father, but the man seems to be suddenly loosening up. He gives a nod to spur me on. I'm on the verge of blubbering, but suck it up and continue. "Um... My favourite is one about how he was hiking in the backcountry of British Columbia once, and came across a stranger named Gus Schmidt who'd been mauled by a grizzly. The nearest doctor was in Chezacut, a good twenty miles away. After hiking for hours, it was looking pretty unlikely they were going to make it. Dad was carrying Gus across a creek on his shoulders when a wild mustang showed up to drink. The horse walked right over to them and lowered his head, as if to tell them to get on."

He laughs. "That's a crock of shit, missy. Ain't *nobody* can get close to them wild horses," he says with a laugh. "Your ol' ma was pulling your leg, sweetheart." The gap in the door returns to where it was a few minutes ago, like the needle on his welcome-meter rolling back.

"I think it's possible the horse was one that escaped from a ranch somewhere. But Gus had lived in that area all his life, and he swore to his dying day it was one of the Chilcotin wild horses that got him to safety. He visited us a number of times after my father died, bringing gifts he made. Elk leather gloves and slippers for Mom and moose jerky for me. Twenty years later, Gus's eyes would still light up every time he told us how the mustang *just walked straight on over* to my father and offered himself as a mount. I saw his scars from the griz attack—the ones on his neck and hands, anyway. So that part's not a myth."

"That is *some* story, lady, true or not. Figure it runs in the family, eh?"

"I guess so. They called me Saint Francis in veterinary college, because of the way animals gravitated to me."

His head jerks back like he's just taken a punch to the jaw. "You're an *animal doctor*?" He studies me intently. "A vet?"

"Yes. My name is Kat Francis. Craig and I went to college together."

The man's face has become almost as chalky as his hair. He takes a step backward, and pulls the door nearly closed, so that only one blue eye is looking out at me. I can't imagine a worse reaction if I had just told him my name was Karla Homolka.

"Go *away*."

"You know who I am, don't you? *What* did Craig tell you about me?"

"Nothing. Never told me jack shit about you. But you gotta go now. Leave me alone."

"I just need to ask you a few questions. Can you tell me anything about the cattle mutilations Craig was investigating?"

"No. Nothing. Now go before things get ugly here."

"All right. I'm leaving. Is there someone else who might talk to me?"

The door shuts with a *ba-lam*, followed by the clatter of a deadbolt.

The big dog rolls around on his back in the dirt, and he moans happily when I bend down and give his pink, freckled belly a gentle rub.

Then I get back in the car and race off.

A few questions answered, several new ones raised.

CHAPTER 18

THE LITTLE TOWN OF ST. PAUL seems anything but exciting as you approach it from the west on highway 28. Driving in, you see a tidy golf course on one side, and a string of typical small-town motels and banal retail storefronts on the other. Further down the way, the Catholic church steeple—the only feature to poke up from the flat horizon in ages—is finally drawing near.

A bizarre object appears to the right. I've seen the thing before on my visits with Craig, but had forgotten all about it. It's a large, round concrete platform centred atop a narrow pedestal, like a giant flat-topped birdbath. A set of stairs runs up the front, and at the opposite end is a curved backstop with a map of Canada embossed in it. Evenly distributed across the top of this are a dozen naked steel masts, on which to fly the provincial flags, I presume. It seems they have yet to accomodate Nunavut, the newest territory.

I'm rattled not by the strange—rather *ugly*—shape of the structure, but by the irony of its very presence vis-à-vis my reason for coming here.

What I'm looking at is the world's first UFO landing pad, built in 1967 as a two-hundred-tonne tribute to Canada's hundredth birthday.

Another structure has been appended to the pad since I saw it last. Though the addition is built in a matching style and from similar materials, it isn't until I get out of the car and walk closer that I manage to identify it as a mock UFO. I climb up the stairs, and stand in the middle of the main platform, spinning a full turn with my arms extended. The pad seems awfully small to accommodate a craft from outer space. Obviously built for an excursion module—or to beam a few aliens down onto—and not for a Klingon D7 starship.

The newer appendage is the tourist information booth, a sign tells me. The boy inside can be no older than fourteen, and I doubt he can offer me anything beyond brochures for local attractions. With a sigh, I go back to the car.

* * *

THE OLD café could use better lighting, and my nose tells me the fat in the deep fryer is overdue for a change. I scan the menu, and am not shocked to see there is no Healthy Options section.

A heavy-set woman in a finger-smeared apron waddles over and gives me an instantaneous lesson in the consequences of neglecting oral hygiene.

"What can I getcha, dear?"

"Do you have green tea?"

"Nope. Coffee. You gonna eat?"

"I'm starved. And coffee is fine," I say with a smile. "It's my very first time here. What's the house speciality?"

"It's all good. From the looks of you, a steak sandwich couldn't do much harm. Our gravy is homemade—none of that powdered garbage you get."

I throw good sense to the wind and order a medium-rare steak sandwich, complete with fries and nutritious home-cooked gravy. You only live once. Steve would be proud of me, engaging in the extreme-sports equivalent of dining.

The steak is a little tough, but surprisingly tasty—at least partly because of how far down Zaina's breakfast toasts are now, but also thanks to a delicious smoky sauce unlike anything I've ever tasted. You've got to go to a rural Alberta café for a proper steak, I suppose. The gravy, on the other hand, is rather clumpy and less flavourful than the *powdered garbage* I'm used to. I can't seem to find a comment card on which to note this.

A man and a woman enter the café, and as if on autopilot, they both go directly to facing seats in a booth across from me. I guess them to be in their mid-fifties. The man wears jeans and a black sweatshirt with a moose on it, and a filthy ball cap. His escort is in flesh-toned cotton pants and a navy-and-tan bomber jacket with a blue Ford oval above her left breast.

"Hi Lottie," the man says when the server emerges from the kitchen.

"Oh, it's only Ed and Louise," Lottie says with a huge cavity-riddled smile. "I'll never get my damn crossed-words done if we stay so busy. Just coffee for the two of youse?"

"Yep. Food's too much money here for what you get," Ed grumbles without making eye contact. "And you probably noticed we don't come around as much anymore since you started charging two bits for a coffee refill," he continues, lifting his cap and giving his scalp an aggressive scratching. A miniature snowstorm descends on his shoulders.

"Oh, cry me a bloody river," Lottie says. "Hang on while I go get my violin. All my regulars sit here drinking coffee and dirtying up my bathroom all day. I can't afford to go taking a loss on all the customers, especially *you guys* who don't even bother aiming for the toilet when they return it."

"He's the same way at home," Louise says, and Ed shoots her a nasty look. "Know what?" she continues, raising her sparse eyebrows at my plate, "I think I'll have a steak sandwich, blue rare."

Ed's eyes bug out, and he clenches both fists. "What, we win the Lotto or something?" he growls. "Just the coffee for me. That's all *I* can afford."

"You're not gettin' even a lick of mine," says Louise.

Ed is clearly taken aback by this, and his bulging eyes dart from Louise to Lottie, then over to me. I look quickly away, but know I've been caught watching.

"How much are they now? Six bucks?"

"Twelve-fifty, plus the tax. It's a ten-ounce top sirloin steak. Best deal in town."

Ed's mouth drops melodramatically, and then his lips soundlessly say *what?* He wiggles in his seat. "You think I got no inkling how much meat that kind of money buys? Ten ounces is about four bites for any real man. That works out to more than three bucks a bite. Who do you people think you're fooling?"

"Just one, then?" Lottie says, stepping away. I have new respect for this woman, not allowing herself to be drawn any further into Ed's game.

"Fine," he snaps, and Lottie winks at me. "Make mine well-done. If I see any pink in it, the damn thing's going right back. Louise can get the Mad Cow all she wants."

"Coming right up," Lottie says, then stops at my table. "How are we making out over here?"

"Just excellent," I say. "I'm from the West Coast, so good Alberta beef is a real treat. We can buy it, but we sure don't know how to cook it."

Lottie smiles warmly, her round cheeks nearly blocking out her eyes. "You here visiting family, or just passing through?" she asks, as if these are clearly the only two possibilities.

"A friend of mine who lives here passed away," I say, sticking loosely to the truth.

"Craig Butler." She immediately concludes. "He was one of my few good customers, 'specially after Lynn left him. Wasn't the kind of guy to cook for himself much. Then a couple months ago, he started to lose it upstairs. Last time he was here, he forgot who I was and left without paying for his supper. Denied he even ate it. Said he hated lasagne and would have got sick if he did. Craig always *loved* my lasagne. His sister came by here the other day, you know. Nice girl. You know her?"

I don't bother to correct her that Isabel wasn't really Craig's sister but a cousin abandoned by his delinquent aunt. "Yes, of course. It's been years since I last saw Isabel. She must be all grown up now. Is she still in town?"

"I take it you didn't make the funeral," Lottie says. "Why in the world would you come all the way here the day after? You don't mind me asking, I hope."

"Not at all. It's a weird coincidence. I had no idea that Craig was dead, or even that he'd been sick. He was actually an old college friend. I came to pay him a surprise visit, if you can believe it." I wonder if she can.

"So you *did* hear about him and Lynn splittin' up then," she says, nodding. I smile, and she continues. "I don't blame you one bit, dear. Craig was a darn good catch. Before, I mean. So sad." She sighs.

"Do you know anything about his research?" I ask.

"What you mean by *that*?" Her eyes have suddenly turned hard. Her head rolls back on her neck and she takes a step away.

"Cattle mutilations. I understand Craig was well-known for some of the cases he worked on. He must have discussed it occasionally."

"Afraid I don't know what you're talking about. I'll get your bill, if you're all done." She walks away, her waddle transformed suddenly into long, practically athletic strides. This time it's me catching Ed and Louise watching, before they look quickly away.

"How about you two?" I ask, knowing full well that neither has missed a word of my conversation with Lottie.

"*What?*" Ed asks.

"Craig Butler's mutilation work. I understand he looked at a good number of cases around here."

"What a load of *crap*," Louise says. "To think the ETs would have nothing better to do than cut bits and pieces off cattle. Craig Butler seemed like a decent guy before he got into that. Devil got him, you know."

I wish I hadn't asked. I pull the wallet from my handbag and take out a twenty-dollar bill. She carries on, undeterred, rolling her eyes around in their sockets. "You could *see-ee* it in his eyes. The pastor at church explained it all to us on Sunday. See, at the Rapture, when Jesus comes like a thief in the night and takes all us Christians away to heaven in chariots of fire, the Antichrist is gonna need some kind of explanation so everyone left behind don't panic. If he says we've all been *saved*, his whole plan would backfire, because that'd start everyone and his dog off repenting like it's going out of style. So he's gonna say the aliens up and abducted everyone. That's why people see UFOs. It's all part of the devil's big set-up. You should steer clear of that stuff, before it nabs you too."

Ed speaks up, still gnawing on a hunk of steak. "She's right. You ought to come talk to the pastor. We can take you after we're done eating if you want."

Lottie returns with my bill, and without looking at it I give her the twenty. "Any idea where I might find Isabel Butler?"

"Yeah. She said she lives in New York," Lottie says.

I shrug. "Thank you. Sorry to be such a bother. I wasn't exactly the best girlfriend in the world to him. I wish I'd had some idea. It's hard to believe he's just *gone*." My hands are fidgeting on the table, and in my peripheral vision I see that Ed and Louise have stopped eating.

Lottie gathers one of my hands in her fleshy fingers, and squeezes it softly. "It's been tough on all of us. Craig's sister said she's acting in a play in Edmonton, at some big festival. I never asked when or where. You might be able to track her down, though."

CHAPTER 19

My motel room is everything you'd hope to find in a small prairie town. Sixty bucks gets you twin beds with matching spent mattress springs and a television that I think is the very same model my grandparents had when I was small.

There is a jungle motif, I notice. The first thing you see when you enter the room is a big bamboo-framed print of a panda bear family, and above the headboard of one bed is another print from the same series, only with an African elephant and giraffe. Essence of China and Africa at no extra charge.

I settle in quickly: this amounts to plopping my handbag and overnight bag on one bed and myself on the other. I relax for a few minutes, then realize I ought to check in with Zaina. She'll be frantic.

R-ring, R-r—

"Kat?" she says, sounding out of breath.

"Yes, it's me."

"What took you so long?" she scolds.

"Sorry, Zane. I've run into a wall here."

"Damn it, Kat, I can't believe you don't carry a cell phone. It's impossible to get a hold of you."

"That's *exactly* why I don't have one. You're the one who told me to get rid of my pager."

"Yeah, but a mobile phone is an essential now when you're on the road. I found out a few things, and I've been going nuts not being able to tell you."

"Me first. I went to Craig's house."

"And? He *was* the one who sent the photos, right?"

"I didn't get the chance to ask. He's dead, Zaina."

"*What?* What the fuck happened?"

"Uh, it was…" I am hesitant to say what must still be a very painful word to Zaina. I spit it out. "It was Alzheimer's. That's what I was told."

She pauses for several seconds. Then: "Is that *possible*? The guy was like, *our* age."

"It might be. I'm honestly not sure. But he was on the same meds as your mom. I've got the bottle right here. I'm going to see if I can find the doctor who treated him and get some more information. That's if he will see me. I tried to talk to his neighbour and got a door slammed in my face."

"No way."

"Yep. And the nice woman who served me lunch turned nasty and almost threw me out of her café when I asked about him. Now your turn. What have you been dying to tell me? I hope it's better than my news."

"You've got to come home, Kat. You can't stay there all alone, especially now. Damn it, are you sure you're alright?"

"I'm fine. I'm phoning from a motel in St. Paul. I'll call the airline and book a flight home as soon as I get a few answers."

"Something really smells, Kat. I tried to check up on the guy who sent the flowers. Checked with Insurance Broker's Association for British Columbia. There's no Tom or Thomas Austin licensed as an agent, broker, or adjuster anywhere in the province. I also checked the Yellow Pages and online. Zip. You can't work in the financial services business and keep that low a profile. Lover-boy doesn't exist."

"What about the phone number?"

"It came up in the reverse directory as a new listing. A cellular number, but I couldn't get the owner's name. When I call it, there's a recording that the mobile customer is unavailable."

"Could be he's unemployed and made up a career to impress me. People do that sort of thing, especially when their self-esteem is screwed up."

"Maybe. Remember those discussion board references to Craig Butler we found?"

"Of course I do."

"They're gone. I can't find a word about Craig anywhere online anymore. The directory links are there, but they're all dead."

"Thomas couldn't do that. I didn't think *anyone* could."

"With the right technology, it's amazing what you can do. A really good hacker can access a server that's supposed to be secure and pull pages down.

And a lot of hosting companies don't shell out the bucks to license good security on public discussion areas. I think someone either zapped the pages or convinced the administrator to take them down. That might explain why no one there is responding to my queries. Maybe they've had a threat from someone they're afraid of. Someone with a lot of power."

"Okay, you're scaring me now, Zane."

"Well, good. I think we might have got ourselves tangled up in something really ugly. You should come home now."

"I can't, Zaina. I came all the way here to find out what happened to Craig, and I'm not quite satisfied yet. I'm going to ask a few questions here, and as soon as I get an acceptable answer, I'll come straight home."

She moans. "I can't believe you're being so difficult, Kat. You'd think you were me or something. Try and get that answer soon, then."

"How is Sasha doing?"

"I only see her when I drop a scoop of food in the bowl, and even then she waits for Muezza to finish up instead of chasing him away like she normally does. The rest of the time, Sasha's vapour. She's being a little weird."

"Of course. She's a *cat*. Give her a big hug for me."

"As soon as she relaxes and sucks those claws back in."

"Talk soon, Zaina."

"For sure. Be really careful, Kat. I'm worrying about you every minute here."

*   *   *

I HAVE an urge to drive back to Edmonton to see if I can track down Isabel Butler, but since I'm here, now seems like as good a time as any to head over to the hospital and try to get an audience with the good Dr. Sampson. If anyone can tell me what *really* caused Craig's death, it should be his physician.

CHAPTER 20

THE HOSPITAL FACILITY IS remarkably modern, and quite a bit larger than I expected. The receptionist sits in front of a computer plastered with sticky notes and colour printouts of many amusing photos that continually circle the world via the Internet. Since many involve cats, I've seen most of them a thousand times before, from *Laughing Kitten* to *Three Kittens and a Pomeranian*. Everyone I know seems to think of me whenever a new one—or one they *believe* to be new—lands in their inbox.

The girl looks far too punked-out to be greeting the public in a medical facility, particularly in a town of only five thousand. Long black hair drapes flaccidly over a cadaverous face, and her hollow brown eyes are made to look even more recessive by heavy blue eyeshadow. Her full lips bear mottled traces of black lipstick and a recent flare-up of herpes simplex. The white smock she wears is open to reveal ample cleavage and part of a giant rose tattoo on her left breast.

She is nearing the final pages of Anita Shreve's *The Last Time They Met*. I try to use this as an ice-breaker.

"Brace yourself," I say, pointing at the dog-eared paperback. "The ending of that one had my head spinning for a week."

"Linda's dead, right?" the girl says. "I always read the last chapter first, but this one's got me all screwed up. Just opened it up twenty minutes ago, though. It's my mom's book. She loves anything that's depressing."

I nod, stunned. With its sections written in reverse chronological order, the novel is one of those disturbing stories about what *might* have happened, had characters made different decisions at critical points in their lives. There is no greater tragedy than what could have been, they say. Not unlike the surprise ending of the movie "The Sixth Sense", the reader discovers only on the last page that Linda, the protagonist, has been dead all along—in this case for decades. Her life for most of the story is nothing more than the fantasy of a former lover. Or at least that's how I understood it.

"Doesn't that ruin everything, knowing how it ends?" I ask.

She crosses her eyes and smacks her brow with the palm of one hand. "At least *my* head won't be spinning all week, will it? I can't stand surprises."

"Then I guess you're doing it the right way. I *love* surprises, and that ending beat the crap out of me."

"Can I direct you somewhere?" she says, her glare leaving no question that I have failed to ingratiate myself here. This isn't good. Receptionists are important gatekeepers. Wise people always befriend them.

I shift gears: "I'm here to speak with one of your physicians."

"Well, you'll have to tell me which one. *Seven* doctors work here, you know," she scolds, her brow knit.

"I'm here to meet with a Dr. Sampson."

"We don't have a doctor by that name. Dr. *Samuelson* is in surgery right now."

"That's what I meant. Sorry, I confused him with a cardiologist I know." I bite my lip. I should have gone with the name on Craig's bottle—or at least confirmed by phone instead of trusting the nutty neighbour to have it right.

She sneers. "I take it he's not expecting you."

"Perhaps not. Can you please have him notified that Dr. Francis is waiting here for him?"

Her head jerks upward, eyes opening wider. That does the trick. She smiles, and I watch her scrawl *DR FRANCES* on a notepad in big, messy capitals. My lips part to correct her, but I stop myself. It doesn't matter if she's spelled my name right or not. Samuelson has no clue who I am.

The seats are standard waiting room fare—not terribly uncomfortable for the first five minutes, though the minimum wait is invariably far more than that. I work through the back copies of *Time* and *Reader's Digest*, paying less attention to content than to making sure I flip the page whenever it appears to be time to do so. Must *look* patient. I'm thinking about what I will ask, and how to word it. The doctor is not likely to provide much information without a good reason. And I *don't* have one suitable to give. Without the cow photos, telling the truth is pointless. So far, the straight-shooting approach has done nothing but get me shunned. For some reason, people around this town seem far from keen on discussing the mutilations.

I watch the clock on the wall. After an hour, I consider leaving. It's nearly four o'clock.

Finally, a man enters the waiting room wearing surgeon's greens, complete with cloth booties over his shoes. His chest is covered with smears of brown. It's fresh blood, the normal bright red neutralised by the fabric's complementary colour.

The doctor's face is round, and his pasty skin and chubby cheeks lend him a Pillsbury Doughboy friendliness.

He offers a hand to me, clean and pink from vigorous antiseptic scrubbing, and I squeeze it. The man's skin is very warm. Or am I just that cold?

"I'm Dr. Kat Francis," I say. It seems easy to smile at this man, which is good. Natural is best.

"Don Samuelson," he purrs in a voice that's almost too deep and mellow to be coming from a white man. I note that he hasn't bothered with the *Doctor*. Of course, *he* has no need to impress anyone. "Sorry to keep you waiting. Was in the middle of an abdominal hysterectomy when they told me you were waiting. Came across adhesions, though. Patient's left ovary had bonded to the bowel, probably from a previous C-section. She's had three. Then, even before I finished, I was told Emergency had admitted a man with severe right lower quadrant abdominal pain and vomiting, so I had the obvious suspicion..." He pauses and looks into my eyes.

"Acute appendicitis, possibly suppurative," I say, feeling I'm being tested. Fortunately, this quiz question is one I could have answered in the fourth grade, when my own appendix ruptured—though the terminology would have come a few years later.

He smiles. "Right. Obvious, isn't it? Rebound tenderness right there and everything," he says, poking himself above the right hipbone. "But when I got him opened up, the appendix was fine. Turned out to be an intra-abdominal abscess."

I nod with feigned empathy, as though I might know this to be an honest mistake from having performed hundreds of similar operations myself.

"All I could do was suction out the area, fix him up with a Blake drain, then close the incision back up. Hopefully, antibiotics and the miracle of healing will do the rest. Always hate to cut someone's skin unnecessary, though. The last thing I need is a malpractice suit for ruining a guy's Speedo-modelling career."

"I appreciate your seeing me without any notice," I say. "Just flew in from Victoria to visit an old friend of mine who was under your care, and got some bad news when I arrived. I'm hoping you can help me understand what happened."

His eyes narrow a little. "And your friend's name... ?"

"Craig Butler."

He shakes his head, and the corners of his mouth drop. "Tragic case, that one. Early onset Alzheimer's. I suspect one of Craig's folks carried the gene. Both of them died of other causes, so it's tough to say."

"What happened to Craig's parents?"

He blinks at me, and I know what he's thinking. *Just how well do you know your dear friend?* "His mother died about ten years back of multiple myeloma. The chemo was more than she could take—did her in before it could be of any use. The old man took his own life not six months later."

"That's horrible. But Craig. He was so young. *Thirty-five.* Are you *sure* about the diagnosis?" I recognise too late that the doctor must still be stinging about his very recent misdiagnosis on the abscess, and I wish I'd chosen my words more carefully.

"*Absolutely* certain. Craig was not an old man by any means, nor was he the youngest to get the disease. Alzheimer's can affect people in their late twenties. Younger still for Down's Syndrome victims, since both are chromosome 21 afflictions. Seems the earlier in life the damned thing hits, the faster it progresses. Craig lived all alone, so nobody was around to see the early signs. By the time he was confirmed, the Alzheimer's was into stage three. Confusion, dementia, memory loss, hallucinations and motor aphysia. Within seven weeks, he became immobile and died of hypostatic pneumonia."

"And the autopsy confirmed it?"

He bows his head, then growls, "There was *no need* for an autopsy."

"What? For such an atypical case?"

"I'm willing to bet you've never worked in a rural hospital, Kat. Sad reality is, facilities like this one all over the country are miserably understaffed. I've been here fourteen hours this shift, and I can't go home to my family quite yet. My two kids haven't been awake to see me in nearly a month. The province has full-time medical examiners in the big cities, but in places like this, they use fee-for-service pathologists. I'm one of them. But we have to give priority to the living. In Craig's case, it was an extremely busy week and there was quite honestly little justification for an autopsy. Fortunately he's got no offspring to pass his genetics to. And he was too much of a recluse to have put anyone at risk, even if what he'd died of somehow turned out to be a pathology that's transmissible. We know that Alzheimer's is *not*."

I nod. "I'm sure you're right. Suppose I'm in shock, and still not quite accepting this. Would you mind if I take a quick look at his charts?"

"Whether or not I *mind* is not the issue. You know I can't show you a patient's medical information. Now, as I was saying, I'm very busy and quite tired." He begins to turn away from me.

"I know your code of ethics limits disclosure to the patient's authorised representative without a court order or search warrant, but—"

"You're not a *medical* doctor, are you, Kat?" he interrupts.

I feel my face warming. "I'm a vet. How could you tell?"

"Among other things," he says smugly, "A *genuine* physician from a neighbouring province would be inclined to know that here in Alberta we have a thing called the Health Information Act. It supersedes the Medical Association's code of ethics. What it does is require us to make that information available if it relates to the cause of death, so long as the person asking for it had a close personal relationship with the deceased."

He flashes a self-satisfied smile, and I do my best to give him one right back. "Well, that's me. Craig and I were *extremely* close."

He folds his beefy arms across his chest and leans back on one leg. "When was the last time you spoke to Craig, Kat?"

"It's been a while."

"How long?"

"About fifteen years."

He chuckles. "That's what I thought. You have a good day, Dr. Francis."

"Can you tell me who the authorised representative is?"

He stops in mid-pivot once again. "The estranged wife. Apparently she and Craig failed to even sign a separation agreement, so she's legally his wife and sole heiress to whatever goodies he left behind. Lives in Lloydminster, I believe. Good luck to you if you decide to talk to *that* one."

This time he does turn, and quickly shuffles away.

CHAPTER 21

I'M BACK ON THE HIGHWAY, doing warp speed in the direction of Craig's farm. I need to drop in one more time on that cranky old neighbour. If I hadn't been so terribly rattled from the way I left Craig's place, I'd have probably been more aggressive and demanded information. The guy was holding out. He said he'd known Craig all his life. And somehow, he *knew* who I was—but not in a good way. It was stupid of me to give up on such a promising source so easily.

Of course, I had no idea how difficult answers would be to come by...

I stop at a field entrance hidden from the man's house by a thick shelterbelt of Scots pines. I have Jack's father to thank that I know what such a thing is. His family farm was in one of the windiest parts of Saskatchewan, and Mr. Colman enjoyed my willingness to absorb his homilies on the importance of soil conservation. As the years go by, fewer and fewer farmers remain who grew up in the dirty thirties like he did, and appreciate the importance of leaving behind rows of trees to slow wind erosion. One good windstorm can steal thirty tonnes of dirt per hectare, he told me—and the topsoil on most of the prairie provinces is only a few inches deep. Yet most new-generation farmers have cleared away the windbreaks left by their pioneering forefathers, just to gain a few measly hectares here and there. You'd think none them were ever told the fable of the goose who laid the golden egg.

The sound of the car door clapping shut triggers a memory of the territorial hound who lives here. If my animal charm proves ineffective and the dog's master is not around, I could be in trouble. But I'm a lot more worried about *owner* than *dog*. Taking people by surprise can be dangerous.

Still, I have a hunch it may serve me well to get a peek behind that broken garage door before I'm chased off the premises again. If I know what kind of vehicle the old fellow drives, I might decide it's worth more effort in questioning him. Or not, and move on.

I'm not a dozen paces from my rental when I realize my quandary about the dog is about to be answered. The beast's claws fling tufts of grass into the air as he tears around the endmost pine at a full gallop, growling and snarling. I try to think of the dog's name, but can't recall the man saying one. I hunker myself down the way I did last time, but this has zero effect on his rate of advance. Perhaps he resents that I've taken a more devious route in approaching his home. Something has got the gears in his head turning differently now.

I know better than to turn and run. That would tell him it's *game on*, and trigger a chase instinct. I pop back upright and make a few quick lateral strides, cutting diagonally across a strip of gravel at the side of the highway, and onto the grass of the opposing ditch. Perhaps the dog will consider this outside his turf.

Apparently not. He keeps coming. I lower myself again, and look him straight in the eyes, giving him the teeth.

He hits me full-on with all his beastly weight. I fly back, my head smacking hard-packed dirt, then continue to tumble down the incline of the ditch in slow motion, my spinning head processing images like film frames. Dog face. Grass. Dog mouth. Sky. Dog teeth...

I stop rolling, and his weight comes down heavy on my chest. A steamy rope of drool streaks across my neck and lips, some of it dribbling onto my tongue. It tastes fetid, and bile rises in my gut.

My arms come up instinctively, trying to cover my most vulnerable parts, and possibly shove him away. I'm all but paralysed by fear, something no animal has *ever* done to me before.

So weak—

His muzzle lunges at me, and I continue to fight despite knowing he is too strong and heavy...

I close my eyes and let out a moan, waiting for the sharp carnivorous teeth to tear into my skin.

The bite doesn't come.

One of my outstretched hands gets a nudge from something moist. When my eyes open, I see it's resting on top of the dog's broad head. His tongue slaps across my face like a hot, wet mop.

He's apparently decided against a late-afternoon snack—in favour of having his would-be prey *pet* him. He growls, and I give his head a shove. He comes back licking and slobbering, baring his teeth in what I now know for sure to be canine roughhousing—the way dogs play with one another—not rage. This crazy mutt likes to play rough.

I give his broad neck a scratch—the most aggressive I can muster after our exhausting tussle. His pink tongue runs the length of my face, his warm breath belting me with a revolting stench. *What does this guy eat?*

"Good boy," I say to him. "Good dog for not killing the stupid intruder."

I sit upright for a few seconds to catch my breath, my head still hurting from bouncing off the ground. Then I stand and brush the dirt and dog hairs from my clothes before walking along the row of trees, on the side they conceal from the house. The dog follows, brushing against my leg and letting out the odd whine for more attention. I really love dogs, but it sometimes annoys me how some tend to perceive the least show of friendship as an all-day commitment.

The branches of the old pines are dense with long, blue-green needles and extraordinarily heavy with clusters of dark cones—the latter a species-preservation reaction to the drought.

It's impossible to see anything through the trees until I come to a spot where a portal was clipped some years ago between two of them. It's grown in considerably since, but I'm able to pass through with only a few pokes and scratches from the spiny quills. I can see the stucco on the side of the house now, brown from field dirt. Having vanquished the pine obstacle, I walk a labyrinth of oily, rusty machine parts, making my way to the front of the building.

The openings in the broken garage door are narrower than I remember, and I wonder if the resident has deliberately closed it up a bit. My pupils still dilated from the sunlight, I can see little in the cluttered obscurity. The dog goes in on the opposite side of the door, and I decide to follow his lead. He's probably wider than I am.

I duck low, almost to my knees, and shuffle in. I smell something resembling the dog's foul breath, and grim thoughts fill my mind. A beam of light from the crack in a boarded-up window cuts a bright squiggle across the dog's motley fur. I hear him licking, followed by the distinct sound of teeth on bone.

Oh, God. Some other, less fortunate trespasser?

He looks up at me, and rolls his eyes downward in the direction of his meal, as if offering me a taste. My eyes have adjusted enough now to see it's a bone, much too big for even the femur of a human. Most likely that of a bull.

Something else grabs my attention, and it makes me forget all about the dog's stinky food.

A car is parked inside the second garage door, mostly concealed from me by a huge metal shelving unit.

It's a Honda Civic. A small circle of light reveals that its paint is a faded blue.

I've found my messenger.

With a *k-bam*, a small door flies open at the rear of the garage, and I'm blinded by a rectangle of white. A short silhouette is carved out of the middle of it, and it shifts in the unmistakable motion of levelling a firearm.

"Shit, it's *you* again," he mutters, and I see him shake his head. "Sam, you're no gord-damn good." The dog looks up at him apologetically, then resumes his gnawing. The gun goes down a bit as the man's voice rises to a shout, "Now what in the hell are you doing back here? Seems to me I told you to get lost." He raises the gun at me sharply, and I can't help but flinch, anticipating a blast. *What will it feel like? Perhaps nothing. Just a burst of light, and then non-existence. A shotgun makes a very big hole.*

"I need your help," I say.

"I ain't hel... Hel... Hel-lll..."

The man is shaking. It's a slight tremble at first, accompanied by a garbled choking sound. The gun begins to go up and down in robotic lurches.

Then the shot. An ear-splitting *KRAK!* and a long, brilliant burst severs the darkness. Seeing the flare's profile, I know the pellets have missed me by a good margin. Sam flees through the opening we came in, knocking over a pile of scrap metal in his haste.

I'm wondering if the gun can hold a second shell, but it doesn't matter. It clatters to the concrete; the man collapses beside it. He writhes there, and there's enough light coming through the doorway to see foamy drool ebbing from his lips. His eyes have rolled back, only the whites showing and lending him a most demonic expression. I know what is happening to him. A generalised tonic-clonic seizure.

Grand Mal.

The man's forehead strikes the rough edge of a vacant steel wheel rim, and a stream of blood immediately begins to flow from the wound. He continues to flagellate on the dirty concrete, smearing the blood into arcs with his hands. I leap beside him and cradle his head, and undo the top three buttons on his shirt. I shove away the metal rim he cut himself on with my foot, and it makes a painful, gritty squeal. The man doesn't notice. He's right out of it. His cut is bleeding profusely as head wounds tend to, but doesn't look as severe as I'd feared.

There isn't much more I can do right now. I've already got the man lying on his side, so if he vomits it's not likely to go into his lungs. Hapless first-aid providers often wrench a poor seizure victim's mouth open hoping to prevent him from swallowing his tongue, which is a myth. It doesn't happen. Perhaps I ought to do it to this old bugger anyway—and give his tongue a good yank for pulling a loaded gun on me.

"Take it easy, Mister. Everything's all right," I say in the voice I use for soothing traumatised animals. He continues to thrash for several long seconds, until the seizure winds itself down.

At last, his body relaxes. Then, suddenly, it tenses up again, and he gives me the look of a racoon caught in a trap. I worry he's about to strike out at me—or grab the gun. I can see now that it's a single-shot, with only one barrel, so even if he could, he'd need to get another shell into the chamber.

"Try to relax. You've just had a seizure," I say, and kick the gun as far away as I can. He doesn't respond.

"Thank... thank you," he finally says. His eyes dart around, and I suspect he is thinking about standing up.

"Shhhh. Rest right here for a minute or so. You've got a cut on your head, but it doesn't look too bad."

"I'm sorry," he whispers, so softly I can barely make it out. "Scared. I'm just a scared old man, living out here all alone. What do you want with me?"

"Let's try not to worry about that for now. I'm not here to cause you any harm." I help him to his feet, and guide him to another door that I presume gives way into the house. It does. "Maybe we can help each other," I say.

He smiles. "You'd like that, wouldn't you?"

I smile back. "Yes. I would."

"I'm Len Gibson. Welcome to my castle."

Cut back to the sticky note at the bottom of Craig's filing cabinet: *For Len.*

"Thank you," I manage a smile. No need to introduce myself, and I really don't know what else to say. The interior of Len's castle is even more of a disaster area than the garage. "Let me get something to clean you up. Which way to the bathroom?"

"Down the hall. First door on the left. No, right. Watch your step. Been meaning to tidy up a bit. Wasn't expecting company, you know."

"Don't worry about it. I'm not here to critique your housekeeping, Len. You should see my place."

The bathroom is something else. I'm surprised to find a clean face cloth in the cupboard, and I moisten it under the faucet of a scum-laden sink. Len's bleeding has already slowed, so pressing a damp cloth against his face for a while will probably be enough to stop it. If not, it's to town with him for some stitches.

Len is seated in a chrome kitchen chair, and I scoop a pile of junk mail off the seat of another. When I try to move the chair by its back, the seat falls right off, and Len chuckles heartily. I smile back, glad I didn't try to sit in it. I move a flat of canned tomatoes off a different chair, and test this one by giving it a shake first. It holds together, so I lower myself onto it with caution.

Len flinches when the wet cloth touches his skin, but after that, we sit together for a while as I apply pressure, without a word between us. The silence is not at all awkward. Rather, I think we both enjoy it.

I pull the cloth away and take a good look at the wound, making sure the bleeding has stopped. No need for suturing, though it probably wouldn't be a bad idea—the wound would heal nicer. But men don't seem to mind scars. Len makes faces like a little boy as I gingerly scrub the surrounding area clean.

"Can I fix you up a cup of coffee?" he offers when I lean back to assess my work.

"Thanks, but I'm fine. Let's just relax here for a bit."

"Suit yourself. Let's get to the meat and potatoes of this whole gord damn deal. What you want to know?"

"Let's start with why you drove all the way to Victoria—more than twelve hours—just to bring me that envelope?" I say. He gives me a stunned look, and I worry he might be getting set for another seizure. "My assistant saw you drop it off at the clinic," I add. "She described you and your car to me."

A sheepish smile. "You know, it took two days to find that crazy place. But

I promised poor Craig I'd do it, and I'm a man of my word."

"He told you to *hand deliver* it?"

"He said it wouldn't do to mail it. That meant it had to be pretty important."

"Did he tell you *why* he sent the pictures?"

"Is *that* what was inside that envelope? I didn't even know that much. What kinda pictures? Naked people?" He laughs, then slaps himself on the hand, as if to say *bad dirty old man.*

"No. Mutilated cows."

He nods, and a chubby pink tongue moistens his lips. "Mutes, huh? Sounds like Craig, all right. Geez, he sure liked those mutes of his, didn't he?"

I smile. "What did the note say?"

He raises his eyebrows and gives me a puzzled look.

"There was a mark on the envelope where something was paper-clipped to it. Was there a note?"

He seems deep in thought for a long moment. Then: "You're right. Yes, there definitely was something on there when he gave it to me. But I don't know what happened to *that.* I walked around Victoria for three days, you know. Must have fallen off somewhere.

"Two."

"What?"

"You said two days a minute ago."

"Did I? Maybe it was two. Tough to say. I used to be better at stuff like that. Sometimes I think I'm going down the same road as young Craig. All senile upstairs."

Seizures *and* forgetfulness. Perhaps he's right.

"What did the letter say?"

"Now how the hell would I know? Wasn't none of my business."

"Any chance you might have left it back here, or in your car?"

"Probably not. Got everything out of the car, and didn't see it again after I came home. But maybe that's how they found me on the island."

"*Found* you? Who found you?"

"Some blond-haired pretty-boy. The kind of disrespectful punk that drags an old man out of his car and slaps him around on the side of the highway with all kinds of people driving by. Said he knew I had Craig's envelope, then got all pissy when I told him he was an hour too late. By then I already dropped it off with you. So he clocked me once more and said to get my wrinkly old ass home and stay the hell away from you. That's what I was doing, 'til you started coming around here all the gord damn time."

This explains why Len was distressed to see me. And perhaps even why I sensed someone was lurking around my house when I was on the patio. Could that have been the man who roughed Len up? I knew it could not have been Thomas who performed the break-ins, though it seems increasingly possible he tried to get me killed by leading me into a riptide zone and abandoning me. I felt so strangely elated out there—could he have put something in that bitter-tasting hot chocolate? I only had one swallow, but it was a big one.

If Thomas *is* involved, and there *is* a second man, how many others are they working with? Was it one of their ilk wearing the spaceman costume in Craig's basement?

Nate and I emailed back and forth about the trip for months. Anyone who intercepted the messages or accessed my computer could have learned that I was getting set to go away.

There must have been something I overlooked in the images, a message that Craig expected me to pick up on or an important detail I ought to have noticed. But if the infiltrator *did* see me with the envelope at my house, then why break into the clinic?

Unless he was looking for something else.

* * *

"DID CRAIG EVER take you on any of his mute calls?" I ask Len.

"Oh, yeah. Four times, maybe more. Same old same old after a couple of 'em, you know. Couldn't tell you how the guy got so worked up about smelly, bloated cows with their eyes cut out and teats chopped off. *You* wouldn't like it, tell you that, missy. Lose your ham and eggs if you ever got caught standing downwind, I guarantee it."

"You said Craig's funeral was just yesterday. Any idea what was done with his remains?"

"You mean the ashes?"

"Uh, yes. He was cremated?"

"Hang on here a sec," he says. "Got em over there." He goes to stand, and appears strangely off-balance. I jump up to help, but he's out of my reach in two impromptu, Chaplin-esque cross-steps. He does a clumsy partial pirouette and miraculously regains equilibrium. He stares at me, wide-eyed.

"Uh, where was I?" he asks, a flutter of fright persisting after he begins to blink again.

"You were about to show me Craig's ashes, Len."

"Yeah. That's right. The ashes." He scowls at me. "What the heck was I gonna do that for?"

"I don't know," I say, feeling like I'm in an episode of *The Twilight Zone*. "I think you wanted me to take a look at them."

"I suppose so. Yeah, that's right. Be back in a jiffy." He leaves the room, and I hear him crashing about nearby. Soon, he returns.

"Had to wait better part of an hour for the funeral folks to make 'em, you know," he says. He is holding a simple black container, two-thirds the size of a shoe box.

"I'm sure it would have taken longer than that," I say with a gentle smile. Mom insisted on being buried *intact* in a simple casket, but Steve had told each of us more than once—perhaps to needle us more than anything—that if tragedy ever struck, he wanted to be cremated, and not "planted in a hole to become worm shit." When I was making the arrangements, I happened to ask the funeral director about the process. The funny little man was happy to explain—seizing what must have been a rare opportunity to explain in detail the cremation process. It normally takes about six hours in all, he told me. Three to turn the body into organic bone fragments, and another three for these to cool and be crushed into minute bits. The actual cremation time depended on how much fuel there was to burn in reducing the remains to calcium. He pronounced the word *fuel* with gusto, spreading his long and bloodless fingers at me in an explosive illustration. Bodies with as little fat as Steve's are apparently stubborn fuel to burn, because they are composed mainly of wet tissues. I expect Craig had a similar amount of body fat, and would have presented the same challenge.

"Just an hour," Len says. "Right after I got back from your place last week, Lynn came by in some guy's truck and hit me with the news. She told me Craig up and died in the night, and then went right into asking how I felt about settling up the estate. Didn't want to get into all that, but couldn't exactly say so. She looked real sad, so I said okay. That cheered her up some, and she asked me to go with her to take a look at the body at the cremating place. Said she was scared to go alone. I tried to tell her it was only Craig's mortal coil without his spirit inside, but it didn't help. Seen too many scary movies I bet. Crap like that'll get *anyone* afraid of his own damn shadow, never mind a lady. Guess you'd understand about women more than I do."

"I don't know about that. We're strange animals, Len. And we're like snowflakes. No two alike."

He laughs. "You're tellin' me. Not even the same from one day to the next."

"Sounds to me like you know women pretty well."

He makes an angry face. "Good enough not to ever marry one, tell you *that*."

I nod, and hightail it from the subject. "So you went along to the crematorium?"

"Yep. Followed her there in my car. We looked at the carcass together, and turned out Lynn was just fine about it. When you see a dead man for yourself, you find out there's nothing scary. Live ones are a whole bunch worse. Folks got her to sign some papers saying it was really him or whatever. Then the guy who owned the truck showed up to drive her back to Lloyd. Don't know where he was, up 'til then. Real winner, that one. Some kinda hippie, I think. Guy had prettier hair than a lotta girls. Impatient as hell, too. So they took off, and I stuck around by myself to wait for the ashes."

"And you thought it was only an hour?" I have my doubts about Len's short-term memory, after what I have seen here.

"*Know* damn well. We got there just after five-thirty. After she did her thing and left, I waited a couple minutes for the six o'clock news to start up, and before sports came on, they said the ashes were ready."

"Really?"

He snickers. "Probably speeded the *brew-rockercy* up when I knocked over a table with a bunch of fancy urns and things on it. Made a bejesus of a mess." I smile and nod while he relishes a rip-snorting laugh at his own antics. He continues: "Suppose they wanted me the hell out of there, which suited me fine. Craig didn't leave no will, but I'm gonna spread some of him in the river valley down by Duvernay. It's a nice place and he liked to go drop a hook there now and again. I'll probably put the rest in Vincent Lake, where his pa used to take him fishing as a boy. Funeral guy said you're not supposed to dump human remains in lakes or rivers, but who's gonna know?" He winks at me and hands over the container. It weighs about the same as Steve's ashes— three kilograms or so. The linkage stings.

I carefully lift off the snug-fitting lid and look at the contents. Len wrinkles his face and steps back.

"You haven't looked inside?" I ask, lowering the lid back, a little askew so it sits loosely atop the box.

His head rocks slowly from side to side. "No, ma'am. Didn't know if it was right. Guess I might have to see 'em when I go out to do the scattering. That ought to be plenty." His eyebrows rise. "I never seen ashes from a burned-up person. What're they like?"

I lower the box a little, so that he can see inside from where he stands. He squints, and takes a step closer.

"Well," he says, "that looks like nothing but sand."

"It does, doesn't it?" I smile at him, and he comes closer still. He reaches a hand inside, then jerks it back once before continuing, making careful contact.

"Just like beach sand, even with little bits of shells inside," he says.

"It's actually calcified bone that they crush into powder once the cremation process is done."

Len's head bobs, stubby digits to his lips. He pulls the hand away sharply and studies his fingers. It was the other hand that touched the *cremains*, but he seems to have already lost track of this.

"You know, Len, I think I'm ready to take you up on that offer of coffee now."

He chuckles. "Instant okay? That's all I got."

"Of course," I say, although I can't stand the *ersatz* taste of the stuff. "Just black for me, please, and maybe make mine a little weak."

"Black's good, 'cause I haven't looked at my milk in a while. Probably cheese by now." He grins widely, revealing a forest of stained stumps to me for the first time.

As soon as Len is around the corner, I pat my hip pocket and feel Craig's Aricept container. I set the ash-box atop a collection of hunting and fishing magazines and dig out the bottle, then align the arrows so that I'm able to pry off its child-proof lid. I palm both pieces, and pick up the box again with my fingertips. Rocking it side to side, I watch the contents flow slowly, a light fog of ultrafine powder rising above the surface. I feel like a prospector, panning for gold. The nuggets I hope to find are not of any material value, but they might help answer some of the questions that have been tormenting me.

From the kitchen, I hear the clatter of pots and pans. "I know I got a kettle here somewhere," Len bellows over the clamour.

"Take your time, Len" I say. I don't want him to catch me at what I'm about to do. I can't imagine how I'd explain it.

The grey powder is far from uniform, but I'm not finding any good-sized chunks inside. I rock the box more aggressively, until a trickling of the contents overflows from one side and drifts to the floor.

"Shit," I sputter to myself, and grind the ashes into the dirty carpet with my shoe. I set the pill bottle on the table and try sifting with my fingers through the powder at the bottom of the box. It feels cool to the touch, and I focus on the sensation to disconnect my mind from the nature of the contents. But it's not possible to ignore that I'm digging through all that's left of Craig's body.

I find a silvery chunk, about the size of a pencil eraser. It clatters like a tooth when I drop it into the pill container. Sifting around, I come across another bit, slightly bigger even. This one is black. In it goes, heavier yet, with a duller rattling sound.

Water is running in the kitchen. Len will probably come back while it's on to boil. I tip the *cremains* the other way, and sift through the bottom some more. My fingernail catches one irregularly shaped fragment right away. I drop it in with the others, and use the plastic container to take a scoop of ashes.

The childproof lid snaps down with a *pok,* and I look up to see Len watching as I'm slipping the bottle back into my pocket.

"Need some water with that, missy?" he says.

"Pardon?"

"I can never just take a pill dry. Gotta have a shot of water to chase it down the hatch."

I fake a hard swallow, accentuated by closing my eyes tight and raising my shoulders. "Went down just fine," I say.

*   *   *

OF ALL the things I've endured the past several days, drinking Len's coffee ranks right up with treading ice-water in terms of overall misery. As I choke down the largest sips I can manage to be rid of it sooner, it seems unlikely my face doesn't betray me. Thankfully, Len quietly takes the cup from my hand before I am finished, and apologises when he dumps the sludge into his kitchen sink.

"I—I don't make a whole lot of coffee," he says softly.

"It wasn't so bad. But I really should let you go. Do you happen to know if any work is being done at Craig's place? Fumigation or something, maybe?"

"Better not be. I'm the one in charge. No one else should be in there but me. And Lynn, I guess, if she wanted. How come you ask?"

"Just wondering. The lock on the front door is broken. You might want to get it fixed for security reasons."

"No kidding? I'll swing by after supper and have a look-see."

"Good idea."

I guess that means I've got to get back there right away.

CHAPTER 22

SOMETHING IS DIFFERENT ABOUT Craig's house. Considering my harrowing departure, I might expect any change to be an improvement. But it is not different in a good way. My knowledge of Craig's death gives the structure and its surroundings a more sombre feel, the emptiness and loneliness intensified.

The black GMC is gone, though, and I'm hoping the same applies to its highly unusual passenger.

I've parked at the back again to hide my car, then entered the way I came out, albeit more slowly. No sense wasting time seeking a new approach.

Inside, I tiptoe into the kitchen and peek through the doorway to the dark basement. I flip on the light, and nervously make my way down the wooden stairs, pausing at the bottom. Not much to see here. It's an old farmhouse, and the basement floor is much too irregular and shallow to be a candidate for developing. There is a massive old gravity-type coal furnace, with a new, smaller natural gas one dropped in right beside it. Next to that is a big cylindrical water heater.

The air is heavy with mildew. At some point, floodwater has stained the bottoms of an empty old armoire without doors and a wooden crate on the floor a matching rust colour. Clearly this is not a place for keeping anything of worth. Then what would anyone—alien or otherwise—be doing down here? There is little for me to investigate. I wouldn't try to open up the furnace if I knew how. The filter must be loaded with grunge—and billions of freaky dust mites.

Good then. Onward and upward.

In the upstairs corridor, everything looks the same—though it would be difficult to say if a dozen people have passed through since I left. There is little to disrupt, and insufficient dust on the floor for footprints. I peek into

Craig's bedroom, then go straight for the bathroom.

With a light tug on the mirror's right edge and a click of its magnetic latch, it swings open to a medicine cabinet. Inside, I find a triple-blade razor, a green can of shave gel, a pump bottle of Cool Water aftershave, a tube of mint Lipsyl, some Visine, and a large steel toenail clipper. I take the razor and pop off its disposable head. There is a bit of sludge in the blades, probably shave gel, blended with the skin and whiskers of a dead man.

I open up a small cupboard on the wall, its wooden door thick with many layers of paint. The shelves hold unused bottles of shampoo, conditioner, and a few rolls of bathroom tissue. Nothing for me here. I take the hairbrush and toenail clipper, which, along with the razor head, should give me what I need.

* * *

IN TOWN, I waste no time in stopping the first pedestrian I see to ask for directions to the Greyhound terminal, though my urgency may be overstated. The buses that pass through these small towns come only a few times a day. It's not likely the very one I need will be pulling away just as I arrive at the station.

* * *

THE YOUTHFUL clerk gives me a collapsed shipping box, and pops it into shape dramatically. *Ta-da*, his smile says. Though the young man—probably near the dawning of his twenties—is far from movie-star material, he has obvious charisma. And he knows it. His hair is dark and wavy, and his six-foot-something frame clearly carries little more than toned muscle. His name is Scott, according to the nametag. Scott looks at me with a broad, toothy smile, and a hungry look in his eyes conveys that he has an interest in an older woman and has sensed reciprocity. He's sensed wrong.

Scott watches in amusement as I drop the hairbrush, razor blade and clippers inside. I decide to be more discreet with the bottle of ashes, and keep it in my pocket for the time being.

"When does the next bus to Saskatoon come through?" I ask him.

"Someone left a few things behind, eh?"

"Yeah," I lie. "My brother is always doing that."

"Could tell it was a guy's stuff. I was hoping maybe you sent a boyfriend packing." He leans forward on the counter and smiles. Suspicions confirmed. I get a heavy whiff of cologne—a pleasant enough scent, only too much of it.

"Nope," I say. "I'm just fine in that department." *The last thing I need now is a child-boyfriend,* I don't add. "Now, when is that bus?"

His smile goes away, and he is suddenly as serious as cancer. It's part of the strategy, I am certain: in order to seduce the older woman, one must be capable of feigning maturity.

The charming gigolo will reappear. He does not come across as the type who gives up easily.

I reach forward and drag the Greyhound memo pad across the desk, rotating it so the blue gumming at the back is opposite me. "May I borrow a pen?"

Scott grins, and smoothly whips a shiny black Montblanc from his shirt pocket, then leans back and watches for my reaction. I pretend to think it's *just* a pen. It writes with delightful smoothness, but I make a point of not communicating this. I do wonder where Romeo got such a fine writing instrument—probably worth two weeks of his wages. Likely it was forgotten on the counter by some hapless travelling businessperson.

"An ex-girlfriend gave me that," he volunteers. "She's a lawyer. Nice pen, eh?"

"I guess. For my purposes, anything more than a gel pen is extravagant," I angle the notepad to screen the words I'm writing from his curious eyes with my arm. I fold the bottom of the sheet upward to the gumming, concealing everything, then tear it free before folding it a second time. "So, what's the secret itinerary for that bus?"

"Gets here at seven-forty tonight, and arrives at six-fifty-five tomorrow morning."

"You're joking. That's over eleven hours. It's not even a six hour drive." Craig and I made it in about five, I recall, including a lunch stop.

"That's about right. You can usually pretty well double the time it takes to drive. Just be glad you don't have to go with it," he says. "So where's it going in Saskatoon?"

I scowl. He's being too nosy.

He smiles and raises an eyebrow. "I need to know. For the delivery slip. I'll fill it out for you."

"Agrigene Labs. In the Saskatoon Research park."

"Think your brother will be at work to sign for it by just after seven in the morning? Might be better to send it to his home."

"You don't know my brother. If I want to be sure he gets something, I'll send it to the lab."

"They got an address?"

"I'm sure they do, but I don't know what it is. It's not a huge facility."

"Hold on."

Scott hits a key on his computer, and the display comes to life. He Googles "Agrigene Labs, Saskatoon," brings up the company's site, and in a click we're on the contact page. While he focuses on this, I put the pill container into the box, and seal it shut.

"Number two thirty-two," he says. "What's your brother's name?"

"That's good enough. Thank you." I don't want Scott doing any more research, although I suspect he will carry on from here as soon as I leave. I do make a note of the telephone number on the screen.

"We need to add it to the waybill," he says.

"I'll fill in the rest," I say, taking the bill away. I write *Tony Fritz* as recipient, and only *Kat* in the sender box. No blood or dangerous goods, no need for insurance.

Scott takes the paper slip. "You should give a number they can call you at if there's a problem with the delivery," he says.

"I'll take my chances. Thank you for all your help, Scott," I say as I make for the door.

"Hope to see you again, Kat Fritz. Come back if there's anything else I can do for you. I'm free tomorrow night."

"... And I just got paid," I hear him say just before it closes.

Not likely, I think, yet it's impossible not to smile back at the guy through the glass. He managed to make me feel a little better.

CHAPTER 23

I HATE MOTEL SHOWERS, but I have yet to find a suitable way to avoid them indefinitely when travelling. The damned things give either no more than a trickle of water or—more often—a blast that attempts to rip the flesh off your bones. Never a happy medium. And then there's the enigmatic hardware that controls them. By the time a person figures out how to balance hot and cold, they've invariably been both scalded and frozen at least once. And may God have mercy on the poor soul who needs to make a temperature adjustment partway through. I've operated some pretty sophisticated diagnostic and treatment equipment, but have never found any of it as confounding as a motel shower.

This one is no exception. The water pressure is of the skin-stripper variety, and the temperature—though I know enough to adjust it in advance from behind the curtain—begins to fluctuate wildly as soon as my body is fully beneath the stream. It must be computer-controlled, I think as I attempt to dodge a particularly scorching burst. *Oh, why didn't I think to shower at home, or brave Zaina's mildew-booth this morning?*

Ever since seeing the movie *Psycho* on television as a teenager, I have been nervous in the shower. I think I was getting over it, until Zane kindly renewed my fear by making me sit through the 1998 remake on DVD to show me how much my new haircut made me resemble Anne Heche, who played Marion Crane in that version. Every shower since, I've regretted that.

Zane said she read an interview with Janet Leigh, who played Marion the first time around, in which the actress said that *doing* the famous scene didn't scare her at all—but she has never had a shower since actually *watching* the finished version. That made me feel *slightly* better about my own phobia.

Even at home, with all my doors locked, I routinely imagine Norm Bates drawing ever nearer with his long and sharp knife, nicely concealed from me by an opaque curtain like this one and enough white noise to obliterate even the loudest of psycho-blunders.

In this motel room, which strikes me now as not all that different from the classic Bates-run one, I'm suddenly even more nervous. There's a thump from somewhere in the complex, and I naturally presume some psycho has found me. They always know when you're in the shower—it's listed as a basic competency in the job description.

I try to calm myself, but then there's another noise. I'm not even sure if this one is real or imagined, but draw the curtain open a little nonetheless.

Nobody is in the room but me, of course. The bathroom door is ajar by just a crack, and I now wish I closed it properly. My rational mind knows that a hollow wooden door with a lock that could be picked with a wax crayon would hardly slow an attacker who has already defeated a deadbolted steel slab to get inside the motel room. But in the land of make-believe fears, it is often the slightest of barriers—whether a door like this one or a thin bedsheet pulled over one's face—that keep the monsters at bay.

I concentrate on slowing my breathing. *Must act like a grown-up, Kat. There is no Norman Bates in this motel room.*

Crash!

This one was definitely real, and it *had* to be inside my room. Without turning off the water, I leap out of the bath enclosure and whip a towel from the wall rack. Wrapping it around my torso, I slam my body against the flimsy door and lock the knob.

Don't lean against the door, I tell myself. *They'll shoot you through it, or skewer your chest with a machete.* I vow never, ever to watch another horror flick.

Then I shout.

"Get out of here!" I mean for my voice to sound powerful, brusque, authoritative. In reality, it is weak, tinny and shrill. I imagine a psycho must relish this part of the attack.

Over the sound of my own breathing and frenzied heartbeat, combined with the concerted drone of the running water and noisy exhaust fan, I can't hear anything.

I just wait. My back slides down the moist door to the floor, where I sit for a time. When there have been no noises for a while—though I have no concept of how long that is—I turn off the shower. And listen some more.

All I can hear is a TV in another room, blasting the obnoxious bells and music of a game show.

Did I imagine the sounds? They were so loud.

So real. Maybe I am losing my marbles now. Just being in these parts seems to have that effect on people.

Still seated on the linoleum floor, I reach up and pull the switch for the bathroom fan to the off position, and the room becomes silent. Next door, someone on *The Price is Right* or *Jeopardy*—I wouldn't know the difference— seems to be winning big, but otherwise I don't hear a damned thing.

Nothing has happened, I tell myself, trying to persuade the sick feeling to depart from my belly. *You imagined it all, Kat. You psychologically set yourself up for it, created your own horror. From now on, only baths for you. At least until you pull your life back together.*

I peer through the crack under the door, with my ear touching the linoleum as I move from one side to the other. No one appears to be waiting for me out there. I climb to my feet, and, elbows on my lap, take a few good breaths. Snugging the big towel around my chest, I crack the door.

Then, louder than ever before, I scream.

CHAPTER 24

"YOU'RE SURE YOU DIDN'T see anyone? Or hear a voice you might be able to identify later?" Ted Kulchisky, the granite-faced Corporal repeats for the third time."

I shake my head. "Just heard some crashing sounds. I actually thought it was my imagination until there was a really loud one."

"You must have felt *horribly* vulnerable," the female constable says. She is not wearing a trace of makeup, which serves only to emphasise her strikingly beautiful face—big hazel eyes, a perfect little nose with a minuscule diamond stud, and full lips. Glossy hair the colour of a Brazil nut's shell is clipped tightly behind her head, apart from a lone curly ringlet that dangles over one Brooke Shields eyebrow. The black nametag on her chest reads JESSICA BOLDUC. Kulchisky glowers at her, and steps to one side, positioning his body to block her from view of where I sit on the side of the bed.

"That's for Victim Services to ask, Jess" he mutters over his shoulder. He looks back to me. "You should get yourself set up with a counsellor as soon as you're home. Now, the manager says she'll move you into the room next to her own for the rest of the night. We're going to need to dust this one for prints. I'll take you to the station and get a set of yours so we can eliminate them from what we find. These rooms aren't the cleanest in the world, so chances are it'll all be a waste of time. But lousy odds are the name of the game."

"You sure nothing is missing?" Bolduc says, a small, arched crease forming at the bridge of her nose.

"I didn't have a lot with me," I say.

She looks down at the items on the bed and points to a CD. "You like Ani DiFranco?"

"Yeah," I say. "Some people find her a little hard to take. But she sort of speaks to me. Maybe that's not a good sign."

"Probably not," she says solemnly. "She's one of my favourites. Just got the new disc."

Kulchisky muscles in. "I'd say somebody wanted to give you a message." He points a thick finger to the wall. I don't look there. I've read it too many times already. The letters are painted with long strokes in dark red spraypaint, no doubt selected because it would nicely approximate the look of fresh blood:

KuRIOsi+Y KiLLs THE KaT

"So what is it you're curious about?" Kulchisky asks.

"Nothing."

"I somehow doubt that."

"Well, *everything*, then. I'm a scientist. Curious by nature. But nothing to bring this on."

He sneers. "Have you had other threats? Run-ins with folks here in town?"

"No. Nothing at all like that. Everyone has been nice."

"And you said you were in town to visit a local ranch owner?"

"An old friend. I found out when I got here that he's passed away."

"Sorry to hear that. Natural causes?"

"Apparently. Alzheimer's, the doctor tells me."

"I'd say that's pretty natural," Bolduc says. "But what a terrible way to go. I had an aunt who died of it. Didn't even recognise my uncle the last couple of years. That tore him apart."

This earns her another stern glare from Kulchisky, and even I can read its meaning: no talking to the victim about things outside of the investigation— especially tiresome details of your personal life.

"Sorry," she says to him in a soft voice I'm probably not meant to hear.

"His name was Craig Butler," I say. Kulchisky nods knowingly.

"We knew him," Bolduc says. "Our paths crossed from time to time. I heard he'd passed away, but not that it was Alzheimer's."

I try not to look surprised at this. "Small town, I guess."

"Yep. Everyone here is all caught up in each other's business." Her tone suggests these words hold deeper meaning, but I don't dare pursue it.

"Did anyone from your detachment ever go with Craig to any of his... *mutes*?"

"Oh, yeah. A dozen times. Corporal Kulchisky and I were the ones who seemed to always get sent out on those calls."

"And what did you think? Were they for real?"

"I think—" she begins, but Kulchisky interrupts.

"Not one of 'em," he says. "Every single case turned out to be the work of predators or scavengers. A complete and ridiculous waste of police resources. We pretty much stopped responding to the calls altogether a few months before Mr. Butler called it quits."

"I don't—" Bolduc begins again, and this time Kulchisky raises a hand to her mouth. She stops talking before it makes contact, and he holds it there until her eyes descend in surrender. I feel her humiliation.

I decide not to discuss the topic any further, not that I'm satisfied but for Constable Bolduc's sake. "You know, I just thought of my car. I've got a rental parked outside," I say, scanning the scattered contents of my handbag on the dresser a second time. "The keys aren't here."

Kulchisky makes a move for the door. "What kind of vehicle?" he says, slowing down for my answer.

"Chrysler Intrepid, dark red."

He waves for Bolduc to follow him.

I got dressed while waiting for the police, but still need to slip on my shoes. I deep breathe for a minute, then go out. The car's hood, trunk, and both side doors are wide open when I get to it.

"They left it like *this*?" I gasp, wondering how the officers could have failed to notice such an unusual sight on the way in.

"Keys were in the ignition," Kulchisky says, "But we opened it all up, just checking it over. Did you leave anything in the car?"

"No. Everything was with me in the room."

"Think you could've left the keys in the ignition yourself?"

"I guess it's possible," I say. "It's not something I tend to do, though. So it would be a weird coincidence."

"Well, it's not likely a thief would get this far and *not* take the vehicle. People *do* get cold feet, though, and you said you screamed. Maybe he decided not to add grand theft auto to his rap sheet. If you haven't got a good hiding place, a stolen car can be a real liability in a community this size."

"Can you check it for tampering?" I say.

"Pardon."

"Sabotage," Bolduc says to him. "She'd like us to look to make sure the intruder didn't mess with the brakes or something."

"I'll give it a quick once-over, make sure the lines are intact and there's nothing else obvious, but you should get a qualified mechanic to do a complete inspection if you're worried about that kind of thing."

"I'd appreciate that," I say to Bolduc. "With the threat and everything."

"Tell you what I recommend," Kulchisky says. "Constable Bolduc needs a signature on your statement, and she'll finish up here while I take you to get printed. Then I suggest you have yourself a good night's sleep, and first thing in the morning get yourself back to the West Coast where you don't have to worry about morons screwing around with cows or spraypaint." He grins at me for a second before his chiselled face morphs into the same reprimanding glare I've watched him use several times on Bolduc. I try to deflect it with my own coldest look, but if there is any effect on him, it's adroitly masked.

*　　*　　*

I SPEND what's left of the evening in my replacement room thinking looping thoughts—like trying to solve a puzzle, but repeatedly using the same strategy—always to the same frustrating outcome. Fortunately, the car checked out okay, and I moved it to a well-lit spot in the open. It's unlikely the intruder would come back tonight, I tell myself. Not with the hotel manager and cops on alert. But I don't buy my own reassurances.

My mind races like I'm hopped up on amphetamines, and I nearly jump out of my skin at the slightest of sounds. If I were in a city, I might find an all-night pharmacy and buy the place out of its Nytol supply. Probably for the best that there is no such drugstore here—if someone tries to enter my room again, I don't want to be trapped in a deep, drug-induced slumber.

When the sky begins to brighten, I feel somewhat safer, and the fatigue overpowers my fears. I drift off.

*　　*　　*

I OPEN my eyes to see the curtains parted, and the oblong heads of two strange beings silhouetted in the morning sunshine.

They look at me with enormous catlike eyes, and a baby's smile appears on each of their lipless mouths. One raises an ultra-long finger in front of its face, as if to tell me to be quiet. The two beings float weightlessly into the room, and land gently on legs proportioned to their ovoid bodies similar to those of a dachshund. I sit upright in the bed.

"Where are you from?" I ask. They warble back and forth in sounds that resemble a CD player scanning through a tune at high speed. I'm not the slightest bit afraid. The creatures exude a strange, benevolent warmth.

One of them spreads its amphibian hand over my face, and I smile.

Contact.

A spasm of electricity jolts through me, and I fall back rigid on the mattress, unable to move. The frog hand descends on my eyes, now holding a black capsule-like object. A brilliant beam shoots from the end, and I feel searing heat as it encircles my eye, a trail of smoke rising in its wake. I lose vision from that eye, and presume the little laser has severed my optic nerve. I smell burned flesh. Strangely, there is no pain.

With my remaining eye, I watch the other creature reach over my face. Its wrist comes down so near that it blurs, then rises, the hand grasping a circular, bright crimson object. My eye, complete with surrounding tissues, canthal tendons cleanly snipped at the back. The other creature's hand returns now, still holding the laser device. I try to scream, to fight, but haven't the slightest control over my physical being. I can only observe as my other eye is cut out, until I can see nothing.

I lay in silence, with no way of knowing what they are doing to me now. There is a booming sound. *My heart?* It seems far too erratic.

What are they doing to me?

* * *

I SIT upright in the bed. My breathing is ragged, and I'm disoriented. In a room above me, a vacuum cleaner is pounding against the wall. I scan my surroundings. The curtains are still closed, with no sign of entry by any creatures, alien or domestic. The clock says it's ten-thirty in the morning.

After what amounts to nearly a full night's worth of sleep, I still feel drained. I go into the bathroom and run the tub, then sit on the bed to wait for it to fill.

Should I call Zaina?

Later. I'll have to tell her about the invasion and graffiti threat, and then she will certainly insist I return home at once. I'd do exactly the same to her.

And in my position, she wouldn't listen either.

I have vowed not to go home until I get my hands on Craig's medical records. And Lynn Butler is the only person who can get me to them.

CHAPTER 25

LLOYDMINSTER IS—OR POSSIBLY *was*, I suppose—home to Sandy, the eldest of Jack's three brothers. Having visited Sandy's family three times during my Saskatchewan tenure, and being endlessly inquisitive, I learned a little bit about Canada's only border city.

"Lloyd," as it is known to locals, was settled a century ago by twenty-six hundred English colonists, when today's prairie provinces were still part of the Northwest Territories. The settlers—who probably did not know (or care) that they were living atop the fourth meridian—named their village by combining the name of Reverend George Exton Lloyd, the chaplain who eased their difficult passage to the New World, with *Minster*, meaning *monastery church*.

Saskatchewan is a sixty-five-million-hectare rectangle, the only Canadian province with four completely imaginary, perfectly straight boundaries. When it and neighbouring Alberta came to be in 1905, the border between them was drawn right through the middle of the town. It's represented today by thirty-metre-tall stakes that run along the city's main street, marking the path of North America's longest surveyed line.

Although it's only a *provincial* boundary, there are some big differences between the two sides. Alberta is arguably the country's most conservative province, much more free-market-centred than predominantly socialist Saskatchewan. But political values, dissimilar though they may be, are seldom the cause of cross-border strife here.

Money is the biggie.

Alberta has it, and Saskatchewan doesn't. The provinces are nearly equal in terms of land area, but Alberta's twin cities of Edmonton and Calgary each have about the same number of residents as the entire province to the east. Not only does Alberta have a bigger taxpayer base, but it also owns incomparable mineral riches. Even the province's extraordinary endowment of natural gas, crude oil and coal are dwarfed by its Athabasca oil sands—the largest stockpile of oil on the planet. With billions in annual royalty revenues, Alberta not long ago became Canada's only debt-free province. It can bankroll massive surpluses *without* a provincial sales tax—while even with the one it has, poor Saskatchewan struggles to make ends meet. The two-thirds of Lloydminster residents who live on the wealthy side also enjoy much higher family incomes and property values, making for economic development nightmares east of Main Street. Jack's brother Sandy loved to lament the injustices done to those like him who lived on the poor side, though he certainly wasn't going to pack up and hike the few hundred metres to cross the border. I would only begin to understand the ferocity of the Colman family's loyalty to their home province when Jack moved with me to British Columbia and was virtually shunned by his brothers as a defector.

The Saskatchewan government recently tried to equalise things somewhat for those living on its side of the city, exempting people in that small area of the province from the sales tax. It seems to have done some good: most residents now do business on *both* parts of town, as do people who drive surprising distances from the interior just to avoid the tax.

* * *

I STOP at a mall payphone and check the local white pages. Number eight at Borders Mobile Home Park—wherever the hell that is. Should be easy enough to find, I suppose. It's not a huge city.

A woman who looks about my age tells me in a condescending tone that she never goes to the *Saskatchewan side*. I try two other people, and get the same kind of parochial indifference. Doesn't anyone ever travel across town?

A man clad in grubby, worn-out clothes approaches me, flashing a gap-toothed smile and textbook gingivitis.

"Excuse me, beautiful lady," he says. *Here comes the pitch,* I think, and he doesn't disappoint. "Sorry to bother you, but I left my wallet at home, and ran flat out of gas. The service station wants a twenty-buck deposit to let me take a jerry can..." He gives me a sorrowful look, and shrugs, as if he can't lower himself to actually *ask* for the money.

It's the oldest scam in the book, but I'm surprised to come across it in such a tidy little city. A whiff of the man's toxic breath—a combination of liquor, tobacco, and periodontal disease—almost knocks me over, and starts my stomach a-jumping.

"That's pretty tired," I say.

He pulls a bankbook from his pocket and starts flipping through the pages, telling me that the bank won't give him any of his money with no ID. I doubt it's his account, and don't bother to look.

"I'm not buying," I say. "But I'll give you a fiver if you can help me find a friend. I'm looking for a woman named Lynn Butler, at Borders Trailer Park."

Big, disgusting grin. "I used to crash at a buddy's house in BT Park. Turned out not to be much of a friend, though. This Lynn a *hottie* like you?"

"Can you tell me how to get there?" He nearly salivates as I reach into my handbag.

"Hey, I'll come along and show you," he says. "For the *whole* twenty. Then I can get that gas and see my kids today. They also need some medicine, you know..."

"Directions is all I want," I say in a tone that I hope conveys there will be no negotiations here. I'm anxious to get away from this guy as fast as I can, and just the thought of being in a confined space together makes me nauseous. Besides, five dollars is my personal ceiling for being scammed.

* * *

THE TRAILER is not one of the newer models that are practically indistinguishable from an actual house—the kind referred to nowadays as *Manufactured Homes*—but a simple, rundown orange-and-brown house trailer.

A White Chevy short-box truck with colourful eighties style striping is parked in front of it. Not something a woman would own. I remember Len saying that a man had been chauffeuring Lynn around.

I park near the foot of the gravel driveway, allowing enough room for the other company to leave—though it's probably wishful thinking.

There is no sidewalk, just a dirty, well-packed dirt trail to the front door, dividing the thriving thistle farm into two smaller plantations. Empty beer bottles and cigarette butts litter the yard. Getting out, I narrowly avoid stepping on a condom probably thrown onto the road from a passing vehicle. I try not to think about it any more than that.

As I approach the trailer, I hear a commotion inside, and harsh voices. *Dear God, please don't get me caught up in the middle of a domestic dispute now.* But I can't turn around and walk away.

Can I?

"Come back here, you little bitch!" a male voice shouts.

Thump! Bump-whoomp!

Crash! Breaking glass.

A woman's shriek. "Stop it, Jerry! *NO!*"

Whoomp-thump!

I dash for the door, with no idea what I'm about to find, or what I will do to help. Maybe in seeing someone here, the guy will knock it off.

Still, my own conscience will force me to report the incident. You can't just walk away from a violent situation and let it perpetuate. There goes the rest of my day, never mind however many future ones will be lost coming back here to testify against some physically abusive dirtbag.

I don't knock. The screen door's partly ajar, and I grab it by the aluminium frame and whip it open. I poke my head inside.

A long-haired man—appropriately clad, it seems in a wifebeater shirt—stands before me, holding a broom. A woman stands on the seat cushion of a worn-out colonial-style sofa, bending the foam into a potato-chip shape. She bears little resemblance to Craig's photos of Lynn. Her skin, tanned to leather, looks fifteen years older than in the photos, and her hair is no longer brown but a straw-like blonde. She is holding the bell-bottomed cuffs of her pink slacks up almost to her knees, and giving me a perplexed stare.

"Who the fuck are you?" Jerry demands. He turns to face me directly, and raises the broom like a quarterstaff. I don't doubt for an instant he'd use it on anyone, man or woman.

"I... I heard some commotion from outside," I croak.

"Yeah? That's because we're trying to whack a fuckin' rat in here," he says. "Who the hell are you, the Rats-PCA?"

I want to turn and run away, but bow my head. "I'm sorry. I heard—I thought someone might be in trouble."

He laughs. "Oh, someone is. That shitty old rat is in big-assed trouble. Shut the door so the damn thing doesn't get out."

I try to, but something is broken in the frame or hinges, making it impossible to close.

"There a rat problem around here?" I ask.

"Shouldn't be, but yeah," he says. "All Lloyd residents on both sides are supposed to be under the protection of Alberta Rat Control, but they only come by like once a year. Rats move a helluva lot faster than that," he grumbles.

He's right. Jack's family was engaged in an endless battle with the rodents on their farm, and I once did some research to see if I could help find a solution. In the end, I learned that the things they were already doing—poisoning, trapping, and keeping everything clean—were about the only means of limiting the damage. One pair of rats can theoretically produce fifteen thousand offspring in a year. The province of Alberta has claimed rat-free status since way back in the fifties, and their Rat Patrol still monitors a strip about thirty kilometres wide along the east border—from Montana up to the unbroken boreal forest near Cold Lake—to keep it that way. Saskatchewan, on the other hand, has a major-league rat problem—its farmers losing around twenty million dollars a year to the voracious critters. Alberta's rat law was extended years ago to encompass the east part of Lloyd, and simplify rat management in the uniquely challenged city.

"Why not just call Rat Patrol?" I ask.

"Yeah, right. Then they'll tear this whole place apart snoopin'," he spits. "No than—"

"—There it is!" Lynn screeches.

A chunky brown Norway rat tears across the room, and Jerry takes a swack at it, knocking a hideous ceramic blob of a lamp to the floor where it smashes to bits. Redirected by the lamp's shade, the broom misses its mark.

There is a mad thrashing of broom straw as Jerry steps onto the back of the couch and knocks it over backwards, launching Lynn almost to the ceiling and forcing her to clamber onto an armchair for refuge. Jerry swings the broom even more frenetically, sending things—celebrity magazines, snack food bags, playing cards, and a hairy brown apple core—sailing across the battered linoleum. Lynn continues to scream like she's having her fingernails ripped out. I see the furry intruder make for the partly open door, which appears logically to have been its point of entry. I move quickly, but don't manage to get there before it scurries—unscathed—past me and outside. Off to replicate itself fifteen thousand times somewhere.

"Good," Lynn says. She continues holding her pant legs up, but at least her terrible screaming has stopped.

"You weren't s'posed to let the fucker out," Jerry mutters.

"I'm sorry. It beat me—"

"Hey! I know who you are," Lynn says to me, climbing down and circling amidst the clutter. "You're Craig's ex-girlfriend. Katie, right? I seen you in pictures. Cut all your pretty hair off, didja?"

"Kat," I say, offering my hand to her. She doesn't seem to see it.

"Ex-girlfriend?" Jerry says loudly. "The *fuck* you want here?"

"I don't have to tell you nothing," Lynn says, out of the blue. *How does she know I'm here to ask questions?*

"No, of course not. Listen, I'm sorry we didn't get off to a good start here. I really don't normally barge into people's homes. I was only trying to help."

"We don't need no damn help," she says. "Especially not from *you.*"

The man leers at me in a way that makes me even more uncomfortable than Lynn's iciness. "Alright, ladies. Everyone's Coolio here. We can talk civilised. Why don't we all just sit down and have a brew. Just everybody *relax*, for Chrissakes. So what brings you to Lloyd? Your name is *Cat?*"

"That's right. With a *K*. Short for Katherine."

"Jerry Girard, he says. He grips my hand and pumps it vigorously. "Lynn's favourite boytoy."

"Yeah, right," she says with a cackle. "You're not my favourite, Jare." She shoots me a nasty look. "Now what *are* you doing here?"

"I heard the sad news about Craig," I say. Of course, this is not *really* a lie. Then again, if she'd asked why I showed up in St. Paul, I'd have given the same answer. "So sudden. At such an early age. I can't get over it."

"Yeah," Jerry says. "But shit happens, man. I lost a brother who was only fifteen in a truck rollover. He was riding in the box and he got the brains squished right out of his head, man. Sucks, but what can you do?"

Lynn grimaces at him. "Jare! That's *terrible.*"

"Sorry, babe," he says, smiling at me again. "It was years ago. I'm done crying about it. Getcha a brewsky, Kittykat?"

"Jare!" She gives him a punch in the shoulder, and from his expression, I'd say it's a good one.

I manage a smile. "That'd be nice," I really have no desire for any such thing, but I'll be harder to throw out with a drink in my hand. "Let me help you fix the chesterfield first."

Jerry smiles. "Don't worry about it," he says. "Shitty thing has no weight to it." He proceeds to demonstrate, grabbing the couch by its back and one arm, then wrenching it upwards. Bits of party snacks fly halfway to the ceiling as it flips back on its feet. "See? No Pablo."

I put the cushions in place. They feel slippery, and I wonder if it's a natural quality of the fabric or from many coats of airborne cooking grease. Lynn sits down immediately, right at the centre.

Jerry flips open the fridge, and I'm near enough to see it's empty except for some nondescript greenish bundles of wilt, a two-litre bottle of Pepsi, and some cheap American beer: a couple dozen cans of Busch Ice and a six-pack of Old Milwaukee. He grabs three of the Buschs and tosses one to me on his way by. The move catches me off guard, and I fumble the can badly, managing to snag it out of the air no more than an inch from the floor.

"Whoa, sweet save, Kitkattie-o," he says. "Let me get you another one so you don't hose Lynn's living room and get the whole trailer reeking like a brewery." It was that way long before I got here, but I keep this observation to myself.

Jerry pops open the beer he'd begun to hand to Lynn and gives it to me, while she glowers from her seat on the couch. She sits there fuming, slouched with her elbows on her knees, waiting for a replacement one.

"So what can we do ya for?" Jerry says when he returns.

"We don't have to tell her *nothin'*," Lynn mutters while digging anxiously in a cigarette pack.

"Have you been talking to Dr. Samuelson?" I chance. It's the only way she could be so sure of my reason for coming. Samuelson must have headed me off.

"Don't have to tell you that neither," she says, flashing a self-satisfied smile as she lights a cigarette and puffs up a smokestorm.

There's my answer. There *has* to be a reason why Craig's doctor would want to limit what Lynn tells me.

I will not leave here without finding out.

CHAPTER 26

"I JUST WANT TO know what happened," I say. "Some of the pieces don't fit, and I want to try and make sense of them."

Lynn's face becomes harder than ever, and I know I am not winning her over. "After what, fifteen years, you wake up one day and think you've got the right to know all the answers? You got no idea how bad you fucked Craig up, do you?"

"Probably not," I say. "And I really don't think I deserve all the answers. But I am concerned that some things might not have been handled the way they should have, and you could end up being impacted."

Lynn's lips twitch and pucker like she's about to say something, but Jerry touches his fingertips to her chin and she takes the cue to pause.

"You mean *medical* things?" he says.

I nod. "Well, I'm not armed to make any accusations yet, but didn't you see a little flag go up when the doctor called in a panic and told you to keep your mouth shut?"

Lynn makes a face. "What flag?"

"It's a figure of speech," Jerry tells her. "She thinks Doc Samuelson might be trying to save his own bacon."

Lynn is expressionless for many seconds, as if her mind has left her body to go think about this somewhere else. When it returns, she appears to be in a much better mood. Her smile is big. "Scared of a lawsuit," she says to him. "Stupid quack fucked up and thinks we're gonna sue his ass, right?" Jerry keeps remarkably quiet, but his delight at the idea is too much to conceal. I suspect if things continue looking up, he'll want to slip a wedding ring on Lynn's finger pretty quick.

"We don't know anything for sure," I say. I feel a twinge of guilt for allowing Lynn to jump to such a conclusion, for fuelling her greed. But I haven't said anything untrue, and the doctor hasn't exactly been forthright and open. If the records show that he's been negligent, let him suffer for it. At least by paying higher malpractice insurance premiums after his underwriter cuts Lynn Butler a hefty cheque. And if he's collaborated with someone who killed Craig by helping cover it up, I hope he gets much worse.

"This is why I've come to talk to you," I say, fibbing now. "There isn't enough evidence to file a suit right now, but that could change fast."

Jerry pipes up: "What you got so far to back up your case?" He sits upright and his eyes twinkle as he looks into mine. For a second, I wonder if he's got some sort of background in the legal world. It's not an entirely ludicrous notion—he seems fairly bright. Not unlikely he's spent some time in the company of a lawyer, and perhaps he picked up a few things.

"First of all, I'm not convinced the diagnosis was conclusive. They presumed it to be early onset Alzheimer's, and treated him accordingly, but I've never heard of that disease killing a person in such a short time. The doctor should have at least referred Craig to a neurologist for a second opinion. He refused to let me look at the charts, so…"

"It wouldn't have been legal to let you see that, would it?" Jerry says.

I smile. "Not *technically*, but unless he had something to hide—" Lynn interrupts me in mid-sentence, jumping excitedly to her feet.

"He'da showed you. She's a doctor," she says to Jerry. "Didn't have nothing to lose by letting you see a bunch of stupid records if everything was on the up-and-up. Then you'd have gone on your own happy way. He wouldn't give two shits about you showing up over here."

"That's how I see it," I say. "All I need is written consent from you to look through the file, and I'll have a much better idea of what you're up against. I'll be able to see the symptoms the nurses noted, what meds he was prescribed, and how his condition progressed."

"And you'll know if they did anything else wrong."

"If there was an overdose or any mishap on the floor, it should be reported in there. More importantly, there might be CT scans and other diagnostic information that we can have re-evaluated by our own experts if we choose to. Will you give me consent?"

She looks at Jerry with her face screwed up, and he gives a crooked smile.

"What am I supposed to write?"

"Something like this, I say, then draw in a big breath. " '*As spouse and next-*

of-kin of the late Craig Butler, I, Lynn Butler do hereby consent to the disclosure of any and all medical files and records resulting from physical exams, blood tests, x-rays and other diagnostic and medical procedures that relate to the medical history of my husband, to Katherine Francis or anyone personally appointed by her.'"

"Whoa. You rehearse that or something?" Jerry asks with a smile.

"Had time to give it some thought on the drive over," I admit.

Lynn rummages through a pile of debris Jerry knocked from an end table with the broom, and comes up holding a note pad imprinted with a caricature of a bearded man holding bagpipes. She gives it to me. *Jimmy Bruce will Sell your Hoose,* it says in barely readable olde-style script. Diving back into the pile, she uncovers a cheap pen with its back end eaten off. With a *woo-hoo* worthy of finding Greyhound Scott's three-hundred-dollar Montblanc, she leaps up and presses the pen into my hand. "You write it. All I have to do is sign at the bottom, right?"

"Right. And Jerry could be our witness. But there would be less chance of it being challenged if the whole thing is written in your own hand."

"That makes sense, Lynn," Jerry says. "Otherwise the doc'll probably tell her to piss off. Then phone here to ream your ass and smooth-talk you into saying you signed it under duress. That guy is slicker than fish snot."

She suddenly looks apprehensive, and begins to chew one of her hangnails. "What do I say if he *does* call?"

"I like the line he gave you for Kat," Jerry says with a chuckle. "You don't have to talk to *anyone.* Better yet, tell the dumb quack you can't talk to him because there's a lawsuit pending, and hang up. Then shut off the ringer."

Lynn thinks about this, her face taking on a smile of grinch-like slyness. She raises the pen. "Okay. Say that BS for me again. And go slow this time."

* * *

"WHAT ELSE do you know?" Jerry asks me after Lynn scrawls a giant signature at the bottom of her girlish, rounded lettering. Contrary to Lynn's bristly, in-your-face character, the orderly penmanship connotes a certain— remarkable—innocence. By the time she's done, I almost expect her to dot the i's with little hearts.

I give Jerry a shrug. "That's about all I've got to go on right now. That and my instincts." I sure don't plan to get into the mutilation photos or the speedy cremation unless it becomes relevant. That could make this a really long visit. Still, I can't help but probe a little further. "Did you decline an autopsy, Lynn?"

She grimaces at the thought. "Was *that* supposed to be up to me?"

"Well, you might have been able to stop them from doing one, say for religious reasons."

Jerry steps in. "You're saying they did one, or not?"

"No. And I think they ought to have. A lot can be determined about a brain disease through pathology that there's no way of knowing while the patient is alive. Personally, I think it was irresponsible to cremate the body without an autopsy. The doctor told me he was just too busy."

"But that doesn't do us any good in a malpractice suit, does it?" Jerry says. "He was already dead."

"No, but it might help further our argument that the case was handled with consistent negligence. If I'm guessing right, an autopsy report could have been worth a lot of money to Lynn."

Lynn is nodding like she is certain that I *am* right. I'm not as sure, but it's nice to be making progress for a change. The first rule of sales is to put the prospect in the habit of agreeing with you.

"Why did they cremate him, anyways?" she asks.

"I presumed those were the wishes expressed in his will," I bluff. Len has already told me that no such document exists.

"Couldn't be. He didn't have one," she says, confirming it.

"If Craig died intestate, then they should definitely have consulted with you."

Lynn's eyes brighten, and she is clearly fighting hard to contain her excitement. "I never said to cremate him. I *hate* cremations. People should get buried, not burned all up. I'm gonna get buried. When I write *my* will, I think I'll put that in."

"Good idea," I say. Jerry nods authoritatively.

"So you also want to find out who authorised the cremation," I add. "Looks a little bit like someone may have been trying to make sure the body isn't exhumed and autopsied some time later."

Lynn looks momentary bewildered, then regains her determination. "I bet nobody *arthur-ised* it."

Jerry chuckles. "That'd be bad on them,"

"Did you know about Craig's condition before he checked into the hospital?" I ask.

"I saw him about three months ago, so not long before. Right here, in this room. He'd been making lots of trips into Saskatchewan for his weird new hobby."

"*Weird?* How so?" *Away we go,* I tell myself.

She laughs. "Chasing flying saucers."

I feign total ignorance. "Did Craig see a UFO?"

"Don't think he ever had any Close Encounters of his own. Not sure he'd have told me if he did, though. He knew I never bought into none of that supernatural BS. And I'm not gonna stop making fun until I see a flying saucer with my own two eyes. What Craig got himself into was *mutated* cows. Ever heard of that?"

"*Mutilated*," Jerry corrects. Some fucked up shit," he adds, shaking his head.

"Can't pretend I know much about it," I say. "What did he tell you?"

Lynn rolls her eyes. "Same kind of BS you see on *Unexplained Mysteries.* A farmer finds one of his steers dead with its eyes and sex organs missing, and they call up Craig. Or they did until he died. He was like the big national expert on *mutel-aided* stuff." She says the M-word slowly, glaring at Jerry.

"You said he was making regular trips to Saskatchewan? How often did he stop by *here?*"

"My place? Not very. Like I said, last time was maybe three or four months ago. He said something like fifteen of them happened not far from here though. *Mutes*, he called 'em."

Something in Lynn's eyes suggests that she is not quite the sceptic she makes herself out to be. I smile. "The space aliens seem to have taken an interest in this part of the world."

"Guess so," she says. "He got kind of mixed up when we were talking about it, though. He kept saying something about the Mad Cow."

"But there haven't been any in Saskatchewan, have there?" I ask, though I'm sure there have not. When Canada broke news of the first-ever Mad Cow raised on its soil in Alberta, disaster followed. Every one of the country's trade partners instantly slammed their borders shut to Canadian beef, all but collapsing the country's cattle industry. Even after the United States found BSE on one of its own farms, Canada's product—including mutton, bison, and other ruminants—remained banished south of the 49th parallel years later. Subsequent BSE finds in Alberta made matters even worse.

"That cow *died* in Alberta," Jerry says. "But it was *born* in Baldwinton, Saskatchewan, just south-east of here. Truth is it spent most of its life at a ranch down there before they shipped it off to Alberta."

"I didn't know that," Lynn says.

"That's 'cause you never read the papers or look at the news. It's common knowledge, but not exactly a thing of pride. Don't think you'll see 'Birthplace of the Mad Cow That Killed the Canadian Farm' on a sign going into Baldwinton," he says with a chuckle. "You know, like they've got over in Floral for Gordie Howe."

"Where's *Floral?*" Lynn asks, looking at me. I give a shrug.

Jerry grins. "Other side of Saskatoon. That's where Mr. Hockey grew up, but it's home to more pigs than pucks now. I did a lot of wiring on a gigantic farrow-to-finish hog operation out there. Quite a shock getting called to work at a place called Floral, then ending up breathing nothing but pig shit for three weeks."

"Jerry's an electrician," Lynn proclaims.

"Is there a lot of work in your industry here?" I ask Jerry, just to be polite.

"Not bad, I guess. It was better before hordes of people migrated over from the East Coast. Damn TV news over there kept reporting how we got nothing but work. Market's pretty well swamped now."

"But you're keeping busy?"

"Most of the time. Been at it a while, so I'm high up on the big contractors' lists. I've thought of moving to Vancouver, though. Think I'd prefer never-ending rain to these prairie winters. Cloud cover keeps the heat in, so clear means cold in wintertime. Last January it was Sunny and Cher here all month, but at the same time we were stuck at minus forty-five. The foam in my truck's seat was like a big block of ice." He tilts his head nearly to his shoulder. "Had to drive around like this all the time."

I smile at the comical gesture. "I'm from Victoria, actually. Weather's similar, but there might be more work to be found in the Vancouver area. Can't say I'm in the loop with the trades."

"I like Vancouver," Lynn says to Jerry with a smile. "I hope you take me with you."

*   *   *

SMALL TALK carries on much longer than I'd like, and it's late afternoon by the time I break away from Lynn and Jerry. I wonder if their lawsuit will get off the ground, or if Lynn will be leaving her trailer to move to the West Coast any time soon.

I pull into a Husky station for fuel before heading out of town. It's not all that far from the mall where I stopped upon my arrival, and I half expect to see the local sham artist working customers at the pumps. But he'd be unlikely to run his out-of-gas scheme here, it occurs to me as I'm filling my tank. Someone might buy him a few litres of fuel instead of handing over the cash. He'd probably kill himself drinking it.

"*Kat*?" says a voice from behind me.

Even before I turn, I know who it is.

CHAPTER 27

SANDY COLMAN LOOKS AT me with an unreadable expression. If anything, I think I detect a hint of a smile on his thin lips. The man seems untouched by the years that have passed since the last time I saw him.

His penetrating blue eyes are identical to my former husband's, but set on a lighter complexion. Sandy has a longer, more slender nose, and his father's flaming orange hair (or so I'm told—what little of it remained for me to see was a yellowy white) instead of the dark brown locks Jack inherited from Mrs. Colman. A matching red goatee—something new—lends Sandy an almost diabolical air. Though he's got to be all of forty-five, I don't see a single white strand.

Thoughts race through my mind, tripping over each other, interweaving and entangling together. I can't possibly follow them all. Finally, the emotion seems to collapse under its own weight. Torrents of tears blur my eyes, flooding down over my cheeks.

I never expected to see Sandy again after divorcing his brother. When I drove into this town, I actually *hoped* not to.

He parts his arms, and I accept the invitation for a hug. He lifts me from my feet, crunching my ribs in his strong arms.

"I missed you," I say when he sets me back down. It's not *really* the truth. I haven't even thought about the guy much, though I always used to enjoy being in his company.

He draws back and studies me. "Missed you too, Kat," he finally says. "What in heaven's name are you doing in Lloyd, of all places?"

I shrug and smile, then take a deep breath, thinking that given a few extra seconds, I might come up with something feasible, but seem to have hit a dead end. What *is* the truth? That I came to visit the wife of a dead boyfriend, and have tricked her into giving me access to his private records?

Yuck. I've got nothing else.

"Long, boring story," is the best I can do. "Just passing through. How are Laura and the boys?"

"Everyone's great. Christopher and Bradley are both in school now. Grades one and three. Laura's enjoying the freedom. Nothing to distract her from the daytime soaps now. Can I buy you a coffee?"

"I'd love to, but I'm staying in St. Paul. I'm even more of a hazard on the road after dark than in the daytime."

"Just a few minutes would be really cool. This is a total stroke of good luck. I can't let you go *that* easy."

With all Sandy's warm fuzziness, I can't help but acquiesce. And I regret it before my backside hits the restaurant chair.

"So why'd you do it?" he says, his tone suddenly sharp, his eyebrows bent into a shallow V.

I don't know how to answer, and fortunately there is no time for a response. It's like he's taken a leap out of a plane and can't stop himself. "Why'd you leave my brother?"

"I... I—"

"Hey, I've known Jack all my life, and I know how he can be. We've had more than our share of scraps. But you were *married* to the guy. I heard you promise to spend the rest of your life loving and honouring him, for better or for worse, Kat. How bad was it? What the fuck's worse than *worse*?"

A waitress comes, in time to rescue me, but Sandy snatches the two menus and waves her off. "You fucking *destroyed* him, Kat. You get what that means? *Destroyed*?"

"He's an addict, Sandy."

"We all have our problems, our vices. Jack is in chronic pain, Kat. The man needs drugs just to have a reasonable quality of life."

"It wasn't just the drugs. I shouldn't have even said that. There were so many things. Too many, and I think too severe to ever fix."

"You *think* Laura and I have had a nice, smooth road? We've been through some damn tough times. She had an affair, you know."

"I'm sorry, Sandy. I didn't know that." The anguish in his eyes scorches deep into my chest.

"I don't even think Bradley is my own biological son. But you know what? I stood by Laura. I made the same vow as you, only mine *took*."

I'm crying hard now, but he doesn't let up: "I never thought you were like that, Kat. When Jack told me he was marrying you, I thought, 'I'm so happy my little brother's found a girl who's not gonna break his heart.' Man, was I ever *wrong*. I encouraged him, and I feel like shit about it now."

"Sandy, I don't expect you to understand. It wasn't just Jack and his drugs and the way he behaved. It was me too. In fact, I honestly think it was my fault more than his."

"Now *that* I believe."

The waitress returns, but continues past us when she sees the red faces and rigid bodies. "Two coffees," Sandy calls to her. "I just needed to get that shit off my chest," he says in a softer voice, with a little smile. "Thanks for hearing me. Now tell me, what are you really doing in Lloydminster?"

"One day, Sandy, I'll write you a long letter explaining what went wrong between Jack and me," I say, surprised to find myself returning to the subject that I wanted desperately to escape only seconds ago. It seems there is no choice. I haven't made any progress on what seems the single alternate topic for us. "As simply as I can put it, I'm not the right person to be in that relationship. I made a really big mistake getting into it. Leaving was terrible, but I think it was the right thing. I couldn't bear the idea of the two of us living out our lives in misery. You and Laura have more. You have a lot in common, including your shared love for the boys. With Jack and me, there really wasn't anything to salvage."

"Sometimes you just gotta wait. Be patient. You went through some tough shit the past few months, Kat, and I feel for you. I mean, *fuck—*" He stops and glances up at the waitress, his cheeks flushed. Her hands shake as she sets down the two rattling coffee cups, both spilling an abundance of muddy liquid onto their saucers. "Thanks," Sandy says, as she beats another hasty retreat. "You know, I think it's fate that we met here. I only come to this station once, maybe twice a year. I just finished filling a propane tank for the weekend when I saw you. Gonna barbecue ten pounds of beef back ribs tonight. Maybe you could join us. Laura and the boys would love to see you again. They won't be as hostile as me, I swear. The wife's never been fond of your ex. Got the boys calling him Uncle Jackass." He laughs at this, but I see pain in his face.

"I'd love to, but I'm hoping to be back home by then. I came to town to visit the widow of an old classmate who died recently," I say, almost inadvertently.

It comes out better than I thought.

"Oh." He flicks his blue eyes down to the cup in his hands. "Sorry to hear that. How's she doing?"

"Not bad, considering. Her husband died of a brain disease that they're calling Alzheimer's. It all happened really fast."

Sandy empties two creamers and three sugar packets into his coffee. I have mine black, as always. It's almost as bad as what Len served me. I wonder when Sandy takes a sip if his syrupy concoction is any less foul.

"Tastes like horse piss this way too," he says, reading my face.

"Now on to the good stuff. Tell me about those boys."

* * *

WE BOTH stick to talking about Sandy's sons—hockey and school and girls—until our coffee is cold. I throw down a couple of two-dollar coins, and we part ways in the vestibule.

"I'll be watching for that letter," he says.

I nod. I might just write it—and not just for Sandy's benefit.

He gives me a final hug, and as his cheek brushes past mine, I feel the wetness of his tears.

CHAPTER 28

A FEELING OF DREAD settles into my belly as I exit the border city, and I know with certainty that staying in St. Paul again tonight is a very bad idea. Call it intuition, common sense—or just learning from past experience for a change.

Whichever, first chance I get, I turn the car around.

I park on a street alongside a really decrepit motel, and backtrack four blocks to an only slightly better one. I catch the slick-haired man at the desk viewing a grainy black-and-white video of two people having sex inside a poorly lit room, and though he immediately changes to a TV receiver showing a documentary about Bhutan, he knows his reaction was too late. Sweat trickles down his temple, and his eyes flit everywhere but to me. I use his nervousness to my advantage, and he is eager to accept the last of my cash—three dollars short at that—to make me and my pointed looks go away. I sign the register with a made-up name, but he doesn't so much as glance at it.

* * *

I MANAGE to sleep off and on, but am up early. My comfort level plummeted upon entering my room last night, when I noticed that it was a dead ringer for the one I'd just seen on TV. Perhaps it was a weird coincidence, but I kept the lights off most of the duration just in case.

Since I'm out of cash and about to skip town, it seems an opportune time to draw a reserve of funds. I take out a cash advance on my credit card for fifteen hundred dollars—a first for me. I feel like a true fugitive. In the spirit of this, I find a local outlet of the rental company the Intrepid is from, and exchange it for a British racing green Mustang. It's a relief to be rid of the car my threat-painting break-in artist would recognise in an instant. I show interest in a black ball cap bearing the Thrifty logo, and get it for free. It hides most of my blonde hair, and combined with my Wayfarers in the dark green car, I think I look positively prosaic.

The morning air and image change gives freshness to my mission. I turn Sarah McLaughlan up loud, and as I sing "Dirty Little Secret," with her, I begin to feel like I'm ready to take on Don Samuelson.

* * *

TO MY dismay, the same receptionist is at the desk. It's a surprise when she flashes a smile—however brief—at me.

"Here for Dr. Samuelson?" she says.

"Yes. He's in?"

"Still here from the evening shift. Seen him in better moods though. He's being a real ass, to be honest. Sure you don't want to come back another time?"

I smile, sensing I have something of an ally. "That's okay. I'm here to piss him off anyway. *The Weight of Water* now?"

"Yeah. Anita Shreve wrote this book first, but the one I just read is a prequel. Kind of whacked."

"But it fits perfectly with the way you like to read," I say. "Back to front."

"Yeah. I do everything backwards. You'd think that'd make me fit well in the healthcare system, yet I stick out like a black fingernail." She shows me her hand, the thumbnail alone painted in glossy ebony polish. "Grab a seat. I'll page the doc."

"Do me a favour. Don't tell him it's me. Say it's a distinguished visitor he'll want to see."

She sniggers and punches a few buttons.

* * *

LESS THAN a minute goes by before Dr. Samuelson emerges, traversing the corridor in long, deliberate paces. He wears a brilliant white lab coat over his greens this time, and equally blinding tennis shoes on his feet. His eyes lock onto mine. I'm expecting him to stop and turn away at this point, but he doesn't break stride.

I stand and offer my hand, trying to behave like a professional rather than the sneaky interloper I am. He curls his lip up at it.

"What are *you* doing back here?" he demands. "*Distinguished,* my ass."

"I've got something for you, Dr. Samuelson." I produce the authorisation, and he snatches it in his fist. His eyes barely scan Lynn's words, and he tosses it at me, wiping his hand on the lab coat.

"I don't appreciate you harassing the family of my patient," he growls.

"I haven't harassed anyone. Now, if you'll let me see the records, I'll be out of your face in just a few minutes."

"I certainly hope so. I don't suppose it's a coincidence that you show up here with a letter from Lynn Butler, full of words she's never heard of the very morning she announces she's going to sue me for malpractice. Absolutely frivolous, and a goddam waste of my time. Ask me how I feel about that, Ms. Francis."

"So you called Lynn today, didn't you? She told me she never wanted to hear from you again."

"I'm sure she did, after you poisoned her simple little mind. Up until now, Lynn trusted me implicitly and never questioned my advice. *Ever.*"

"And blind faith is the proper doctor-patient relationship? Give me a break. The records, please."

"You stay here. I'll have a nurse pull the file."

* * *

THIS TIME, my wait is much longer. I wish I had insisted on accompanying Samuelson. Finally, a nurse with frizzy shoulder-length white hair and tired, drawn features enters the waiting room. She stops, looking at no one and says blankly: "Kat Francis..."

I hop to my feet. "That's me."

"This way." The nurse turns around and walks down a corridor, and I follow. She opens the door to a room containing a pairing of dark folding tables, encompassed by ten well-worn brown chairs. A Coke machine is in one corner, and in another there is a small table with a three-hole punch, stapler, and paper shredder on it, the last of these above a plastic garbage bin on the floor.

A thin-looking file sits alone on one of the large tables. I pick it up without sitting down, and find it to be every bit as lightweight as it appears. I flip it open, then look up to the nurse, but she is gone.

* * *

THE FIRST page contains the Emergency Room RN's triage notes from Craig Butler's admission the day he arrived here, eight weeks ago today.

Patient is in acute distress. Continues to wheeze, dizziness increasing, nausea, some apparent dementia. Trembling of right ant. quadrant suggestive of Parkinson's. Blood obtained. Urine obtained—100 cc, return clear.

There are only two other pages, trivial information gathered during the next few days. Furious, I close the file and slap it back on the counter.

The nurse is back in the doorway, wearing a mean face.

I poke one finger down on top of the file. "Where is the rest?"

"What are you talking about? It's *all* there."

"Nothing is here. Just admission information and maybe three days of notes. Craig was here seven weeks. Where are his intake and output logs? What about medication information, vital signs logs, or pain scale data? There's not a scrap of information here from any other consultants. This file has been stripped."

"It's *all* in there," she says dourly. "I looked through it myself before I went to call you in." She picks up the file and her mouth drops open. "What have you done with the file?" she snarls. She looks across the table at the shredder and howls: "Oh, NO! Oh, my goodness. I'm calling Security. This is *criminal*."

She jogs out the door and down the hall wailing, "Help! *Haay-lp!*" as if I've just held a knife to her throat. It doesn't seem to me like an act. Did she *really* see a complete file before ushering me in? I check the garbage can, and it's a quarter full of small bits of white, yellow and pink paper. I grab a handful and examine them. It's impossible to tell what they once were. The shredder is the cross-cut kind that creates minute diamond-shaped scraps with no more than one or two partial characters on each.

I now have two choices:

1. I can stick around and somehow try to prove that I did not use Lynn Butler's ill-begotten consent to shred her husband's confidential hospital records.

2. I can bolt *now* and try to get the hell out of town before the police capture me.

If I stay, I'll go to jail—maybe for days—even though they've got nothing on me but circumstantial evidence. Dr. Samuelson is a convincing—and credible—adversary. But if I can make it to my lawyer's office in Victoria, he can probably make sure any charges they lay don't stick.

Perhaps I can even locate Isabel Butler in Edmonton—on my way to the airport.

*   *   *

I SLIP out the door and sprint down the corridor the way I came in. Dr. Samuelson rounds the corner at the end, and stops. He stands and folds his arms across his chest. My shoes squeak on the floor tiles as I make a knee-straining one-eighty and streak back past the door to the shredder room, then round blindly into an adjacent hallway.

"Stop... at... once," Samuelson calls out, the pauses between words a sure indicator that he is now giving chase. I see a red EXIT sign glowing at the end of the hall, and go for it. The door's red panic bar is marked in big letters EMERGENCY EXIT ONLY—ALARM WILL SOUND. To my right, at the end of another corridor, I see a similar door with the same warning. If my bearings are any good, that one should get me out in the vicinity of the staff parking lot, which I noticed to be separated only by a concrete barrier from the public one where I left the Mustang. I hit the door at a dead run, and nearly snap my wrists slamming the bar.

It flies open. Instantaneously, an alarm begins to whoop, and a red strobe pulsates behind me. "Over there!" hollers a voice that does not belong to Samuelson.

Without looking back, I charge across the lot and take the waist-high barrier on one hand like a gymnast on a pommel horse.

CHAPTER 29

WHEN I RETURNED TO the island during the spring of my third year in vet school, I bought a blaze orange Volkswagen Beetle convertible—which I decided to drive all the way back to Saskatoon for the fall session. Mom assured me I wouldn't make it as far as Revelstoke, but I was twenty minutes past Edmonton when the head gasket finally blew and my radiator emptied itself onto the Yellowhead Highway. It was Friday afternoon, and I found myself with three days to kill before a mechanic could get it fixed.

Edmonton is called *Festival City* for good reason: it plays host to a long chain of world-class cultural events every year, the Fringe being the summer's grand finale. I arrived just in time for the closing weekend. I befriended a street performer from Northumberland who had juggled neon clubs and flaming swords in the farthest reaches of the world, and he happily recounted for me the festival's history—originating a short jaunt north of his own birthplace in England's North Shields.

In the summer of 1947, while Europe was busy rebuilding from the terrible war that had ended just two years before, a few great minds in Edinburgh enacted a different kind of reconstruction. The psychological wounds were still very raw between nations that had recently been mortal enemies, and posed a very real danger of erupting into new turmoil. The Edinburgh International Festival was launched that year in the hope of leveraging artistic culture to emotionally reunite Europe's war-torn countries.

It was a huge success from day one, every venue filling to capacity with performers and patrons alike. A number of theatre companies showed up uninvited, and were surprised to be denied a stage. Eight of these decided to set up on the periphery of the festival and put their shows on regardless.

Thus was born the Fringe.

Fast forward more than a quarter-century to 1982. That year, North America's first Fringe festival was held in Edmonton, with the same theme as the Scottish original: anything goes.

Similar annual festivals subsequently popped up in cities all over the globe, but none could keep pace with the Edmonton event. Boasting more than a hundred and fifty performing groups, the Edmonton Fringe remains the largest one outside of Edinburgh—and the continent's biggest annual *whoop-de-doo* of any kind. For eleven days, streets in Edmonton's Old Strathcona district are closed to traffic and clogged with half a million show-goers and thousands of others who come purely to take in the party atmosphere.

*   *   *

THE LAST time I saw Isabel Butler, she was a sweet nine-year-old with an incurable Anne of Green Gables fixation. Isabel was a brunette—not a redhead like her idol Anne Shirley—but in her long braids, and flowery cotton dresses, anyone familiar with the character could tell at once who the girl was emulating. Upon my first visit to the Butler home, Isabel proudly carried her repertoire of straw boater hats down to the living room in a stack, where she painstakingly explained the differences to me. I told her I'd been an Anne Fan too as a girl (albeit with a lesser degree of commitment), which gave the two of us some common ground. Isabel had received the entire CBC miniseries—newly released on videocassette—as a Christmas gift, and I promised to watch all the episodes with her. The way things turned out, we managed to see only one tape together before Craig and I split up.

As I drive, I smile at the thought of how Isabel saw Anne Shirley as not just a fictional character invented a hundred years before by an author named Lucy Maud Montgomery, but a *kindred spirit* of her own. "I truly wish Anne could join us here tonight," she announced at the dinner table. "She would certainly love this meal, and I would be happy as a queen."

I smile at the same reminiscence later, as I scan the countless playbills photocopied onto multicoloured paper and stapled one over the other to a plywood barricade, hoping to find one bearing Isabel's name. My reverie, and perhaps the memories themselves, shatter when I find it:

(i)
Isi Butler's
The Vagina Soliloquies
Cunning Linguistics from the Land Down Under
ADULTS ONLY — EXPLICIT CONTENT

I stare at the poster, reading it over again. The second time, I catch the meaning of the lowercase *i* in parentheses. Not merely the first and last letters of Isabel's nickname, but a pictogram.

The act appears to be some kind of tribute to Eve Ensler's *The Vagina Monologues*. Considering Isabel lives in New York—and her involvement in the performing arts—it's no surprise she has been exposed to the off-broadway sensation. I haven't seen it myself, but I once browsed through much of the follow-up book in a store, in the end feeling too intimidated by the title to carry it up to the cashier. Ensler, a feminist playwright, travelled the world asking hundreds of women from all walks of life a series of questions about their most private of parts. She assembled many of the interviews to create a stage production—which spawned a book, then a movie. I recently read about a parody called *The Marijuana-Logues*—directed by the creator of *The Kids In the Hall*—that's become a runaway success. It's hard to imagine what Isabel might have done to make her version unique.

I'm eager—and a bit *scared*—to find out. A show is scheduled to start in just minutes, a few blocks from where I am now.

Perhaps it's not too late to get a seat.

The mature content warning was probably more an attempt to arouse interest than to keep children out, I tell myself as I dodge half-naked teenaged girls then step over a prostrate panhandler. As on my one previous Fringe encounter, the acts continue to vie aggressively with one another for maximum shock value—with a hundred and fifty other shows, it must be quite a challenge to stand out. From the titles on playbills stapled one on top of another—*Nymphomania, To Shag or to Sew, Chainsaw Love, The Tit Show, Aspects of Sex, Double Climax*—replete with equally suggestive imagery, it appears there hasn't been a shift toward conservatism.

I approach the doors to the venue—which fifty weeks of the year is a regular Celtic pub—and am at once pleased and disappointed to see that there is no queue. Getting a seat will probably not be a problem, but it's sad to see Isabel is not drawing a long line of interested show-goers.

"Are there still tickets available?" I ask a thin young woman dressed in *Addams Family* who leans against the door, partly obscuring an oversized version of Isabel's playbill. She gives me a blank stare. I point to the poster above her rump, and she glances back, then takes a drag of her cigarette, forced to do so from the corner of her mouth. A large round ring runs through the middle of her upper lip, straddled by two even bigger hoops projecting from the pink tissue of the lower one. I wonder how she must feed herself.

"Sold out," she tells me with a face of alabaster and harsh makeup. My eyes follow the movements of all the lip rings, despite my effort to fight this. "Again," she continues. "Today's show is starting now, but you can come back in about an hour for drinks."

"Really? I see the poster lists just one showing tonight. Does she do any others?"

She gives a heavy nod, strands of poker-straight black hair sweeping forward over her painted cheekbones. "She should. Opening night was only yesterday, but she's already one of the biggest draws, 'cause of the stuff she does. Advance tickets sell out the week before, soon as they're available. We hold a quarter of the day's tickets here, but if you want to make tomorrow's show, be sure to come real early. I had more people waiting than tickets three hours ago."

I am surprised that Isabel is doing so well, selling out all her shows. Her soliloquies must be supremely profound and touching. Apparently after experiencing the Eve Ensler versions, many people break into tears and claim to have been *transformed*. I'm disappointed, but try to resign myself to the fact that I won't be seeing Isabel perform.

"That's no good," I say. "I'll be back home in Victoria then. Isabel—*Isi*—is an old friend, and I haven't seen her in years. Is there no way at all? I could pay you a commission…"

"'Fraid not. There's a fixed number seats based on our liquor license, and I need to be strict about not going over capacity. Get us shut down during our biggest week of the year, and I'm canned for sure. Assholes from Gaming and Liquor go on a rampage during the Fringe. Two places got their licenses yanked last night. Sorr—."

The door bursts open, and the girl narrowly avoids being pasted against the entrance's stone wall. A scrawny little woman with cotton-white hair, bright red lips, and painted-on eyebrows charges out and elbows me aside.

"Give me my money back," the old lady sputters at both of us, shaking her head vigorously. "That's *re*-volting." Her lower lip curls down so far when she pronounces this last word that it stamps a horizontal red line across the middle of her chin.

"Sorry," the hostess says. "Can't give refunds. Seeing Fringe shows is always at your own risk. Says so right on the ticket."

"What?" the woman sputters. "That will not—"

"Hold on," I interrupt, digging in my handbag. "I'll buy your seat."

She looks perfectly stunned. "That wouldn't be proper. I am *going* to get a refund. It's not about the money, you know. I wouldn't have bought the ticket myself. My son bought a bunch of 'em, but got called out of town for the weekend. Money is not the issue at all. There is a principle at stake here."

I find my cash. "Eight dollars, right?"

"I don't know. And I'm not interested..."

"You're not going to get a refund," I say. "You heard the young lady. The festival management *never* does that, and their volunteers have a lot more time and energy than you or me. Here's ten. Where were you seated?"

She grabs the bill from my hands and pinches it precisely in two. "Second row from front, left of centre," she sputters, her jowls wriggling like living creatures, and shuffles down the sidewalk. "You'll be *so-rry*," she warns loudly without turning. I reach for the door.

"Hold on, miss," the hostess says, raising her voice now. "There's a strict no-latecomers policy—"

I look at her, stunned. "But I'm not a latecomer. I'm replacing that old hen, and she was on time."

"No re-entry either."

"Nice of you to stand there and let me buy the ticket, then. Listen, I won't tell if you don't." Instead of waiting for her to consider this, I jerk the door open and jump into the darkness, then feel my way around a corner to the performance area.

The room is dim, but I spot the narrow aisle between chairs and rush for the front. It's only when I'm passing near the stage that I grasp what it is that everyone is watching. At the centre of a miniature, rose-velvet curtain is a rostrum for what appears to be a face. Except it is smaller than a person's face. The eyes are clear plastic domes with free-floating black irises—the kind you might find on a child's hand puppet—and the rubber nose sits atop a furry beard. The mouth is not that at all.

I should have guessed.

* * *

AFTER THE SHOW, workers hustle in, some carrying with them tall round tables and others folding up chairs to turn the space back into the pub it was designed to be.

I mill around, with no idea of what I'm going to say. Isabel extricates herself from the mini-stage wearing a pair of loose-fitting silk pants, and I finally get to see what she looks like.

"I've missed you, girl," she says to me.

CHAPTER 30

"I CAN'T BELIEVE YOU RECOGNISED me, Isabel," I say.

"Oh, come *on*. I thought the world of you. And it's *Isi* now.

"You looked up to *me?* I'm not Anne Shirley, you know."

She snickers—the very same laugh I remember from the sweet little girl in braids and eyeliner-daubed freckles. This is probably the first comforting thought I've had in this room. "I know *that*. You're Kat Francis. God, I bawled my eyes out when you and Craig broke up. Knew we'd never get to watch the rest of those silly videotapes together. Funny thing—I thought about that just three days ago, at the funeral. Kind of hoped you might show up there."

"I'm sorry. I had no idea what happened until the day after that."

She shrugs, but wears new sadness on her face. "You know, I recognised you as soon as you got to the front of the aisle, even with your hair so short. The bright lights don't shine where my eyes are. It's one advantage I have over conventional performers. I can see almost everyone in the audience through slits in the curtain."

It's not nearly as hard as I thought it might be to reconcile the face in front of me with my memories of little Isi. At about twenty-four, she is still a young lady. She wears no makeup—on her face—and has retained much of her little-girl cuteness. Her eyes are still big and light brown, widely spaced above the bridge of her slightly upturned nose, giving her the appearance of a pixie. And like a mischievous sprite, her broad-lipped smile belies a seductive blend of innocence and naughtiness.

"Why don't we go have a seat in a booth?" she suggests, pointing to one towards the back. People are starting to flow in and line up at the entrance, so I nod and follow her. I slide onto one of the wide benches, and she sits facing me. She leans way forward and sucks in a deep breath.

"So," she says. "What did you think of the show?"

"It... It blew me away," I say, looking up at the large copper ceiling tiles.

She laughs. "It's not for everyone. I could tell you were shitting yourself. Made it hard keep my eyes off you."

"I think I would have found it easier if your—uh—*character* belonged to a complete stranger. But what about for you? It's got to be—I mean, isn't it...?" I can't find the right words.

"Uncomfortable? Embarrassing?"

I nod. "Yes, both. It must be hard, being so *exposed*."

"Not really at all, anymore. I find it invigorating and empowering now."

"That's unreal."

"Can't honestly say it was like that at the beginning. I sat up the whole night after my first performance, saying to myself, 'Omigod, I just showed my wazoo to a roomful of strangers!' But then people started coming up and telling me how brave they thought I was, and how they wished they could be so free from their own self-limiting inhibitions. Ever heard of *Puppetry of the Penis?*"

"Two Australian guys, right?"

"Two *very* well-endowed Australian dudes. You've seen their act?"

"No. My best friend saw them in Barcelona. Said it was quite amazing. I didn't think I could sit and watch something like that, but maybe now..." It occurs to me that I was made much more uncomfortable by Isi's show than by the thought of two men tying knots in their willies onstage. And *I'm* a woman.

Perhaps that's why.

She does her Anne laugh again and rolls her eyes. "Glad to see I've helped you *grow*."

"Or something."

She laughs. "I've seen *Puppetry* twice. And to tell you the truth, it blew my mind that normal people would pay money to see Simon Morley and Paul Friend twist their junk into different shapes. *Genital Origami*, they call it. I thought it was sort of unfair men could do that kind of dick tricks, but there's nothing a woman can do to entertain with what she's got."

"Well, aside from the *traditional* way." I nearly say *the way it was* meant *to be used*.

"A few months later, I went to see *The Vagina Monologues* in New York. Have you been to *that* one?"

"No," I say. "Guess I don't get out much."

"The playwright explained that she went around the world, asking women questions about their vaginas like 'what do you call it?' and 'what would it say if it could talk?' I joked to a friend that mine would tell dirty jokes. We both laughed, but it was right at that moment that I came up with my concept. Thought it would be great for someone *else* to do, someone real brave. But I couldn't stop thinking about it. I suggested it to a few performers I know who are pretty bold, and they thought it was a fabulous idea. But they'd never actually *do* it. After a while I realized if it was ever gonna happen, it'd have to be me."

"And just like that, you went up on a stage and started doing *this?*"

"It wasn't nearly that easy. I gradually came up with an act, wrote notes whenever I got a new idea and then started privately rehearsing it. I did a lot of homework. A former classmate of mine owns a small club in Manhattan that brings in a lot of avant-garde acts. One night after a few drinks, I told her what I was doing, and she begged me to let her book me when I was ready. She even referred me to a friend on the showgirl circuit in Vegas. He hooked me up with an entertainer who used to be one of the biggest acts in Southeast Asia."

"I hear they do some wild stuff in the clubs down there."

"You heard right. And this woman was nothing short of *amazing*. She could do things I doubt I'll ever be able to, like pick up coins and crush an egg. She told me how to exercise, and where I could get special equipment to work the right muscles. I practised for sometimes two or three hours a day, for months."

"So that's how you learned to do the thing with the smoke rings. And what you did with the sword..."

She hides her face. "That seems to be a favourite. I think it's the real reason why I'm a sellout. Did you recognise the tune?"

"It sounded very familiar. What was it?"

"'Sabre dance,' by Aram Khachaturian. He composed it for the ballet *Gayane,* but people seem to know it more because of Ed Sullivan. I guess he used it on his show for years, whenever he brought in plate-spinners. Before I was born. I saw the ballet and thought it fit that segment of my act—and I just love the crazy tempo."

"Got my heart racing," I say, and have to look away for a moment. "Wow, Isi. I'm not surprised you had to train so much. How did you know when you were ready?"

"Guess I never really did. There were complications. Always are, right? Not long after I started my training, I broke up with a really bad boyfriend named Joe Manucci. He liked to play rough and was super possessive. *Scary* possessive. When I told him it was over, he said the thought of another man with me made him insane, that the next guy better watch his back. Scared the shit out of me. His eyes were so—so *evil*. I didn't want to risk dating anyone. Finally, I got myself a gun."

This throws me. "You're not packing it *here*, are you?" I ask in a hushed voice.

"Naw. I don't like to tote a piece around the festival. Plus I feel safe here, so it stays in the motel room. It's not registered, probably stolen. An *illegal firearm*. Woo."

"How did you get it here? Into the country?"

She hides her face behind long, tapered fingers. "Oh my God, it's so dumb, Kat. It came through in my checked luggage. I'm lucky it didn't get picked up in there by some kind of scanner, or I'd probably be sitting in that terrorist jail in Guantánamo Bay."

"No kidding. I can't believe you actually carry a handgun, Isi. Aren't you afraid that an attacker might sense your fear and grab it away?"

"Sure I am. That's why the only thing to do is shoot first and ask questions later." She rotates her body so it's at forty-five degrees to me, and extends one elbow in my direction at shoulder level. The other hand braces it from below, and she aims a loaded index finger at me, cocking her thumb. She stares unblinkingly, then points her finger away, doubtless seeing my uneasiness with the gesture. "If Joe showed up, he'd get just one warning: 'Make a move and I'll shoot.' And if he did, I'd switch my brain off and just pull the damn trigger." Her arm is knocked back and upward by a well-fantasised recoil. "Otherwise, you're probably right. *I'd* be the dead one, and I'm nowhere near ready to die yet. I feel like my life only *started* a few months ago."

"Unreal. Anne of Green Gables, armed and dangerous." I try to laugh, but the thought rams a shaft of ice down through my core. I shiver it off. "Looks to me like you know what you're doing."

"Have to. My gun's a Smith & Wesson .357 Magnum seven-round revolver."

"I take it that's a *big* gun?"

"For a girl, yeah. Took shooting lessons at a monstrous indoor range in Woodhaven. She resumes the shooting gesture. "This is the modified weaver stance. It's how I'm most accurate on any more than a single round. See how my arm works like a rifle stock?" She twists her shoulders parallel with mine and extends both arms directly in front of her face, like one of Charlie's Angels. She makes a point of aiming the imaginary gun over my shoulder now, instead of straight at me. "This is *the isosceles*. Faster to assume, but gives lots of bounce in the recoil. You want to make the first shot count with this baby." She demonstrates with a sudden up-and-back jerk, flinging her bunched hands up near her forehead. A .357 Magnum must indeed be a mighty gun.

"So, anyway, when I put on my first show, I got cocky and sent Pal Joey a ticket. He had no way of knowing what to expect."

"No shit. Why would you do *that*?"

She shrugs, and gives me a funny smile. "Guess I wanted to show him he couldn't control my body or who I shared it with."

"Did it work?"

"Yes and no. Two bouncers had to drag him outside near the start of the show. One of them knew Joe and drove him home, and the other one escorted *me* out afterwards. I slept with the Smith under my pillow for weeks, but never heard from him again."

"Wow. What a story. You grew into a brave lady, Isi."

"That was probably more dumb than brave. But you didn't come here to learn about my artistic career and love life, did you?"

"No. I needed to talk to you about Craig. I'm so sorry, Isabel."

"*Isi*," she corrects. "It was a fucking *shocker*, Kat. I figured something wasn't right with Craig, but I didn't know he was *dying*. Nobody even looked me up to say he'd been put in the hospital, or I'd have come right away. The way things went, I only got here last week. In time to watch him wriggle and moan and die. I babbled at him a lot, but doubt if anything got through. It's funny, the two of us were never close as kids. Too much of an age gap. But these past few years, we were really getting to understand each other. He was an awesome listener. Didn't like to offer advice, but whenever he did, it was right on the money. I can't imagine I'd be in the arts if he hadn't pressured me to get out and follow my dreams. About a year ago, when I told him I was working at a bar in Manhattan, he got really pissed. Thank God I didn't mention it was a topless place." She laughs at this, and for some reason, I'm a little startled by it. "Told me I'd never make it if I threw away my best years serving drinks to all the successful artists."

"Did your clientele include any big-name artists?"

"One or two, actually. I even got some work as a life drawing model that way. Didn't tell Craig that either, though. Then I met Joe, and he made me quit both, so it became a non-issue."

"Did you and Craig talk a lot?"

"Email and MSN mostly. Up until about two or three months ago, Craig and I would connect online at least once a week. Half the time we'd just bitch to each other. The very last time, I complained about my crummy apartment, and he told me I was lucky to be in New York. He griped that the dust in his house was driving him crazy. We did talk about deeper stuff sometimes, like our feelings. I'd tell him some of my worries, the ones I thought he could handle. We could *never* do that on the phone. The Internet is great that way. People—especially men—have a hard time saying emotional stuff, but everything changes if they don't have to talk out loud."

"When was the last time you were home, before this?"

"You mean St. Paul? Two years ago, I guess. No, even more than that. I don't have any friends in the area anymore. Which is probably good. I don't think I'd have done a show here if I thought half my graduating class might show up in the audience. It was a last-minute gig. Way after cutoff, actually. On the plane in from JFK, I sat next to a guy who turned out to be one of the organisers, and we got to talking. He ended up driving me to the bus station, and on the way, a call came in on his cell phone. A one-man show from New Zealand pulled out, and he said if I was up to it, he might be able to pull some strings. I really needed the money, so I called up a friend in New York and got my gear shipped over, and managed to get the penalty waived for rescheduling my flight home. The airline gave me a bereavement discount in the first place, so they didn't make a fuss when I said my family needed me here for another week. It's sort of true. My family is the arts community now."

I bow my head. "Did Craig know about your show?"

She smiles. "Not yet. Guess I'd have told him sooner or later. Or not. Some people just aren't comfortable with nudity, and Craig was probably the biggest prude you could find. I guess you'd know."

I look away again. "I think he might have loosened up," is all I say, deciding there is no need to mention the fetish magazine.

"But I did tell him I've got my own act, and he seemed real happy. He tried to get me to tell him about it, but I said it defied description. I actually wrote him one message with a link to my website, but never sent it. Did you and Craig keep in touch by email?"

"No," I admit. "We never emailed. And I haven't spoken to him since…"

"That's what I figured. Since you *dumped* him," she says, then stares at me blankly.

Tears cloud my vision. After facing Lynn yesterday—then Sandy's ambush—this is too much. I've never been made to feel like such a rotten bitch in my life. "I swear, Isi, I had no idea it would hurt him so, *so*—"

"Hey, it's all right. I'm sorry, Kat. God, me of all people. Sometimes you're the dump*er* and sometimes you're the dump*ee*. That's just how it goes. It's wrong to stay in a relationship for one person. Both parties need to see a future in it or no one's really happy, right? Not like I could get Joe to understand that. You only did what you needed to do, like I did, I guess. Now I just wish Craig could've done the same and let the fuck go."

"He never tried to contact me," I say. "Not until…" I stop myself, and I realize Isi is still clueless about what brought me here.

"Until what? Craig called you before he died?"

"Not exactly. He sent me a package. Photos."

"Holy crap. He mailed you all his pictures of you and stuff? Now *that* surprises the hell out of me. I tried to take those things away years ago, after Lynn got hosed one night and flipped out. She said he was still in love with his old girlfriend, and showed me the box. I thought it'd help if it was all out of the house. Wasn't my place, but you know what they say about hindsight. Craig grabbed both my wrists and squeezed until I dropped it. Then he just glared at me and took the box away. Things were pretty chilly between us for a while after that."

I shake my head, then blurt, "No, the photos weren't of me, Isi. They were of dead cows."

"Oh, *that*," she says with a dismissive wave of her hand and an audible sigh of relief.

"You know about the *mutes*?"

"Sort of. I've never seen pictures, which is cool with me. Now and then Craig would write that he'd just got back from an especially freaky one."

"What do you think?"

"I sort of worried about him at first. Kind of a nutty pastime, even to me. I mean, I might show my pooch to a roomful of strangers, but you sure wouldn't catch me out chasing UFOs. I wouldn't mess with someone who just flew like a billion light years to steal the cock off a two-thousand-pound bull."

I smile at Isi's indomitable, albeit warped, sense of humour. "Did Craig ever mention if anyone wanted him to stop conducting his investigations?"

An introspective furrow creases her brow. "One night he wrote he'd just met with someone who gave him some really eye-opening info, but said he had to be careful what he sent out on the Internet. I laughed when I read that. 'Too much X-Files, bro,' I wrote. He replied with, 'Something like that Isi, something like that.' I never pressed the issue."

I see that she is studying my face.

"Why?" she asks. "You don't believe it was Alzheimer's, do you?"

"It looks like he *did* have a brain disease of some kind. I dropped in on Lynn in Lloydminster yesterday, and she gave me written consent to view his medical records."

"*What*? She cooperated with *you*? That doesn't sound like the Lynn I know."

"I told her the records might give her grounds for a lawsuit."

Isi laughs. "Now it's starting to fit. Popped some dollar signs in her eyes, huh? So you actually got to see the records?"

"Only after most of them had made a trip through a paper shredder. And the doctor set it all up so it looked like I was the one who did it."

"Shit. I swear, this *is* the fucking *X-Files*."

"I'm beginning to think so too."

"Guess it's your ass Lynn'll have to sue now if she wants her lawsuit. She'd enjoy that. She's already taking all Craig's assets, stunned little bitch."

"So I gather Craig's family never officially adopted you? I remember him calling you his little sister even way back, but he explained the whole story to me on the drive home after I first met you."

"He really was my big brother in my heart. I desperately wanted to be adopted. But Dad—*see?*—Craig's father—thought it would be like stealing me away from his own little sister. I think he always felt a bit of guilt about taking custody. Even though it's the best thing that ever happened to me."

"Where *is* your birth mother, if you don't mind me asking?"

"Craig told me about a year ago he heard she was living in downtown Vancouver. Selling herself for a pimp she considered a husband. Probably her and six other gullible whores. I guess she'll die out there on the streets." Isi says this with only a hint of sadness.

"Did you ever see her after you moved in with Craig's family?" I ask.

"She came around the ranch twice. Last time I was about fourteen. Stayed two nights, then ran out of crack or whatever. She got so strung out and freaky that Craig's dad actually took her to town to look for some. That's what I heard him tell her, I guess probably just so she'd get in the truck. He came back two hours later, alone. My guess is he gave her some cash and put her on a bus, but I'll never know. Doesn't matter."

"I'm sorry."

"Don't be. So what do you think *really* killed Craig?"

"I'm not sure," I say, "But I suspect there is a connection between his death and the cow pictures he sent. I just don't have a clue yet what it might be. Seems like I'm getting warmer, though."

I tell her about the break-ins at my home and clinic, the spraypaint on the hotel room wall, and the instruction from Corporal Kulchisky to go back home. When I stop, we both go silent.

A voice comes from over my shoulder, startling me. "Sorry to interrupt, but would you girls like something to drink?" Isi smiles at the person doing the speaking.

It's Goth Girl from the door.

"Nancy, have you met my old friend Kat?"

"Sort of, out front," Nancy says. "I actually wasn't gonna let her into the show, but she paid off the old lady who wigged when you came on."

I smile. "Nice to properly meet you, Nancy."

"Yeah. Sorry about earlier. I'm not allowed—"

I raise a hand, and she stops. "You were trying to do your job, and came up against a desperate woman. Don't even think about it. I *am* glad I got in, though."

"Are *not*," Isi says.

I smile, and give her a light slap on the shoulder. "I'm happy I found you. Nancy, do you have a house Merlot?"

"We do, from France. It's a little on the dry side, I'm told. I also have a Chilean Shiraz that's supposed to be nice. A hint of wild berries with a pleasant aftertaste. That's what's printed on the carton, anyway. Red wine gives me brutal headaches."

"I'll go with the Merlot. Thank you."

"Same for me," Isi says.

Nancy smiles. "Getting together with your brother tonight, Isi?"

Craig? Does she have a real brother? Isi looks as bewildered as I am. "God, no. Not for a few years, I hope."

Nancy gives a half smile, tugging nervously with a thumb and forefinger at the ring in her upper lip. "Want me to tell him that if he comes by again?"

"Sorry?" Isi says, deep wrinkles across her forehead now. "Rewind."

"A guy came by maybe fifteen minutes ago asking when you'd be leaving. I said I didn't know, that last night you left right after the show, but now you were in here talking to an old friend. I invited him in, but he said he'd grab a green onion cake at a stand and wait. He was back again like a minute ago. Asked where you were staying. Told him I didn't have a clue."

"Just great," Isi says. "Now some fucking loony-tune is after me. If you see him again, say I'm gone to the mall, and staying in the penthouse at the Sutton Place tonight."

"You got it," Nancy says with a little laugh. "I'm real sorry. The guy seemed totally sincere."

"What did he look like?" I ask.

"Come on, Kat," Isi says, shaking her head. "Get your own homicidal maniac."

Nancy's eyes roll upward in contemplation. "He had a really cool pair of Revos on, so I couldn't see his eyes. Hair down to the middle of his back, streaked sort of blond. Had it back in a ponytail and a blue bandanna on top, but I could see it when he walked away. Oh, and he had like a goatee, trimmed real short. Probably in his forties, but I'm not good at people's ages. Big nose and kind of weather-beaten skin. Friendly smile."

"It's not Joe," Isi says, her shoulders dropping in relief.

She squints at me. "What? Someone *you* know?"

CHAPTER 31

"CANCEL THE DRINKS, NANCY," I say, sliding out of the booth. "We're out of here. Is there another exit?"

"There's a back door at the end of the kitchen," she says, motioning to a doorway beside the bar. "Supposed to be for emergencies, but we use it to take garbage and grease out, and to go into the alley for a smoke. Want me to call the cops or something?"

"I don't think so. But if that guy comes by again, tell him we left town together."

She squishes up her features. "Not Sutton Place, then? *Where* do I say?"

I look at Isi, and she shrugs. "We don't live here. Be creative."

"Calgary?"

"Perfect. Tell him his little sister got called down for an impromptu audition. Let's grab your stuff, Isi. We gotta go."

"My gear can stay here for tomorrow's show. Kat, what's up? You're really freaking me out."

I pull her close and speak in a low voice. "When my house and clinic were being ransacked last week, I was on an ocean kayaking trip. I was actually lucky to make it home alive. I think a man tried to kill me. And the description Nancy gave of your so-called brother fit him to the letter."

"My god, Kat. You didn't tell me about *that*."

"I'm sorry," I whisper. "There's been so many things." I raise my voice again to a level that Nancy can hear, reaching into my bag. "Thanks, Nance. Tip's on the table."

I smile at the cook and dishwasher. They look startled, but seem to relax when Isi comes in behind me. I spy the dishwasher giving the cook a nudge when she passes.

There are several people in the narrow paved lane between the old brick buildings, some of them using it as a shortcut and others huddling together to share weed. A teenaged boy, evidently lacking patience to endure the porta-potty lineup, wavers from side-to-side as he unabashedly pees on a stack of boxes.

We make good progress until the end of the block, where a wall of Fringe revellers brings us to a standstill.

"Which way?" Isi asks, yelling in my ear to overcome a thousand rival conversations.

"I'm parked by a row of little houses. That way," I holler with a directive roll of my eyes, hesitant to make a hand gesture in case we're being watched from somewhere. "Let's go a block or so the other way, then break out of the crowd and double back."

"What if he's already waiting for us?"

"Let's watch for that. But I want to make sure if he spots us around here, we don't give any clues where we're going."

"Good thinking. 'Cause there he is." She tugs at my arm.

I quickly scan the myriad of faces around us, but don't see anyone who fits the image in my mind, a fusion of my own recollection of Stompin' Tom and Nancy's version with fancy sunglasses and a blue bandanna. I grasp Isi's hand, and tow her along, using my free elbow to part the crowd like an icebreaker uses its double-hulled bow to pry open a shipping lane.

"Excuse me; sorry; please excuse us," I say, to replies of "No shovin'!" and "Fuck you!"

Three blocks of this before we break free of the humanity.

"Do you think he saw us?" I finally say. "I couldn't pick him out myself."

"Maybe this is a different guy. He *was* sort of facing our way. But I doubt he's as good at crowd-cutting as you are."

"Basic shopping skill. Now let's head this way a bit, then we can turn and go back down to my rental. You said you're in a motel?"

"Yeah. Just off Gretzky Drive. Swanky place. Thought the room I had in St. Paul was something. Here, I get to watch the hooker action right out the window. Nice reminder of my heritage."

"You'll have to point me the way. Where's this Gretzky Drive?"

"Oh, sorry. Used to be Capilano Drive. They renamed it a few years ago, I guess because it goes past the big bronze statue of Wayne Gretzky where the Oilers play."

I smile. "You'll still have to point me there."

*   *   *

TWO MINUTES LATER, we're at the Mustang. It *appears* untouched, but I wish I had a way of knowing for sure. If it is indeed Stompin' Tom Austin following us, that pretty well confirms my "accident" was his handiwork.

Isi does her best to guide me to the motel using mostly small roads, to lessen the likelihood of encountering Thomas—or any associate of his who might be on the lookout for us. Judging by the break-in at my house and Len's talk of a blond "pretty-boy," he isn't operating alone.

"So what the hell does this character want?" she asks.

"Beats me. You got any ideas?"

"Yeah. I'll bet he's part of the government conspiracy to keep UFO activities secret from the public. Like Roswell, you know? They must think you're close to blowing the lid off the Canadian version."

I shake my head. "If that's true, I wish someone would let me in on it. You don't have *any* idea what Craig might have been on to that was special enough to attract this sort of attention? He didn't exactly *discover* cattle mutilations. They've been going on for decades."

"Well if he *did* have anything, I'll bet he kept a record of it, and we can find that at his house. He set up an office in his bedroom."

"No. I've been to Craig's house," I confess. "The back door wasn't latched securely, so I sort of let myself in when I first arrived. I still didn't know he was dead, and was afraid he could be inside, maybe injured. Anyway, the office was empty. I could see where he kept a computer, but it was gone. Any clue who might have gone by and taken stuff?"

"Only person I can think of is Lynn. She's still his wife, and you probably noticed she's kind of an oddball. I wish I'd known that lock on the house was broken. She wouldn't even let me go inside one last time—said if anything turns up that pertains to me, they'd ship it. Collect, I bet. At the funeral, I only spoke like three sentences to her. The two of us were always oil and water."

"I understand why. But I doubt Lynn has anything to do with this. She seemed totally oblivious, and then signed a consent so I could see the records. I'd pretty much cross her off the list. But there's one more thing I should tell you."

"Fire away," she says, clearly apprehensive.

"When I was at Craig's place, someone else came in. Didn't know I was there, I'm guessing, since I'd parked in the back. He went straight down into the basement. Scared me half to death."

She looks confused. "I suppose with the door broken, it could have been anyone. Did you get a look at him?"

"Yes. And no. I thought it was an alien being."

"Total freak, huh?"

"That's not what I mean. I think he was wearing something on his face, like some kind of special mask. And a suit that looked like blue rubber."

"Nothing strange about that."

"No?"

She grips my shoulder and gives it a shake. "Sarcasm, Kat. That is fucking *unbelievable*. In Craig's basement? What was he doing?"

"Holding a metal box of some kind. I don't know. I ran. Nearly crashed into a black SUV on the way out. I went straight over to the neighbour's house. He chased me away, but got more accommodating the second time I went by."

"Len?"

I nod. "You know him?"

"Very well. Was he any help the second time around?"

I bite my lip. "Looks to me like Len's got whatever Craig died of. I saw him have a seizure, and he was having all kinds of short-term memory problems. His balance was screwy too."

"Omigod. This really sucks. Len's a sweet guy. He *did* seem really scattered the times he came by the hospital when I was in, but I figured I was probably no better. And he took a tumble the funeral, blamed it on a lumpy carpet."

"Doesn't look good, huh? It was Len who delivered the photos to me last Friday—fulfilling Craig's last request. He said a guy shook him down on the island, told him to back off. I'm guessing that was who did the break-ins."

"No shit? Len drove all the way to Victoria and back? He didn't come around for a while after I first got there. The nurse mentioned he was normally there all the time, so she got a little worried when he didn't show up for five days. When he came back he said he'd been sick and didn't want to give it to people. He tell you anything else?"

"Did you know Len was holding Craig's ashes?"

"No. I'd have guessed Lynn would take them."

"Only if you could pawn *cremains* off somewhere. Len's planning to spread them where Craig liked to fish."

"I guess that's a good idea." She sniffs.

"I took a sample of the ashes and sent them to a friend who works in a lab, hoping he can run some tests on them. It might have just been Len's memory, but there were some inconsistencies in what he said about the cremation timing."

"Oh my god, Kat."

"I'm sorry."

"Don't be. I'm just blown away by how hard you're working. You're really on the case, aren't you? Quite an investigator yourself."

I shake my head. "Truth is, you're the end of the line for me. I was hoping you knew something that would bring me closer to understanding what's going on. I hate to just walk away now, and pretend nothing ever happened, but I can't stick around here either."

"Well, you've got me now. I'm booked for evenings all week, but my days are wide open. We'll sort this out together."

I'd almost forgotten about Isi's strange show-biz life, but I am comforted by the offer. She knows more about Craig than I do, and might open some doors in her old hometown. "I'd like that."

"You doing anything in the morning?"

I laugh. "Well, I thought maybe I'd go home and start to put my life back together. But I haven't booked a flight yet."

"Perfect. If you pick me up, I'll take you to a little café that serves a great Parisian breakfast. The only place in town where you can get a real *pain au chocolat.*

"I'm in," I say, not completely sure what a *pain au chocolat* is, real or counterfeit. "What time is morning for you?"

"Eight o'clock."

"Wow—early for a performer. See you then." She gets out, and gently closes the door. I wait, and watch her work her key inside the lock to her motel room.

Lucky number thirteen. The steel numeral three is even screwed on a little crooked, as if for effect. Isi's not superstitious.

Neither am I—normally—yet a peculiar apprehension stirs my insides.

Just nerves, I tell myself.

CHAPTER 32

I SLEEP REMARKABLY WELL in my elegant downtown hotel room, though not without some sense of guilt for being in an opulent suite with a king-sized bed while Isi is holed up at a one-star cockroach inn.

It's almost seven when I haul myself out of bed, and I immediately run a bath and enjoy a brief soak. I try to call Zaina, and feel some relief in reaching her answering machine. It would be hard to keep a conversation short. I apologise to the tape for not calling sooner, say I'm all right, and promise to call before getting on the plane to let her know when I'll arrive.

Then I jog the two blocks to the car park I opted to use instead of the one directly beneath the hotel. It may have indeed been a little over the top to forfeit my complimentary parking and check in under a fake name, paying cash. (With a forty-dollar greasing for a front desk girl who maintained—even after pocketing the first twenty—that this was against company policy.) But it *did* afford me a decent night's rest despite last night's Stompin' Tom sighting. That alone makes it worth the trouble.

* * *

WHEN I arrive at Isi's motel, my levity begins to evaporate. Four white police cruisers fill the lot near Isi's room. She mentioned that prostitutes frequent the area. I feel bad for her. An early-morning raid has probably ruined her sleep.

Yellow police tape is staked around the entrance to her room. I roll back my memory to when I dropped her off. *Number thirteen*, with the crooked three. That is definitely the door I saw her go into.

I try to leap out of the car, forgetting I'm seat-belted in. I wrestle with the belt, fumbling hands and clouded vision making it impossible to free myself. I take a deep breath, blink a couple of times, and release the buckle with a solid *click*.

I dash out, leaving the door wide open.

One of the cars has vinyl letters on the back quarter panel that spell COMMANDER. *Shit.* This is no minor affair.

An officer is seated behind the wheel.

I pound on the glass. He jolts back and glares up from his paperwork, then seems to soften a little upon seeing it's not another cop. He looks about fifty, with tinted wire-rimmed spectacles, short salt-and-pepper hair and a lantern jaw.

He hits a button and the glass rolls all the way down. He removes his glasses, and blinks. "What can I do for you, miss?"

"Afriendamine-is-is-is-stayinghere," I blurt, the words running into each other in my panic. "Whatwhat-what-whathappened?"

He flashes a calming smile. "Slow down a little, please. Just take it easy. What room is your friend staying in, Ms.—?"

"Francis. Kat Francis. Roomthirteen. Withwith-with the tape."

"You're sure about that, Ms. Francis? Can you tell me your friend's name?"

"Isi—Isabel Butler."

He sucks in his upper lip and looks downward, then back up at me. "How about you have a seat with me here in the car?"

I stand there feeling dizzy, guts knotted, until he gets out and guides me around to the front passenger door. Having heard about things that happen in the back seat of police cars, I'm relieved he doesn't put me there. The dashboard is full of radar and communication equipment, including a small computer screen. I read the information on the top line and look away.

Victim ID: **Isabel Cynthia Butler**

The officer takes his seat, and presses a button to clear the screen. "Ms. Francis, I'm afraid the news is not good at all. Your friend is dead."

I let out a shriek. Then a lengthy whimper. "What happened? Please tell me what happened."

"How well did you know Ms. Butler?"

"I knew her when she was a little girl," I say.

"Would you be able to help us get in touch with the immediate family? Apparently we're having a hard time..."

"There is no one, anymore. What happened to Isi?"

"It's being treated as a suicide," he says flatly.

"*Suicide?*" I feel absolutely sick, but even more than that, I'm angry. "That can't be. She told me yesterday she had so much to live for. Said her life was just beginning."

"Depressed people can have some violent mood swings. Up real high, and then *crash!* We found a bottle of Paxil, a common antidepressant."

He leaves a moment for this to sink in. "Do you know how Isabel might have got her hands on a firearm? She was found with an unregistered revolver."

"Yes. A .357 magnum. Smith & Wesson, I think. She told me about it just yesterday. It was only to protect herself from an ex-boyfriend. Please listen to me. Isi wouldn't have killed herself. We made a date to have breakfast together. We're supposed to be eating a goddam *pain au chocolat* in some French café right now."

The sergeant nods. "I hear you, but I'm afraid all indications are that your friend took her own life, Ms. Francis. I'm going to have you write up a witness report. You can put all your concerns in there, and if we see a need for a further investigation, or if the forensic and ballistics boys find anything that looks suspicious, we'll follow it up. Always do."

"Will you want me to testify in court?"

He clamps his big jaw. "Not likely, ma'am. Suicides don't often end up there."

"With all due respect, officer, someone damn well *did* this to her. Have you dusted for prints?"

"We have. Listen, the victim's body was found locked in her room, with a handgun next to it and no sign of forced entry or any kind of struggle. The weapon has no one else's fingerprints on it. In a few minutes, they'll be taking her away."

"Will there be an autopsy?"

"In the course of procedure, certainly. Any time a death is unnatural or suspicious."

I nod. "Right."

"I'll need to have you write up a report. And I might need you to give a visual confirmation on the body's ID."

I feel terribly ill. "I don't know if I can."

"Just takes a minute. We can have you come by the morgue later if that's better."

"No. I'll do it now."

*   *   *

THE REPORT I write in the cruiser—the third I've given in a week for as many different police forces—fills the front of the form and half of the reverse side. I include the things I've already told: seeing Isi last night, and my prior knowledge of the gun. Then I give the best description I can of Stompin' Tom, including things derived from my previous experience with him like the tattoo on his shoulder. Perhaps it will match something in the files. I write that this man lied to Nancy, the hostess, saying he was Isi's brother, then he tried to follow us. The officers investigating this case are employed by the city, and though their systems and databases are linked to those of the RCMP, they work autonomously. My fear is that if I mention anything about the federal police, the people interfering in Craig's case might muscle in and quash Isi's investigation. Instead, at the bottom of my report, I write in large letters, PLEASE INVESTIGATE DILIGENTLY. ISABEL DID <u>NOT</u> KILL HERSELF.

Cops probably hear that kind of thing a lot after suicides, from people who are left in shock and denial.

When the sergeant returns, he introduces me to two constables, DeGroot and Fitch, and tells me he's been called to an apparent homicide scene in the inner city. The other officers escort me past the police tape and into the motel room. Fitch enters first and then DeGroot waves me inside. I've been trying to steel myself for what I am about to see, but it proves useless. As soon as I enter the room, I am met by a smell that I've never experienced before, and will quite certainly never forget. It's not outright rot, nor is it remotely pleasant. It's death, rendered more unbearable by the room's stale air. I would have expected the odour to be more similar to the blend of smells an animal gives off when it dies. Maybe the difference is psychological, and linked to the kick-in-the-guts revulsion from what I see.

Isi's form is clad in a lacy spaghetti-strap nightgown, and crumpled chest-down beside a bed that looks slept in, as if she was sitting on the mattress and slumped over forward. One arm is pinned beneath her torso, and the other is raised above her head, looking strangely poised, as if in dance. I expect her to be outlined in a halo of white chalk—marking her position for investigators to reference after they haul her body away—but she is not. The only outline is a chunky delineation of a pistol, made from strips of tape. It is about a metre away from Isi's extended hand, in perfect alignment with her shoulders, and pointed away from the body.

Isi's face is china white, but otherwise looks perfectly normal. Her eyes are both open just a crack. Right beneath her chin, there is a black hole about the diameter of a ballpoint pen, from which a river of dark blood has spewed, draining from her inclined trunk to create an immense ovoid pool on the carpet. The back of her head is a mess of spiky white bone fragments, coagulated blood, matted hair, and fatty grey tissue. A pulverised matrix of the same has been flung messily at the upper half of the wall behind the bed.

Seeing for myself the position of the body, the bullet hole, and spray pattern, I begin to doubt my own belief that someone other than Isi did this. I visualise her sitting on the bed, with the gun under her chin. The terrible thing that happens next in the theatre of my mind fits what I see.

Either she did this to herself, or someone went to a lot of trouble to ensure it looks that way. Was Isi *really* depressed? Or was the Paxil planted?

Then I see it.

On the night table by the bed.

My white envelope.

CHAPTER 33

I TAKE A STEP closer, and look at it.

The very same grimy handprints, very same coffee cup ring. A rectangle has been cut away from the middle where my name used to be, right through both layers of the envelope. I can see the wood of the table through the window, and it's obvious the pictures aren't inside.

That fucker Thomas left this here—for me.

Only *I* would recognise it.

He's taunting me. Did he kill Isi just to get to *me*?

My head spinning, I step away, try to walk to the light of the doorway.

"It's..." I start, but find myself wondering what's befallen my voice.

"Pardon me, ma'am?" DeGroot says. I choke in the most air I can manage and try again. "It's. Her. Isi. For. Sure," I manage to say to him, spitting a short word between each choking sob. I need some air. I turn and walk out, then crouch and vomit on the sidewalk.

*   *   *

I TELL DeGroot he should fingerprint the envelope because it didn't belong to Isi. Problem is, they won't find anything but Len's prints—along with Pam's and my own, I guess. Thomas is no fool. *God, how I hate him. I want to find him, and kill him myself.*

DeGroot seems interested in my comment about the envelope. I shift the conversation to the man who followed us last night. I tell him I think it's the same man I met on a trip, an insurance salesman and former member of the armed forces who called himself Thomas Austin, and that the details are all in my statement. He promises to look into it personally. I suggest that he notify the Fringe management of Isi's death—she's got a show scheduled for tonight—and maybe try to track down her theatre-owner friend in Manhattan. I don't even know the woman's name, or what the place she runs there is called. I tell him that there is also a former boyfriend named Joe Manucci in Manhattan who might be of some use—but don't reiterate what I mentioned to the sergeant about Joe being the reason for the gun's existence—not wanting to throw a red herring into the investigation. As for family, Lynn Butler would want to know, and might have information that'll help find a certain prostitute in Vancouver.

* * *

I FEEL bizarrely detached from the world around me as I drive across the North Saskatchewan—the river that snakes diagonally across the city— then turn right and make my way to the crest of the valley, then past the mansions of Ada Boulevard. I take the narrow road that descends steeply to the clubhouse of a picturesque golf course, and get out and teeter in the middle of its nearly empty parking lot.

I can't drive anywhere now. I can hardly think. For the next hour or two—it's impossible to know with a manic mind and no watch—I merely walk, keeping my distance from the few golfers. A light mist hangs in the air, and dark clouds threaten of a rainstorm that never fully materialises. I pass within inches of a huge Canada goose standing at the rim of the asphalt path, eyes pleading for a handout, and I observe a beaver attempting to resolve the enigma of many layers of chicken wire wrapped around the trunk of an elm tree to deter him.

I have my own hunger, my own puzzles to solve. Can it somehow be possible that Isi really *did* commit suicide? Without the envelope, I might already think so. If someone stalked and killed her, it's obvious who must surely be next.

It's partly my fault that Isi is dead, and it may be all for naught. I'm no closer to knowing what happened to Craig Butler. I'm still only guessing it's not what his doctor said.

I need access to a computer. Better yet, a medical library. With the right information, I might get somewhere.

My last year in Saskatoon, Helen Stoddard—the college librarian—left for a better-paying job at an Edmonton hospital. The Royal Some-Damned-Thing.

Oh, what *was* it?

I jog back to the car, and drive up the hill. I find a gas station and borrow a telephone book.

The Royal Alexandra Hospital. That's it. I check a map at the front of the directory, and it jumps right out at me. Helps that hospitals are well marked. It doesn't look like it's very far away, either. I hope Helen still works there.

* * *

AT THE hospital, I luck out and get a parking spot near the main entrance to the Active Treatment Centre. So far, so good.

Inside, a woman at the information desk tells me the library is just around the corner. But it's closed Sundays.

"I know," I lie. *Fuck.* "But could you please have someone let me in? Helen is my sister-in-law. She's at the airport now, waiting to board a flight to Toronto because of a family emergency. She asked me to come in and retrieve the confirmation number. The airline won't let her on without it, and her online account was set up to automatically email the information to her work computer. Those discount carriers don't use paper tickets anymore. I'll only need a few minutes, I'm sure. Helen gave me her password."

I feel myself breaking a sweat. I wish I'd come up with a story that would buy me more time. What if someone has to *watch* me?

"And your name?"

"Isabel Butler," I say, feeling rotten about assuming Isi's name. But I can't give my own, or Helen will know when she returns who it was that made up an appalling lie about her family circumstances to get access to her library.

"Hold on a minute," the woman says, typing something into her computer. I take a peek and see she has accessed a staff directory. *My God, she's going to call Helen at home!*

She hits a wide button on her telephone, and the dial tone hums aloud through the integrated speaker. She punches seven keys, and I stop breathing. *Ring. Ring. Ring. You've reached the voice mail of Dan and Helen Stoddard. We're not able to take your call...*

After a long beep, and the woman hangs up. I'm glad she does not leave a message, in case Helen gets to her voice mail soon. I release the air in my lungs, and try to be subtle about drawing in a few deep breaths.

She dials another number, this one only three digits. "Yes, Eric, there's a woman here who needs to get into the library..."

* * *

ERIC IS a short, balding Neanderthal with a single unbroken eyebrow, a spud nose, and a die-cast scowl. He seems to have been genetically engineered to be a Rent-A-Cop. Without speaking, he gestures for me to follow. He leads me down a corridor, with slothful torpidity most befitting of *Homo Neanderthalensis*. After a short distance, Eric stops, and draws a set of keys on a retractable string from a chrome disc clipped to his belt. He wriggles one into the lock, and pops the door open, then flicks on the lights.

"How long you need?" he asks.

"I'm not sure. You can just lock the knob, and I'll close it behind me. That way I won't need to take up your time."

Eric ponders this deeply.

"Five minutes, tops. And no touchin' anything."

I offer my most puerile expression. *No touching anything! What could I possibly achieve like that?*

I watch Eric dawdle down the corridor. When he rounds the corner, I turn off the lights and close the door. Upon his return, he might presume I've got what I needed and gone. And hopefully the information clerk isn't paying careful attention to time. I'll need *at least* half an hour here.

The computer is in low-power sleep mode, and hitting the space bar brings it to life. That saves a good two minutes of boot-up time. I launch Medline, the library's database program. Medical journals are indexed similarly to the scientific and veterinary periodicals I've used extensively in my research. The computer was probably set up by Helen—a good thing. There are a host of database applications used by different libraries, but this facility happens to license an app that's analogous to the CAB Abstracts tool I use regularly.

I'm immediately prompted to enter a password. If only Helen *really* had given me hers.

Now what?

Helen tended to be absent minded, so she assigned the same passcode for everything. What was it? That was a long time ago. It was a pet's name. But she didn't like dogs or cats.

A bird. That's it—she had an umbrella cockatoo that liked to nip at people. It was called something goofy. Started with an S, like Saskatoon.

Scooby Doo? No. But it was kind of similar to that, wasn't it?

Scrappy? Skittle? No, no. Come on, Kat. It brought to mind an amusing image whenever she spoke of the bird. I close my eyes and visualise a dog, squinting and dragging its hind end across a carpet because of an irritated anal sac. *Scooting.*

Scooter! That's it!

I key it in, hoping she hasn't since acquired a new pet. Umbrellas have a life expectancy of about seventy years, but you never know.

Just like that, I'm in. This is going well. Too well. Any second now, the security guard will surely return.

As if choreographed to that very thought, I hear a rattle from the doorknob. A knock.

"Hello," an indistinct male voice calls.

I freeze. The grinding sound of a key entering a lock cylinder. I hit the power button on the monitor, and the display goes black. Three long steps get me to the librarian's desk, and I dive beneath it just as a wedge of fluorescent light spreads across the ceiling.

"Anybody here?" Eric's voice says. I watch as two navy running shoes with Velcro closures shuffle over to the computer, then stop and linger. Can he be perceptive enough to notice the green LED on the central processing unit is glowing, but not the one on the monitor? Eric coughs, then snorts back a substantial mass of phlegm, and coughs some more.

With each fulmination, I instinctively recoil, coming close to whacking my head on the bottom of the desk. Then the shoes begin to meander back the way they came.

They stop right in front of me, and I hear papers being shuffled just inches above where I'm hiding. *No touchin' anything, Eric!* The feet move in close enough that I can smell them, and I hear a jingling sound, like pens and pencils being moved about inside a jar. What a snoop.

He walks away, but does not make for the door. Instead, he drifts down an aisle between bookcases, stopping halfway down. After a loud flutter of pages, a thick book lands heavily at his feet.

"Cock-*sucker!*" Eric mutters. I recognise the book's cover. A gross anatomy atlas. The boy's a budding physician. He picks it up, then stands there and flips through the pages, pausing occasionally for a distressingly long time. This huddled position of mine—chosen for quickness over comfort—has become outright torturous. *For God's sake, just steal the damned thing,* I want to cry out.

The agony is too much. I try to find a more comfortable position, and my knee makes a cavitative *pop*.

The guard's posture stiffens. My new position is even worse than the previous one, but I don't dare budge again.

I hear the book clap shut, then slide back and knock against the rear of the wooden shelf. Eric walks straight to me.

Oh, no.

There's another rattling in the pen jar above my head. Perhaps he's known I'm here all along, but is just being patient. Tormenting me, just like Stompin' Tom with the envelope. *Anyone else want a turn?*

He takes a few steps back, then waddles out the door, stopping to bump it shut behind himself. He tests the knob, and delivers a parting hack-snort.

Hopefully Eric is not off to the information desk to compare notes. The lady there hasn't seen me leave—mind you, she would know better than anyone that this hospital has at least a dozen other exits I might have used.

I extricate myself, and, in the middle of a glass container on the desk, spot what the guard was so interested in. A plastic magnifier complete with built-in light bulb—the better to see those sexy anatomical plates with.

I lean backwards and press my hands into my lower back, stretching and trying to shift my vertebrae back into alignment. I rush back to the computer and punch the button to power the monitor back up.

Where to begin? I enter the terms:

Alzheimer's + "early onset" + "accelerated progression"

Three articles come up, one from *Scientific American* entitled "Early Onset Alzheimer's: a New Epidemic", another from the *British Medical Journal* called "New Gene Associated with Alzheimer's," and a third from *JAMA*: "Vascular Basis of Alzheimer's Pathogenesis."

I click the first one, and begin to scan as soon as the copy comes up. It seems Dr. Samuelson was right, that Alzheimer's can indeed affect people Craig's age—and it seems to be happening with increasing frequency. The "Early Onset" tag has been more or less arbitrarily assigned. It applies to anyone under 65. And the disease does indeed seem to progress faster in younger victims. Still, according to this article, they live an average of eight years after symptoms begin.

Craig Butler died after about seven weeks.

I'm more suspicious. I continue to dig. I already know a fair bit about Alzheimer's, and my learning curve quickly levels off. Thirty minutes later, I'm no longer discovering anything new.

Think, Kat! Craig's medication was for dementia. I mentally travel back to his house, where I found the bottle. To the fine dust that covered everything. Even Len—a veritable slob—didn't have a similar problem, only a mile away. You'd expect his place to be much dustier. And Isi mentioned that he'd complained of it in one of their last communications. All that dust was not normal in that house.

Perhaps the mystery creature in the basement had something to do with it. Down there, he would have had access to the house's water, electricity— and *ventilation!*

I key in a new search, deliberately omitting the word Alzheimer's:

dementia + dust + airborne

Oh, my. This is it.

CHAPTER 34

BEFORE LEAVING THE LIBRARY—and nearly four hours after I arrived—I find the number I wrote down at the Greyhound depot, and dial up Agrigene Labs in Saskatoon.

"H'lo?" comes the answer—a male voice. Not so surprisingly. It's Sunday, so Trudy, the receptionist, wouldn't be in. It must be one of Tony's colleagues.

"Is Tony Fritz around?"

"No doubt. Tone hasn't left in days. Hang on two shakes."

He lets me listen to hold music, which is a radio tuned between two country music stations. Shania Twain enticingly warns, "I'm Gonna Getcha Good" over top of Johnny Cash droning out a sickly version of Depeche Mode's "Personal Jesus." It's a freaky duet:

You're a fine piece of real estate, and I'm gonna get me some land, sings Shania.

Lift up the receiver, I'll make you a believer, Johnny murmurs. I'm immensely relieved when Tony Fritz picks up *his.*

"Tony, it's Kat. Did you get my package?"

"Kat. Yeah. You really weirded me out with that, hun. What's with it? And how come my phone says you're at the Royal Alex. In *Edmonton*?"

"That's right. I'm just borrowing the library here. I'm afraid I'd really better not tell you any more than I have to right now. Have you had a chance to analyse the samples?"

"You know you can trust me with confidential stuff, Kat. What *is* this shit you sent me?"

"I don't expect it to make sense. Were you able to get DNA from the material in the pill container?"

"Wasn't too hopeful at first, but one of my texts said it was possible. Got on it right away. Took a while to try all the samples. I did the hair in the brush, but there was nothing to work with on the razor blade or the nail clippers."

"That should do, right? What did you get?"

"Well, the cremains had me stuck."

"Nothing, huh?"

"No. Just not what I expected. Where did that sample come from?"

"They're from a man who was cremated not long ago."

He laughs. "No they're not."

"What do you mean? You got DNA?"

"The small particles were no good for sure, so I ran them through a sieve. The shiny white chunks have nothing in them to test. Those are like solid porcelain. But there was a larger black one that had me kind of hopeful. Turned out that one wasn't entirely converted to mineral. Hit mtDNA in it."

"Mitochondrial DNA? But that's good, isn't it? You couldn't use it to match to the hair?"

"It won't match *any* person, Kat," he says with another little laugh. "It's *bovine* mitochondrial DNA."

"Are you sure? Could the sample have been contaminated on your end?"

"I'm absolutely sure, Kat. I use ethidium bromide stained agarose gel, which makes it easy to tell the difference. Know what a PCR primer is?"

"PCR? Educate me."

"Stands for Polymerase Chain Reaction—it's a method we use to amplify extracted DNA. The PCR primers from human and bovine mtDNA differ in shape and size so much that even if the two were thoroughly blended together, I'd be able to easily distinguish between them. What I've got here is pure bovine. You need this stuff back?"

"Not now. Maybe hang onto it until I get home. Thanks for doing this, Tony."

"No problem, Kat. But now you've got to tell me why I gave up a day of my life to find out if a hairbrush and razor belonged to a freaking cow."

"I promise I *will* tell you, Tony. I just can't do it right now. And please don't speak to anyone about this, okay?"

"Okay. But you owe me a date, as soon as you're ready."

"I suppose I do. But you're too good for me."

"I'll be the judge of that, hun."

I hang up, and am left to contemplate this new information. Why would someone substitute a cow's ashes for Craig's?

There is only one reason I can think of. Somebody needed Craig's body—or at least part of it—for their own purposes.

CHAPTER 35

I PULL INTO THE desolate and dusty parking lot of the Spedden Motor Inn at sundown. I'm about half an hour's drive from St. Paul, which is already close enough to impact on my comfort level in a *big* way. I've developed a new phobia of motels, and parking a car anywhere in or around that town is certainly asking for a rough night, one way or another. Even before getting out to arrange for a room, I tuck the car in out of sight behind the building.

For the first time since I opened that dirty envelope in my office nine long days ago, the balance of questions and answers in my mind seems to be tipping in the right direction. Yet some of the most daunting riddles remain.

I need to try contacting Constable Jessica Bolduc. Maybe she will speak to me. I suspect that outside of her partner's sphere of oppression, she might behave somewhat differently.

The hotel clerk here is happy to take my cash without any questions, and she doesn't blink at my name-of-the-day being Eve Ensler. Of course it means nothing to her, and I doubt she'd give a rip if I'd called myself Martin Scorsese. The cash goes into her shirt pocket before I'm out the door. *Must make a mental note to think a story through ahead of time nonetheless.*

Inside the room, I set my stuff down and pick up the phone. I punch Zaina's number, and get her machine again. My heart sinks. Where can she be? I've got to be careful what I say, and keep it very short—just in case. "Hey, Zane. Couldn't get away today. I'm okay here. I'll keep trying you." I hang up. "Shit, Zaina. You'd better be safe."

I'm relieved to find that the local telephone directory includes listings for St. Paul. I flip to the B names. Bolduc is a common name in the largely French community. There are nine Bolducs listed in the area, and two of them are J. Bolduc—plus one J.D. I don't know Jessica's middle name—and with no way of telling what part of town she lives in, the addresses are no help.

My intuition, perhaps? I close my eyes and concentrate. I visualise the three listings, and the top and bottom one seem to fade out just slightly.

I pick up the phone and dial the middle number.

Ring. Ring. Ring.

"*Allô?*" It's a man.

"Uh, may I please speak to Jessica?"

"Dare no one 'ere by det name," he says with a thick French accent.

"I'm sorry." Two to go. I reach for the plunger to hang up.

"You looking for da cop?"

"Uh, yeah."

"Her *numéro*, it not listed."

"Oh, *no*. Listen, it's an emergency, sir. Do you have it?"

"*Bien, oui.* She my *nièce.* Of course I do. What *sorte* of emergency?"

"It's not safe for me to say. But I'm in danger, and I need her help."

He laughs. "Dat's a new one. It's 555-7093. Tell her *mononcle* Jacques say hi."

"Thanks, Jacques. Bye."

I hang up and dial quick, before my eggbeater brain scrambles the number.

"Pick up, Jessica," I plead out loud as it rings. Three times. Four.

There's a click. "Hey, you got Jess. Can't take your call at the moment, so just leave me a digital voice imprint, and the minute I've got a free tongue and fingers, I'm all yours..."

I'm hardly able to wait for the tone. "Jessica, it's Kat Francis. You and your partner were at my motel room the other night after someone painted up the walls for me. I'm staying at the motel in Spedden for the night. My phone says 555-2949—if that gets you the desk, I'm under the name Eve Ensler, room twenty-two. Think I'm the only guest tonight anyway. Please call as soon as you get this."

I drop the phone in the cradle, and fall back onto the bed, feet still on the floor. My head spins, and as I feel myself drifting away, I have to wonder how much danger I'm about to put Jessica in.

If she even calls.

* * *

I WAKE up twice, each time roused by an involuntary twitch—*hypnagogic myoclonus*. Cats and dogs experience the same thing when they sleep. I'm not sure what triggered the first one, at which point I removed my shoes and jeans and climbed under the covers. The second twitch comes at the beginning of a dream in which the miracle of sleep allows me to believe I am a little girl again. I dance and run happily through a sunny Rocky Mountain pasture of beargrass fronds taller than me—until my foot drops into an unseen hole, and I kick out hard against the bedsheets.

Jack hated when I woke him up like that.

* * *

I FIND myself sitting upright like a racecar driver, my fingers planted into the mattress's upper layer of low-density padding. In my wearied haze, I think the sound echoing in my mind might possibly be a remnant of yet another dream, something I neglected to leave behind when I awoke. I feel disoriented, and look to see if Sasha is at my feet.

Then it starts up again, just as I begin to comprehend that I'm in a hotel room, and that someone is banging at my door. Panic grips me. I think immediately of the intruder who came while I showered, and the one who killed Isi. It's another terrible moment like those. I look at the digital readout of the clock radio beside my bed. One nineteen.

I wasn't careful enough. Must have been the calls I made. *From your own damned room—how stupid can you get, Kat.*

The bastard has found me.

I take in a big, shuddering breath as I scan the room for weapons. The little clock radio, a flimsy lamp, a wooden chair. Nothing suitable for doing battle with an expert assassin.

The knocking starts again, this time decidedly harder, as if the visitor has switched from his knuckles to the heel of his fist.

"Kat?" a voice says, barely audible. *Shit. He knows it's me.*

"Who is it?" I roar from deep in my belly. I almost scare myself.

"Constable Bolduc of the RCMP." Her tone is firm, but falls well short of mirroring the severity of mine.

I doubted Bolduc would even call, but she's *driven* over.

I sit upright on the bed and grab my jeans from the floor. "Hang on a minute," I say, pulling my leg out of the wrong hole and trying again. "I'll be right there."

The outside door was hard to close, and now sticks in the frame. When I pull harder, it jerks open sharply, glancing off my cheek and striking my shoulder.

I feel a blast of cool wind on my face. It really *is* Jessica Bolduc, though it would be easy not to recognise her without the RCMP uniform. Her dark, curly hair hangs down over her shoulders, and flutters in the stiff breeze. Jessica managed to look pretty even in her cop outfit, but it gave her a slightly androgynous quality that has now vanished outright. She wears a snug white T-shirt without a bra, cut high to reveal her navel, and navy sweatpants with RCMP embroidered across the waistband in white block letters. She has goosebumps on her arms.

"I was scared to open the door," I say, my voice quavering. "I'm glad you spoke up."

"*You're* glad. I'm freezing my ass off out here."

"I'm sorry. Come in, please."

She rubs the skin of her arms and enters, closing the door behind herself. "Cool evening. Right after that second week of August, it always feels like summer is over."

"I can't believe I left you out there so long. I was sleeping, and didn't expect you to actually come here."

"You kidding? Your message scared me. Figured you'd be back home on the coast by now. Heard you were at the town hospital yesterday. Caused quite a stir."

"I was. What did they tell you?"

"Wasn't on shift. But word is you faked a consent letter from Craig Butler's wife and then shredded all his medical records."

"It was a setup."

She nods, but I don't know if she is agreeing, or acknowledging that my answer is what they all say. "You know, I must have driven past this place a million times, but this is the first time I've been inside. Looks okay."

"Didn't think it'd be safe to go back to St. Paul."

"Safe from the guy who broke into your room, or from the police?"

"I called *you*, didn't I?"

"You did. And I still can't believe I'm standing here. We've got a warrant out on you."

"I can't believe it either. But thanks. I really need your help." I pull the chair from the desk, and angle it slightly to face the bed but leave direct eye contact optional. She takes the chair, and I plop down on the side of the mattress.

"From the hospital, I went and found Craig's cousin Isi in Edmonton yesterday."

"I never met the cousin. Craig mentioned her once though, sitting in my cruiser. One night about a year ago, Ted Kulchisky was sick and I had to go out to a mutilation site alone. I asked some questions I normally wouldn't get to, and was surprised how Craig opened right up. Normally he wouldn't talk to us much. But with just me, you couldn't get him to stop. Talked about losing his folks, and selling the ranch. Even about *you*, believe it or not. You *are* the one he never got over, right?"

"Oh, God," I say, shaking my head.

"Probably not your fault he kept living in the past. I've met Lynn," she says with a little laugh. "And Craig never blamed you for anything either. He said he just made bad decisions. The investigations were the only thing he ever did in his life that he really wanted to. Bet he talked more than an hour straight that night. This cousin of his is an actress or something, right?"

I nod.

"So how is she? This must be a hell of a tough time..."

"She was fine when I met her."

"Oh, that's good," she says softly, then hesitates. "You said *when you met her*."

"Yes. Last time I saw Isi, this morning, she was dead. Gunshot wound in the throat, out the back of the head."

I doubt if any dentist could get Jessica's mouth open wider than it is now.

Seeing that she's not yet able to speak, I continue. I go way back to how the photos arrived at the clinic, then to my near-death experience in the ocean, and the mysterious apparition in Craig's basement. I try to round out all the important background stuff before I get to what really happened at the hospital, how I tracked down Isi, and our escape out the back of the pub. I describe how we planned to go for breakfast, and the horror I was met with instead—including the envelope's re-appearance. At Jessica's gentle prompting, I even explain how the body was positioned, and can't help but notice how easy it is to move from my sitting position on the bed into the one the body was found in. I need only fall slack to demonstrate.

I finish with my walk in the park, and subsequent visit to the hospital library—but skip over the part about lying my way in with a story about a crisis in the librarian's family. Though it now seems a smaller deception than it did at the time, Jessica might disagree.

"You don't think there's any chance Isi killed herself?" she asks.

"No way. Not just because of the envelope. Can't say I've ever talked to anyone the day before they committed suicide, but Isi's attitude was amazing. She was high on life. And we were both looking forward to our breakfast together."

"I wonder if she was high on more than just life, and came down hard. It's possible there's another explanation for the envelope. Maybe someone slipped it in the room under her door, knowing Isi would find it odd and show it to you, and she was the one who put it on the table where you saw it. We have to make sure we never rule out the real truth because of one scrap of evidence. Could have easily been things in Isi's life that were unbearable to her. She just lost a cousin who was her only real family. She was a young actor, so it's highly possible there was money trouble. Who knows, maybe she was pregnant from that badass boyfriend. You couldn't possibly know all the shit someone is facing from a single conversation. We all tend to gloss over our situation when we're talking to someone we haven't seen in years. God knows I've done it."

"I have too. But this is different—"

"You told me the police doing the investigation felt they had every reason to believe it was a suicide, though."

"Yes. The sergeant said they confiscated a bottle of antidepressants. I think *that* was a plant. That the police were fooled only means we're dealing with a killer who is really thorough. What—you don't believe me, do you." I resent that Jessica is wearing a hint of a mocking smile now.

"I believe you're being completely honest about your feelings, Kat. And you could be right. But as a police officer, I'm programmed to be objective. Don't misinterpret my questions as me doubting your word. I owe it to Isi to think through every possibility, not blindly connect dots that may or may not have anything to do with each other, just because it makes the picture you expect—or really want—to see."

The room is quiet as a crypt while I contemplate this. *Have I been jumping to conclusions?*

Finally, I break the silence. "What do *you* think about Craig Butler's death?"

"Not much to think about, I guess. He died of a non-contagious brain disease, so no one did it to him. You can't go and *give* someone Alzheimer's."

"Actually, you probably could, if you fed them the brains of another Alzheimer's victim. It's been done with apes. But that's not what happened."

Her eyebrows lift. "I'm all ears."

"When I went inside Craig's house, the place was covered with fine dust. It was on everything. And I saw someone in the basement who looked like he'd just taken something out of the furnace."

"Now you're confessing a *B and E* to me?"

I smile and hold out my wrists. "Guilty. Cuff me and stuff me."

She waves them away, trying in vain to keep a poker face. "So while *unlawfully trespassing* in Craig Butler's private residence, you found out he was a lousy housekeeper. We *are* talking about a bachelor here, and one who had Alzheimer's at that."

"There was a lot more dust than you'd normally find in a house. He commented about it to Isi, which to me suggests the house wasn't usually like that."

"Possibly. But it might have just finally *got* to him. He lives on a farm, and we've been through some of the driest years in history. Keeps getting dustier out there every year. Watch a truck driving down a gravel road, and you'll see it leaves behind a yellow cloud a mile long."

"That's the way I dismissed it when I was there. His jeep had the same kind of dust inside, and it made sense that if you drove around the area where he lived, you'd stir it up and it'd get sucked inside."

"Forgive my impatience, but what does any of this have to do with Craig developing Alzheimer's."

"It wasn't Alzheimer's. I think someone tampered with the ventilation in Craig's house and car, and exposed him to a form of BSE."

"BSE? *Mad cow disease?*"

"More like mad person disease. Technically it's only BSE when it's inside a bovine. It's called variant BSE when it comes from eating beef, and Creutzfeld-Jakob Disease or CJD when people get it *spontaneously*, which really just means the cause is unknown. I'm not sure exactly what form Craig had, but I am certain that the dust contains pathogens of a transmissible spongiform encephalopathy similar to BSE.

"You're *certain?* So you *did* see his medical records?"

"Yes, I did. And I really did get permission from Lynn, and then demanded the file from Dr. Samuelson. But I made the mistake of letting him out of my sight. I think he was the one who shredded most of them, and made it look to the head nurse like I'd done it."

"You said *most* of them? What *didn't* get shredded?"

"Nothing useful. But when I was doing my digging today, I came across a series of articles in medical journals about the spread of Mad Cow disease to humans. The most eye-opening were written by a scientist named Joseph Gibbs, who pioneered research on prion diseases like Creutzfeld-Jakob in the mid-60s. Dr. Gibbs said every single CJD victim he knew was an avid rose gardener."

"So? Aren't roses big in Britain?"

"This man lived and worked in the States. I haven't conducted any surveys of my own, but I'd bet that fewer than one-tenth of all Americans are into flower gardening of any kind. Yet we're talking about a hundred percent of these victims growing rose bushes."

"Interesting. But you've really lost me. Craig didn't grow roses."

"Gibbs theorised that these people did not acquire CJD by eating infected meat, but through the bone meal growers use on their roses for its high phosphorous and calcium content. Roses need phosphorous as a nutrient, and the calcium neutralises soil acidity."

"So? No one *eats* bone meal."

"Of course not. But it's ground extremely fine, and creates a lot of dust when you apply it. Just like the dust in Craig's house. Know what a *prion* is?"

"I've heard the word, in the context of Mad Cow. It's like a virus, right?"

"If *only* it were like a virus. A prion is a cellular protein that somehow becomes folded wrong, and then bullies similar proteins into misfolding themselves in the same way and carrying on the replication."

She nods. "So it's the Heaven's Gate cult of the protein world. *Become one of us, and then help convert all the others.*"

"That's how it works, except probably more belligerently. In no time, the forced replication causes a runaway reaction in the victim's nervous tissues. Like molecular dominoes tumbling in all directions. The nerve cells that go down get shrunken to mats and tangles full of gaping holes. It's messy."

"Sounds terrible. But it can't be worse than what some viruses can do. I've seen pictures of anthrax and smallpox victims."

"One big difference is that prions are pretty well indestructible. The high temperature of the heat-digestion process used to make bone meal would easily destroy any bacterial or viral agent, but not a prion. It would only make prions in the bone marrow more accessible. Probably even selects in favour of the most virulent and resistant strains."

"So intense heat doesn't kill it, but makes it stronger. You think the dust in Craig's house was full of *prions*?"

"Exactly. I think the guy I saw in Craig's basement was taking out a device that used his furnace to disperse it into the air."

Her eyes go wide. "You breathed it too, then."

CHAPTER 36

"WE'VE GOT TO GET you tested," Jessica says, leaping up from her chair.

"Relax. I think the supply of pathogens was probably exhausted. Craig slept in there, and might have breathed it in for months, and then he was in the hospital for seven weeks. Anything in the air should have settled. Besides, there's no test. Another thing that makes prions worse than bacteria or viruses is that they contain no DNA or RNA. That makes them really hard to detect. An infectious prion is also chemically identical to the normal protein, so it doesn't prompt any kind of immune response."

"I thought there were new tests for Mad Cow. I'm sure of it."

I shake my head. "Not according to the most recent journals. Believe me, I read everything. There *has* been a footrace among scientists to be the first to come up with a fast and reliable diagnostic tool, something working with blood testing or heart rate sensors. There's a test called the conformation-dependent immunoassay that seems good, but only works with liquefied brain tissue. And right now, the standard means of positively identifying a prion disease is by looking at the victim's brain under a microscope."

She winces. "Either way they're taking out parts of the brain, right?"

"Which means you've got to be dead. Or not need your brain anymore."

"I'm sure I can find out if they did an autopsy on Craig Butler."

"Already did that. None was performed. The doc says he was too busy."

"Crap. But that could be true, you know. Doctors are probably the most overworked people in town."

"That's what I hear. The body was supposedly cremated. Lynn left the ashes with Craig's neighbour, and he was going to scatter them. What he told me about the cremation didn't make sense. You don't cremate a body in an hour, and yet he seemed certain it had only taken that long—from seeing the body to going home with the ashes. So when he stepped out of the room,

I borrowed a sample and sent it to a friend at a lab for testing."

Jessica wrinkles the bridge of her nose at me. "You stole human remains? Shit, Kat, you can go to *jail* for that."

"Who said they were human?" I give her a grin of petty one-upmanship. "The test showed my sample was bovine."

"*Cow* ashes?"

"My researcher friend was sure of it. I think whoever developed the prion had a reason to take Craig's body, maybe struck a deal with the funeral director. Threatened him or gave him money, possibly both. Len volunteered to disperse the ashes, so after signing off, Lynn left him at the crematorium. He started acting up and broke a few things, so they handed him the replacement ashes earlier than they were supposed to, just to make him go away. How would a delirious old farmer know how long a cremation took, or confirm the ashes..."

"*Delirious?* Don't tell me-"

"Unfortunately, yes. Len had a seizure when I was at his house. His equilibrium was off, and his memory all over the place. I'm guessing he contracted the disease by accident, in Craig's house or riding along in the jeep. Or maybe they were worried Craig told him too much."

"Shit. But why didn't they just cremate the real body if they wanted to get rid of it? What could anyone *need* it for?"

"A couple of possibilities. Could be for research, or worse yet, to harvest the infectious agent."

"*Harvest?*"

I nod grimly. "Diseases like Creutzfeld-Jakob normally take as long as ten years to take hold, then anywhere from a couple months to two years to be fatal. If you're interested in killing lots of people, that might be fine. It leaves ample time to make sure no mark is missed and to cover up your tracks. Or your needs might be better met by the *instant* version."

"So you think this stuff is being engineered in a lab somewhere."

"That's *exactly* what I'm guessing. Like the biopharmaceutical labs that develop new treatments for diseases like cancer or diabetes."

"More like the opposite of those. Turning it into some kind of biological weapon."

"And what do those labs do when their testing on animals—in this case cattle instead of rats—is a success? They move on to human trials."

"On Craig Butler."

"They must be feeling pretty smug. I presume Craig's investigations were getting a little too close for comfort. Maybe he was nosing around their facility or asking all the right—or from their point of view, *wrong*—questions. They not only tested on him, but turned him into a prion factory for their new product. They can probably get enough proven, human-ready infectious agent out of his brain to wipe out a small country."

"So," she says, looking very nervous. "What are we going to do?"

"Find out where they're doing their work, and shut them down."

"Yeah, right. Wouldn't be easy, you know. To be doing what you think these guys are up to, they're not a bunch of amateurs or thugs. If they've even got the federal police under their thumb like I'm thinking they have, this thing would have to be somehow connected to *parliament*."

I nod sombrely. "Either originating from there, or from someone who's got a lot of pull with our guys. Like a more powerful nation we rely on to defend us."

"I like that. Blame the bad old U.S. of A. But it could just as easily be Britain. That's where Mad Cow started."

"Whoever's involved, the lot of 'em are breaking international laws. They need to be reported to the United Nations."

"Yeah," she says, biting her lower lip. "Any idea how one goes about doing that?"

"Not a clue."

"Same here."

"I guess first, we'd need something to show as proof."

We both go quiet.

CHAPTER 37

"GOD IT SUCKS BEING a cop," Jessica finally says, bringing a fist down hard on her lap. "Never mind being a fucking girl cop in a small town."

"I'll bet," I say, somewhat taken aback. "Didn't look like Corporal Kulchisky cuts you much slack."

"Might be different if he was that kind of a dick to all the constables, but he's not. Just me. When I signed on nine years ago, every cop in my division was male. The administration was under huge pressure to recruit women and minorities to make the force a better reflection of Canadians. There was a running joke they'd have to turn away Robocop to sign a one-eyed native chick in a wheelchair."

"I guess you were a shoe-in, fit and able bodied."

"Getting in was the easy part. You can legislate hiring practices, but not respect. I read about a survey where eighty percent of female RCMP officers said they'd been sexually harassed on the job. But only two percent reported it. Think about that. These are the same people who tell victims they're *fools* not to report that shit."

"A close friend of mine talked a lot about becoming a cop in the nineties, because she'd heard it was a good way to get a decent salary with no post-secondary." I almost laugh to think how long Zaina would have lasted in such an environment.

"Good on her for staying out. At five years, they gave me a meaningless stripe to sew on my shoulder. The big five-year constable chevron. More of a slap in the face than a thank-you—in recognition of being exactly where you started out, only five years older. If they tell me I've made corporal before I retire, I'll probably drop dead of a heart attack. Nobody gets promoted anymore. *Especially* not a woman."

All I can offer is a gentle smile. Jessica seems to need to vent. After all the talking I've done, I guess I ought to let her.

"Women have been in the force for nearly thirty years now," she goes on, "but it's still a man's job. Even the equipment we have to carry. My waist is fifty-eight centimetres, but all the junk I have to put on my duty belt— my baton, flashlight, ammo, cuffs, pepper spray, and holster—add up to seventy-one. But no point complaining. You just grin and wear the bruises. It's an impenetrable bureaucracy," she continues. "When you're a constable, you're not even at the bottom of the totem pole. You're below ground. I've been on dozens of those cattle mutilation calls. Most of them, Craig Butler got to before us. Farmers in the area knew it was his area of expertise—and he *gave* a shit—so they'd actually call him first."

"Yet *you* believed they were all caused by predators?"

She expels air out her nose like an angry bull. "A few I've seen were, for sure. The ones lying in a lake of jellied blood, with tooth marks all over what's left of the body. Only makes it more obvious the other ones aren't. When it's a *real* mutilation case, no dog or predator goes anywhere near the carcass for weeks. Coyotes sometimes circle at a distance, but that's about it. Still, the unwritten rule is to say in our reports we've examined all the evidence and determined without a doubt that the animals were killed and chewed up by predators or scavengers."

"The *unwritten rule*? Whose directive is that?"

"For me, it comes from the staff sergeant. The Chief. But I'm sure it doesn't start with him. Check out reports from any division in the country and you'll find exactly the same thing. One that comes to mind is a high profile case in British Columbia a couple years ago. *Anything* but the work of predators. The CBC did a national radio piece on it. A farmer in the area saw bright lights the night it happened, and the body was carved up with tools that seemed to have cauterised the incisions. The tissues around some of the cuts actually had hemoglobin on them. People joke that the coyotes out there have laser teeth."

"Even that wouldn't do it. Extracting hemoglobin from blood is tricky. Takes multiple centrifugations in a well-equipped lab. But you're telling me even *that* case went into the reports as an attack by predators."

"Clear-cut."

"God. So for talking to me now, what would happen to you?"

"I'd be disciplined for coming here, unless it was to arrest you for tampering with those medical records." she says. "But for talking to you about the way we handle mutes, I don't even want to know."

"So why'd you come? You must have had some idea what I was calling about."

"Not really. Guess I didn't believe you were the villain Ted Kulchisky made you out to be. Figured your call had something to do with Craig and his work. The incidents happen so often around here. There was an attempted one on a farm just north of town earlier tonight. It's what took me so long."

"Attempted?"

"The farmer was immunising a calf in a small barn, and he heard a noise outside. He walked out, and saw nothing but bright lights filling up the sky. Said it was a spaceship, lit up his whole pasture. Told us he had a deer rifle with him, and fired a shot to scare it off." She shakes her head. "Not exactly."

"What, you don't think he shot?"

"Oh, he sure did. But not just *once*. We found six fresh shell casings on the ground. The guy emptied his whole clip."

I smile. "Guess he really *was* shook up. I thought you didn't respond to mute calls anymore."

"We don't. But when the guy phoned in, the operator couldn't make out what he was saying. She took it down as a rural home invasion."

"The bullets didn't hit anything?"

"Can't say for sure. I walked in the pasture with my flashlight and didn't spot any chunks of glass or debris. Ted was in a hurry to go, even though it was the first time either of us ever heard of someone opening fire like that. But if your theory is correct, they'll still be back, right? There'd have to be an animal in that herd they're interested in."

"I guess. And this stuff is time sensitive. So you're suggesting if someone were to camp out there for a few days, it seems logical the bad guys would show up to get the parts they wanted."

"I don't think I'm suggesting anything of the sort. That *someone* would be in serious fucking danger. Don't forget it looks like these freaks are killing more than cows now."

I nod. "What about the farmer? Won't *he* be keeping an eye out?"

"Doubt it. We had to go check out the scene without him. He said he's never going there again except in broad daylight. Not an atypical reaction. Anyone who thinks ranchers mutilate their own animals for insurance money has never been there after one happened. These people are *scared*, Kat. Some carry a Bible with them any time they have to go back to where a mute occurred. And when we tell them it was the work of predators, they always look like the weight of the world has been lifted off their shoulders. This one probably got enough of a scare to last the rest of his life."

"Think that'll concern your superiors?"

"Probably not. In case you haven't noticed, people don't talk about these things much. Trust me, you don't want to be branded in a small town. Craig Butler wasn't immune. About a year ago, he had coffee with a woman at the A&W. *Coffee*. And it was the talk of the town."

"Just once?"

"Think so. A second sighting would've made front page of the paper here. Ted pointed the lady out to me once, getting into her car by the post office. Right about this time last year. Carol something-or-other. Good-looking blondie. I don't think I've seen her since."

"Hard to blame her if she left town."

I stand up from the bed and walk around Jessica to the desk. In the drawer are a pen and note pad, both bearing the motel's logo in fecal brown. I give them to Jessica.

"Can you draw me a map?"

"Of where the pasture was? I guess."

She draws a small rectangle. "You are here," she says.

She runs a remarkably straight line off to the right of this, and then another that snakes outward, then hooks sharply.

"This is fifteen kilometres," she says, writing *15 km* above the straight line. "Then you go about a mile off the main road. This probably isn't to scale, but there's a big feedlot. Even in pitch darkness, you couldn't possibly miss it." She wrinkles the bridge of her nose and waves a hand in front of her face. "Go another two kilometres or so up this dirt road, and you'll come to a pasture with a good hundred head of white cows. That's the spot."

I take the map. "Thanks."

"I don't think this is a good idea, Kat."

"Well I *know* it isn't. If they catch me, it's free laser surgery."

She stands from her chair and turns away. "You'd be sausage. And I don't know what the hell I'd do."

"It sure wouldn't be your fault. You haven't told me to do anything here. This is all my own idea."

"I'm not worried about getting blamed." She turns so that I'm looking at her in profile. The soft highlights and shadows on Jessica's fair skin give her the appearance of an ivory cameo. "I just don't want anything to happen to you. I'm sort of hoping we run into each other again."

I put a hand on her hip. She raises it and kisses my knuckles gently, then, looking into my eyes, puts her lips to my fingertips. Inside of my torso, an orb of heat is rising. She gives me her hand, and I do the same. Her skin smells of subtle perfume—lavender and citrus maybe—but has no taste. No saltiness, nothing.

She kisses me on the lips, so gently that I can feel warmth but am unable to tell when we touch. They are the silkiest that mine have ever touched.

She draws away. "You okay?" she whispers. I get the words from reading her lips more than from the soft susurration that comes from them.

"*Very* okay," I say. It's as though she's been reading my mind, though I can't imagine I have given any perceivable hints.

I fall over backwards, and both of us giggle as she topples on top of me. I feel nervousness creeping in from all sides, and consider shoving Jessica away.

Screw that.

"What?" she says.

"Uh, nothing." *Did I speak, or is she truly reading my mind now?* I give her a smile and reach down, grabbing her thin shirt at its bottom hem. I wrestle it up over her athletic shoulders and arms to fully reveal her jaunty little breasts and six-pack abdomen. She gives me a mischievous grin, as if sensing my approval, then kisses me again, this time more forcefully.

It's a delight I've never experienced from contact with a man. So *this* is what a first kiss is supposed to be. I feel like I have been waiting my entire life for it.

It seems that Jessica knows my body better than I do, navigating adeptly through the folds of my skin, stroking me in ways I've never conceived of that jolt me with almost unbearably glorious pulsations of neural electricity.

I have in fact only been with three people before—all of them male. Jack and Craig, of course, and a boy named Kurt Hogan whom I dated in the eleventh and twelfth grades. Those wayward tongues and fumbling digits now seem utterly ridiculous compared to a truly proficient lover like Jessica. When it's my turn, I'm delighted to watch her find similar ecstasy in the kind of touching that years of sexual starvation have driven me to near-mastery of on my own body.

I discover another perk of being with a woman—no sudden disintegration of libido. Again and again, we make love, and each time, I somehow experience a climax more intense than I've ever conceived possible. We continue until both of us are pinned to the bed in exhaustion, gasping for breath.

We snooze for a while, then I wake up and whisper her name. She kisses me, and we proceed to work one another to orgasm yet again. When we lie together after this, I bring myself to ask something that's been tickling at my mind.

"So tell me, Jessica. How did you know?"

"Know what?"

"That I..." I start to laugh, unable to say it.

"That you liked me?"

"No. That I like... *girls*?"

She snickers. You're shitting me, right?"

"No."

"Oh, *God*. When I saw you the other night, my gaydar was pinging so damned loud it gave me a migraine."

"*Gaydar*? Me? I don't believe you, Jessica. Nobody's ever guessed before."

"Yeah, right. Get real, Kat. Or should I say *Eve Ensler?*"

"Eve Ens—Why? *She's* a lesbian?"

She roars. "Big time carpet muncher. You mean you didn't know that?"

I didn't. "Carpet muncher?" I laugh and squirm in delight as soft kisses tickle the skin of my tummy on her way down.

CHAPTER 38

A BLINDING RAY FROM outside slashes across both my eyelids, prying its way in. One thing I liked about my room in Edmonton was that it faced north, and didn't subject me to any unwanted early-morning sunlight.

I moan. "Morning already?" I say to Jessica, then realize that her side of the bedsheets are nicely smoothed out—and vacant. *Just like a man*, I think, but feel a big smile creasing the skin of my cheeks and up near my temples. I realize it isn't a feeling I've had a lot of lately. It might be good to develop a few wrinkles in places other than my brow.

I don't want to spoil my own elation, but it's hard not to wonder if last night meant anything to Jessica. The thought feels terrible, and lingers like the taste of bitter medicine. Did she come here purely because she saw me as a prospective sexual conquest? Though I wish it didn't matter, somehow it really *does*.

Yet regardless of her motivation, I don't regret anything.

Nor do I want to be alone now. The alarm clock's red LEDs say it's 6:22. Earlier than I want to get up, but I climb into my jeans and top, and carefully move to the window. Instead of looking through the existing gap between the drapes, I raise one end just a little and peer outside from the corner. There is no activity yet, but probably soon will be. It's Monday. The few people who live in this tiny town will soon be going off to wherever it is they work.

I grab for the telephone, but stop short of lifting it. It's five-thirty where Zaina is. She'll have finished her morning *salat* and be back asleep. I should give her another hour, although I feel desperate to call her right away. She could be in danger. I can't just let something happen the way I did with Isi.

I collapse back on the bed and use the time to worry and cry a little.

* * *

I'M ANTICIPATING Zaina's now too-familiar answering machine message, but the phone doesn't even have a chance to produce a ring tone before she grabs it. "It's me," I say.

"You're alive."

"I am."

"Good. But I'm *so* pissed at you, Kat. Where the hell are you calling from?" Her voice is so deep and hoarse I might not recognise it.

"In a motel not far from the town I talked to you from before. Are you okay? You sound funny."

"I picked up cold, maybe a sinus infection too. Probably worried myself sick about you, but I'll be fine once you're back home. I've been checking constantly with the airline you flew out on, and there's never any booking. I've also left a dozen messages at your place and at the clinic. Pam's gonna shit when she gets in. Kat, I was *that* close to reporting you missing."

"Oh, I'm so sorry. Maybe call Pam at home and update her, okay? Didn't you get my messages?"

"You call those *messages*? They sound just like how a hostage talks after they warn her not to give any clues. I keep expecting a box to show up with your finger in it."

"I'm sorry, Zane. There's been some shitty incidents, and I had to keep moving around. Didn't know who might hear what I said to your machine."

"Incidents? Kat, are you OK?"

"I'm fine. Shaken, not stirred. Shaken quite a bit, actually. Somebody came into my room when I was in the shower and left me a love letter on the wall in red spraypaint. Then a girl I visited in Edmonton—Craig's cousin Isabel—was killed."

Zaina gasps twice, then continues, her voice quavering. "Shit, Kat!" She continues breathing loudly.

"Please take it easy, Zane." I'm getting worked up talking about it, and can tell my own tone is far from soothing. "I'm fine now."

"Oh my God. Kat, you've got to go to the police."

"I did. I've given witness reports to two different police divisions, not counting the one at home."

"Well, you can't stay there any more. You're in *trouble*, Kat. Are the cops protecting you there?"

"One of them stayed with me last night," I say.

"That's a relief. So tell me you're leaving it up to them now."

"Afraid not. The police aren't being much help, actually. The officer who stayed here was off duty and taking a big risk. It's looking like the cops are tangled up in this."

"Wouldn't that figure? Kat, I talked to Nate."

"You called him, or did he call you?"

"Neither. He called *you*. I've been doing some tidying up at your place—which is why I missed your calls—and I heard him leaving a message. Really agitated, so I picked up."

"Is he alright? Is Sylvia?"

"They're both fine. You were right about that guy Thomas skipping out on Nate at the ferry. Pissed Nate off, but that wasn't why he called. Kat, a fisherman found the kayak you were using. Down by Neah Bay."

"*Neah Bay*? That's in Washington State."

"Yes, it is. Nate's logos are silkscreened on the sides, so the guy phoned him, and they met up at Port Renfrew."

"Wow. That put both of them out. I hope the boat's still good."

"He didn't say. He was too busy flipping out because the float bags had been taken out of the bow and stern. He said they couldn't possibly have come out on their own the way they were installed. Someone had to have messed with your kayak."

"Oh, shit. Can't say I didn't suspect something like that, though. Dammit, I shouldn't even be talking to *you*. There's not a thing you can do to help, and if they get me, they might go after you next. You're at as big a risk as I am. Maybe worse, since you're easy to find. Right now would be a really good time for you to take that vacation. As in *today*."

"*Today*? Yeah, right. I'm not ready. And you know I can't afford to go to—"

"STOP! Don't say the place. I'll buy you the ticket online as soon as I can. Pack now and grab a coffee at our Saturday spot in two hours. I'll call you there with the particulars."

"No one's bugging my phone. At least I don't think..."

"I hope not too. But it looks like someone is pretty damned serious about stopping *me*.

"Kat, I can't go. I just *can't*—"

"You sure can. Pam will look after both our cats until I get back. Don't let a living soul know where you're going. No one. Come up with an alternate place to tell Pam and your landlady. Okay?"

"Okay," she says with a sigh, though I don't think she believes herself yet.

Zaina will be okay. She's got to be getting itchy feet to travel anyway.

"And first chance you get, see a doctor and have him prescribe an antibiotic for your sinuses. Make damn sure you keep taking the pills until the last one is gone, or you'll build a resistance to the meds and get an even nastier relapse. Talk to you in two hours."

"Kat, watch out. Fuck, this is crazy."

"I know. Bye, love."

I depress the plunger.

* * *

I DECIDE my crinkled white shirt and the stretch denim pants will do for today. I've worn both of my outfits for two days each now, but this one looks much fresher than the capris and T-shirt. Good thing I don't perspire much. Still, I don't think I've ever worn pants or a top three times between washes. It is definitely high time to go home.

I check out of my motel and pay the manager for my two long distance phone calls. The office has bulky metal shelves where it displays a few products for sale: chewing gum, candy bars, disposable cameras and film, over-the-counter medication, batteries and some postcards of tourists in the area circa 1980. I buy one of her two cardboard cameras with a built-in flash. The first one I look at has an expiry date of last year, but the one shelved behind it still has a few months left on it. She is visibly displeased when I choose the newer one.

I'm not planning to return to St. Paul, especially now that I know for sure I'm *Wanted* there, so I drive forty minutes east to Bonnyville, a town of similar size that seems a virtual clone of its neighbour. I wear the Thrifty cap and sunglasses, not knowing how seriously an All Points Bulletin for an alleged document shredding felon is carried from one community to the next.

Fortunately, an electronics store is running a demo of its high-speed Internet service. The young salesman sees me head for the computer, and begins a lame pitch for what *even I* can tell is an outdated and overpriced system. I tell him I'm just interested in trying out the connection. I might subscribe to the service if I'm impressed.

He launches a Web browser for me and begins a canned run-through diatribe. I interrupt and politely tell him I've got a migraine and am far more likely to get in a buying mood if I play around by myself.

At this point, another twenty-something man enters the store. The two grunt *Hey* at one another, do a strange handshake, and abandon me to share a conversation about High Definition TV systems and debate the fastest way to download movies for free.

"Gimme a shout if you need any help, 'kay?" the salesman says in a low voice.

"Sure will," I reply, squeezing my temples.

"*Heyy.* Who's tha...?" I hear his friend ask, just before the discussion gets relocated to the home theatre section.

I try a few airlines, quickly learning that no one on the planet flies direct from North America to Khwaja Rawash airport in Kabul. I find the fastest route, then book the connecting flights through Expedia.

I've used the discount travel service before, and know that if anyone follows my credit card trail, they'll end up at Expedia's Las Vegas address. I used the service to book a hotel in Seattle, and was confused when the front desk clerk asked me a sequence of questions about life in the Casino City. I happily played along, and it was only later when I looked at the printout of my receipt that I realized the misinformation's origin. Instead of my address, the surrogate buyer's office was listed.

I don't think it's possible for someone to extract my true location from Expedia or the credit card company. Even if it is, by the time they do it, I plan to be somewhere else.

It's a good thing Zaina is a seasoned traveller. She's looking at a long, arduous trip. The first leg—a prop plane to make the short hop from Victoria to Vancouver—departs tonight at nine. In addition to the considerable flight time, she'll have a two-hour layover in Toronto, and eight long hours in Frankfurt while waiting for the once-daily Ariana Afghan Airlines haul to Kabul. I'll remind her to bring a few thick books.

I'm done. I delete my history from the computer, purge the cache, exit the browser, and make for the door. "What did you think?" the salesman says, barely glancing at me from a giant screen where Eminem is mouthing off at a topless woman. His friend seems torn between checking me out and watching the video.

I smile. "I'm sold. It *is* very fast. I'll talk to my husband tonight."

He pries his eyes from the screen and pulls a business card from his pocket, squeezing it back into shape as he approaches me. *JIMMY D, AUDIO AND VIDEO AUTHORITY.* "Hope to see you again real soon," Jimmy D says with a prefab smile before turning his attention back to Eminem.

*   *   *

"All packed?" I ask Zaina from inside a telephone booth with a busted door. I feel a flood of relief in knowing she's still safe, but will be better still after nine when she's up and away.

"Got everything, I think," she says, with all the enthusiasm of someone going to the gallows. "You know, I've done it a million times, yet I still always forget at least one thing."

"It's a mechanism to make sure you come back. Brighten up, Zane. You must be looking forward to this at least a *little*."

"I'll do my best. Are sure this is what I need to do?"

"I'm sorry Zaina. I'm really sure."

"All right then."

"What will you do in Kabul?"

"Not sure. When my reporter friend was asking me to join him, he told me about a European women's magazine seeking English writers for a new publication they're tailoring to the emerging female audience. If that's still available, it might be fun for a while. But how am I supposed to know *you're* all right?"

"Try me at home as soon as you get settled. Hopefully this will all be a bad dream by then."

I give her the details of her flight, and she has me repeat it all to make sure she's written it down correctly.

"Take care of yourself, Kat," she says. "You're my very best friend, and I need you."

"I need you too, Zane," I say. The truth is I've loved Zaina deeply for years, though from beneath many heavy layers of self-inflicted denial. Unfortunately for me, she is chronically heterosexual. I yearn to tell her I've met someone here whom I believe I also love, because I think it would make her happy. I often suspect she knows me well enough to see through my ruse anyway. When I finally do come out to her, I expect she will say, "Well, *duh*, Kat."

"I'll see you real soon," I say, hoping this is a promise I can live up to. "Look after that infection of yours. You still sound like shit. And don't you dare agree to marry that man unless he's willing to relocate to Victoria."

"No need to worry about that. Even *I* know better than to marry a reporter. *Ila'l-liqa, insha'Allah." Until we meet again, if God wills.*

"*Ila'l-liqa*, love. And thank you." I hang up and stare out at the street for a while.

I ask myself why I am doing this. What do I have to gain? Not much, other than the satisfaction of knowing who or what it was that really killed Craig, and why it's so damned big that the police and medical community seem to be in league with them. It's more what I have to *lose* that motivates me. Would it be possible to go back to work at my clinic, and pretend nothing had ever happened? I don't know. I might never feel safe again. It's pretty clear that someone powerful considers me a threat. How likely would they be to leave me out there, with a head full of potentially damaging knowledge? I've already proven I'm not good at putting such things out of my mind. Sooner or later, I'd come back to haunt these people. They suspect it—and I *know* it.

BOOK II

CHAPTER 39

Six months ago

THE ICE CHIPS CRUNCHED and chirped under the frozen rubber of Duncan Henderson's winter radials as his truck slowed and pulled up to the NutraPet security gate. Everything sounded different at these frigid temperatures, in part because the sound waves travelled more slowly in the less dense air, and also because the heavy snow-cover provided a unique acoustic environment. Henderson flashed his picture ID tag at Randy Farrell. The first weeks of February—or *Feberwarry*, as you called it back in Scotland—had been the most bitter he'd yet experienced here, and the TV meteorologist had lamented seeing no sign of the cold snap ending anytime soon.

Randy gave a stoic nod and pushed a button to raise the heavy steel gate arm. Henderson waved and drove ahead, smiling to himself at the name on the guard's ID badge. *Randy* was an adjective in the U.K.—not by any means a proper given name. It would be as bad as naming a kid *Horny*.

Outsiders must wonder why such high security for a factory that makes animal kibble, Henderson often thought. *If only they knew...*

Henderson turned left after passing the guard tower. The buses that brought in the *authentic* factory workers went straight ahead to the main entrance, where everyone piled out. The factory ran two consecutive eight-hour shifts, from seven in the morning to eleven at night. Many factory workers knew that people worked in a facility below them, but believed these to be an elite collection of management—"animal nutritionists" like Henderson, and the various members of the R&D, public relations, sales and marketing departments. People above ground were required to come or go only on the buses, enabling Henderson and his associates to avoid ever being seen by them.

The superstructure was shaped something like the head of a golf putter, the jutting heel a new addition to the ground floor—built only four months ago.

Inside, collagen from the skin and bones of cattle was now being processed with lime and hydrochloric acid to make gelatine, then formed into two-piece capsules bound soon for the global export market. There was strong demand for a pork-free product, and the new capsules would be a much more profitable use of the animal hides and bones than grinding them into pet food. At least that's what the PR department's new release had said.

When he'd first arrived here, Henderson had wondered why a pet food factory was selected as a cover operation for the facility. He now wished he'd never found out. It was that kind of disclosure that undoubtedly got Dr. Carol Benson—the only colleague here he'd truly liked—transferred away to Kansas, just about the time the new wing was finished. The example made of Carol had definitely served to stifle gossiping among the co-workers.

Even Henderson's wife, Mairi, knew virtually nothing about the *real* work he did here, and she seldom asked questions. Which was good. His distrust for the organisation was such that he remained mindful of his words even at home. Perhaps especially at home. *They* had built the house.

He drove up not far from a semi trailer docked in a loading bay, pulling up close to the grey wall of the complex. When his bumper reached precisely eighty centimetres from it, a stucco-covered wall panel swiftly rose, and rolled inward on a set of titanium tracks. He advanced and flicked the wiper lever—the exterior of his windows having fogged over immediately from the sudden surge in air temperature—and drove down the moist spiral ramp to his spot on the second of three parking levels.

He rode alone in the elevator down to the fourth basement, and unzipped his parka to avoid perishing of heat exhaustion from the eyeball-shrivelling forced-air heating. Maintenance always cranked the furnaces too bloody high in the winter, and then went crazy with the air conditioning all summer long. It was a virtual reversal of seasons within the facility—never quite comfortable either way.

Practically everywhere Henderson had ever worked, he'd been relegated to a sub-basement two storeys below ground, and here it was all of four. Not that it truly made any difference once you were lower than the grass. He'd accepted years ago that a subterranean existence came with the territory as a pathologist—floors with windows were of psychological benefit to living patients. And morgues were always shoved as deep under ground as possible. Others liked it that way.

Here, however, all the *real* work was done below the main level. The upper floor of the facility was both figuratively and literally a cover.

The first and second basements were occupied by management, security and operations personnel. All these offices were generally off-limits to worker bees such as Henderson. He was fine with that. Whatever went on in the secured areas was probably not good for his mind to know about. Henderson was allowed to move freely about the third and fourth sub-basement, which was where pathology and histology, various other labs, the morgue, and the cafeteria were located. Everyone thought it was someone's demented joke to have the eating area on the same floor as the morgue, but it actually came down to HVAC planning and the shared need of both facilities for robust exit ventilation. To Henderson, having the cafeteria next door was one of the facility's few intrinsic conveniences.

He had only been to the fifth basement once, during orientation on his first day here. The floor was split into two sections. The larger of the two contained several advanced protein engineering labs, where new prion strains were developed and tested on rodents and primates. The engineering itself was really quite simple when it came down to it. Different strains were generated from particles of the very same protein, simply folded into various intricately shaped conformations. Under a powerful microscope, a prion looked much like the bow on a Christmas present. Making a minor modification to the way a bow was twisted or relocating the folds would result in amazing changes in the pathogen's effects and virulence. It only had to be done one time: once a new prion disease was introduced, it would force the surrounding healthy proteins to mimic its shape perfectly. Though the scientists here were becoming quite good at creating the new prions, they remained baffled as to exactly how the replication worked.

Security for the engineering area was even tighter than for the rest of the facility. Before going down to the labs, Henderson had been required to have his *irises* scanned. (Not his retinas—the blood vessels at the back of his eyes, as with other ocular scanners he'd seen—but the visible pigmented part.) A temporary profile was created for him in Engineering's independent security database. After this, he was required to look into a second scanning device, which electronically advised a body-heat monitor to admit one warm-blooded being into the staging chamber. Then, like up in the morgue, he'd entered a space between two submarine-style sealed doors, where he donned a Chemturion "blue suit" before proceeding.

The laboratories themselves were quite ordinary, he thought. No shortage of high-tech equipment, but nothing especially exciting. It was the test animals in various states of mental decay that had really impacted on Henderson. A rabbit had entirely chewed away the skin of its own belly, and lay with one foot thumping incessantly against the bars of its little prison. A larger cage held two chimpanzees, one of which appeared to have expired, while the other sat frothing at the lips, grinding its teeth aloud and crying as tremors rattled his little body.

And there were horrid—although largely muted—squeals and wails escaping steadily from inside some of the rooms that he had not been taken into.

He did not intend to ever go down there again. The only true benefit derived from the visit was that he now considered himself fortunate that his work was limited to those whose suffering was over.

Engineering took up slightly less than three quarters of the fifth basement. The remaining portion was divided into bright and cheery—yet hopelessly cell-like—residences for two dozen scientists. These included Henderson's remaining morgue colleague, Dr. Jean Letendre—among others who, for some inconceivable reason had agreed to live down there. Perhaps these people's talents and backgrounds were not quite as unique as Henderson's, and they had been offered no choice. More likely, none of them had a spouse with Mairi's bargaining skills. She had insisted from the outset that a move to Canada and the five-year contract would only proceed under a list of specific circumstances—all of which were agreed to on the spot, with no compromises proposed. Mairi had expected *some* measure of negotiation in response, and still mused that she must not have asked for as much as she should have. A winter cottage in Cancun might be nice, as would a couple of weeks a year of vacation time for her husband, she'd recently suggested.

Henderson's own wishes were quite a bit simpler, yet ironically less probable. He spent much of his free time fancying ways of getting out of here. Sadly, none of the schemes he'd dreamt up so far could safely include Mairi and the kids. And no way he was going *anywhere* without them.

* * *

WITH ITS staff of sixty-eight, GATSER Northwest was a relatively small team, but in matters such as those dealt with here, small was undoubtedly the only way to go. Large organisations could not trust their many members to keep their mouths shut—or quickly identify any mouths that happened to work themselves loose. It was no secret that such things were monitored here, and that the consequences of even the slightest indiscretion were most severe.

Henderson hung his heavy coat on a peg, and removed his big Sorel snowboots, then scrubbed up like any good doctor—though it was probably really of negligible benefit—and entered the staging chamber. There, he folded his clothing and dropped it into an airtight canister before inspecting and pulling on the bright blue "space suit": a pressurised outfit made of chlorinated polyethylene that covered his entire body except his face and hands. Some pathologists who worked on victims such as these continued to rely only on only a second pair of rubber gloves to protect their hands, but not here. Henderson had yet to completely adjust to the sacrificed sensitivity from wearing an additional gauntlet of scalpel-proof chain mail on his left hand, underneath a latex one.

Then the air-filtration hood. *Don't want to inhale any particles of this kind when the bone dust is flying.* As an intern, Henderson had occasionally been capricious about wearing a mask—it made conversing and dictating notes a chore, and forced one to taste his own halitosis for hours on end. After he'd caught TB from a diseased lung, that changed forever. He'd been diagnosed early and recovered with no permanent damage, but the experience taught him an important lesson early in his career. It would serve him well, for the pathogens he worked with here made tuberculosis look like the hiccups.

He exited the staging chamber and sealed the second door, then passed through the claustrophobic stainless steel environment that marked the entry to the morgue. He saw his weight displayed on the wall in large green letters as he walked over a scale embedded in the green-tiled floor. Ninety-four kilos. He was down six—nearly a full *stone*—since coming to Canada, though Mairi remained an excellent cook. Part of it may have been the daily running, though he'd been at that for a decade. His appetite just wasn't the same any more. He simply had too many burdensome thoughts on his mind.

Above the entrance to the autopsy suite was a sign that Henderson had brought with him overseas and hung with double-sided tape soon after he began working here. It read, *Hic est locus ubi mors faudet succurso vitae. Here is the place where death rejoices in coming to the aid of life.*

He could no longer bring himself to look at it.

Henderson heard a rattling sound from within the autopsy suite. He glanced up at the clock on the wall. Still twenty minutes before showtime. Uncharacteristic of Jean Letendre to ever be here early. With all of Jean's peculiarly diverse responsibilities, he generally ran anywhere from five to fifteen minutes late for morgue duty.

Henderson stepped into the autopsy suite, and then took two quick steps back. What his eyes beheld set him reeling like a heavy fist to the guts.

A blue-fleshed cadaver lay fully exposed on a stainless steel morgue cart, legs hanging off the sides. A man stood over the end of the cart, his face hidden as he fondled the body with one gloved hand and himself with the other. A rubber respirator might have concealed the degenerate's identity, had the shock of blond hair at the top not given it away. It was Kyösti Talo, GATSER Northwest's Director of Security.

But there was something even worse. The corpse was that of Dr. Carol Benson.

CHAPTER 40

As the line of trees obscuring Len Gibson's house draws near, I can't help but wonder how the poor old guy is doing. My foot hovers over the brake pedal. Perhaps I should stop and check on him.

I'm ready to dismiss the thought—the man's house is not exactly a happy place—when I notice that he's gone and done something unusual. His picture window—previously bare—is now adorned by a strange new drapery.

I brake to a stop, and the engine whines in its low reverse gear, back to the entrance road. The yard appears unchanged, and Sam the dog approaches my car like a dart, barking. This time he loosens up when he recognises me and begins to wag his tail. It seems safe to get out.

"How're you doing, Sam?" I say, giving him a scratch. He replies with a strange whimper.

"Something wrong, pal?" From here, the new window treatment is more discernible. It looks like the soft patterned fabric on the interior of an old sleeping bag. A similar one and a wool blanket cover the two other windows on this side of the bungalow.

That's odd.

I ring the doorbell, yet somehow don't expect an answer. I pound against the beat-up wood and call out Len's name, then eventually try the knob. It's not locked.

The mess seems somehow even worse now. And what a smell!

In the living room, I see what I feared. A pair of legs and feet—toes down.

It's Len. I rush over. His cheek and nose are pressed to the floor, complexion drained to a dreadful pallor.

"Len!" I drop to my knees next to him, and touch my hand to his face. To my horror, he jerks away violently.

My God, he's alive.

He appears as terrified as I am, his features twitching randomly, mouth open, lips silently working.

"Len. Can you speak? It's Kat."

"I... I'm bli-ind," he moans softly. Then he yells: "I've gone *BLIND!* Mom! *Help me, Mom-MA!*"

I delicately stroke his arm. "It's all right, Len. Momma is coming. You just try to relax for a moment." Starting with his shoulders, and then his hips and legs, I roll him as gently as I can onto his side. He grimaces and grunts, but it will be a better position for him if another seizure comes on before help arrives. I slide the coffee table a few feet further away for the same reason.

Poor Len can't be at all comfortable, if he's aware enough to notice. Coming in, it was immediately clear to me he'd lost control of his bodily functions.

In the kitchen is a red wall-mounted rotary telephone. I grab it.

It's dead. *What the—?* Then I notice the white plastic plunger protruding from the side. It's an old party line model, designed for multiple rural residents who once had to share a single phone line. Surely Len has a private connection—everybody does these days—but he was probably too cheap to upgrade his still-functional telephone. I pull out the plunger and the receiver purrs in my ear.

I spin the dial. It seems to take forever for it to return all nine clicks, and I am glad that the two remaining digits are both ones.

"Nine-one-one Emergency," the operator says. But my attention has been ripped away by a few words on a business-sized envelope that's crammed along with Len's power and gas bills into a wooden letter tray beside the phone.

KAT

READ THIS ***FIRST!***

It looks like it was printed using the same bad inkjet as the one Len delivered. I grab it. It's sealed, so I work a finger under the flap and tear it open.

"This is Emergency Nine One One," the voice on the receiver repeats. "Are you able to speak to me?"

"Pardon me, yes," I sputter. "I've got a man here who has collapsed. He is breathing and can talk, but he isn't ambulatory. Says he can't see, and he doesn't seem coherent."

I tell the operator roughly where I am located, but am barely able to pay attention to my own conversation. I close my eyes, forcing myself to cease reading Craig's words until the call is complete, then I squat down, lowering my bum to the floor.

"Ma-aaa-om," Len whines.

"Mom is on the way, Lenny-boy. Just try to breathe easy a minute."

The letter is dated eight weeks ago—just before Craig was hospitalised—and written by an unsteady hand. I know it's Craig's writing, but from the penmanship, you might think an arthritic ninety-year-old wrote it.

> *Dear Kat,*
>
> *I wanted to deliver this to you myself, but haven't been well. My neighbour Len owes me a few favours, and offered to bring it to you. (Before I told him where you live!) I've decided to take him up on it, and Len's a man of his word. I reckoned it might help to explain what is in the big envelope before you see it. The contents are a little on the strange side.*
>
> *The past few years, I have gradually retired from cattle breeding. It never was what I wanted to do. Now Mom and Dad are gone, and there is no reason to stay in it. Looks like my timing was good for once, considering what's happened to the industry. I'm far from wealthy, but I've had the luxury of being able to take some time to think about what to do next.*
>
> *I got married eight years ago, but Lynn and I have been separated since last April. I think we love each other, but we are two different breeds. Can't say I think things will work out for us. The more time goes by, the more doubtful it seems. That's all right. As you know, I've never been too lucky that way.*
>
> *Don't worry! I'm not writing after all these years to talk about THAT.*
>
> *A while back, I took up a new hobby. I investigate mysterious animal mutilations. If that sounds weird, it's because it IS. Started out by accident, when farmer a few miles down called on me to look at a bull that got carved up overnight. He knew I'd put in some years at vet school, and hoped I could tell him what the hell happened. I sure couldn't! Since then, I've looked at a lot of what we call "mutes," yet it seemed every one brought me farther from understanding.*
>
> *Then last summer, I got a call from a woman who said her name was Carol. She asked me to meet up with her—said she had important info that might help my research. We met in a restaurant, and she told me she worked for a*

secret government organisation that has been monitoring diseases like Mad Cow for years, with databases that track darn near every head of livestock in the Americas and Britain. Quite a claim! It gets crazier. The company she works for is supposedly behind the mutes! She also told me the folks at the top were up to something terrible, but wouldn't elaborate. Too dangerous to talk about in public, she said.

We planned for Carol to come one week later to my house, but she never showed. I was really disappointed. She was to bring me important info on the operations she talked about, so I could write it into my research findings and expose the operation without putting her at risk. This lady was scared shitless, Kat. I still don't know if she lost her nerve, or if something BAD happened.

Maybe you can help me now. The photos in the envelope are just a sampling of what's in my collection. I am hoping that you will take a look and decide for yourself if the mutilations are consistent with what Carol told me. You'll notice there are some differences between the two sheets. The first ones were shot about three years ago, and give you an idea what I was seeing at the time. The animals on the second sheet are from just a few months ago, and have more than the normal parts removed. The brain and backbone are gone. Seems to be the new trend, and from what I've learned about BSE, it makes Carol's story that much more credible. Why else, all of a sudden, would they be going after THOSE parts?

We should talk. I'm a bit of a hermit, and haven't got a lot of good friends left. You are the only person I trust who has the credibility and connections to assess this and maybe take it straight to the scientific community. I've read some of your work. You turned out to be everything I expected, and more, Kat Colman. Other scientists will pay attention to you—the same people who'd reckon I've gone off the deep end and laugh me out of the room.

Please give me a call when you've had a close look.

I'm really sorry to involve you, Kat. Please DO NOT go discussing this with anyone before we talk. I'm afraid it might be dangerous.

Take Care,

Craig
780-555-3584

CHAPTER 41

Six months ago

"WHAT THE *FUCK* ARE you doing?" Henderson spat, his voice weak and frog-like. Talo paused for a nanosecond, then squeezed one of the corpse's full breasts, and began stroking himself anew, his insolent blue eyes fixed behind the respirator's round lenses.

"Step back from the cadaver and put that goddam thing away, or I'll rip it clean off ya." Henderson's boiling rage made his chest feel like it was ready to explode, and his voice reverberated loudly under the big hood. "NOW!" He ordered, and strode ahead.

Talo continued as if oblivious to the other man's presence. Henderson bulldozed him away from Carol's body with the palms of both hands.

Talo stumbled, but stayed on his feet. He stood up straight, wrenched his rigid member into his trousers, and zipped up. He lifted away the respirator to reveal a full-faced sneer, then peeled away the latex gloves and dropped them nonchalantly into the biohazard disposal bin. Shoulders back and head high, Talo glided over to the large steel sink and began to scrub his hands and forearms with soap, then turned on the water and rinsed the suds away. Only then did he turn to face Henderson, who stood trembling, fists clenched at his sides.

"*Kuolematon rakkaus. Immortal fondness. Or To Each His Own*, if you're a film aficionado," Talo said blandly with a shrug, and headed for the door.

"This is reprehensible," Henderson roared. He wanted to pummel the filthy bastard. He was not sure why he hadn't already done so—or carried out his initial threat and yanked Talo's ugly pecker off. The Fin was years younger, and could possibly be more vicious in a fight, but Henderson was solid—and would have blind rage to fuel his punches. A few years ago, *nothing* would have held him back. Henderson pulled his own hood off, and threw it down, glowering at Talo. "I won't stand for this bloody crap. In my morgue, we have *absolute respect* for the human body."

It was true. Although to an outsider, it might appear that cadavers were sometimes thrown about like slabs of meat—especially when a pathologist had to move one alone—Henderson had always tried to envision the owner still present in the room. He now hoped this to be false, that Carol's spirit had not been watching today.

"You saw nothing," Talo spat.

"I will report *exactly* what I witnessed here to Director Weissmann. Personally and in writing."

Talo cocked his head like a bird. "Oh, you do just that. And I'll be sure the next stiff I have my way with is you, Doc." Talo cranked open the door to the staging chamber and went inside.

Henderson could not remember a time when he'd felt so damned helpless. Talo was not likely bluffing. As Director of Security, the bastard's word was worth far more to the superiors here than that of a mere neuropathologist on contract with the lab.

He walked over to the corpse, and lifted its legs back onto the cart.

"Oh, what have they done to you, Carol?" he sobbed. "I'm so bloody sorry. I did nothing to protect you from them—or from *that* sonofabitch."

He looked down at the face. Though it had changed some, it was without a doubt Dr. Carol Benson, his colleague who had purportedly been transferred to a similar facility in rural Kansas. Though he knew that GATSER Northwest—this place—was one of three similarly concealed facilities in Canada, he was not sufficiently privileged to be have been debriefed on the operation's full scale or organisational structure. He did know for certain, though, that there were other GATSER locations—*including* Kansas—with in-house pathologists competent to handle Carol's autopsy.

The cadaver had been sent here purely as a message to the people who worked in this morgue—and perhaps Henderson in particular. Rumour had it Dr. Benson had made contact with a local man who'd previously taken interest in some of GATSER's activities. Many believed this to be largely the cause of Carol's transfer. No denying it was *possible* she had contracted a prion disease in the course of her work. But Carol was so bloody *careful*...

Even if accidental infection was the cause, it didn't explain the body's return here for autopsy. Carol was an American citizen.

Most of what Henderson knew about GATSER came from the literature they'd left briefly with him—after he'd sworn an oath of secrecy and signed a meaty non-disclosure document that went practically so far as to include a "pain of death" clause. The material—strategically vague, it in many respects appeared—was even printed on red paper, so that a photocopier would turn out nothing but solid black pages. A throwback to the days before the simplest photo manipulation program could be used to remove the type from its background, but the colour still stood to reinforce an underlying statement: *tell no one.*

GATSER was a much-needed acronym for the Global Alliance for Transmissible Spongiform Encephalopathy Research. The project was a joint venture between the governments of the United States, Canada, and the United Kingdom—with generously remunerated contributions from Argentina and Brazil.

The program had seen its beginning almost four decades ago, not long after the first-ever discovery of a prion disease in North America.

Several theories remained as to where the disease came from—of which Henderson thought the *kuru* one most plausible. In the Eastern Highlands of New Guinea during the mid-1950s, the Fore aborigine tribe had become plagued by a bizarre fatal disease known as *kuru*, the natives' word for *tremor*. Victims developed shakes and lost co-ordination, then became unable to swallow. Then they would starve themselves into a coma and die. The diseased cerebellums were consistently covered in dark, gummy plaques where the dead tissues accumulated—leaving behind countless tiny, sponge-like holes.

In 1957, the United States army sent a man named Carleton Gajdusek— who studied diseases of "military interest"—to New Guinea to observe *kuru* victims, and to send back tissue samples.

The medical community had been baffled by the disease—and its limitation to Fore women and youths—until the means of transmission was discovered. Whenever one of the natives died, the family would cook and consume the body. The men got to eat the most tender and flavourful parts, leaving women and children with the remaining tissues. Not surprisingly, these scraps included (among other niceties) the brains, which were whisked into a thick grey liquid, warmed, and slurped by the lower ranking tribe members.

Kuru's remarkably long incubation period—often ten years or more—had made identifying its cause quite a job. When a person finally displayed symptoms, food consumed years before was not initially taken into consideration by doctors seeking the origin of the holes and plaques.

By 1958, Gajdusek started to send his autopsied *kuru* brains to Dr. Joseph Smadel, chief of the biologics department at the National Institute of Health in Bethesda, Maryland. From there, brain extracts were forwarded to the U.S. Army Biological Laboratories (today the Army's Medical Research Institute of Infectious Diseases) in Fort Dietrich Maryland, to be injected into lab animals of every foot and feather.

Then something went awry. The prions either got out or were deliberately released from their laboratory environment, and began showing up in the form of Chronic Wasting Disease in deer and elk.

Prion diseases like scrapie had existed in sheep for at least two centuries (the Fore people may have initially contracted *kuru* by eating the brains of sheep imported to New Guinea by the ruling Germans in the late 1800s), however these had previously remained confined to a single species.

That is, until sheep became a popular ingredient for MBM—Meat and Bone Meal—and fed to cattle to promote rapid growth. In 1986, BSE was first identified in a British cow, followed hot on its hooves by nearly two hundred thousand subsequent confirmations in the U.K. alone. With nearly simultaneous prion disease outbreaks in North America and Great Britain, the experts knew bigger trouble was on the way.

And then it happened. By eating the cattle, humans began to get infected with variant BSE.

But what no one could understand was *how*. The natural firewall that prevented virtually every known disease from jumping between species proved impotent against this new pathogen.

Prions were nothing more than chains of amino acid molecules, lacking the genetic instructions for copying themselves. Although physically incapable of dividing to multiply like a bacterium or commandeering cellular replication like a virus, they used a simpler—and more deadly approach. The villainous protein would grab hold of a neighbouring protein and force it to assume its own shape. The new prion would also take on the same bullying behaviour.

Henderson had worked with prion diseases for ages, but only recently was he beginning to truly comprehend the mechanisms behind them.

Upon beginning his speciality in neuropathology in 1979, Henderson had often travelled from his home in Glasgow to work on a number of brain-related deaths at the Western General Hospital in Edinburgh. When the facility opened its now-renowned Creutzfeld-Jakob Disease Surveillance Unit in 1990, he accepted an invitation to become its first resident neuropathologist. It was all about helping people, despite the fact that the ones he worked with happened to be dead. He knew his research had contributed to some major progress made at the CJDSU in developing ways of detecting the disease and prolonging the lives of people who suffered from it. Perhaps their collective work would someday lead to a cure.

Here, though, the work had allegedly started out with a similar objective, but at some point had seen its focus altered. The data gleaned was often shared with researchers in facilities including CJDSU as promised, but that was no longer GATSER's *modus operandi*.

Prions were being mutated right beneath Henderson's feet. Just as medical research and defence budgets were blended in financing GATSER, decades of research was re-purposed within its facilities to create a weapon unlike any seen before.

Better than, the converted liked to say.

It needn't be an evil thing, he tried to tell himself. One had only to consider how many lives might have been saved if the food supply of Adolf Hitler and his "inner circle" been targeted with prions like those developed here!

The incubation period could be set to anywhere from weeks—if results were needed immediately—to decades if a large group were to be infected with no chance of early detection. With such a long incubation period, by the time the first people started showing symptoms, it could be ensured that every one of the targets had contracted the disease. And as long as no one consumed the dead bodies, there was virtually no chance of it being passed on.

It was a truly self-limiting weapon.

If it had been available sooner, such a thing could indeed have conceivably been used to stop Hitler—as well as Josef Stalin, Kim Il Sung, Mao Tze Dong or Saddam Hussein—avoiding the millions of terrible deaths caused by these men's regimes. Not to mention the countless civilian casualties of economic sanctions and war that surrounded them!

And the governments working on the project could be trusted, he reminded himself. *Couldn't* they?

He wanted to believe so. But what if someone else got hold of the technology? Unlike nuclear warheads or other WMD, prions were dreadfully easy to conceal and transport. Once they were acquired, anyone of means could arrange a method of delivering enough of the pathogen to infect a great many people.

It was this concept, he believed, that was the genesis of his nightmares. The crazed, twitching and convulsing figures that attacked him, ashen faces foaming from the mouths as the bodies piled up atop him. Only after the fourth or fifth recurrence did he realize that many of the faces bore ethnic similarities—including dark hair and eyes. Many of the men had long beards and prayer caps, and women wore dull-coloured gowns and headscarves—*hijabs*.

For God's sake, the victims were all Muslims.

But what was happening? Why were the dream people angry with *him?* He had never taken issue with Islamic people—or those of any particular faith.

The combined spasms and oral frothing, typical of seizures, carried an implication quite obvious to Henderson. They were dying of a prion disease. His worst fear was being realized in the dream, his subconscious mind alerting him to a terrible possibility. That the prion diseases being engineered by GATSER had frightening potential as a genocide tool.

And Muslims, through their adherence to the Koran, shared (as well as abstained from) many common foods, placing them among the easiest targets—and thereby possibly the most likely victims. Contaminate the food sources of the Middle East, Indonesia and South Asia, and you could wipe out nearly three-quarters of the world's Muslims. Henderson shuddered at the thought, not only the vast scope of such an atrocity, but because it struck close to home. His sister Heather had converted to Islam years ago. Her husband, Fayaz, was a devout Muslim and the best father one could wish for to Henderson's two delightful nieces.

He also had several Muslim friends and colleagues, with much to admire and not a thing to fear in the lot of them.

Whom might GATSER empower to carry out such evil?

Hard to say.

Unlike their Jewish brethren, the Muslim world had never fallen victim to a massive-scale genocide attempt that Henderson could think of. Sadly, if Jews were the target (which was a different, equally terrible concept), the suspect list might be longer. There was a growing number of well-organised and equally well-funded anti-Semitic organisations like al-Qaeda, Hezbollah, and Hamas, plus many neo-nazi groups from Aryan Nation to the White Order of Thule who would happily do away with the Jews, but Henderson could not think of a single anti-Islamic terrorist group. Even in Israel, lethal attacks typically went the opposite way—aside from those sometimes targeted against leaders of groups such as Hamas.

Most other significant religion-motivated attacks on Muslims typically came from other "cult" factions of Islam—such as *Sipah-e-Sahaba* and *Lashkar-e-Jhangavi*—terrorist groups in Pakistan known to kill Shia and Sunni Muslims alike. These were Wahabis, the Afghani faction of which were known by a more familiar name: the Taliban.

Henderson was certain there was no way GATSER, however corrupt it may have become, would collaborate with the likes of *them*.

Not that the idea of such a weapon had not in all certainty crossed the Taliban's mind—just not for use against other Muslims. When the U.S. army raided the al-Qaeda caves in Afghanistan searching for Osama bin Laden, hundreds of pages of American agricultural documents were found. To the CIA, the documents' existence might have made little sense. In the context of the potential of prion warfare, however, Henderson fully understood the implications.

There was another unbearable possibility: perhaps it could be a nation or alliance of nations—not a terrorist group—that might implement the genocide of Henderson's nightmares, in the name, say, of pre-emptive self-defence. Through a fomite vector—like a prion-infused rendition of the yellow packages dropped into Afghanistan by the U.S. military—any impoverished population could be enticed to unwittingly infect itself.

Although there were still plenty of crazy dictators around to fear, *none* of the governments involved in GATSER could claim an entirely clean conscience. The original three had collaborated on the only two atom bombs ever used against humanity.

Yes, even Canada—proud peacekeeper and human rights defender—had its own genocidal secret. Its British settlers had wiped out the entire population of Newfoundland's gentle Red Ochre people, butchering entire families and hunting the natives for sport. England had done it before, placing a bounty on Tasmania's aborigines, ultimately killing every last one. And Lord knew they'd tried to render the Scots extinct enough bloody times! Generations passed and times changed, but a people's nature was inherent, it seemed.

Little remained unsaid about the Americans when it came to looking out for their own interests. It seemed their leaders could justify *anything*. Quite sadly, public support of an attack against Islam was not something in dire need of cultivation.

That left Argentina and Brazil. Though the southern accomplices were apparently not full partners in the JV, they could be frightening enough in their own way. GATSER's South American division had so far proven a challenge to keep in check and had more than once gone so far out of line as to implement *human* mutilations, including one autopsied and widely reported case in Guarapiranga.

All of this said, Henderson could not believe that in these times, any civilised democratic government would set out to annihilate at once a race and a major world religion.

Could the recurring nightmare be nothing more than a dream, a manifestation of Henderson's own guilt combined with his ungrounded fears?

Or was it really a prophetic vision—of a fate that could not be allowed to realize itself, yet one already impossible to avoid?

CHAPTER 42

I STUDY THE MAP Jessica drew, wondering where the hell I am in relation to it. About every mile, a gravel range road runs north to south, intersected at twice that interval by perpendicular township roads. I wish I'd counted the ones I've passed, rather than contemplating the dreadfulness of my situation as I drove. I *think* I'm six miles north—and probably just short of a mile east—of St. Paul. But I could be four miles north. Or even eight. I do the math, multiplying by one-point-six to convert these numbers to Jessica's kilometres.

Too complicated. It seems the more I think about what to do—or try to actually *do* anything—the worse it all becomes. A week ago, the contact sheets aside, things were quite bearable. Now Craig and Isi are dead, with Len not far behind. I may be infected too, and I've got mysterious people threatening and probably *trying* to kill me. And the police want to throw my ass in jail. All except the one constable I've endangered by sleeping with her. If I thought I might see Jessica Bolduc again, it might give me something to hope for. But I must try to be realistic.

Also because of me, my best friend is about to board a red-eye flight to one of the most dangerous countries in the world. If Thomas and whatever other assassins don't get to her first.

And now—*NOW* I'm off to see if I can photograph a cattle mutilation in progress. If everyone is *really* lucky, I might get abducted by aliens.

*   *   *

I FINALLY find a farmhouse, complete with an ultra-ripe stink that assures me it's the one, and drive a distance up a narrow strip of gravel to a large pasture—packed with a good hundred head of white charolais. As white as a cow can be, that is. These animals sleep on muck and manure, and don't exactly groom themselves with feline diligence.

The young aspen trees around here are sparse, and I can't see a hiding place for a moped, let alone a Mustang. I carry on, until the road is crossed by a rickety fence about five hundred metres beyond.

It's been many years since I last opened a barbed-wire gate. This one is a kind I've used before: crudely built, with the most rudimentary of locking systems. The gate itself is a series of wooden fenceposts suspended by the tension of three braided steel wires. Tufts of yellowed cowhair are bundled on many of the barbs where cattle have rubbed themselves. It's hard to imagine aggressively scratching an itch on sharp metal spikes, but that's how tough cowhide is.

Two loops of smooth wire tether the gate's movable end post to the fence. I squeeze the floating post against the fixed one, and pop the top loop up and out of the way. Then I lift the gate free of the bottom loop. *Open sesame.*

I drive in, close the gate behind me, and motor into the field. The car's taut sport suspension is not cut out for off-road driving. I bounce on my seat so high that the top of my head bumps the ceiling several times.

Good thing I'm driving a rental.

I come across a rotting building with an open front, possibly once used as a woodshed. It's seen better years, but is just what the animal doctor ordered. Big enough to park a Buick in, but already partly occupied by an old steel-seated tractor. It's a Massey-Harris Pony like one Jack's father had restored—this specimen probably also from the late forties, but almost certainly rusted beyond rehabilitation. I'm not sure there is enough room beside the ancient tractor for even a car the Mustang's size.

My rural parallel parking proves better than in an urban environment though—the absence of spectators surely helps—and I've got her tucked neatly under the drooping roof with only a few small corrections.

Everything can stay where it is in the car except the disposable camera in the glove box—and I take the windproof fleece jacket from my overnight bag in the backseat. I pull it on, though I'm not feeling remotely cold. The temperature will surely drop while I wait. The camera fits nicely inside one of the jacket's zippered pockets.

I close the door gently—not so much out of fear of being heard as that I'm not sure what it would take to bring the old shed crashing down on top of me.

As I start off on foot, I am astonished at how still and quiet it is out here. Occasionally, I hear a despondent *mooo-aw* or the ominous cawing of an unseen crow, but there is otherwise no discernible sound. Then leaves on a nearby bluff of spindly aspens whisper in a breeze, and I shudder, though I should be warmer than ever walking in my cotton shirt and fleece.

I trudge from the clearing into the trees, stepping over fallen branches and the vital organs of long-dead machinery, left here ages ago to rust into oblivion. There will not be an abundance of hiding places, I confirm as I draw nearer to the penned-in cattle. *Where will I wait?*

There is a fairly new wooden structure close by, which I presume must be the one from which the landowner fired his shots last night. I'd expect the mutilators to check inside for him—or perhaps vaporise the building immediately. They might not know how scared he is.

This isn't going to be as easy as I expected.

But it didn't seem there could be much to it. I'd sit here a few hours, and hope something happened worth photographing. More truthfully, I'll hope nothing at all happens. Then perhaps I can allow myself to go back home in the morning. Solve this from there, or maybe just do what I can to forget. *Sometimes you just have to live with shitty things, Kat.*

I come to the barbed-wire fence that separates me from the cattle. The bottom two wires have barbs wrapped in clumps of hair, but the top one is completely smooth. I look at the wooden fencepost nearest me, and see why. The other barbed wires are stapled to the wood with U-shaped spikes, but the top one is seated on ceramic insulators. It's electrified. Good thing I didn't try crossing using *that* wire for balance.

I've been zapped by a fence once before, and it felt like being clocked by Mike Tyson. That was on a ranch just south of Saskatoon, where I stood in when the regular veterinarian was out of town, to help deliver a Hereford calf from a mom with a twisted uterus. The farmer was a cantankerous giant named Sean Shanahan, his size accentuated by an enormous waxed moustache and an equally oversized stetson hat. He was in a state of panic to begin with, augmented to borderline hysteria by his surprise at seeing me. Yammering like an auctioneer, Shanahan warned me that he'd already suffered three calving fatalities that spring, and could *not* afford another DOA. This while driving me out to the nearby pasture where a calf had been stuck for more than two hours in the birth canal.

The calf's head and front legs were out, he said, and from his description my guess was its hips were securely hooked over the mother's pelvic bone.

Shanahan parked his half-ton at the side of the highway, as near as he could get it to the cow, but neglected to mention that all three wires of his fence were electrified—still too caught up in voicing his disappointment at a rookie vet showing up to help. I spotted the cow and immediately made for her, Shanahan grumbling close behind as I glonged onto the topmost wire.

It was such a jolt, I thought the big walrus had punted me from behind. I turned and rang a fist off his slate-hard chest, the green canvas of his jacket abrading my knuckles. He didn't seem to feel it, and roared with laughter, saying he'd *electri-cised* the fence a week prior—after his cattle had perfected a method of busting out, twice causing accidents on the highway.

The calf's delivery wasn't to be easy. Shanahan and his blue heeler, Smokey, stood and watched as I tried rotating the frightened baby animal forty-five degrees in one direction, then the other. The hind legs appeared not to be turning along with the upper body, as it remained locked, partially born.

After twisting, tugging, and wrestling at length, I had Shanahan help me get the cow to lie on her side. With several eye-popping pulls, it worked.

While we watched the mother lick her weak but healthy calf, I urged Shanahan to keep Smokey from interfering. I explained to him that the amniotic fluid the cow was ingesting created an analgesic effect, easing her birthing pains. Then the dog's ears pricked up, and he tore off in pursuit of a big brown jackrabbit that had hopped into the pen to munch some spilled oats near a trough. I couldn't bear to watch the nature scene that followed. Soon, as Smokey proudly dragged the bunny's limp form toward the farmhouse, Shanahan boasted how the dog was a Natural Born Rabbit Killer, and sometimes rid him of two or three of the varmints in a week. I was barely able to hold back my tears.

Blue heelers are not big dogs, and Smokey had no problem fitting between the bottom and middle wires of the fence without making contact, but his kill got snagged. When the shock travelled through the rabbit's body and hit him, the dog let out a startled series of yips and made off. I chuckled to myself. He returned a moment later, snarled at the blood-soaked rabbit draped over the wire, then chomped angrily into it. With a yowl, Smokey ran all the way home.

When I ran into Shanahan a year later at a grocery store, he was quick to tell me the rabbit's corpse had remained on the fence wire until he removed it himself because it was weakening the current. Smokey never killed another rabbit, he said with dismay.

* * *

PICKING A spot midway between two fence posts, I place one foot on the bottom wire, and my weight is enough to sink it to the ground with a plaintive *ree-aark*. I reef upward on the middle wire, and squat under it with care not to let my hand come in contact with the electric one. I get through unscathed, and with nary a zap.

One of the big, off-white beasts has become bold enough to approach, and a few others follow behind, not wanting to miss out if I happen to have come bearing alfalfa.

"Sorry, girl, I'm empty-handed," She stares at me with huge, moist cow eyes. *What a beautiful animal.* The others gather around me in a deformed semicircle.

Which one of you is getting cut up today? I wonder silently. *Didn't Mama Cow ever tell you it's all good fun until someone loses an eye? Or her genitals?* I shake my head at the grim thought, and caress the first cow's muzzle near her wide, glossy pink nose, feeling her steamy breath. "Hi, baby," I say. "You're a friendly gal, aren't you?"

I stay with the growing assemblage of cattle a few minutes, and finally heed an inner warning that I ought to make an effort to be detached from the animals.

Making my way across a minefield of hoof craters punched deep into the hardened mud and cow-pies, I take care not to twist an ankle or slip on something fresh. Three times, I nearly tumble into the manure, muttering curses as I lurch and squint in the twilight, scanning for more reliable footing—then whispering thanks whenever I find some. My respect for cattle ranchers multiplies every time I go out into a minefield like this.

I am headed for a pile of toppled trees, to assess its potential as a lookout spot. The trunks were pushed, probably by a 'dozer, into this corner of the pasture to make a clearing, leaving a single long windrow. Some time ago, judging by the grey wood denuded of its bark and roots rain-washed clean of all but the odd great mass of clay. In the sediment that has collected between many of the parallel trunks, clusters of grass and some willow saplings grow. A red squirrel scurries the length of the biggest log and chatters at me, then relocates to a new spot midway up a standing poplar to give it to me some more.

I seat myself on a stump—and it disintegrates under my weight.

One look at the crumbled remains on the ground between my legs and I see why. Carpenter ants have consumed the wood from inside, leaving only a sawdust-filled husk that had the *appearance* of a stump. I leap back up in a panic upon seeing all the ants, and feel sharp stings to the exposed skin on the back of my waist. I swat wildly at my rear, envisioning it thick with the big black bugs, angry with me for flattening their home. It's a moment before I piece together enough equanimity to think straight. I've never been especially squeamish about insects in small numbers, but swarms of them freak me out. I twist to look for the little nippers, and find nothing but rust-coloured sawdust clinging to my jeans and the fleece of my jacket. Behind me, though, I see the sharp willow branches that speared me. The soft new growth has been chewed away, perhaps by the incisors of cattle—but more likely a moose, judging from how high up the pruning extends and the way some larger branches have been broken off. With their stilt-like legs, moose step right across fences like the ones here and tear down whatever tree limbs they desire.

I cover my bare waist, and move to a log protruding from the far end of the windrow that looks both clean and solid. Still, I give it a manual test before sitting down. Seems good.

The seat is a prime one indeed—not just for its stability, but for the view and cover it offers. From where I sit, all but the middle of my face would be concealed from anyone in the pasture. A small tree, whose roots are embedded between logs near my right elbow, provides a nice canopy of leaves over my head. I could hardly design myself a better camouflage. Even in full daylight, I would probably be hard to spot here, except from behind. With dusk's Cimmerian blanket settling heavily into place, no one will see me.

It's a rare comforting thought. I still don't actually know whom I'm hiding from, but I am quite certain that whoever it is, they would not treat a spy with kindness.

Assuming there really *is* anyone to hide from tonight.

The first hour or so I spend watching the cattle mill around, focusing on keeping my breathing slow and steady, pushing away negative thoughts. It's not easy. Nocturnal animals make many sounds you never hear in the daytime, and a surprising number of these I cannot identify.

Still, my mind tries to assign something it knows to each one. It attributes an eerie shrieking to a raven, simply because that particular corvid has an infinite repertoire of voices. They'll imitate anything—humans, dogs, cats, a squeaking gate, or an alarm clock. The raven becomes my catch-all for unknown noises.

An animal begins to whine and howl not far away, soon answered by another even nearer. The voices seem almost too deep for coyotes—this far north, they may be wolves. And they seem to be getting louder. Are they coming this way? *It's only a couple more ravens, Kat.*

Perhaps the cattle have taken a vote, as they now advance toward me as one. I try to spook them away with a cougar-like hiss. This seems only to intrigue them, so I resort to clapping my hands hard and yelling, "Shoo! Get lost!"

The herd lurches away. Minutes later, they approach more carefully. I make even louder noises, before they draw as near as before. That seems to do it.

The waiting gets more difficult. The log is no longer my easy chair—more like the hard plastic seats in a McDonald's, engineered to work in unison with the sub-comfort-level air temperature to prevent patrons lingering too long.

I've definitely outstayed the comfort rating of this log. My toes tingle, the onset of numbness from pressure on my sciatic nerve. I lean back to put most of my weight near the back of my butt, near my tailbone. This is fine for about five minutes, at which point it quickly turns so agonising that I decide numb toes were really not so bad. I move my meat off the log entirely, and go for a short walk. I do hope these mutilators come soon.

Maybe it's time for me to go. I've given it a fair shot.

I hear a drone in the distance, and my entire body instantly goes as taut as the rope at a Klump family tug-of-war.

It becomes louder, and I return to my post and scan the sky from between the leaves of my cover shrub, looking for any movement, anywhere. The starlight seems to intensify under my scrutiny, the Milky Way looking like a trail of white paint spatters from a loaded brush swung by the hand of God. The distant sound comes and goes, and I write it off as a noisy truck miles away. Aside from the coyote-ravens—which have toned it down somewhat—silence returns.

A while later, a faraway hum sounds promising. It seems to come from higher up, and I am soon certain it's an aircraft of some kind. The wingtip navigation lights, red on the port side and green on starboard, confirm that

I'm looking at a small airplane, single-engine from the throaty buzzing. It passes almost directly above me, with enough air under it that I know it won't be touching down anywhere nearby. After it's gone, I find myself feeling more disappointment than relief. Not that I have become interested in putting myself in greater danger, but nor do I care to suffer here all night for absolutely nothing. If there are to be cattle mutes tonight, *please* bring the damned things on!

For the moment, I stay put. My soft-tissue discomfort eventually turns into dull pain. Sitting in a different way or squatting above the log no longer offer relief, and I don't really care. Shivering has become my new obsession. I stand, then hop up and down for a while, but have to give this up when I notice it's troubling the herd. I straddle the log like a cowboy on his horse, and find this a nice change. It also enables me to arch my spine and lessen my exposure a little. Soon, my lower back starts to hurt.

It's got to be age. As a girl, I could sleep all night on the hardwood floor of my mother's bedroom, wrapped only in the wool blanket I dragged over from my own bed. Climbing in with Mom would get me sent back to my room, but I was usually good on the floor until morning. This wasn't without its own dangers. Once, I took a toe to the mouth. Mom was deeply sorry, until she found I was uninjured.

Now, not even a log as ergonomically accommodating as this beauty can offer anything to keep me happy for longer than a few minutes, though time is not something I have much of a grip on. I should have replaced my watch. How long have I been here? Hours, for sure. What a dumb idea.

At last, I decide to call it a night. All the pain, chill and numbness remain, but have given way to exhaustion as my predominant source of displeasure. I haven't slept properly in more than a week.

I try to stand, and go straight down. My legs are asleep, numb as posts. I haul myself back onto the log, and rub the deadened muscles. Got to get the sensation back. If not, I will surely drop a leg into an unseen hoof-shaft and snap my tibia and fibula. The way things are going, that's probably when the sky would fill up with lights.

The sky *is* getting brighter. Dawn will soon be near enough to provide the visibility I need for a safe departure. Then I will go. Into the car and straight to the airport, baby. Zaina has probably got my house all tidy, bless her, and my bed will be so soft and warm.

Pain and fatigue have softened my ambition, and I can't say I believe any more that I owe it to Craig or Isi or anyone else to probe the world's cow pastures for a truth that has never had anything to do with me. Why did Craig have to bring me into this?

What if this is all a hoax—a setup by Jack? Maybe Craig is still alive, laughing at me over beers in Lynn's trailer with Jack, Len and Isi. Watching me on a hidden webcam, right this fucking minute. The whole world might be watching, on some sick new reality TV show!

I catch myself looking for a spot in the logs that might be a good place to stash a small transmitter, and clench my jaw. I lean way forward and bounce my forehead lightly against the log above my knees. My first real bout of denial—and a fairly impressive one at that. *If only* it were nothing more than a great big practical joke.

"Easy, Kat," I grumble out loud. Must get some sleep soon.

I no longer trust my own reasoning. Do I hear the hum of another approaching aircraft? I dismiss the thought, but the sound gets louder. It's of a deeper pitch than the airplane, accompanied now by the heavy *wuppa-wuppa-wuppa* of big rotor blades. I glance upward, then bring both hands to cover my open mouth.

This can't be real, Kat. Relax.

CHAPTER 43

Six months ago

JEAN LETENDRE ENTERED THE autopsy suite later than usual. Henderson watched as his colleague sealed himself in, all suited up and masked. The suite was outfitted with two fixed tables: a standard rectangular one for humans, and an oversized circular slab custom-built with features to facilitate handling even the biggest grain-fed bovines. Out of principal, Henderson used that one for any animal, even ones that would be adequately served by the human table.

He had moved Carol's body from the autopsy cart to the appropriate fixed table, and made some preparations, then covered it again when he heard Jean enter the staging chamber. He hoped to prepare his colleague, limit as much as possible the kind of shock he'd himself experienced upon coming in here.

"Sorry I'm late, Dunc. Delayed again in the admin bin. Ready to rock and roll?" Jean spoke loud out of habit, to be heard through the hood. "Body block's in place?" He pointed to the vacant space on the countertop where the big rubber brick otherwise sat.

"It is. Initial measurements are down and I've drawn the fluids. There's something I must tell you before we begin, Jean. This will be a difficult one, but we'll have to reach within ourselves, gather up every ounce of our professionalism…"

Jean's eyes moved behind the glass of his hood, down to the covered body. "It's Carol. I know."

Henderson stepped back. "What? Why is it *I* didn't get any warning?" His eyes took on a wild expression.

"Hey, whoa. I had a chat with Director Weissmann just now, and he gave me the heads-up. Chopper dropped her off a couple hours ago. I think it's no secret Dr. Benson got more than a little bit loose with a whole pile of privileged info. Spilled the beans to an outsider, damn near ruined *everything*. Weissmann didn't come right out and say it's why she's on the slab, but we're not stupid, right? We all sort of knew what was going down. Dammit, you did too, Dunc. Quit fooling yourself."

"Good God, *no*. Who the hell did she talk to? *The New York Times*?"

"That might have been next. I hear it was some guy in town who was already nosy about our in-herd retrieval programme. From what I was told, sounds like *she* actually approached him."

"And blew herself. Oh, dear God. When did this happen?"

"Early last summer. June, I think. But symptoms only started eight weeks back."

Henderson's mind flashed back to the conversation he overheard in the Director's office in June of last year. The *information leak* was indeed Carol.

"And the gentleman Carol spoke to?" Henderson asked, already dreading the answer.

"We'll be seeing him by late summer, I'd say. Heard the boys are getting set to test a new dispersion idea."

"Heard from *whom*?"

"Admin bin chitchat. No big deal, Dunc. I only know because when he goes, I get the privilege of sweet-talking Mr. Funeral Director into some swapsies. One used cadaver for a fresh side of veal."

"*Sweet talking*?"

"Yep, and slide him a tip in the order of fifty large. We've got a working relationship. He'll do a little-sleight-of hand on his end, cremate the cow instead of the cowboy, and you and I can do another autopsy. All in a day's work."

"Bloody hell," Henderson said, shaking his head. Was there *anything* Jean wouldn't stoop to, couldn't somehow justify? Henderson whipped the sheet away from Carol Benson's pallid body, watching Jean's reaction. His blue-green eyes held nothing to read.

"What a shame," Jean finally said, still expressionless. "Let's get busy, pal."

"I caught Kyösti Talo in here today."

Jean shrugged. "Guess he can go anywhere he wants."

Henderson closed his eyes. When they opened again, they shot pure fury. "He was way the fuck out of line. I caught him here, touching Carol's body."

"Oh, *shit*. Have you done cavity swabs?"

"I don't think he penetrated her. But we'll do the swabs. If he did, it's damn well going in the report."

"We can't do *that*."

"Bloody hell we can't. What's wrong with you, man?"

"Just think about what you have to lose, that's all I'm saying." He leaned close to Henderson's ear and lifted the hood to uncover his mouth. Even so, it was hard to make out his words over the rumbling of the big ventilation fan. "Who do you think blew the whistle on Carol? It was Talo who planted the idea in her head of talking to that guy, and then hid a fly on her."

"A what?"

"Fly. A microtransmitter, so he could record the conversation."

"What the hell did he do that for?" Henderson roared.

"Quiet," Jean whispered, eyes big. "He had a thing for her. Everyone knew that. But time after time, she kept turning him down. Good looking guy like Talo isn't used to that. Word is, the asshole tried to force himself on her in this room, but she got her hands on a scalpel and put it to his throat."

"So he decided to off her? There has got to be more to it than that."

Jean shrugged. "Maybe for you or me there'd need to be. But I've seen how the fucking guy works. Textbook sociopath. Motivated solely by his hunger for glory and his own giant ego. And there's nothing worse for the male ego than rejection."

"Good *Lord*."

Jean gave Henderson a slap on the back. "Try not to think about it too much, pal. This'll be hard enough for both of us already."

*   *   *

JEAN MADE the thoracoabdominal incision, diverting the two upper cuts around the contours of the corpse's rounded breasts so that the arms of the Y were made up of two arcs. Together, the men worked with scalpels and brute force to strip the muscle, skin and soft tissues away from the chest wall. Henderson felt a certain amount of relief when Jean pulled the chest flap up to cover his dead colleague's face. Behind his respirator, he could not smell the delicate lamb-like scent of fresh human flesh, yet his mind recreated it perfectly for him. That and rot were two odours that never left you once you'd worked with them. There'd been many times when he could have sworn after washing several times he could still smell one or the other on himself, despite Mairi's assurances that it was purely his imagination.

He grimaced a little as the bone cutter crunched through rib after rib in making the two long cuts that would allow the entire chest plate to be lifted away. The two men systematically removed the organs from the chest cavity, working through from top to bottom. Jean expertly did the slicing necessary to remove the organ block from the trunk, and Henderson helped him to move it in one piece to the dissection table.

"I've got all this," Jean said. "Go ahead and pop open the brain box." Henderson reached up and grabbed a handle on the massive stainless steel exhaust hood—similar in appearance and function to the ones used over cooking grills in restaurants—and pulled it downward, allowing just enough clearance above the deceased's head to do his work. He turned a dial on the wall to MAX. The large fan that drew the morgue's air up through a series of ultra-fine filters immediately went from a throaty growl to a near-deafening roar.

It was normal for the men to work independently from this point on, though there were no hard and fast rules. Jean dissected the organs, weighing each on the autopsy meat scale and writing the numbers on a board, while Henderson moved on to the brain. His element.

He pried the rubber body block from beneath the empty chest cavity and positioned it beneath the head, temporarily uncovering the familiar face but trying not to look. He made a deep incision from the top of one ear across the dome of the scalp to the other, then wrestled with the tissue to peel the front flap down over the face and the back one down to the nape of the neck.

He used the Stryker saw to cut around the equator of the exposed cranium, going *almost* all the way through the skull, but not quite. A visual check confirmed that no brain tissue had been cut. Henderson used a T-shaped chisel aptly called the *skull-splitter* to part the halves, then, to the expected slurping sound, lifted the calvarium away and set it aside. The *dura mater*, literally the *tough mother* of the brain, came off nicely, leaving the glossy grey whorls exposed. He snipped the spinal cord and tentorium between the cerebellum and cerebrum, and lifted the brain out.

Under ideal circumstances, the brain would be fixed for a few weeks in a jar of formalin, which would give it the feel of ripe, slippery avocado flesh. At GATSER, Henderson had yet to be allowed such an extravagance. Fortunately, this brain was relatively firm. The last human one he'd worked on had fallen to pieces on the way out of the skull cavity.

Henderson severed the cerebellum from the brainstem, and then sliced the cerebrum into long strips. He began to prepare slides for the microscope, adding drops of pigment to make the holes and fibrils more pronounced. In many cases, this was needed to make a prion disease identifiable. With this specimen, the gaps and dark, gooey tissue bundles were sufficiently advanced for him to make a naked-eye diagnosis.

"What you got?" Jean said.

Henderson grimaced behind his mask. "You've heard me say it before, but I've truly never seen anything quite like this one. You sure *this* only took eight weeks from onset of symptoms?"

"That's what the Director told me," Jean said, bending to take a close look. "Holy Christ, Dunc. Want me to do the blots?"

"Please," Henderson said. Western blot tests were the standard way of charting prions, dividing proteins into three vertical and forty horizontal bands based on their composition. It was tedious work, and while Jean began, Henderson busied himself writing notes, then began dictating the findings.

"The body is that of a well-nourished, well-developed Caucasian female, thirty-eight years old..."

"Make that *very* well-developed," Jean said with a smirk.

"Don't you fucking start with me," Henderson snarled.

"Just trying to keep things light."

"You just don't *get* it, do you? There's not a damned thing light about what's happening."

"Listen, Dunc. You and I have our jobs to do here. Neither of us understands the whole scope of what goes on in this place, and believe me, it's better that way."

Henderson nodded. "We both know that Carol's body is on this slab to drive that very point home to us. Or to me, at least."

Jean nodded, then pointed with an index finger to his ear and waved his hand across the room. The message was clear. *Be more careful what you say.* The fan still roared, but it was probably good advice nonetheless.

Henderson continued his dictation, holding the little recorder close to his lips, white noise filter on. "The body weighs fifty-eight kilograms and measures one hundred seventy two centimetres from crown to sole. Hair on the scalp varies from light brown to blonde." He cursed, then returned to the cadaver, where he rolled the front scalp flap back a few centimetres. He peeled back the eyelids and looked carefully at each of Dr. Benson's eyes. "Eyes are hazel, pupils fixed and dilated."

* * *

JEAN FINISHED the blots and placed representative parts of each organ, including the larynx and thyroid, in a solution of ten percent formaldehyde.

"Anything noteworthy on the organs?"

"Everything more or less unremarkable," Jean said. "No sign of sexual entry, if that's what you're after. Some ventricular enlargement, consistent with atrophy. Want to grab a bite?"

Henderson repeated the part about the enlarged heart chambers into his voice recorder, then shook his head at Jean's offer. It was in fact very normal for a seasoned pathologist to have a strong appetite after an autopsy. "I'll just grab a PowerBar. I need to lie down for a bit before I try to take on this bloody report."

CHAPTER 44

THE LIGHTS REMIND ME of the ones at Royal Athletic Park two years ago, when Jack took me to see the Victoria Capitals play host to his beloved Saskatoon Legends. I've never been much of a baseball fan—I can tell you who won that night based only on Jack's foul mood afterwards—but I was truly impressed by how the steel trees of lights illuminated the whole ballpark. The cow pasture is much the same way, bright as day. The omnidirectional top lighting here is different from daylight, though. It's an icy blue-white, and stencils the blackest of shadows under the motionless bovines. I expect the animals to scatter at any instant, but they do not. Perhaps they are as terrified as I am. Deer in the headlights, all of us.

I've almost forgotten—pictures!

I unzip my jacket's pocket and pull the little camera out, then move in tighter to the bundle of timber that hides me from the helicopter's view. Making sure the flash is off, I snap a few shots of it. The wind from its rotors blasts my eyes and fills the air with particles of dirt and dung. The cows seem less stunned now, and glance about nervously, probably looking for somewhere to take refuge. The one nearest to me—a big one—takes a few awkward steps, and I sense a flood of panic surging through the rest of its mob.

Then something drops from the helicopter with a resonant clatter, and one animal collapses, the others around it scattering simultaneously. Normally, cattle stampede as a group, preserving the safety of numbers. Here, it's every cow for herself. I'm taking another picture of the helicopter as a pair of them charge past me, and there is a crash as one stumbles over a log, rocking the entire windrow I'm sitting in and throwing up a heavy cloud of crud. I cough, but can't even hear it over the helicopter's roar. A third animal comes racing around the back of the log pile, so close to me that I get a solid whiff of its pungent hide.

When I look back to the pasture, raising the camera for another shot of the fallen animal, I see it is no longer on the ground. A pair of harnesses have been locked around its abdomen, a narrow loop around the brisket and a more substantial one just ahead of the hind quarters. I get a shot of the cow, its head hanging slack as the distance steadily increases between its swinging hooves and the pasture below. I've seen cattle lifted on livestock slings before—to relocate them after suffering birth paralysis or milk fever—but this is different. The slings of my experience were either wide belts of PVC or bulky steel-and-canvas mechanisms, both of which had to be manually attached to the fallen cow, then suspended at the front of a tractor by a hydraulic lift. The ones here must have attached themselves automatically upon contact. And from the way the animal collapsed, they must have somehow stunned it at the same time.

The cow's form blocks out the light source, and I see nothing but its dark silhouette against a brilliant back-glow.

Total eclipse of the moo.

Then a growing crescent appears beneath its abdomen, and I get one more photo just as the cow disappears inside. It's not terribly far away, but with the camera's wide fixed lens and questionable optics, some skillful enlargement will no doubt be needed to make anything of this shot.

The bright lights go off, leaving only greenish highlights on two oval faces that hover above the cow in the doorway. The helicopter begins to move away even before its catch is fully inside. I am overcome by a sense of relief, until it occurs to me that they will be back. That's how it works, isn't it? They take the parts they want, and return the rest.

As I wait, I begin to shiver erratically. Has the temperature suddenly dropped? God, I've got to get out of here. I'm terrified, frozen and revolted, and I've got my pictures. I stand, and just as I step away from my hiding place, I hear the helicopter's rapid drumming again. What was that, five minutes? These guys work too damned fast.

Where the navy-blue sky is now turning orange to the north-east, I see the helicopter's black insect-like silhouette rise above the treetops and grow larger. I let out a sigh, and sit back down.

It hovers over the precise spot where it was before—*a creature of habit?*—and begins to descend. This time, the lights stay off. When the aircraft is no less than ten metres from the ground, the cow emerges from its side door.

I snap a picture of it hanging limp in the harness, spinning as if on a swivel. This might be the best shot I've taken, provided it's well enough exposed to show anything. *If only the lighting was better.*

There is a clatter, and the cow drops fast, meeting the dirt with a sickening *phulp.* The helicopter descends halfway to the ground, then lurches in my direction. I feel a blast of chilly air as the stabilising rotor swings downward and the aircraft draws back slightly. It plunges to the ground, just the other side of my windrow. A pounding in my chest is heavy and rapid, and I don't even know if it is my heart or the rotors.

Two men in dark suits and matching knit caps leap out the open side door. One is tall and thin, and the other much heavier set. The heavy one barks an order, and they split apart. I understand immediately that the plan is to come at me from both sides, so as not to allow me an out. I dart off in the only remaining route, straight opposite the helicopter. Maybe I can make a sweeping turn and end up somewhere near the cowshed where the Mustang is parked.

I run for it.

"Get back here!" one of the men bellows over the din in a voice that seems vaguely familiar.

"We'll shoot!" booms the other.

I glance over my shoulder. Both men have rounded the windrow, the slim man already a bus length ahead of the heavier one—putting him perhaps three or four times that distance behind me. Neither appears to have a weapon in his hand. *They're bluffing!*

I hope.

I come to the barbed-wire fence, which I'm hoping will act more in my favour than in that of my pursuers. I go for a fencepost, where the wires have the best support, springing up off the middle one to get my other foot to the top of the post. A stabbing pain in my arch tells me a barb has punched through the rubber, hooking into my flesh. It grabs enough to wreck my balance, and the camera goes flying as I grab the top wire to throw myself forward. A jolt of current paralyses me, and I hit the ground in a heavy tumble.

Dazed, it takes a few seconds to gather my senses. Seeing the first dark figure draw near in my peripheral vision helps. I stumble to my feet, and, seeing the yellow camera, grab it. Within eight or ten strides I'm moving pretty good. Perhaps a little electricity helps.

A quick over-the-shoulder glance tells me that my pursuers are even less adept at fence-climbing than I am. The slim one is attempting to wrestle free the leg of his suit from the barbs and just learning about the top wire when the other arrives.

"Fucking thing's electric!" he shouts. Both men spout curses befitting of two villains.

I run harder. My lungs feel constricted, and a sour, coppery taste rises into my throat. My thighs are on fire. I trip over something—*a root?*—but miraculously manage to keep upright despite several exceptionally graceless steps.

A tree clips my shoulder, and I am thrown into a full-on tumble, clutching the camera to my chest like a running back holds a football. I stuff it in my pocket, and try to pick myself up, willing my body back upright, but I seem to have lost track of which way that might be.

My fall seems to motivate a burst of speed in the slim man, and he is suddenly upon me. In the dim light, I get a look at his face for the first time.

Beneath the dark cap are cheekbones, piercing eyes, and the outline of a goatee. And when he swings his head to look for his partner, a thick ponytail whips from the back.

Stompin' Tom.

"Don't move!" he barks, his hands reaching for my neck.

Instinctively, my foot drives for his groin. It connects beautifully, and my attacker grunts and folds in half, then begins to topple in my direction. I try to roll clear, but he comes down hard on top of my right knee. I can't help but whimper softly, tears of anguish filling my eyes as I wrestle the leg free of his weakened grip.

"Thomas, you asshole," I gasp, trying to get up. It hurts.

He grimaces at me. I wonder if it's out of anguish, rage, or shame. Then his hand shoots out at the ankle of my hurting leg. I manage to kick it beyond his reach, then roll further out of the way.

Picking myself back up, I hear the other man's ragged breathing behind me. Between gasps, he manages the word, "Freeze."

I opt not to.

Off my good leg, I lunge back to my feet, and try to run. Searing pain seizes my knee and shoots upward, nearly knocking me back to the ground.

I can see the woodshed where my car is stashed. With two good legs, I'd be

BRAD STEEL

just seconds away. I manage a few more agonising strides before my feet go
out from under me. I'm lying face down in bent grass, and it takes a moment
to realize I have been tackled.

"Stay put, for Christ's sake," Thomas wheezes. He crawls up over me, and I
feel his hard elbow in the middle of my back. There's a metallic jingling, then
he grabs one of my wrists and slams cold, hard steel against its bones. Then
the other.

"Doesn't look like I've got much of a choice." Even as I say it, though, my
mind is racing, and I'm searching for even the briefest, least likely opportunity.
I doubt Stompin' Tom will give me another clear shot at his groin.

"Just don't you fucking move." He raises his voice: "Eddie, call for Derek to
bring the helo. No way I'm carrying her ass back over that fucking fence."

The other man is near now, one hand at the base of his ribs. "Runner's
stitch," he says, as if to exonerate the hundred or so extra pounds he's
carrying. He pulls a small device from a belt clip, punches some buttons, and
studies a glowing display. He barks into the same unit, "Come get us, Derek.
Me and Jean nabbed 'er. Six hundred forty metres north-northwest, plenty
of space for you to set down."

CHAPTER 45

Four days ago

HENDERSON WAS RELIEVED *NOT* to recognise the face of this new man who lay on the table. In spite of the inevitable wasting from having been fed intravenously after loss of consciousness, the subject remained reasonably well-muscled. He had been young—probably in his mid thirties, Henderson guessed. The deceased man's hair, the golden colour of ripened wheat, had no white in it, and the only wrinkles on his skin were the start of crow's feet and two straight creases across his brow. Thirty-five, the tag confirmed. No name was given. Treated by Dr. Donald Samuelson, expired Monday—that's three days ago. Normally they got here much quicker than that—must have been complications with this one.

A youthful cadaver was sadly nothing unfamiliar to Henderson. Many of the ones he had examined in Edinburgh were in their late teens and twenties. One was only twelve—a boy named Michael Donovan. The disease had taken young Mike in only nine weeks, yet the fibrils it had manufactured in his cerebellum during that short time were awe-inspiring. Of course, that was before Henderson had come to work here. Mike's had been an *unintentional* exposure.

The sealed door creaked open behind him.

"Morning, Jean," Henderson said.

"Good morning." The voice startled Henderson, though he recognised the accent immediately. He turned and focused on the elegant, chiselled features of Kyösti Talo. *Oh, Jesus. Not now.*

Henderson had managed to steer clear of Talo since the day of Carol's autopsy. The mere thought of the bastard was still enough to fill his space suit with steam.

"What do you want?" Henderson said, taking a step toward Talo, to keep him from advancing any closer to the cadaver.

Talo laughed. "Relax, doc. I've got something to share with you."

"I don't think so. I choose not to hear anything you have to say."

"You sound very sure of that. Why not give me a chance? I expect you'll change your mind."

Henderson's cheeks reddened, his head sweeping slowly from side to side. "Out. Get *out!*"

Talo smiled, and raised his hands shoulder-high in capitulation. He looked down at the cadaver. "You know, I just saw this fellow's old college squeeze. Not bad looking."

"I don't want to know," Henderson said, scratching nervously at the skin of his neck. Noticing Talo's eyes were still on the cadaver, Henderson reached into the pocket of his lab coat and pressed a button on the side of the digital voice recorder that he used for dictating lab notes.

Talo looked up—just as Henderson withdrew his hand—and continued, "Director Weissmann sent your associate Jean on a West Coast kayaking trip with a former sweetheart of our dead chum here. Kat Francis is her name, a veterinarian. Very *nice*. She received a package from him, part of the ongoing ripple effect from Dr. Benson's bad behaviour. Mute photos, keying in on some of our procedural changes. Accompanied, I was told, by something of a deathbed exposé. So while Jean was off playing watersports with Kat, I paid a visit to her clinic in Victoria. Wasn't there, so I tried her household. Nice place. Have to admit I left it in a bit of a mess. Never did find the blasted note. Bitch must have destroyed it."

Talo stepped around Henderson and tapped an index finger on the dead man's forehead. "I'd like you to meet Craig Butler. He was your friend Dr. Benson's outside confidant. Was looking like he might just keep his mouth shut to the end. Turned out he got someone else to take Kat Francis his little package. Of course, in no time *she* started nosing around. The Director's solution was fine, but badly executed. Jean performed a small downgrade on her kayak, slipped her a hallucinogen, and took her out paddling in a riptide. She was as good as gone. But seems she ingested a partial dose of the drug, and the tour guide—a friend of hers—proved unexpectedly heroic. And like sand through Jean's fingers, she slipped *away*..." He let his voice trail off dramatically.

Henderson reluctantly bit. "Away to where?"

"Home to Victoria. And now she's coming here. Isn't that nice?"

"What the hell do you mean, *here?*"

Talo grinned, leaving Henderson to contemplate this a moment. "She spent the night at a friend's home. Jean tailed her to the airport. Direct flight to Edmonton International."

Henderson's back stiffened. "Christ. How much does she know?"

"Just enough to be sure she's sitting on something *big*. So far she doesn't even appear to have learned the fate of her old flame here. But once that happens…"

Henderson bit his lower lip.

Talo shook his head, but continued to smile cruelly. "And it all comes back to Dr. Benson and *this* naughty boy."

"Which is my business, not yours."

"Oh, it's mine too. I had the task of getting him to you. It was more complex than you may think."

"You injected the prion?" Henderson said, a leading question. It was fast becoming clear that Jean had spoken the truth.

"That would have been my preference. But they wanted to test a new method. Aerosol particulate. I don't think it's got a future, frankly. Particles have to be a very specific size, between one and five microns. Anything smaller gets exhaled, and bigger than that and they get hung up in the upper respiratory tract and washed out by mucous. So I erred on the side of prudence, something our Jean could stand a lesson in. Installed a twenty-litre dispersion unit in the furnace, and a miniature version in his jeep. Overkill, quite literally. Both units put out nicely, powered by fuel cells. Which reminds me, I've been meaning to return and take them out. Hasn't been easy, with the new programme here and then my blasted field trip. Suppose today will have to be the day, with company coming. You know, I captured the installation on video with my handheld. I'll be sure to send you a copy."

"That's quite alright. Please don't."

"Oh, you *must* be interested to know what's going on in your place of employment, are you not? I'll leave you to work now. Perhaps you'll be seeing the old girlfriend soon. *I* certainly hope so." Talo said, then snorted and turned away.

"I beg of you, Mr. Talo. Please don't share these things with me any more. I'm just a doctor in the morgue."

"Just thought you might like to know. Careful, though, Duncan. A little knowledge is a dangerous thing. Here more than anywhere."

Henderson could feel a build-up of sweat on his brow. He sensed Talo was making reference to his upcoming meeting. Weeks ago, Henderson had booked a couple of hours with the very busy Director Weissmann, to talk about some issues. The date selected by Weissmann's officious EA had seemed distant at the time, but was now only a few days away. He was planning to give his resignation—and would use the opportunity to speak candidly at last about Talo.

Henderson had tried to think of a way to lock all the cadavers safely away, but nothing could be out of the reach of GATSER Northwest's Security Director. Perhaps the incident with Carol was an isolated one—indeed nothing but Talo's sick way of getting the final word, massaging his bruised ego. It seemed too much to hope. The man had been too casual about it. On top of all else that distressed him here, Henderson could not work with an unrestrainable necrophile on the premises. *Had Talo somehow learned of the meeting?*

For certain there were pathologists who regarded dead human bodies as nothing more than slabs of meat, but to Henderson, each was still the mortal coil of a real person, deserving of every dignity that could be afforded them. Throughout his career, he'd taken his fair share of ribbing about lewd relations with corpses. Henderson had always tolerated the jokes. They were merely words, and ones unworthy of his consideration.

It was impossible not to take *some* interest in the subject—however unsavoury, it was grotesquely intriguing. He had read that more than half of known necrophiliacs worked as medical examiners and morticians, and could think of a few suspect individuals—whom he did his utmost to avoid—he'd met at conferences and in hospital morgues. He'd heard of various bizarre cases over the years, including that of an Italian gravedigger who admitted to violating hundreds of corpses. It was in fact an ages-old depravity: the Greek historian Herodotus reported that ancient Egyptians kept the bodies of their beautiful deceased wives at home until decomposition was severe, to discourage embalmers from ravishing them. And according to legend, after King Herod executed Mariamme, the most beloved of his ten wives, he continued to have *relations* with her for seven years.

Such things were hard to imagine, even—perhaps *especially*—to a man accustomed to working with the dead. But how would Talo—a glorified security guard—develop such a nefarious obsession? Perhaps, as with so many things, Henderson did not want to know. He wished to Christ he'd never known this hellhole existed.

It had become unbearable—and now...

Now Talo had crept into his nightmares.

CHAPTER 46

I HEAR AN ENGINE fire up in the distance, and the heightening whine of it gaining velocity. It isn't long before I'm hit by a blast of wind from above as the darkened helicopter comes over us low, headed for a large treeless area near the woodshed. An instant before its skids touch the ground, any notion of escape vanishes as the old wooden structure crashes down on top of my car.

"Where's the camera?" Stompin' Tom—now *Jean*—demands.

"What?" I'm astonished that he could possibly know I've been taking pictures. He begins to pat me down vigorously, his hands groping considerably higher than necessary.

"Try the pocket of my jacket," I say.

He grins at me as he tosses the camera to Eddie.

* * *

THE HELICOPTER'S interior is illuminated only by green strip lighting along the edge of the floor, plus the soft glows emitted by wall-to-wall video screens and digital displays. I stumble inside after Eddie and ahead of Jean, dizzy from terror and the stabbing pain in my knee. Jean shoves me down onto a round stainless-steel platform with a number of different sized straps built into it. They look like they're made of polypropylene webbing, like automotive seat belts. Smears of mud and blood, puddles of spumy drool, and tufts of cow hair are all over it. "Keep a close eye on her," Jean says to Eddie. "I gotta chew the fat with Derek."

The platform shifts under me just enough to confirm that it's a rotating turntable, now locked in place. Makes sense. A lazy-susan style of table would make it easy to operate on one part of a large animal using equipment fastened out of necessity to the floor, then move quickly to another. Arranged around the platform are three bulky consoles, one of which I can see clearly from this perspective, with a robot arm extending from its side. At the end of this is what looks like a microkeratome—a laser scalpel. Nestled in form-fitting compartments on a large tray angled toward me are traditional steel scalpels, along with vessel clamps, a Maryland dissector, obstetrical forceps, biopsy punches, ovariectomy hooks, emasculators for castrating, and a couple of nasty looking implements whose function I don't even want to guess. Above me are a pair of hinged arms, each supporting the kind of halogen dome heads used in operating rooms. The lamp closest to me has seven bulbs—one at the centre, encircled by six more—and the other has four.

On the wall are brackets holding towel clamps and sponge forceps in place. Overtop of these, a green LCD panel reads 63.451 KG.

My weight. Am I on the table simply out of convenience? Or to be dissected? Perhaps just to make me wonder.

The entire rear of the long cabin is a big white machine with an arched portal at the bottom. A set of heavy-duty tracks holding the machine to the ceiling extend to overhang the turntable, apparently designed to allow it to ride right over the patient. I'm guessing an MRI magnet or a CT scanner. Not far from that is a big black crane, mounted via a swivelling platform to its own rail system, this one bolted to the floor.

This is what they use to lift the cows. It's retracted now, but I can see it is outfitted with an arm that would telescope when it rotates, to make it project outside. The mechanisms of this thing are unbelievably intricate, and are surrounded by hydraulic cylinders, hoses, and several modules that look something like security cameras. The cow harness still hangs from the end, the two beefy swing-locking mechanisms open at their hinges. I'm guessing it works something like the handcuffs on my wrists: the two loops are cantilevered near the top so that on contact with a cow, the curved lower segments are knocked skyward, flipping up over the top hinge. Then gravity would pull them down around the target animal—while being engaged in a ratchet mechanism. Before she knows what hit her, the cow is locked in and ready to lift. There's probably a high-powered cattle prod built in, from the way tonight's victim went all limp.

Inside the cockpit, two men sit with their backs to me. The one to the right is Jean. Behind them—on opposite sides of the cockpit partitions—are a pair of black leather seats, positioned for operating individual keyboards as well as dozens of switches and buttons. Eddie sits in the one behind Jean, alternating between monitoring me and looking out the window, into the distance.

Each of the computers has its own widescreen display, the one at the empty chair giving a frozen bird's eye view of glowing green cattle, and the one near Eddie displaying what looks like a colourised magnetic resonance cross-section of a bovine cranium. Jean returns, takes the vacant seat, and slaps a few keys. At the edge of his screen, I now see a view from above of a seated person.

Me.

I'm embarrassed at how plainly visible I am, all hunkered down and presuming myself hidden. Like a silly pup hiding his head.

"Smile," Jean says, clearly enjoying my alarm. "See how good you look?" He drags his finger across a trackpad. A rectangle appears around my form, and it moves with me to the centre. He taps the pad, and the rectangle grows to fill the display. Two more quick taps, and the image becomes animated. I can see myself fidgeting, then suddenly drawing back. A moment later, the on-screen me raises the camera and starts to shoot.

I am stunned by the clarity of the image, and how the brightness varies from one part of my body to another depending on the intensity of my body heat. The viewing angle changes as the helicopter descends, and there's a bounce when it touches down. Then the image of me runs away and two other glowing figures take after it.

"Green suits you," Jean says. "It could render you in any colour, but green is best because it doesn't make our pupils constrict, so we can still see if we have to run out in the dark," Jean says. "Excellent quality, isn't it? Thermal imaging, digitally enhanced on the fly. Best night vision technology there is. It can see the heat of your footprints half an hour after you make them."

"Spotted you on the initial approach," Eddie says. "Can see inside a building too, if the operator is paying attention." This is directed at Jean, and I assume it to be a reference to last night's snafu.

Jean gives him a look, and grins at me. "This is our second visit for the same cow, and be damned if we weren't going to get her. Last night, we got *shot* at, for fuck sakes. But you know that. Got connections, haven't you?"

I ignore the question. The last thing I want to do is betray Jessica.

Jean continues: "I knew it was you. Heard you were in the area. I told Eddie you wouldn't be going anywhere 'til we came back. You're too damn *curious*. Got to understand you pretty good on our little adventure, didn't I?"

The word *curious* slaps at me, all but confirming it was Jean who spray-painted my motel wall, though I don't want to flatter him by mentioning it. "I guess so," I say, my voice shaky. "That's because *I* didn't lie about who I was."

"Shit, Kat. I sort of *had* to use a different name, and I made up the bit about selling insurance. But what I told you about my military past was all true. It's what got me picked for this job when I was still in Med school."

"You're a doctor?"

He smiles, a glimmer of pride in his blue-green eyes. "I'm an oncologist-pathologist-immunohistochemist."

"You left out *assassin*."

"Guess you can't take the soldier out of the boy. Really *is* nice to see a bit of action now and again. And the military training makes me unique enough to get the odd outdoor assignment.

"Like raiding my motel room," I say. "And following me to Edmonton . You killed Isi Butler, you rotten fuck." A surge of rage seems to take the edge off my fear. I want to throttle Jean.

He smiles. "Guilty on the first charge, but no, not *that*. You're the one I was after—all along. The Butler girl was one of my colleagues' doing. And he *is* one rotten fuck. You'll have the good fortune of meeting him, and see first-hand."

"But *you* drugged me. And tried to get me drowned."

He laughs. "A little bit of E in your hot cocoa was all. Damn rude of you not to drink it all. Listen, Kat, I was there to achieve one of two things. Recruitment, or removal. Remember our little campfire chitchat?"

"*That* was your best shot at recruiting me to work for you? Asking me if I'd sacrifice my loved ones for a good enough cause?"

"No. That was when I determined you weren't suitable. We could have found a place for a good smart vet here, but you'd have to be willing to get your hands dirty. Squish a few grapes. And it was pretty damn clear you couldn't. We've put up with enough fucking bullshit from people who don't dig the corporate philosophy."

"Sorry I didn't make the grade. So then why the flowers?"

"That wasn't work-related." He winks at me. I glare back, and he roars, loving it. "Obviously I wasn't done with you yet. You hadn't signed on with us, but you were still breathing. If you hadn't hopped that damn plane, guess I'd have tried harder to court you. Create another opportunity to fulfill my assignment. Matter of fact, I was planning to take you on a fishing trip."

"I don't fish."

"Doesn't matter," he says, deadpan. "You would have been the anchor."

"Alright, enough true confessions already," Eddie booms. "The bitch is a goddam terrorist."

"Whatever," Jean says with a wave of his hand. The playful smile returns to his lips. "Not like she's going anywhere, right? She's been fucking FFD for like a week."

"*FFD?*" I repeat.

"Flagged For Deletion."

How enchanting. These people have created their own acronym for such a thing.

* * *

"WHERE ARE you guys taking me?" I give in and ask.

"You'll see," Eddie says, shooting Jean a look that warns not to divulge anything further.

"Back to the ranch," Jean says, ignoring a glare of even greater severity. "Where we take all the toxic bovines."

"Except the ones you drop. Why do you do that?"

Jean chuckles. "The sixty-four thousand dollar question. I'll tell you why, you *lucky* girl. It was never part of the original plan, actually. We used to just incinerate them. But back in the early seventies, a few loose cannons down stateside started dumping the odd one. Just for kicks, they said. They were disciplined, with alarming severity even to an old warhorse like me. Only afterwards it was discovered that the results were quite positive."

"How's that?"

"The first ranchers who found the mutilated remains kicked up a fuss—and became laughing stocks. Same time, a phenomenon began. We became *alien* mutilators to all who believed. Up 'til that point, our risk of being exposed was big. Sampling needs had become dangerously high. But by dropping a few carved-up carcasses here and there, we made the quantum leap from clandestine to *supernatural*. A realm only a balked minority will admit buying into."

"So you hide behind people's doubts and insecurities."

"Yep. Simple as hell, but it's worked for decades. The mutes reported are a very small fraction of what we do. No one *believes*." He snorts, and turns away.

Outside, the sky is becoming light. Sunrise must be only minutes away. Jean goes back to his computer, and Eddie no longer takes his eyes off me at all.

It can't be more than a minute later when the helicopter banks to one side, enough that I get a good look at a fenced-in compound on the ground below us, the electrical lighting all around it remaining effective despite the impending daybreak. It's a sprawling, roughly T-shaped building, with a number of gigantic silver vessels around it and a singular windowless tower on one end—all contained within an enclosure of chain-link fence topped with barbed coils.

In the yard of the compound, a large square area suddenly becomes brilliantly illuminated. A yellow ring marks the helipad's periphery, and we hover momentarily above it, then descend.

As soon as we touch down, Eddie jumps out of his seat, evidently making a point of getting to me ahead of Jean. "Up," he says, reaching around me to give a hostile jerk of the handcuffs. In agony, I struggle to my feet.

"Guess I'll carry the histology specimens," Jean says. "Lock her in the kennel Weissmann uses for his big dumb mutt. I don't want her downstairs."

"We should gag her."

"Nah. The factory's loud," Jean says, then scowls at me. "But any noise gets you that, plus a bonus ass kicking." He slaps Eddie on the back. "On that note, maybe put some duct tape on those legs of hers, before anyone else gets kicked in the boys."

Jean picks up a box that looks like a large plastic cooler. I presume it contains the parts that have been excised from the bovine victim. The helicopter door glides open, and he sets it by the doorway, then climbs out before picking it up again.

I soon wish Jean had escorted me. Eddie is a brute. He shoves me out of the 'copter, and then jerks back up on the handcuffs so I trip over the skid. Then he shoves me forward again. The metal cuffs cut into my wrists as he uses them to lift me up.

"Don't fuck around with *me*," he says. "I don't go for that."

Jean stops at the building and sets down his load to open a steel door. He props it open with the box.

"Ladies first," he says.

"What—what's going to happen?" I ask, an irrepressible shiver of fear cutting through my words.

Eddie smiles. "Know what we do here?"

"Animal experiments?"

"Yeah, down below. Up on the ground floor, we make dog food."

"So you're going to put me in the food?"

He gives me a sly smile. "Think so. But first I'm thinking there might be a little fun to be had."

CHAPTER 47

HENDERSON DRANK THE BITTER cafeteria coffee in gulps, chasing each with a swallow of bottled mineral water. Last night had been another sleepless one, followed by a miserable five-kilometre jog before leaving for the office. It had felt more like a death march.

He seldom drank coffee, but today exercise alone would not be quite enough to keep him alert—and the cafeteria had nothing but caffeine-free mint and jasmine teas in stock. Canadians didn't know squat about tea. It didn't help that the altitude here, at more than six hundred metres higher than Glasgow, was too high to brew a good pot. Water boiled at ninety-six degrees—not hot enough to release the more complex flavours.

He peeled open the foil wrapper of a chocolate-flavoured PowerBar, and bit in. The hard, sticky bar removed some of the lingering taste in his mouth, but plenty of bitterness remained elsewhere.

A handful of other workers shared the cafeteria with him now, all of them keeping to themselves the same as he tended to, or huddling quietly in small groups to discuss secrets. He did not notice the figure approaching until a chair beside him skittered away from the table on its back legs.

Talo spun the chair around, and plopped down, crossing his forearms atop its back. Henderson closed his eyes tight for a moment. Having other people looking on took his uneasiness with Talo to a whole new level.

"Mr. Talo. Everything okay in the security world?" A quiver in his voice spoiled the attempt at sounding casual.

"Excellent, Doc." The characteristic element of cruelty that often exuded from Talo's perfect smile was present now, and Henderson presumed that things were truly *not* well at all.

"Good to hear. I'm just finishing a quick coffee and energy bar here. I recommend it."

"My doctor tells me coffee is bad for the heart," Talo said with a shrug. "Perhaps it's a matter of opinion."

"Perhaps a person has to have one," Henderson grumbled.

"Pleasantries aside, are you aware that we're expecting a special guest?" Henderson looked away. He slid his chair back.

Talo continued. "Apparently our Mute team discovered a *voyeuse* on the early morning run."

"A voy*euse*?" Talo's deliberate invocation of the feminine piqued Henderson's curiosity in spite of his impulse to escape.

Talo nodded. "The very one Doc Letendre allowed to slip away in the Pacific Ocean not long ago. The boys just radioed that they picked up Kat Francis at the site of a chop-and-drop. Sounds like she got an eyeful. Stupid little bitch even took pictures."

"Shit." Henderson's gut was wrenched by thoughts of what would happen to the woman now.

"You should try to get a look at her if you've got a chance. She's a pretty one. Shame she has to die."

Henderson squeezed his pounding temples with one hand. "Yes. It's a *bloody* shame. Thanks for sharing this, but I'm afraid I must excuse myself."

"You've been getting my files?"

"I have. And I've deleted every one upon receipt. I'll thank you to stop sending them." He raised himself from the chair.

"Perhaps you'd like to discuss them in your little meeting today with the Director."

Henderson's legs went soft beneath him. Thankfully, the seat was still there. "So you *do* know about it."

Talo made a *t-t-t* sound with the tip of his tongue, shaking his head. "I know *everything* that goes on here. And by now, I'd say *you* know a lot more than you have clearance for. That can get a person in a very grave situation, mind the pun."

"I don't read the files. They go straight to the recycle bin as soon as I see something has come in over the network."

"That's not terribly gracious. You've missed out on some gripping stuff, complete with stills and video. You're telling me you didn't even see the part about the capsules?"

"I saw nothing."

Talo laughed. "*That's* what I like to hear. It would be healthy to take it up as your mantra. But I must recap for you. See this?" Talo held a closed fist in front of Henderson's face.

"Looks like the hand of a degenerate. Begging your pardon, but I really haven't the time—" Henderson began to stand again, but Talo used his other hand to exert great force on the bigger man's shoulder, digging his powerful fingers in and driving him back into the chair. Henderson turned his body away slightly, rubbing his pained shoulder with one hand and bringing the other up behind it, into his coat pocket. The record button made an inaudible *click*.

"Everyone is busy. Sometimes we have to *make* time." Talo rotated his fist, and unrolled his fingers to reveal a small red and yellow capsule. Taking it with his other hand, he rolled the capsule between thumb and index finger only inches from Henderson's nose.

Henderson drew back, scared now. Was Talo about to force a drug on him?

"Just *look* at it," Talo said smugly, clearly picking up what the other man was thinking, savouring it. "This little bomb will win the war against terror."

"Bomb? It looks like a bloody pill to me."

"It is. And anyone who swallows one like it will die."

"Brilliant. Now all we've got to do is convince all the terrorists to pop one, correct? Perhaps go drop them in al-Qaeda's caves, with a note: *Free vitamins*. Please, Mr. Talo." He reached to push the hand out of his face, but Talo retracted it first.

"Here, hold it," Talo said, then slowly returned his hand, the capsule rolling slightly in his palm. Henderson reached carefully, expecting it to be pulled away once more as the show of dominance carried on.

Talo allowed him to take it.

"It's empty," Henderson said. He grasped the two sides with his fingertips, and Talo gave a slight nod. Holding it over the table, Henderson carefully twisted the red half away from the yellow half.

Talo sat upright and thrust his chest forward. "As you can see, there's absolutely nothing inside. You're holding a certified *halal* capsule, made right here in our fancy new facility."

"*Halal*? So Muslims are allowed to eat it. As opposed to *haram*, which means forbidden."

"That's right. Not many non-Muslims know that."

"My sister married a Sunni and converted."

"I see. Then you'll be glad you stayed for this."

"You didn't allow me much choice." Henderson reassembled the capsule and set it down on the table. "Looks quite ordinary."

Talo took the gelcap, and began rolling it between his fingers again. His face took on a particularly menacing expression. "That's the idea. As I'm sure you already know, it's made without pork. Couple days ago, we brought in a real-live imam, to monitor the process onsite and put his stamp on every batch."

"Good of us."

"Not really. It was necessary. Final bureaucratic hoop to ensure a stronghold on the global market. Standard gelatine-based capsules are made primarily from the skin and bones of pigs, and are thereby blacklisted by Muslims as *haram*. That creates a problem. Over ninety percent of medications use two-piece gelatine capsules, including common antibiotics like amoxicillin. So Muslims have always been forced to make a choice. Either obey the Koran and stay sick, or use gelatine-based capsules, and chance forfeiting Paradise. A few manufacturers have tried to introduce substitutes made out of veggie matter, seaweed mostly, but those are much more expensive to make. Ours are pure bovine, a by-product of our existing processes—and production is subsidised, so the cost to pharmaceutical companies is less than any independent manufacturer could possibly compete with. *Far* less."

"So the hope is that all the drug companies will use our product, and then virtually all Muslims of means will buy it."

"You're catching on. But it's more than a hope. The sales team has exceeded expectations, albeit with the help of several million dollars slipping into the right suit pockets. Initial orders are sitting at over 50 million units, to begin arriving at pharmaceutical facilities around the world in seven days, pills hitting the market two or three weeks after that. And they will certainly not go only to people with money. The poorest ones will receive free vitamins and antibiotics, compliments of their friends at NATO."

Henderson's mouth hung open. "*This* is what the capsule manufacturing venture is about. Good Lord. But it's not only Muslims who avoid pork…"

"That has been planned for, and collateral damage will be minimised as much as possible. There is also a *kosher* certified product that's completely safe. Very few Jews will want a product with CERTIFIED MUSLIM HALAL written on the packaging in big letters, especially with our alternative close at hand. Nothing has been left to chance."

Henderson shook his head angrily. "I doubt anyone has come close to imagining the full scope of consequences. My God, what about all the bodies? You're talking about something in the neighbourhood of one-fifth the world's population. Ashes from the mass funeral pyres would spread harmful prions to anyone who inhaled them or ate food the particles settled on. I can't believe those *goffs* never consulted me about the dangers. You can't kill a billion people to eradicate perhaps a few thousand dangerous individuals." He slumped forward, his face apple-red.

Talo cast him a look of disdain. "So worst-case scenario, the global population gets set back a decade. That's how long it takes to add another billion people nowadays. Not so bad, hm? We'll need to do a hell of a lot more to solve our overpopulation problem before this fucking planet implodes."

"You don't even *consider* the humanity. I could strangle you, you bloody—"

"Mustn't be angry with *me*, Dr. Henderson. I just work here. As do you, don't forget. There's a war going on, and so far we're on the losing end. Militant groups are everywhere, with more layers than an onion. They're growing and spreading like a cancer, much more quickly than they can be flushed out."

"Security is up a thousandfold. And intelligence is improving."

"Not as fast as the terrorists are advancing their own technology. And unlike our side, they're tripping over one another for a chance to die for the cause. Hamas members are taught the Koran promises every martyr seventy-two dark-eyed virgins waiting in paradise. Hell, I'd blow myself up tomorrow if you could convince me of that."

"I'll get to work perfecting my argument."

This made Talo smile. "I've already seen some of the best. Palestinian TV runs recruitment ads for suicide bombers showing gorgeous maidens with flowing hair and white gowns. I'll send you one of those commercials. I also recorded a live telecast on the Palestinian Authority's official news where an imam led the viewing audience in prayer. Know what he said?"

Henderson shook his perspiration-soaked head, a sneer of distrust raising his upper lip. "I suppose you're going to tell me."

Talo grinned. "I quote: 'O Allah, destroy the Jews and their supporters.

O Allah, destroy the United States and its allies.' Word for word, I swear to you. This is what many Islamist leaders out there are preaching. I've seen numerous tapes of virtually the same message, echoed by different Muslim clerics.

"Hold on a moment. All these imams were speaking in English on Palestinian TV? I find that odd."

"There were subtitles, of course. What I'm telling you is that the call to *jihad* is constant, and it's working. The Western infidels—that's Islam-speak for you and me, Doc—are looking straight at a blueprint for holocaust. Desperate times call for desperate measures, and it doesn't get any worse than this, short of the first really big attack. Our governments are in the same position as Winston Churchill in the thirties, watching as Germany built up its army. The difference is that we learned a lesson from history. We see it coming, just like Churchill did. But we've learned to strike first."

"We have. For threats real as well as imagined. Case in point, Iraq."

"I'll tell you what's real. I'm sure you've heard of scenarios like the one in which a killer virus released by a terrorist wipes out most of the world's population. That's the kind of thing our governments are bracing themselves for today."

"It sounds to me like that's what they're *unleashing*."

Talo smiled. "Pre-emptively. But at least ours has controls built into it, unlike whatever new strain of Ebola or Smallpox a terrorist would be using that could kill everyone on earth. Al Qaeda has trained thousands of people to make ricin—one of the most deadly agents there is—out of fucking castor beans. If we don't eliminate these guys—not a word of a lie—it's only a matter of time before they get us. You think these guys can't afford to buy nukes and hide them in all our cities? Think again. And their consciences sure as hell aren't stopping them. You can bet your ass it's already in the works."

"It doesn't justify the casualt—" Henderson began, but Talo had too much momentum.

"Bullshit. In war, civilian casualties *always* outnumber military ones. Tens of thousands of innocent Iraqis had to die for the U.S. to get its hands on a handful of people. Half of those were just kids. Sounds extreme, right? Not at all. World War Two killed more than thirty million civilians. That is the kind of collateral damage to be expected in modern warfare. The Allies have finally woken up and smelled the Arabica. I hope it's not already too late."

Talo stared directly into Henderson's eyes, and waited for the doctor to blink before continuing. "Tragic that you can't tell the bad ones from the good ones, so they've all got to go. *With us or against us,* my friend. Sleeper cells of radical Islamist organisations are waiting for their marching orders all over the fucking world. The enemy is *inside* the gate. And you've helped engineer the most important preventative military operation in history."

"That is bloody *insane,*" Henderson said, his voice raspy. His face was so completely red now, it appeared the blood vessels were on the verge of bursting. The nightmare was only weeks from becoming reality. Henderson's features contorted, then he tightened his lips and buckled forward, clutching his abdomen. "Pardon me, Mr. Talo. I'm about to bring up."

Talo smiled, and patted his holstered pistol. "Be *very* careful what you do next, Dr. Henderson. As director of security for GATSER Northwest, I cannot let you get up from this table and set out to subvert our operation. It is my duty to kill you right here and now if I think that's what you are going to do. Think about your wife and children. A little boy and girl growing up without a father, and for what?"

"So you'll kill me, if that's what it takes to shut me up."

"Something like that. Suppose I'm funny that way. Loyalty is a rare commodity nowadays, something you wouldn't understand. However, there are still invisible files on your computer that Director Weissmann would find highly interesting. I've prepared a memo notifying him of their existence. All I've got to do is click one button. Or, I can kill you right now, and use the files you have as proof of your treason. The director seems to favour you, but given the circumstances, I'm sure he would understand. I've already taken the liberty of cancelling tomorrow's meeting on your behalf. I expect you'll agree it was good judgement."

Henderson did not respond.

"Well, got to run, Doc. Off to the Big Asshole now—GATSER Centre. Weissmann is coming too, you know. Momentous things going down. *Historic* things. Guess I'll have deal with our silly little spy when we return tonight. Don't assume I'm not watching. Open your mouth, and I'll strike where it hurts most." He stood and took a few steps then turned. "Oh, and don't forget to turn off your little voice recorder now."

CHAPTER 48

FOR A FACTORY, THIS building seems disconcertingly quiet.

It has a concrete floor and a very high roof, and is packed with stainless steel—machines, conveyors, and big silver vessels. The air is sour with the odour of old meat. I'm somewhat familiar with the making of pet food, because it's something I sell in my clinic. I have to know enough to advise my clients as to which brand and product to buy. I even toured a manufacturer's facility once, where I saw the grinders and extruders used to convert raw animal parts into the variously shaped pellets of dry food. The machines looked similar enough to these big and nasty ones.

Once inside, Jean turns and trudges off with his plastic box, and Eddie directs me forcefully ahead, across the factory and into a corridor. He opens the door to a room where cellophane-wrapped pillars of what looks like colourful empty pet food bags are stored. Pallets of these fill most of the room, the remaining space taken up by a large custom-fabricated dog kennel. It's taller than I am, and equally deep. On the floor of the cage is a blanket covered in short black dog hairs, and an empty bowl made of red plastic sits in one corner.

Eddie opens the door and shoves me inside so hard that I fall to the floor, wrenching my injured knee. Down here, the disagreeable meat odour combines with the smell of unclean dog, to less than pleasing effect.

Without speaking, Eddie slams the door and secures the cage with a massive padlock, then goes away. I wonder at first if he's gone to get duct tape for my legs and mouth as Jean recommended, but after a time, it seems he's forgotten all about me. I wish I could feel relieved, but the wondering is unbearable. Nothing good can happen now. But what? *What will they do to me?* I allow myself weep for a while, then manage to deep-breathe it away.

* * *

EVENTUALLY, I hear footsteps. My body tenses up. Instead of Eddie or Jean, a tall, slim-faced security guard stares in at me. He gives a curt nod, and walks on.

The guard checks in on me regularly, which I find a little weird. The cage is secure. I've checked for any weak spots—a corner that was not assembled properly, perhaps. No such luck.

I hear one of the machines in the factory start up, followed by another. Before long, every corner of the building has come to life, each piece of equipment in turn adding a grinding, rumbling, or rattling noise of its own to the mix. *Which of these am I destined for?*

I sit on the floor and close my eyes. From time to time, I can hear a voice shouting over the sounds of the machinery, never seeming very far away.

What are my captors going to do to me? I pray to God Eddie was pulling my leg about grinding me into dog food, not to mention the *other* part.

Luckily I have other things to think about. For example, my mouth is parched, and I really have to pee.

"What'd you do?"

I bang the back of my head against the cage.

It's the guard. He is a tall, funny-looking man. His nose long and pointed, with a big lump midway down its bridge. The murky green of his irises is contrasted to rather festive effect by several pyrotechnic bursts of red blood vessels. Greasy black hair is pasted forward across a forehead you could show a film on, and without smiling his lips part to reveal teeth merged together under a heavy veneer of plaque.

"To get yourself thrown in here," he continues. "What'd you do?"

"I don't know if I'm supposed to tell you."

"No, it's okay. I'm security. Cleared for pretty well everything."

"Shouldn't you already know, then?"

"Normally I would. But our DOS—that's Director of Security—is gone off to New York for the day, and I never got a proper debriefing this morning. That's procedure. Ask me anything about procedure, and I'll tell you the answer. All's I know is that I'm supposed to come up topside from time to time and keep an eye on you. But you weren't what I expected."

"How's that?"

"I don't know. I guess you look *nice*. Not like most terrorists, I s'pose."

"Thank you. I think I *am* nice. And I sure wouldn't call myself a *terrorist*.

Saw something I wasn't supposed to is all."

"What kinda something?"

"I got caught taking pictures of a cattle mutilation."

He whoops with laughter. "No *way*! Well, you're a brave one. Give you that."

"So what are they going to do with me?"

"Don't know. Guess Mr. Talo wants to interview you when he gets back."

"Then what? I get made into Kibbles 'n' Bits?"

He laughs. "That's crazy."

"Really?"

"Yeah. They don't make that here. I can tell you who makes all the brands if you want to know. Kibbles 'n Bits is Del Monte. This here is NutraPet. You're funny, ma'am."

"A hoot, aren't I? Do a lot of people get locked in this cage?"

"Oh, no," he says, serious now. "Some crazy shit goes on here, but you're only the second one I've seen locked in *there*. First one used to work here. Don't know if they're really gonna put you in the food. Never know. You got to admit, what you did was pretty dumb. What else are they supposed to do with you?"

"Can you help me?"

He smiles. Then he laughs, and gives me a sample of his breath I can almost bite into. "Yeah, right. Then I can be complete and balanced nutrition for pups too. Nice try, lady. Don't ask again, okay. I'm a trusty kinda guy."

He slaps the side of the kennel with his long fingers, and walks away. I underestimated the man.

It's a long time before he returns again, and even so, he takes only a quick look before turning away. My searing bladder forces me to call out to him. It's that or the dog dish. "Hey, excuse me!"

He sticks his head in and raises his sparse eyebrows. "Whatta you want?"

"I was just wondering something. What's your name?"

He scowls, and begins to turn away.

"I'm Kat, short for Katherine. I thought it would be polite to call each other by name. Couldn't hurt, could it?"

"Dennis," he says, eyeing me with suspicion.

"A strong name. Very appropriate. Listen, Dennis, do you think I could make a real quick visit to the ladies' room? I've been in this thing all day. I've really got to go, and I'd hate to do it in here."

He looks surprised at this, and his cheeks flush a little. "Guess no one's let you out to pee, huh?"

"No. You're the only one who's come around. I swear I won't be a problem."

"You make a run for it, I'll have to kill you." He pats his holstered sidearm.

"You don't have to worry about an escape attempt. I wouldn't do that to you, especially when you're having mercy on my bladder. Besides, I'm handcuffed, and this factory is full of workers. I've got nowhere to run to."

Dennis nods, and smoothly withdraws his pistol. He takes a set of keys from his waist, and uses the biggest one to release the padlock. The door squeaks open.

He waves the gun, and I step out of the kennel.

"Got the safety off," he says. "I've killed before, you know." I believe him on both counts.

He guides me down a corridor, to a door with a hand-written and sullied "NOT FOR FACTRY STAFF" sign taped to it. I push the door open and see a sink and a toilet. I walk in, and he follows.

"We got some other bathrooms over on the east side, but they're big," he says. "This is better for a prisoner."

"Could I have some privacy?" I say.

"You won't try nothin' funny?"

"What can I do in here? I've given you my word, haven't I?"

Dennis wrinkles his face and turns. "Wait," I say. "Would you undo my jeans for me? I can't do it with my hands cuffed back there." I demonstrate how far I can reach, not nearly to the closure.

His tall head looks like a big, red Roma tomato. He nods, and steps closer. I restrain my breathing to avoid taking in full-on Dennis Odour as his fingers bumble with the button, then I hear my zipper going down. Dennis steps away, wavering like he's about ready to pass out.

He leaves the room, partially closing the door. I push it the rest of the way with my knee until it latches with a click. I consider depressing the button on the knob to lock it, but reconsider. I don't want him to panic and smash the door down before I relieve myself.

And I have never needed this kind of relief so badly in my life. My bladder is so distended that it has become difficult to empty. I wonder if I have permanently ruined its elasticity.

As soon as I finish, I pull my pants on as well as I can and rush to the sink.

With my butt to the porcelain, I manage to reach the cold water tap, then turn around and guzzle thirstily. I try not to drink too much, not knowing if or when I'll get to come back.

Only now do I look for an escape route. The ceiling is drywall, not tiles. There are no windows. I pull open an access panel under the sink, but find the opening filled with plumbing. I'm as trapped in here as I was in the cage.

Just as I close the panel, the washroom door opens.

* * *

BACK INSIDE the cage, I get two more brief visits from Dennis, but no one else comes by. Is this part of the game, or am I just so minor an issue that I've been forgotten entirely? I try to rest on the floor of the cage, but it's impossible to get remotely comfortable with my hands cuffed behind me. My shoulders ache, and the metal has cut and badly bruised my wrists.

The next time Dennis comes by, he informs me that it's time for him to punch out.

"Does everyone in the factory go home for the night?" I ask.

"Yep. At midnight. I don't do night shift anymore. Had to for years, and it's the boringest thing in the world. That's *senior-ty* for you. Been here two years now, and put in another three in Kansas 'fore that."

"You're a veteran."

"Yep. It's an important job, security. My hero is Frank Wills. Know who he was?"

"Can't say I do."

"*No*? Frank Wills was the security guard who busted Richard Nixon's ass. Found a piece of duct tape on a door in the Watergate office, stuck there to keep it from closin' up proper. Not for him, Nixon never woulda got caught. Some security guards don't take much pride in what they do, but not me. I'm *damn* proud. Mr. Talo says I'm his number one most reliable man. He's my boss. Prob'ly be back from New York any minute now."

"Well, I'm sure your director is right about you."

Dennis's face takes on a severe expression. "You be careful with Mr. Talo. He's the kinda guy you got to butter up a little, get what I mean? And you don't never do *nothin'* to piss him off. *Never*. Got that? You hold your tongue, no matter what."

"Got it. Dennis, before you go, is there anything you can do about these terrible handcuffs?" I turn and raise my hands in his direction. The pain is intense, and I feel a tear descending my cheek.

"Wow, that looks *real* bad. You been bleeding like a stuck pig," he says. "Guess they coulda taken those off once they locked you on up. Bring 'em here."

I turn and grip the bars with my fingers, and hear the jingling of keys. The handcuffs go searingly taut as he tugs on the chain. I feel one pop off, then the other. He bunches the two cuffs together and drops them into one of the big pockets on his cargo pants.

"Thank you, Dennis," I say. "You're a man of compassion. Have a nice night." I hope Dennis goes out and gets lucky tonight.

He bites his lip and walks away.

I flop down and rest in the cage for a time, less uncomfortable without the handcuffs yet far from at ease. Finally, one after another, the big petfood-making machines grind down. Even after the last one stops, my ears continue to ring.

The silence is a relief. I pull off my fleece jacket and roll it up, then place it between the back of my head and the bars. I close my eyes, and gradually drift away.

* * *

MY BLADDER burns again, and I realize it's because I'm hearing running water. It seems to be coming from down the hall—the washroom Dennis took me to, probably. The sound continues at length, and after a time I listen with my eyes closed, wondering if someone turned it on and went away. When it finally stops, a door slams. I turn to watch the entrance to the room, expecting a person to appear—and am startled nonetheless when one does.

I have never seen such a handsome man. *Too* handsome, I think—the kind of face that seems in its symmetry and flawlessness to have forfeited all character. His hair is platinum, and I wonder at once if this is the blond "pretty-boy" who roughed Len up in Victoria.

I look away, and though there is not a sound, I can *feel* him approaching.

"Well, well," he says. "Look at the animal we've caught, hm? Out doing some early morning sightseeing, I'm told."

I clench my jaw.

"Oh, come, Katherine. Kat. You can talk to me. My name is Kyösti Talo, and I'm in charge of security. You'd do well to stay on my good side. Perhaps we can work things out. What have you got yourself into here?"

The phoney, patronising son-of-a-bitch. My anger gets the best of me.

"Your people killed two of my friends," I cry out.

"My people, you say?"

"This *organisation*."

"No, no. I believe in credit where credit is due." Talo walks closer to the cage, then grips the bars and touches his cheek to the metal. "I think you're referring to *my* artistry. Tell me, Kat, where were you hiding when I was with Isabel Butler in her room, while she pleaded for her life? She made it easy, you know. I told her I was your brother, that you'd left home without your medication and were delusional. Paranoid schizophrenic. Every time you forgot your pills, the whole world was out to get you. Like Russell Crowe in *A Beautiful Mind*, she said. Seemed to have no trouble believing it, you know."

He laughs, a truly wicked, mocking cackle. I have never seen such an ugly man. "As soon as I was in, it seems she recalled you no longer had a brother, and pulled a gun on me. Big mistake. I had to stop being nice. Little wench gave me false information, though. Told me you were staying with a man named Blythe."

He grabs the cage, white-knuckled. "Why are you smiling like that?"

"*Gilbert* Blythe?" I say, feeling proud of Isi. "That's the character Anne of Green Gables marries in the books."

He sneers and snaps his hands away from the bars. "So perhaps I'm not as well-read as I believed. Sweet Isabel was surprisingly competent with her gun; I suppose it was foolish to presume her too innocent to tell a story. Nothing easier than taking a gun from the hand of a woman, you know. Just make puppydog eyes—they want *desperately* to believe you're really not so bad. And the gun is yours for the taking. Isabel couldn't believe it. She started to cry, begged me not to kill her. So I promised not to, as long as she told the truth about where to find you. As we know, she didn't. I sat her down on the bed, stroked her face with one hand. Relax, sweet Isabel, there's nothing to..." Talo's voice is gentle, and goes too soft to hear. He smiles warmly, *lovingly*.

"*BANG!*" His hands slam the bars.

I draw back with a shriek, to his all-too obvious delight.

"Hey, she's the one who lied," he says, chuckling.

"You didn't fucking know it."

"True, if you must be so particular. Did you like my message? Subtle, yet powerful, hm?"

The envelope. "*You* destroyed my home. My office. Everything I own."

"Indeed. Seems I excel at things that others find too difficult or unsavoury. It's what got me where I am today. *Today*, I spent helping our leaders plan things that will shape the future of the entire world."

Things others find too difficult or unsavoury? What is Talo going to do with me? I will not do him the favour of asking. The narcissistic brute is enjoying this far too much already.

His voice softens again. "I know all about you, Kat. Everything. The student loans and mortgage you recently paid off with money your mother left behind. Which she got from the proceeds of your grandfather's sawmill businesses. Your former husband's drug addiction. Your friend Zaina's escape to Afghanistan—*that* one's a laugh. I had my people plant bugs and wiretaps in your car, your home, and your clinic. Anything that you said, read or typed came directly to me. I *know* you inside and out, Kat."

"Oh, God. Please don't..." I say, feeling numb and sick. "She's gone, and she doesn't know anything."

"I'm not too concerned about that one," he says with a wry smile. "Some problems take care of themselves, as they say. She's fairly low on my list."

I breathe a sigh. "And Thomas? Or Jean—whoever. What was *his* role? He followed me to Edmonton the day you killed Isi."

"Jean," he whispers, shaking his head. "Jean, Jean, Jean. He has this *need* to be at the hub of everything, yet he can never seem to complete any one of the assignments he takes on. But the Director just *loves* him. Jean of all trades, master of none. Getting things partly done, that's Jean's role here. The man may be a satisfactory doc and have a good military résumé, but he can't seem to get it right in his operational duties here. Leads troublemakers into deep water to *almost* die, or eavesdrops on people in a pub from across the road and *almost* tracks them home. Others like me then spend all of our time trying to tidy up the messes and do the damned job right. *If you want something done*, you know."

He produces a key like the one Dennis used to open my cage. Except now, I'm more comfortable with the lock where it is.

The door squawks as he swings it open, then he ducks inside and pulls a handgun from the holster on his hip.

"Now, you are going to tell me some things. Answer all of my questions *truthfully*, and I will do my best to have you released."

I can't help but smile at the suggestion, shaking my head. "I'm sure you will do *precisely* that. I know I can't possibly be released. I'm FFD."

He smiles. "Jean again, right? Our boy certainly has a mouth on him. Get one thing straight, Kat. You do *indeed* want to answer my questions."

"I really don't know anything," I say. "Certainly not that you aren't already on top of. You who knows everything about me."

"Who have you spoken to about our activities here."

"No one alive. You've seen to that."

"You're *lying*." His hand swishes up, and the pistol's barrel connects with my cheekbone with a terrible *krak!* I fly back, bouncing off the cage's wall and dropping to the floor. One of my hands comes down on the empty dog dish and it clatters aside. I stay there, unable to move. The sound of the blow still echoes inside my head. I touch my fingertips to the throbbing cheek, and feel a ridge of soft, torn flesh. My fingers are coated with an abundance of hot blood, and seeing it brings on blinding pain. A wave of terror makes my whole world shake. I let out a whimper.

"Gets worse from here on in, I'm afraid," he says. "I *really* didn't want to do that, you know. You've limited my options, should you be foolish enough to remain uncooperative. I was hoping not to leave any physical evidence of our interaction. There *is* a bright side, I suppose. Mother used to say that whenever the Good Lord closes one door, He opens another."

CHAPTER 49

FROM THE MISERABLE POSITION I'm in—doubled over on the hard floor of the cage—I spot something I didn't notice before. Beside the dog dish, partly hidden in a fold of the blanket, is a wedge-shaped chunk of bone. It must have been underneath the hollow-bottomed food dish, which moved when I struck it on my way down. One side has been deeply knurled by sharp teeth, and the other end probably cut by a meat saw, creating a cusp that looks sharp.

Probably sharp enough to pierce skin.

A pretty crude weapon to use against an armed man who has already taken a loaded gun from a trained handler, but it's something. This, and the element of surprise.

I pull my knees together in front of my chest make sure the bone is blocked from Talo's view. I feign being startled, drawing suddenly back and allowing my jaw to fall open while looking wide-eyed at the doorway behind him. He glances that way for only an instant, but it's enough for me to get a hand over the weapon.

"What is it?" he says. "You fucking with me?"

"No. I swear. I thought I saw something move back there."

He makes a strange growling sound. I *know* I don't want to get his adrenaline flowing.

"Listen," I say, and begin to slowly pick myself up, getting a better grip on the bone as I push off with my free hand. "I give up. I'll tell you anything you want to know. Just don't hit me again." I feel my features twitch, on the verge of exploding into tears, and focus on channelling that energy. *This is it, Kat. It's either you or the piece of shit who killed Craig and Isi. This is it.*

Talo sneers. "Give me some names."

"The only one who knows anything is already dying. Craig's neighbour,

Len Gibson. He's got the disease. Anything I've discussed with him, he's forgotten."

"*Bullshit*. He hasn't been infected."

"He spent time in the house and jeep. He got it the same way."

He smiles. "You're telling me we've got some small-scale collateral damage. That's interesting. This man hasn't sought treatment. I would know if he had."

It's hard not to smile at this. "Not to discount your omniscience, but I called an ambulance to his house yesterday. Gave the operator directions from Bonnyville, though. He's nearly equidistant to both towns, and I wasn't eager to subject him to Dr. Samuelson's bedside manner."

His lips twitch, but he doesn't say anything for a moment. "Who else?"

"No one. I swear it."

He makes a threatening gesture with the gun, rotating it in his hand, then aiming the barrel at me. "You're lying. I know about Zaina. And you visited Lynn Butler in Lloydminster. What did you discuss there?"

"I asked her for written consent to see Craig's medical records." I keep eye contact, engaging Talo in a staring contest while I work the bone forward with my thumb, so that half its length is projecting from my fist.

"Which you received. And you told her and the boyfriend about your suspicions, didn't you?"

"I knew that would put them both in danger. And I didn't think she was smart enough to keep a secret. I didn't tell Lynn anything."

"You're LYING!" he shouts, eyes bulging from their sockets.

A flash like a giant spark, as metal hits bone again.

And an instant transition in what I see—Talo's contorted face, then the wall beyond the side of the cage. Dots of red appear on it, then melt into vertical stripes.

Talo has hit my raw wound again, the way a boxer continues to target a cut he's already opened. I focus all my concentration on staying conscious, on continuing to hold the sharp wedge of bone in my hand, keeping it out of sight. If I drop it, I'm dead.

He gives me a hard shove. I bounce off the bars behind me, and step back on one leg, propping myself up like a bike on a kickstand. Then I do a controlled fall in Talo's direction, thrusting the weapon up at his throat as I draw near.

He cannot have anticipated this, yet his hand snaps up and seizes my wrist, clamping it like a vice. He stares at me icily, then looks at the piece of bone and bursts into laughter. He stoically squeezes with augmenting force, entrenching his manicured fingernails deeper and deeper into the tendons of my battered wrist. The piece of bone falls to the blanket without a sound.

"Nice try, *Kat*." He spits my name like a scrap of rotten food. "Your friend Isi should have made so valiant an effort. His hands slam into my chest, the barrel of the gun stabbing into the tissue of my breast. I'm knocked back into the wall of the cage again, dazed but still standing.

When I focus, he is clasping the gun in his teeth. I gasp when I realize why. His hands are working his belt buckle.

"Stick me with a bone, will you? Now that's just unkind. How about you tell me what else you know while I'm *fucking* you? While I'm cutting off your pretty nose with your own little weapon. How about that?"

He pulls his khaki pants and small briefs halfway down his thighs, holding them there with the tension of his slightly parted legs, and grins down at his own erection as he palms the gun again. I avert my eyes, but the glimpse of the engorged organ has etched itself in my mind, a menacing Waffen SS officer in a purple helmet. Poised to inject me with poison while shredding apart my self-respect. I am sickened by the notion that it will soon force its way into the most intimate part of my physical being—to break my spirit, demeaning me in an ages-old display of ignominious male dominance.

This while the dirty fuck disfigures me.

No matter what he does to your body, he can't have your dignity, I promise myself. *No one ever can unless you empower them to. Especially not this lousy piece of shit. NEVER!*

He grabs my shirt at the neck with his hands and drags me along as he takes three short paces backward, so that he stands outside of the cage but I remain confined by its walls. The veins in his neck bulge out as he whips several of the snaps on the front of my shirt open. He presses his thumbs deep into the soft tissue beneath my clavicles, the cold barrel of the gun pressing into my larynx, and forces me to my knees. I close my eyes and draw in a breath, knowing I'm about to let out a scream despite my intense will to repress it.

Before I can, the back of his hand strikes my face hard, and a heavy mist of blood flies from the cut on my cheek, dotting the blanket and the concrete floor beyond it. My senses muddled by the blow, I perceive motion somewhere behind Talo, and strain to see. *Oh, God, has a second person arrived to share in my humiliation?* I shiver at the thought, letting out another unwanted whimper.

Talo chuckles wickedly, shaking his head. It seems he presumes I am trying to divert his attention a second time, reusing the same technique. I *ought to* be that clever, with my life depending on it.

With a heavy *bomf!* his head lurches into an unnatural position. There's another sharp blow to the humerus of his gun arm, and the weapon skitters a few feet across the floor, stopping at a wall. He buckles at the waist.

With Talo's upper body out of the way, I get a clear view of the man behind him. He is heavy-set, in a white jacket, with a gleaming bald head and a thick moustache. An unlikely saviour, it seems to me.

"Henderson, you shitfucker," Talo grunts, reaching to retrieve his gun. Henderson strikes again, and his weapon—something that resembles a shiny length of pipe—bounces off Talo's shoulder and rings against the cage's doorway.

I can't help but notice that Talo has lost his erection.

Talo spins and lunges at Henderson, one hand working to pull up his pants that are still absurdly at half-mast. Despite this handicap, an instant later he has possession of the pipe.

I reach for the gun. Before I get a hand on it, the pipe smacks Henderson's head with a ghastly *whuk!*

I stand, fumbling with the weapon like a spud hot off the barbecue.

It terrifies me.

Henderson falls heavily to the floor and lies there motionless. Talo prepares to whack him again, then notices me. He turns, and steps my way, hiking his pants most of the way back up.

"Please, Katherine," he says, his expression incredibly calming, the evil seemingly drained from it. He takes another step towards me, and lets the pipe clatter to the ground, raising his empty palms.

I know it's all a sham.

Yet I don't think I can shoot.

CHAPTER 50

"YOU DON'T WANT TO kill a person," Talo says with tearful eyes. His lips are bloodless, stretched tight over his teeth. I cannot recall ever seeing such anguish expressed in a face. Phoney though it is, it's *working*! My hands go into a palsy-like shake, the gun suddenly unbearably heavy. As Talo lurches in a sob, he tugs his pants on properly.

An instant before they are up, I see that his organ is getting engorged again.

Nothing easier than taking a gun from a woman.

"The *fuck* I don't." I squeeze all my fingers with everything I've got—including the one on the trigger. There is an eardrum-splitting *krak!* and a fantastic jolt impacts my wrists, elbows, and shoulders.

A red dot appears on Talo's forehead, and his expression turns to one of bewilderment. Poor Henderson, who hasn't moved, gets a shower of bloody mulch. Talo collapses like a sack of meat. Sitting loosely in his hand is a big folding knife, its blade partly open. He must have taken it from his pocket under the pretence of pulling the trousers back on.

I remain in my shooting position for a few seconds, gripping the gun with both hands, one arm locked at the elbow. A modified weaver stance, more or less.

"Thanks, Isi," I whisper, fighting back tears.

I rush around the dead man, to Henderson. He is motionless. I press my index and middle fingers to his jugular, and feel a pulse. He's alive.

"Mr. Henderson," I say, slapping at his cheek. "You with me?" He reacts, turning his face slightly away.

"I'm getting up, Mairi," he groans in a Scottish brogue, rolling the *r* and pronouncing the words *gittin' oop*. "Good Lord, what time is it."

A gentle smile crosses his face, and becomes a grimace. His eyes open just slightly, then close again, tight.

"Oh, *Christ* that hurts," he says. What happened, lass? Did I *save* you?"

I smile at him. "You did, Mr. Henderson."

"You know my name."

"Talo said it."

He closes his eyes again and twists his features, gingerly stroking the knob on the side of his head where the pipe struck. "I suppose he did." Henderson lifts his head and turns it to Talo's crumpled body. "Christ, I *killed* the son-of-a-bitch?"

"No, that was me. With *his* gun. It made quite a noise, Mr. Henderson. Someone must have heard it." I notice Henderson's eyes flitting nervously to my chest, and realize my top is still wide open. I swivel on my hips and do up a few snaps. "Sorry. I'm really not an exhibitionist."

"This floor is solid concrete, three feet thick," he says, looking away. "May still be possible sound got through, but it was expected. Talo is the security chief. He sent out an e-memo saying it might be necessary for him to fire a single shot up here in concluding a security issue. I expect he didn't want to be interrupted, the sick piece of shit. Now come, we must waste no time in getting you out of here."

"Isn't there any security up here, Mr. Henderson?"

He laughs heartily, as he takes the hand I offer, but makes little use of it in climbing to his feet. "Call me Duncan, please. There's no shortage of *that* all around the exterior perimeter, as well as at the entrances and throughout the lower levels. Nothing to speak of in here, though. This whole factory is only a front, and the fences and guards are more than it needs. There are five floors below us where the *other* work goes on. The kind to which you presented a threat."

"I got inquisitive after a former boyfriend of mine died of a brain disease. Got caught taking pictures of a helicopter stealing cow parts. I'm told that's a no-no to the powers that be."

He laughs again. "I'm sure it is. I do my best not to get involved in *that* part of the business. I'm a neuropathologist. I examine the nervous systems of dead bodies. Animals mostly, since leaving Edinburgh."

"What's wrong with animals? That's *my* specialty."

"So I'm told."

"They notified you *my* body was coming your way?"

"Mr. Talo here let me know you'd been captured. The lad's been trying to get the drop on me for months. A bit of a one-sided power struggle. But I got the distinct impression your death would not call for a medical examiner. They were planning to, uh…" His voice fades to nothing, then he grimaces and tries again. "You were to be…"

I help him out. "Disposed of? Talo was kind enough to allude to that. Wasn't quite the gentleman you are. You probably noticed his pants were down when you got here."

Duncan looks at Talo's crumpled form, and then down at the spatters of gore on his own white lab coat. He uses his boot to move the dead man's head in its large halo of blood. The exit wound is immense, I think, comparing it with the only other one I have ever seen—in all too recent memory.

"About two metres away when you fired, correct?" he says.

I manage a weak smile. "Showoff."

He strokes his chin for a moment. "I'm not a ballistics man. I was mostly gauging the distance from his feet to where you were. In any case, I'm going to need your help if we expect to pull this off. I've got to gather a few items downstairs to tidy up and perhaps buy us some time. You might prefer to wait around the corner, where you don't have to look at our nasty lad here."

We walk into the corridor together, and I indeed feel relieved to be away from the corpse. I can't fathom how people like Duncan can bear to be around dead bodies on a regular basis.

"Just wait here," he says. "There's a lavatory down the hall." He points to the one where Dennis took me. "Try to clean up the lacerations to your cheek the best you can. Use soap. Then see if you can find us a mop and some hot water." He removes his lab coat and uses it to casually blot the spatters and bone fragments from his neck, then rolls it in a bundle with the soiled part inside.

"Thank you," I say, and watch him hustle off and disappear around a corner. I go inside the washroom and splash cold water on my face. It bites into the cuts like needles. The two deep wounds look even meaner than I expected, enhanced by swelling, thick borders of clotting crimson, and long built-up drips. I squirt a little of the amber soap onto my fingertips, and gingerly rub it along the edges of the wound. I clamp my jaw, and work the soap into the meaty interior, creating a pinkish lather. The searing pain is more hellish than when the wound was inflicted. After many unbearable seconds of this, I throw a few scoops of cold water over it, and dab the new blood away with a paper towel.

I stare at my own image in the mirror, incredulous. *What a wreck.* My eyes are bloodshot, one of them swollen nearly shut, my hair is tangled, and my cheek looks like I've just been on the sorry end of a rumble with the Hell's Angels. The cuts *do* look better now, but it's hard to imagine they'll heal up nicely.

I look away. Not the time for vanity. I've still got to get out of here, past all that security at the exits and at the gate. *What does Duncan Henderson have in mind for my escape?*

I walk back into the corridor, wondering where one might find cleaning supplies. There are three doors here in addition to the washroom. The first one is made of reinforced steel, with a heavy-duty knob. It's locked and bolted. The next houses what appears to be a large furnace and a utility sink—filled nearly to the rim with water.

This would be where the running water sound came from.

Talo filled the sink before coming to me.

Why?

After he struck me with the gun the first time, he said he'd limited his options for getting rid of me. Was he planning to *drown* me in here? *Damn, this is weird.*

Next to the sink, I see a metal shelving unit stocked with sponges, rubber gloves, and bottles of cleaning product. *Jackpot.* A broom and a metre-wide industrial dust mop are on one side, and on the other, two mop-and-bucket combos—both on wheels.

I roll up my sleeve, and reach into the sink to pull the black rubber drain plug. The cold water makes the bones in my arm ache, a chilling reminder of the seawater that nearly took my life not very long ago. I visualise Talo plunging my head into this sink, and shiver. *What is it about these people wanting to drown me? Is my goddam destiny to die like my brother?*

With the stopper out, the level drops quickly.

Just as it empties, I dump the brown water from the emptier of the two mop buckets into the sink, then refill it with hot water, adding a generous shot of Pine-Sol.

I pad back and forth in the corridor for several minutes. Duncan should be back by now. Has something gone wrong?

A door clicks shut. Then the squeaking of wheels that could do with a squirt of oil, and a hand truck appears, followed immediately by Duncan. Stacked on the dolly sit four flats of half-litre mineral water bottles, topped by a big white plastic pail with a lid. Draped around the back of Duncan's neck and over his shoulders is the kind of PVC bag used to draw blood from donors, complete with collecting tube and venipuncture needle.

"Glad you're still here," he says. "That looks *much* better. Ought to heal up just fine."

"Thanks. But I'm sort of focused on survival right now. What's happening downstairs?"

"Pretty quiet—people going about their drudgery like any other night. Appears no one heard the shot."

I point at the vinyl collection bag. "Why *that*?"

"Patience. First, let's get our dead *badling* out of the way. Come with me." He returns to the room where we left Talo, and I follow with my mop and pail. Duncan lifts the lid from the bucket partway, and slips out what looks like a blue bedsheet. He partly unfolds it, leaving it doubled over once. Then he makes a face at me, lays it just outside the puddle of congealing blood, and grabs Talo on the hip and shoulder. A pro with an audience, he flips the body over, plopping the head messy-side-down on the edge of the folded sheet. Duncan draws the rest of the sheet up over the corpse, concealing it completely. From the yet-covered bucket, he pulls a roll of duct tape, and rips off a piece a metre long. He wraps that around Talo's head. Another goes at the feet, and a third midway in between.

"Want me to clean up?" I offer.

"Soon. First, let's move this bloody scoundrel. Grab that end, if you will."

I do so—taking the feet side—and we begin to drag the neatly packaged corpse. Duncan gives directions as he leads, and we enter the factory area. He takes me to a narrow opening in the floor that's covered with a metal lattice on both ends, the middle third of it open. The old meat stench that has become familiar to my nostrils augments in intensity as we approach, becoming unbearable. Like the smell of a skunk, it takes on a completely different, far more vile character at full-strength than when dispersed. The reek is clearly coming from this pit. When we're near the edge, I risk a look.

I almost *yarf*.

In the belly of the stainless steel abyss, I see the brown-and-white carcasses of two Hereford steers, amidst dozens of chickens with yellowy plumage.

Both steers are missing their eyes, ears and genitals, and then some. The bottom ends of the carcasses have been slit from the rectum wounds to the necks. Similar thing at the top: from a dark void in the top of each animal's head runs a long carved-out channel that extends beyond the white oval cross-sections of the ribs all the way to where the tail used to be.

The brains and spines have been removed, like the ones on the second contact sheet. *So not all of the mutes get dumped back in the pasture.* Beneath the heap of putrefying animals are the gleaming spiral blades of a corkscrew-shaped auger.

"Did those two necropsies today," Duncan says. "Jean and Eddie brought them early in the morning, couple hours before you. Came up clean, though. Eyeballs gave a false positive in the chopper. Have you heard of CDI?"

"Conformation Dependent Immunoassay," I say. "Read up on it a couple days ago. That's what you go by here? I saw what looked like a centrifuge in the helicopter."

"We *invented* it. Version we use is tailored to detect prions in the synaptic layers of the retina, where their concentrations tend to be comparable to in the brain. As you may know, benign prion proteins occur naturally, and we still get some false positives where precursor prions look like BSE ones. I only know for certain by looking at stained brain tissue slides and once we've run hybridisation and blot tests. As I said, these two gals were clean. This organisation may do some cruel things in the pursuit of its evolving mandates, but they would never deliberately put infected material into the food or feed chains. Not outside a *controlled* environment, at least."

I nod facetiously, and look at the bundle that is Talo. "We're not going to—"

Why not? It's the fate that awaited *you*. The chef's probably already expecting some human tissue in the mix. Probably already modified the ingredient list for this batch."

I'm unable to even acknowledge Duncan's black humour. "I don't think so. Talo got upset when he first cut my face. He said he hadn't wanted to leave any physical evidence."

"Really? He had another plan then—in which your body was to be discovered somewhere. Look, we haven't the time to deliberate this. Let's toss him in the pit, and we'll tidy up the mess you made with the gun. Trust me, you *don't* want to be around when I switch this baby on. I've been up here during working hours, and this machine is the worst of the lot. Makes noises to gag a pathologist."

Duncan picks up Talo's top end again. "Let's try not to think of the poor pups who'll get a bellyache from this shitburger," he says, trying once again to inject some levity into a purely macabre matter. This time, I force a smile.

Although Talo is very lean and cannot be particularly heavy, he might be a whale now that I'm trying to lift his lower body off the floor. Duncan raises his end high, taking on as much of the load as he can. I notice now that the duct tape holding the blanket over Talo's head has slipped up and twisted. One of his eyes and the entry wound are staring out at me through the gap. I feel suddenly weak, but don't let go.

"On three," Duncan says, and nods to begin with a short swing in the direction opposite the pit.

"One," he says as Talo sways back a few inches the other way. "Two." He grunts when the body comes back a second time.

"*THREEE!*"

Duncan releases first, throwing me off balance. I frantically put down the heel of my shoe at the pit's rim. It slips on the shiny steel, and I glance down to see Talo's buttocks bounce off the far wall as he lands, his head jamming in the spiral of the auger. The sheet has come off his head altogether, and his jaw wedges open against the gleaming metal, leaving him frozen in an awful, noiseless scream.

I let out a desperate shriek of my own at the thought of joining the scene below. Can I jump over? Not with my legs so far apart.

I close my eyes.

Expecting to feel cold steel and stiff flesh, I am surprised by a hard tug at the waist of my pants. I'm towed two swift paces backwards, and my legs go rubbery. Duncan's arms encompass my chest, and he holds me up until I manage to support myself again.

He releases me and steps away.

"Thank you," I gasp.

"Think nothing of it," he says. "I simply couldn't bear the thought of climbing down there to get you back out. Let's be off now. Time for me to mop up."

"No you won't. I may be a liberated woman, but you *are* saving my life here. I can clean up my own wetwork."

He shakes his head. "You've got more important work to do now. I need you to *bleed* for me."

I stare at him in bewilderment. "Here's where I get really nervous."

"We only need a pint," he says. "About half a litre, one glass of Guinness. Needn't worry."

We return to the cage, and only now do I begin to have serious doubts about Duncan Henderson's plan. Perhaps he's insane—and here I am going along with everything he suggests.

But what choice do I have? The last madman tried to kill me, and Duncan hasn't done *that* yet.

He picks the collection bag from atop the bucket, and motions for me to sit in its place. He twists the protective cap off the needle. I extend my right arm, and he rolls up my crinkly sleeve, then expertly finds a vein and inserts it. My blood begins to flow into the bag.

"You're a natural," I tell him. "Better than a lot of pros I've seen."

"Thank you. Been awhile since my days as an intern. Hold this in place, if you will," he says. I hesitate, and he raises one eyebrow. "Unless you prefer I use the duct tape."

"No, I'll hold it."

Duncan grabs the mop and gets to work, beginning with the spatter trail from Talo's exit wound. After a good wringing, he starts on the puddle. He works fast, and my blood flows nicely into the bag. On the numerous occasions I've donated blood, the process has taken about eight or ten minutes. Perhaps an accelerated heart rate speeds it up. I've almost filled the 450-mil reservoir by the time he is finished—which hardly seems half that long, even in my anxious state.

He walks in line with the bullet's path, to the closest wall, and inspects it carefully. "Slug's in here. There'll also be some matter in this area, but nothing anyone is apt to notice. Not after I'm finished with *that*," he says, pointing to the bag of blood.

CHAPTER 51

DUNCAN EMERGES FROM THE cage and hands me my fleece jacket, still rolled like a log cake. "This yours?"

"Yes, thank you."

"Hang on to it. You'll be glad later on." I have no idea what this means, but give a nod. He disconnects me from the tube, and a little pearl of blood emerges from the hole in my arm. I smear it away with my finger. No antiseptic-dabbed cotton for me, I guess. Shivering, I roll my sleeve back down, then pull the jacket on.

Duncan removes a red Swiss Army knife from his coat pocket. He flips out the biggest blade and sticks it into the side of the PVC sac. Then he walks into the cage and withdraws it, folding it in his hand on the way into his pocket. He begins to squeeze the bag, holding it away from himself at arms' length. My blood shoots out in spurts, governed by the varying pressure he applies on the reservoir. Duncan directs some of the spray into the cage, and vacillates long gushes onto the surrounding floor and walls. He sprays with particular copiousness in the area where Talo's blood puddle sat. I'm amazed by the coverage a mere half litre can achieve.

"Very important that it appears you were bleeding profusely," Duncan says. When he's wrung the bag empty, he approaches me with a smile, and places a hand on my back. "Almost done, lass," he says, giving me a playful rub on the back of the head. Then he grabs hold of my hair, and pulls away violently. My head kicks back, to a ripping pain in my scalp. Duncan smiles sheepishly, holding a lock of the blonde fibres.

I glare at him. "What the fuck was that for?"

"Far easier on you without warning. Apprehension is the worst of it. Here, take some, and smear it around in the blood. And give me some nice handprints on the floor and bars.

I understand now, but my head still stings. "Jerk," I say. Duncan's eyes sparkle at me.

The blood still feels warm on my skin. Might as well do a good job, I think to myself, plunging both hands in and slapping them against the bars. I consider how I might be positioned if facing an attacker and turn around, then make two handprints, one with the fingers straight out and the other with them slightly curled.

"I think I'm done," I say.

"Rather like finger painting, isn't it?"

"I suppose. In some whacked-out playschool. Care to come turn on the water for me?"

"Yes, mind not to touch anything now. You can give the mop a good rinse once your hands are clean. I'm going to smear my coat into some of your blood and drag it over to the pit, to leave an obvious trail. No question as to what was done with you."

"What if they find the fabric? Or run a DNA test?"

He gives an abrupt laugh. "Not bloody likely. After the initial shredding, the raw material goes to another grinder where it's chopped to fine bits. Then it all gets rendered for an hour at three hundred degrees—before the meat and bone gets pulverised in a hammer mill along with grain and other dry ingredients. After that, it gets cooked some more. It'll be at minimum that far along before anyone might be interested in checking it. Mr. Talo was at the tail end of a very long workday when he finished with you, so he'd be expected to go home and sleep awhile. In all likelihood, he will have been extruded, enrobed and packaged hours before anyone questions his whereabouts and tries ringing him. Tomorrow is a big shipping day, I believe. He may well be on his way to nourish pets in Europe or Asia by then."

"And what happens when they don't find him at home or here?"

"There may be a search, but I expect his disappearance will remain a *mystery*." He whispers this last word, apparently relishing it. I get the sense Duncan had a very strong dislike for Talo.

"Does he have a family?"

He laughs. "Wife and kids? Of course not. You don't believe I have thought this through, do you? I'll move his SUV to the bottom floor of the parking garage. That level never gets used, and there are a few stalls conveniently out of sight at the farthest end," he says, pulling a key from his pocket and holding it up so that I can see the GMC insignia embossed in the plastic. "They over-built everything here. I'll be wearing my latex gloves, of course."

"Won't it seem unusual he's left so much blood on the floor?"

"You're a tough kid. No one will be surprised you put up a fight. And knowing Talo, it would in fact be far more unusual for him to have tidied up after himself. *Especially* if he was incensed about the way things went. Now you really must trust me, Kat. We've wasted a lot of time."

Duncan turns the water on, and squeezes a glob of soap into my waiting palms, then sets off to make some bogus drag marks. I expect he will throw the blood bag and coat in the pit to be ground up and cooked with Talo and the other dead beasts.

I finish washing up, then dump out the bloody water and rinse the mop in the sink. The bits of bone and fatty clusters cling to the fibres, but a few vigorous rinses in scalding water get it clean. I place the mop in the bucket and transfer most of the brown water into it from the pail I left behind. It now looks as though our mop was used to clean a dirty floor rather than a bloody one.

Duncan returns without his lab coat. "I think we're still all right," he says. "Come with me."

He begins wheeling his dolly down the corridor. I follow, very interested in knowing what he plans to do next, as its success might well determine whether or not I live to see morning.

We round a corner into a shorter hallway, and come to a set of double doors under a sign that says SHIPPING AND RECEIVING.

"What, you're going to FedEx me out of here?"

"Something like that," he says, and punches a code into the keypad.

* * *

THE WAREHOUSE is bigger than I would have guessed, half of it a labyrinth of pallets topped with cellophane-wrapped towers of brightly coloured animal food bags. The remaining area is stacked even higher with tidy brown cardboard boxes. The air is filled with a different scent than the reek of the rendering and processing area—one I'm familiar with. It smells like pet kibble.

"What's in the boxes?" I ask.

"Gel capsules. We make them in a new wing on the other side there." He points to a set of closed double doors like the ones we just came through.

"New product. That's probably the first batch, waiting for all the export permits."

"That's a funny thing to make in a pet food factory."

"Not really. Uses some of the same key ingredients. Best I not say more now. Come."

Duncan's tone has changed. He seems uncomfortable and restless, and his face is flushed. But these are hardly comfortable circumstances—even for a man resilient enough to work elbow-deep in death all the time. If anyone were to walk in, he'd be screwed. And I'd be lucky to get thrown back in the cage alive.

There are two loading bays, with a semi trailer backed up to each. The twin doors of the first trailer are wide open, revealing a completely empty interior. The other has its doors closed. Duncan walks directly to the second one, then stops.

He's going to get me out of here in the back of a truck.

"I've got to cut the seal off, and we're in business," he says, grasping a yellow tag threaded through a pair of holes in the doors' locking mechanism. The style of tag is familiar to me. It's the same kind of tamper-proof device Jack received from the Saskatchewan government for tagging big game: a flat metal strip with a ball-lock mechanism on one end. Once the strip has been inserted into the ball—Jack would wrap it around the animal's hind leg tendon or lower jawbone—it cannot possibly be removed and resealed.

"But they're numbered," I say, pointing to a string of digits stamped into the metal.

"The tracking system they use is simple. And the computer is right here. I'll just go in and change the number. But first things first."

He picks up a set of long bolt cutters that are leaning up against the wall, and easily slices through the slim metal tag. He drops it in his pocket, and replaces the cutters. The two levers on the truck's doors squeak as he lifts and swings them outward, disengaging a system of tall shafts that lock both doors at the top and bottom.

The truck is packed to the ceiling with cello-wrapped pallets of red bags, their gussets labelled NUTRAPET PREMIUM ADULT DOG FOOD.

He takes his Swiss Army knife, whips a blade out, and begins to cut away the clear wrap, starting at the bottom and working upward.

"Help me load these on our dolly," he says, sliding the hand truck out from beneath the bucket. By jumping up a little, he manages to grab the topmost bag. He slides it off, followed by the next one down, and hands both to me at once.

"Where are we going to put them?" I ask through clenched teeth.

"Back in inventory." He points to a pile of similar bags near the end of a conveyor belt that comes in through a square opening in the wall. I load the dolly with twelve bags, and wheel them to the pile, where I place the bags around the parameter of the existing ones. Hopefully nobody will notice if it grows by a few bags in each direction.

I make eight trips before Duncan tells me to stop. We've created a gap in the back of the truck that's more than big enough for me to tolerate a few hours in. After all, it's nearly the size of the cage where I spent my entire day.

Duncan places the plastic bucket inside the truck. "So," I finally ask, "Where is this thing bound for?"

"Europe. Not sure what port."

I laugh. "I've always wanted to go there by truck."

"This is a forty-foot shipping container, on the back of an articulated lorry. I believe you call them semi-trailers here. This food is for export. It'll cross the Atlantic in a barge."

"Surely I don't need to go overseas."

He shakes his head. "If this container gets opened before that, nothing good will come of it. You don't want to find yourself in the hands of the border guards. Who do you think runs *this* facility?"

"The Border Service Agency?"

"No. Nor the RCMP, but you certainly don't want to turn to either of them. Those companies both have the same *heid bummer*. That's how we say *boss* in Scotland. The CBSA turns anyone caught attempting an unauthorised border crossing over to the RCMP. That's who holds the ultimate responsibility for patrolling the border. And the prime minister considers this operation's privacy to be a matter tantamount to national security. I'm certain he would endorse having you branded a terrorist if you were caught. The new Anti-Terrorism Act would then allow your 'preventative arrest' and the stripping of your rights."

"At least I'd be *alive*."

"Don't be naïve, Kat. They couldn't allow you to talk to a lawyer. If they did that, in their eyes, they'd be setting the stage for a national security crisis that would endanger all of the NATO allies. There are plenty of ways a person can die in custody. I would expect nothing short of top-shelf creativity, given what you've got in that head of yours."

"*All* the allies? Who is involved in this? I got the impression it was a national initiative."

"Not *all* the NATO chums. Just Canada, the States and Britain, as far as I know. Possibly others, I suppose, to varying depths. Perhaps even the Kremlin now, the way things have been going. Hard to be sure when it's classified all around."

I nod, though not sure I'm truly grasping anything. "Now I know why you brought so much bottled water. But what am I supposed to *eat?*" I turn and look at all the bags of dog food, feeling instantly sick.

Seeing my expression, Duncan pivots his head side-to-side, smiling. "Oh, come, Kat. I wouldn't do *that* to you. I've got four cases worth of PowerBars in this bucket. I buy them from a wholesaler. Now if you're inside here for four weeks, that gives you a little less than two per day. Not a lot, but with a low activity level, it should sustain you just fine."

"That's a *month.* I'll be locked in there for a MONTH? You must be joking."

"Relax now, lass. These shipments go express. It should take no more than three weeks to make the full journey. But delays happen in transit. You'll have to ration yourself expecting the worst."

"Oh. Only *three weeks*," I say. "This is crazy. What about air? I read about a container they opened in Montreal and found two dead Romanian stowaways inside. They suffocated."

"I recall the story. Terrible way to die, gradually running short of air like that. These containers are built to be watertight, which means they're *air*tight too. I've got a cordless drill in there with your food. Be careful, though. Air holes can get you killed too, if someone sees them or hears you doing the drilling. There's also a small torch." He smiles as I'm envisioning myself cutting through the steel with an acetylene flame. "*Flashlight* to you."

"And what about washroom facilities, Duncan? This is a *terrible* plan."

"It's a perfectly sound one, Kat. I even thought to bring a bucket with a lid. You'll be glad for that, I assure you."

"I'll go nuts. That isn't a ride to freedom. It's a sensory deprivation chamber. Solitary confinement-slash-coffin. I'm going to *die* in there."

"Some people *might* die. But not you. You're too strong for that."

He reaches into his pocket and pulls out an antique watch. Its case is tarnished silver, with raised roman numerals engraved around the porthole, through which the hands—shaped like highly elongated infinity symbols—can be seen. Inscribed in the face are *Hebrides* and *Scotland*.

"Use this to keep track of the days," he says. "That will help to preserve your sanity."

"This looks old. Like an heirloom," I say.

"So it is. A truly significant one at that. It holds a million memories."

"Can't I just grab a desk clock or something?"

"Please. You *must*. There are still things to get in order here. We're chancing—"

Duncan's words are cut short by a crash, not far away. His eyes grow wide. "Stay here," he whispers, swinging one of the two doors shut. He then closes the other, which is made to slightly overlap the first and sealed by foam stripping.

It becomes absolutely black inside, without even the most minute hairline of light leaking in. I hear another squeak as he works the levers to latch the door in place.

Stay here?

I doubt if a wild elephant could get out.

CHAPTER 52

HENDERSON EXITED THE WAREHOUSE and ran through the corridor to the manufacturing area. The lights were still low, in night mode. He peered into the pit and saw that Talo was still in the same position. No one else appeared to be present.

Not far away was a big red wheelbarrow used for hauling animal parts and small carcasses that did not require one of NutraPet's propane-powered Bobcat loaders.

The wheelbarrow lay on its side, in the middle of a walkway. Earlier tonight, Henderson recalled with certainty having seen it leaning on its handles against the blade unit of an extruder—wishing he'd known it was there *prior* to dragging Talo across the factory and bloody near having to retrieve Kat from the pit. It would have made the hauling and dumping far easier.

It was sure as hell not lying in *that* position.

Henderson could imagine how it must have got that way. He visualised someone looking down into the pit, and then knocking over the wheelbarrow while running down the walkway in a panic. He looked all around, and prepared to be pounced upon.

All was silent.

He considered shouting a *Hello*, but what good would that do? Instead, he rotated the black dial to activate the conveyor below.

The machinery roared to life, followed instantaneously by the ghastly sounds of dislocating joints, snapping bones, and bursting organs. Henderson glanced about the factory once again.

He set off at a dead run, back to the warehouse.

Panting a little, more from hysteria than from the brief exertion, he rapped on the door to the trailer. Kat was too smart to answer. "Just me," he said. "Everything good in there?"

"Dandy," was Kat's stifled retort. "How's life on the outside?"

"*Not* good. Someone was up here. I'm going to put a seal on these doors, then I must go."

Henderson fired up the shipping department's computer. He then returned to the container's doors and threaded a metal seal through the two eyelets, then clicked the loose end into the locking mechanism. He tested it.

Sealed.

He returned to the computer and waited a few seconds for the operating system to finish its startup routine, then launched the tracking application. All of the shipments of the past few days displayed, ending with this one.

Henderson selected the field with the tag number, and began to type the replacement one. He hit *enter*, and the computer responded with a series of castigating beeps.

A warning message appeared.

INVALID ENTRY
SEQUENCE VIOLATION

There had to be a workaround. There always was. What if a tag ever got spoiled, for God's sake, or if a sealed truck needed to be re-opened. The blasted things could not be reused.

Since they all ran in sequence, there *had to* be a beginning. Henderson scrolled back through all the shipments, one week at a time.

This would take all bloody night. He selected the field at the top with today's date, and attempted to change it to one five years prior.

INVALID ENTRY
DATES IN ADVANCE OF FEB 2, 1999 NOT PERMITTED

Okay, he thought. *February 2, 1999 it is.* He entered that date, and four shipment numbers appeared. He advanced the first by one integer. The next three automatically updated themselves. He returned to today's date. The last entry matched the number on the new tag. If a prior shipment had to be tracked now, it would be a nightmare for the clerk on duty. But it would take time to identify the source of the problem—hopefully a *lot* of time.

Henderson's heart was pounding now. Someone had surely seen Talo in the pit, and may have already reported it. He hoped the observer's own fear might prevent this. That Talo was loved by no one could also stand to help. Perhaps whoever knocked over the wheelbarrow—most likely a member of Talo's own department at this time of night—will be glad to have seen the bastard down there. Henderson knew that he, for one, would have been relieved—just as soon as the initial shock subsided.

But there was also enough fear in this building that many employees might squeal to avoid becoming the next one in the pit.

He had to be very careful. If he gave away Kat's hiding place now, they'd both be killed. No question about it.

He moved in close to the container's doors, and spoke softly, hoping to appear to be simply talking to himself if someone were spying. "All done my dear. Remember to pace yourself. Must leave you now."

He needed to say more, but did not dare. Kat must have sensed the panic in his voice, for there was no reply.

Not a word.

CHAPTER 53

A WHILE AFTER DUNCAN says his strange goodbye, I hear the reverberation of other machinery in the factory coming to life.

Perhaps it's his doing—or it could be the material gets moved automatically from one part of the process to the next. If that's the case, Talo seems to be done rendering and is now being transferred onward to the next step. It seems like it's been in the order of an hour.

I've always been a little suspicious of pet food, though I have on occasion had to comfort apprehensive customers about its safety. Every now and again, a rumour makes the rounds that the popular brands are full of antibiotics and drugs like sodium pentobarbital—a barbiturate used to euthanise animals. I've always counselled clients to feed their pets products that use only human-grade ingredients, and to avoid brands that list such obscurities as "meat meal". That particular tag leaves the manufacturer too much leeway, opening the door to the use of virtually *anything* dead, often including roadkill, zoo animals and other people's pets.

I've noticed the human-grade claim printed on NutraPet's bags. The batch presently in production would definitely give those words an altogether different meaning.

* * *

I HEAR muffled voices entering the warehouse, and sit dead still on the double-wide layer of dog food bags that Duncan decided to leave at the bottom of my pod. It was probably good judgement—the bags should make for relatively soft bedding later on. Anything would beat sleeping on plywood.

Over the factory noises, it's impossible to discern what the voices are saying. I'm hoping this truck was loaded and sealed before the last shift of the day ended for a reason—that it's scheduled for pick-up first thing in the morning.

It's hard *not* to contemplate all the things that could go wrong now. Someone could clue in to the tag number having changed. I don't even know if Duncan was successful in editing the tag tracking system. If one worker suspects tampering, and another notices that too many bags are piled near the conveyor, I'm dog food.

And then there's that noise Duncan went to investigate earlier. He said someone was nosing around up here.

Could they have stopped the cooking process already, and somehow determined that it's Talo's body and not mine in the mix? Or what if Duncan was caught hiding the SUV? Far too many individual things could do me in.

Duncan was wrong. The more I think about it, the more I'm convinced this is an absolutely lousy plan. Yet it was fairly detailed. When did he have the time to assemble it? Had he been plotting to get *someone else* out in this way?

"When was this seal put on?" a deep voice I don't recognise enunciates, very close to me.

"Last night, sir. Right before I left." The other party sounds further away, and clearly quite nervous.

"You put it on *yourself*? And it hasn't been tampered with?"

"Yes, sir. I'm the only one who seals the containers on evening shift. I can double check the number in the system. I'm reading NTP 452 876."

There is a pause. The mechanism that secures the door rattles as if someone is testing it.

Or opening it. It rattles harder. I try to regulate my breathing, expecting at any instant to be blinded by the warehouse lights. What would I do? To run or fight would surely be a waste of energy.

"Very good, Jim," the deep voice says. "Your boys can go ahead and start their day."

"Thank you, sir."

* * *

ALL OF a sudden, the entire container begins to quake. A series of sepulchral *ba-booms* assail my eardrums, and the container's floor rumbles again. Then it lurches into motion.

I want to leap up in celebration. Though I'm still utterly trapped, I am buoyed by a terrific sense of emancipation.

What will I see when the doors open again? Armed border guards? Dock workers in St. John's—or Southampton?

After a short distance, the truck stops again. *Damn*. We must be at the compound's gate. I'm not out yet.

It's a few terrible minutes before we begin to move again. The hum of many tires tells me I'm on the open highway at last.

I wonder if it's time yet to use the drill. Surely I still have enough air to last quite a while, but there is no chance of being heard now. I remove the lid from the five-gallon bucket, and dig around for the flashlight. There are so many plastic-wrapped energy bars, I can hardly imagine eating them all. I really don't *want* to imagine that.

Buried midway into my food supply, I find a cold, cylindrical object. It seems to be a flashlight, but one smaller than I expected. I hold its narrow metal barrel and feel for a button. Finding none, I twist the head. It comes on, illuminating a harsh oval on the door's plywood liner. I direct the beam inside the bucket, and snoop through its contents. Energy bars, energy bars, and more stupid energy bars. Nearing the bottom of the pail, I find a sealed orange-and-black package of eight alkaline batteries. I wonder how long that will last me. It was thoughtful of Duncan to supply them, but I will nonetheless have to be conservative in the use of my tiny personal sun. I'll have plenty of time to estimate the remaining hours later on, based on how long the existing ones last.

At the very bottom of the bucket is a small blue Makita cordless drill. It's already got a quarter-inch bit installed in the chuck.

I play the flashlight's beam around the inside of my new home, in search of the best place to put an air hole. The ideal spot, it seems to me, would be facing forward, to benefit from air movement. (It might whistle in the wind and drive me bonkers, but the extra fresh air would probably still be worth it.) I suppose it should also be positioned to offer a decent view, since it will be my only window into the outside world. Most importantly, it must not be easy to spot from the outside.

I put the lid back on the bucket, then turn it over and slide it up against the wall of the container. I place the flashlight between my lips—suddenly glad that Duncan furnished a miniature model—and step onto the bucket.

I guess the wall to be a little short of eight feet high. It is corrugated with oblique vertical grooves, no doubt to add compressive rigidity like the channels on the side of a tin can. I pick a spot at eye level that will allow me to lean into the corner, against both the door and wall for support, and place the tip of the bit into a forward-facing corner of the corrugation. A hole a foot or so from the top of the container should not be too conspicuous. I *hope*. The drill screams, and seems to make the entire container rumble.

A poorly timed bump on the road—not even much of one at that—and the drill bit skips skyward. With the surprise loss of its resistance, I lurch ahead, and inadvertently kick the bucket out from under my own feet. The flashlight drops from my mouth onto the plywood floor, followed by the drill. I manage to moderate my own fall somewhat by sinking my fingers into the cellophane on the nearest pile of bags. Fortunately, my light and the drill appear unharmed. *Dumb Kat. Imagine if you broke the bit off, or wrecked the mechanism! Suffocation city.*

I replace the bucket and try again immediately, using the cone-shaped divot I created on my first attempt as a starting point. This time I'm careful to brace the drill with my arms, and my body solid against the two walls— together with a more positive stance. The bit soon begins to spew small metal filings. A moment later, it punches through, but I'm ready and remain upright. When I withdraw it from the hole, I'm stunned by the brightness of the little circle of light, and instantaneously feel a tiny blast of cool, fresh-smelling air. I'm tempted by the delightful sensation to start drilling several more holes.

A quarter-inch is small, but with my eye very close to it, I'm able to see the pink early morning sky and the blue-green leaves of poplar trees. Nothing passing by outside looks even remotely familiar, but then I don't know this part of the country well enough to orient myself readily even if I had a panoramic view.

I gaze out for a long time, utterly lost until I see the skyline of Edmonton zip fleetingly by when the truck makes a turn. Later, as the suburban sprawl begins to appear, a McDonald's truck pulls alongside—and stays there—my mouth watering at the truly super-sized fries. By and by, it pulls ahead, and I see a sign roll by that says CN INTERMODAL TERMINAL. After a time, we pull alongside train cars stacked two-high with containers marked COSCO, the name of an international carrier whose units I've seen on shipdecks and in great stacks around the harbours of Victoria and Vancouver.

The truck inches forward many, many times, an ongoing clattering outside growing gradually louder. Then my stomach sinks as the blackened compartment around me begins to rise like an elevator in a crooked shaft.

The plastic wrap securing the bags squeaks as they start to shift, and I hear the rumble of countless kibble pellets rolling within.

I begin to wonder how securely the bags themselves are held in place by the wrap, and what degree of harm has been inflicted on the load's stability by the void Duncan created in it for me. Neither the person who engineered the container's filling, nor the crane operator, have counted on it having an empty pocket on one end. The side I'm on stops rising—

—Then begins to *drop*!

Hearing the mounting thunder of tonnes of shifting dog food, I stand and apply pressure to one side of the stack nearest me, with no idea whether my strength is enough to do any good. I do a fast calculation of the weight I'm trying to hold back. The pallet we removed contained one hundred eighteen-kilo bags, in twenty layers of five each—less the five we left inside. If the container is forty feet long as Duncan said, filled with four-by-four pallets, that leaves nine eighteen-hundred kilogram bundles between me and the other end.

Just under eighteen tonnes.

If anything were to cause the container to fall and stand on this end—say these bags start to slide and it falls off of the loader—that's how much weight would be on top of me. I doubt it makes much difference after the first tonne or so. Still, I continue to apply pressure. Might as well do what little I can to preserve my own life.

Not like I've got a lot of other things on my to-do list.

CHAPTER 54

Henderson raised his id tag for the security guard. It was Frank Roosen.

Not good. Roosen was an absolute motormouth. Bad enough Henderson's departure time would go in the log, but Roosen would probably gab about the anomaly to the next forty people who came through.

"Workin' pretty late?" Roosen said, in a tone that begged an explanation.

"It's embarrassing, Frank," Henderson said, shaking his head. "Fell asleep at my desk. I just woke up not ten minutes ago. Still got the impression of a cerlox binding on my cheek. Could you do me a tremendous favour and log me out at the normal time? The Director caught me snoozing last April and chewed my bloody head off. The way things have been, I don't know what he'd do next time."

"Sorry," Roosen said. "Do it if I could, but the system is fully automated. I punch your security code, and the computer adds in the time. Probably for cases 'zactly like this. I'll put in the comments field you worked late. Director Weissmann's one to talk, though. Hear he falls asleep during presentations all the time. They say he's got that condition that makes you fall asleep at the drop of a hat. What's it called...?"

"Narcolepsy, I believe."

"Yeah. Necrolips. I'd like to come down with some of that. Have trouble sleeping a lotta nights. Drive my wife crazy talking. Know how you always think of real important things when you can't get to sleep?"

Henderson smiled. *Necrolips. Sounds like the punchline to a bad pathologist's joke.* "I'd better be off. I truly do appreciate your discretion, Frank. You're a friend."

The gate rose, and Henderson drove out into the darkness. Buttering Roosen up about his non-existent circumspection *might* help, but he wished he hadn't said anything. The nodding-off-at-work story would only make tonight more memorable, and be prime fodder for Roosen to yak about. What the hell would have been wrong with just saying, *Yeah, working late*?

Henderson certainly did not have to worry about falling asleep at the wheel. He was buzzing with fear. Would he be rustled awake at home, dragged away for his role in killing the security director and helping Kat to escape?

The thought was interrupted by flashing red and blue lights in Henderson's rear-view mirror.

He pulled over and cursed aloud. Inside the glove box, he quickly found his diplomatic passport. When the officer approached, he pressed the express down button for his window, and tried to appear casual as he showed the document.

"Not this time," the officer said. "Please get out of your vehicle, Dr. Henderson. And keep your hands where I can see them."

The cop's gun was drawn.

CHAPTER 55

THE BIG BOX SWINGS laterally, jerking like a midway ride—then plunges downward. Mercifully, it makes jarring but non-injurious contact with something solid below. It slides to one side before making a short, teeth-rattling drop. In my mind's eye, a set of grooves across the container's bottom have just locked into place atop a flatcar chassis.

I sit up, listening wide-eyed in the dark to the sounds of other cars being loaded, until the train finally begins a slow advance. Quite some time later, after its speed has levelled off, I stand atop the bucket again and take a look out my minuscule window.

The rich green tones of boreal forest blur by, and though the scenery must in fact be quite pretty, watching it only makes me more aware of how trapped I am.

I step down and lower myself blindly onto the small pile of lumpy bags that are to become my chesterfield and bed for the coming weeks. As the car's steel wheels clatter along, the pinprick of light dances in the blackness. Eventually, my eyes close, and the train's relentless rhythm gives way to yet another dream of simpler days.

After what seems a long nap, the train's horn wakes me—but I am instantly distracted by raw, pulsating pain. My entire face throbs, and when I touch the wound under my eye, I yelp, then feel like puking. My cheek is puffed up like a zeppelin, oozing something wet and sticky. It hurts terribly, the eye glued shut. Precious little I can do in here except try not to touch again.

I get up and peek out the little hole with my good eye. I've entered a city. One I know well.

Saskatoon, my college hometown. I feel my spirits lifted, if just a little. I wonder if I'll be able to catch a quick glimpse of the University, with its Yale-style collegiate gothic architecture. As the train passes through downtown, though, it occurs to me I've drilled on the wrong side for that. When it traverses the South Saskatchewan River, I get a peek at the chateau-like Bessborough Hotel on the low west Bank. Not far from that, I can see the Cathedral of St. John the Evangelist—hard to miss, thanks to the tallest spire in Western Canada. I let out a sigh when the buildings disappear behind more typical nondescript Saskatoon architecture, feeling for the first time that I can recall a deep stab of longing for my former home. I don't know if I'm yearning for what I left here, or if it's an intuition that I will never see this place again.

Despite that I forfeited a look at my alma mater because of it, the hole is certainly on the best side for a trip eastward. The sun will shine in most of the daytime. Right now, it is still up, but has moved out of sight behind the train. I find Henderson's pocketwatch, and hold it back far enough from the hole that the circle of light grows by three or four times in size. Eight o'clock. I've been on the rails for barely eight hours. *God help me.*

* * *

AFTER THE train exits Saskatoon, I settle back down, and doze off quickly. When I wake again, it takes me a few seconds to remember I'm inside a railcar. The reality of it weighs heavily against my chest, and I want to retreat to my initial inkling that this is all a dream. The air is cool, and the light from my tiny porthole has disappeared. I bumble around on the floor for the small flashlight, finally remembering that back in Edmonton I left it in the pocket of my pants. Of course—hence the mysterious pain in my right hip!

The beam's brightness hurts. I get on my bucket, turn off the light, and peer out.

I see… nothing. Scanning the sky, I locate a narrow sliver of moon. As my night vision returns, stars slowly begin to appear around it until flecks of white fill the little circle of sky, everywhere I look. The crescent moon is too insignificant to illuminate what is outside, I presume, until a lone tree sails by. Then I realize there is simply nothing to see here. I'm somewhere in the bald prairie of central Saskatchewan.

Not that there is nothing to see in the province—though this is in fact a belief held by many who drive only the flat stretches of highway from the major cities to others in Alberta and Manitoba. I am fortunate that Jack showed me much of Saskatchewan's unsung beauty during the summers we spent here together.

One summer we hiked part of the Athabasca Sand Dunes to the north, the hundred kilometres of Sahara-like terrain along the south shore of Lake Athabasca. Though they closely resemble a desert landscape, the thirty-metre orange dunes are home to at least ten plant species found nowhere else on earth. Perhaps the most astonishing thing about the dunes is that in spite of their magnificence, few Canadians know they *exist!*

Then, at the province's southwest corner, we visited the Cypress hills, projecting the better part of a kilometre above the surrounding plains, and topped by Saskatchewan's only lodgepole pines. Scattered in between, throughout the province, are more than a hundred thousand lakes. Most offer world-class fishing in unpolluted freshwater. I can't claim to have experienced all of these, though Jack made sure we gave it a good run. Reality is, if you fished in one lake a day—year round—it would take nearly three centuries to try them all.

Then there is Big Quill, the biggest saltwater lake in Canada. And Little Manitou, fifty percent saltier than Jordan's Dead Sea. Like the Dead Sea, Little Manitou has legendary healing properties, possibly due to disease killing anti-organics. Fascinating from a medicinal perspective, but I liked Little Manitou because of the buoyancy it gives you. The water's phenomenal specific density makes it physically impossible for a person to sink in it.

* * *

HAVING SLEPT much of the day, I'm left with nothing more than my own sombre thoughts and the now-familiar sounds of the train. Perhaps I can adopt the sleep patterns of a death row inmate—or a cat—in here, eighteen hours or so a day. That would eat a nice chunk out of my voyage.

I find myself thinking about Jack again from time to time, but in a surprisingly different light since my run-in with Sandy. Initially, I'm uncomfortable with this strange open-mindedness, but soon surrender to it. Perhaps I can make constructive use of my weeks in transit, rather than allowing it to psychologically dismantle me. It's practically unheard of in Western civilisations—*especially* for a workaholic freak like Kat Francis— to devote days at a time to self-examination!

I decide I will force myself to emotionally travel through my relationship with Jack from *his* point of view, to the fullest extent that my imagination can recreate.

I begin by envisioning myself a self-centred and vindictive drug addict, which—however gratifying—will not do. In order for this exercise to work,

I've got to be willing to really *try* to experience what Jack might have felt, to imagine his life and our relationship as he would have perceived it, and then to confront myself on his behalf.

I take a deep breath, and begin with my ex-husband's early life.

*   *   *

I AM Jack Colman, the youngest of four children—all boys—growing up in a perpetually struggling farm near the south-eastern Saskatchewan town of Melville. Jack's—I mean *my* father—is a man who seldom talks much, except for after he has had a few too many beers and goes on a rant about how unfortunate he was to have given his entire life to trying to grow wheat in a veritable desert.

I'm stricken with a rare case of cholera as a young child, with fluid loss so severe that I am not expected to live. I persevere, but illness continues to plague me in my childhood. I miss months on end of primary school, and upon returning am constantly bullied by classmates who gossip that I am contagious. I'm small for my age, and timid. An easy target for anyone—boy or girl—looking for someone to push around for an ego boost.

In my teen years, my health improves. More a product of my work ethic than natural talent, I become star running back for the Melville Cobras. Until early in my senior year, when an opponent's helmet splits the outer capsule of my spleen, causing internal bleeding that nearly kills me before I get under the knife. For many people, a missing spleen's functions are taken over by other parts of the lymphatic system and the liver, but not me. I apparently *needed* those particular lymphocytes. Over the next few years, I develop a chronic bladder infection and twice come down with pneumonia severe enough to require more than a week of intravenous antibiotics.

In college, I take another crack at football. I play running back again, this time for the U of S Huskies. Minutes into the second game of the season, I find myself eating turf underneath the University of Manitoba Bisons' hundred-and-fifty-kilo defensive tackle. My fourth lumbar vertebra is fractured, and my new girlfriend Kat cries beside me while we wait for the ambulance. I feel unlucky about the pain most of the time—the only exception being when I see someone confined forever to a wheelchair.

Kat and I marry, and I leave behind everything I have ever known for her hometown on the West Coast, where I undergo two major operations that do little to improve the constant pain in my back. I can't bear to sit in a car or at a desk, which makes it nearly impossible to work. Without medication, the pain is often so acute that I have trouble even sustaining a conversation. I can only make love to my wife lying on my back. It's the least painful position in general, and I find myself spending more and more time that way, night and day. I try a narcotic analgesic called oxycodone, which does an okay job of numbing the pain.

In about two weeks, I'm an addict. After months of zoned-out numbness, I try to quit, but the withdrawal fever and extreme pain that returns to my back soon have me doubling my previous dose. The drug obliterates my sex drive, but my wife doesn't seem to care. I'm a disappointment and a burden to her. One night, when we're arguing, she tells me so. She tries to take it back the next morning, but you can't take shit like that back. Ever.

I *do* manage to go back to work, keeping my meds to a minimum during the daytime. I learn my way around the island, and even begin to feel a little bit at home. Meanwhile, Kat's life takes a few major blows. Her brother dies, and then her mom. I put in extra work at home, doing the laundry and cooking meals. We still fight from time to time, but things seem to be looking up.

One day, out of the blue, Kat tells me I have to move. She never did love me, she admits. Never will. Broken, I quietly pack up and go. The only thing I say to her is that I hope one day she knows how deeply she has hurt me. She falls to the floor, bawling, but I have no reason to believe she is sincere. This is the woman who once claimed she loved me more than life itself. I step over her collapsed form on my way out the door, taking only my most essential belongings, which include my dog, Arnie.

Knowing I may soon be permanently incapable of working, and that Kat has a lucrative career ahead of her, I let my lawyer pursue half of my recently deceased mother-in-law's estate. But Kat has a better lawyer who portrays me as a pathetic money-grubbing addict who'd sink to any depth for drug money. To the judge, she's a fatherless girl who made good against all odds and is now suffering a string of misfortunes. The judge says I'm lucky to get even a portion of the assets, the distribution of which he schedules to make sure I don't blow it all on meds.

But why *shouldn't* I spend it on my one true lifelong companion? *ENOUGH!*

* * *

I blubber, then weep aloud. Real loud. And—strangely—it feels…

...*Good*. It's the first time I've cried with absolutely no selfishness, not for anything or anyone except Jack. I would not want to be in his place. I may even be better off here, in my mobile prison cell. At least I have some hope of getting out at some point and then possibly even living a normal life—under an assumed name or otherwise.

The train begins to slow. I use the flashlight for a time check. Three o'clock in the morning. I climb up, and see lights of what appears to be a small city.

A slender white railway sign tells me the knife in my gut is more than déjà vu: MELVILLE.

Jack's hometown.

* * *

DURING THE second day, with its lengthy stops in Winnipeg and Kenora, I spend more hours digesting my life with Jack, reassessing things that I may have never considered had I not been locked in darkness for days on end. I have a few more crying sessions. And I still have plenty of time to worry about what will happen to me if the doors are suddenly thrown open. And to wonder— simply *wonder*—what I will do when I climb out of here if I am *not* arrested.

Which could only mean I'm no longer in Canada, it seems. It's possible that I will never be able to return to my house and clinic in Victoria. The people I'm escaping from are still around—I haven't done a thing to stop them. I don't even know what the *terrible thing* was that Craig referred to in his letter, though I fear it was something to do with an imminent prion attack. I've done nothing to prevent it, yet so much harm. And I can never go home.

An unbearable thought, but if I want to survive this, I have got to be willing to accept a very different future. It would be easier, I think, if my home no longer existed—if the next big Cascadia earthquake from a submarine avalanche caused a seismic *tsunami* that wiped out Victoria.

Grim, but not impossible. Some experts say a major event on the seafloor could cause the 500-kilometre-long island to break in two at the Alberni inlet, sinking its entire south quarter. I try to imagine this has already happened. *Your life no longer exists. Let go.*

It seems to help. A little.

For about half a minute, and then I start to cry. I can't stop myself wondering what is happening with my clinic, with poor Pam. Am I officially missing yet? Presumed dead?

* * *

I've been wide awake for hours the third morning in my compartment when the train rolls into Sudbury, Ontario. The outskirts of town bring a sulphurous stench that makes me wonder if the lid has come off my bucket. It was last night, not long after pulling out of Thunder Bay, that I was forced to dump out the PowerBars and make first use of it.

That was relatively easy. The daytime heat inside the container is sure to ascertain that each subsequent use is increasingly dreadful. I hope I am able to resist drilling a hundred new ventilation holes in the wall after a week.

The lid, however, is still on nice and tight. The smell is pure industrial-strength Sudbury. I am now the farthest from home I have ever been. I spent three weeks here when I was twenty-one, after Zaina had left her mother's Victoria flat to marry her new lover. She stayed here eleven months—practically eons in the history of Zaina's love life.

Her short-lived husband D'arcy liked to talk about the nickel mine he managed, and was fiercely proud of his hometown. Sudbury is known around the world for its nickel production, and last I heard the region still produced more of the stuff than anywhere in the world—plus huge quantities of platinum, gold, and other metals. And, evidently, sulphur.

Unlike Alberta, which credits most of its mineral riches to long-dead creatures of inland seas, Sudbury's wealth of metals is a bestowal from outer space.

No joke. Geologists say that two billion years ago—give or take a few millennia—a gigantic meteorite crashed into this area with the energy of ten billion Hiroshima bombs. The cataclysmic impact created a metallic basin sixty-five kilometres long and twenty deep. Just over a century ago, it was in the making of the railroad tracks I'm riding on now that the minerals were discovered.

* * *

The train stays in Sudbury for a long time, doing the back-and forth rolling and crashing I have learned to expect at most every stop. I presume this is done to load and unload cars, and sometimes to move the train from one track to another. God knows these railyards have enough of them. I flick on the flashlight to check the watch, noting it's almost time for another change of batteries. I decide to treat myself in commemoration of reaching Sudbury, and pick a Peanut Butter Chocolate Chip bar, the kind I like the best (which is to say they disgust me only a little), rather than using my customary luck-of-the-draw method. The vast majority of the bars are Chocolate—naturally, since these are the most revolting of the lot—and the oatmeal ones are only a small step up. I have always had a miserable time choking energy bars down, so being left with nothing else for sustenance makes my purgatory complete.

I take a bite of the sawdust bar, and swish it down with a gulp from my half-finished bottle of water. Rationing has gone well so far. It's not hard to keep my food consumption down, and I've drunk less than my quota, in spite of the amazing mouth-desiccating effect of the bars. As I twist the head cap of the Mini Maglite to turn it out, the beam pans across the gusset of a big red bag on the floor. The words continue to repeat in my mind while I chew on my flavourless meal. Complete and Balanced Wholesome Nutrition.

I can't help but think that the diet I'm lamenting is probably more exciting than what most pets get. I tell clients their dogs and cats don't need anything besides the tinned or bagged food—*especially* not table scraps. But wouldn't I salivate now at the sound of turkey and mashed potatoes being scraped off a plate!

Just as I choke down the last bite of my breakfast, the train rolls out of Sudbury.

* * *

I HAVE been forcing myself to stay awake during the daytime, which is not easy in the intense, stagnant afternoon heat. There is little to see outside at night, and I prefer to sleep away the chill. Every evening, I thank my lucky stars Duncan retrieved my fleece jacket from the cage. Without it, the late-summer nights would be insufferable.

Today, I get a look at Ottawa just past noon, and then Montreal in the early evening. I see a lot of graffiti in every city, and I have yet to identify what the connection is between railroad tracks and spraypaint. The breathtaking murals in Montreal place among the most amazing artwork I have ever seen. Everything from big-eyed Japanese anime girls and dark fantasy worlds dominated by giant insects, to deviant Disney characters and nightmarish, demon-filled wastelands. Many of them have been rendered in exquisite detail by hoodlums with world-class artistic talent. People must spend *days* on these projects, all the while managing to avoid being caught at their art.

Once again, I wish I knew what I am missing on the other side of the tracks.

* * *

I THINK about my aunt Justine—my father's only sister—who lives in this city. The last time I saw her was more than fifteen years ago, when she was in Seattle and Mom and I took the ferry and met up with her for lunch. Aunt Justine sent me two cards in that time, one crammed with words in every available writing space when Steve died, and the other three weeks after Mom went. That one read only, "Sincere condolences, Justine." I guess she said it all the first time.

I probably wouldn't recognise my old aunt if we brushed past each other on the sidewalk, yet I would like nothing more than to bust out of here and go find her. After all, she's now my closest relative.

When the train begins to steadily pick up speed on the outskirts of Montreal, I begin my nighttime exercise routine. I have customised my normal strength and flexibility workout to suit these restrictive surroundings. The cramped space forces me to modify my push-ups—diagonal across my square cell, with knees bent. I keep the pace slow and avoid things like static lunges that would cause me to break a sweat I can't wash off, which would also mean drinking more water and inevitably peeing more frequently. I can spare the time to stretch my workout into three or even four hours—so I do.

I do my special pushups, and—since the rails are especially smooth and I'm feeling brave today—handstand pushups, with one foot on the wall and the other against a door. I also do calf presses, one-legged deep knee bends and a variety of crunches, followed by two gruelling Pilates ab exercises: *One Hundreds* and *Leg Circles*.

Then my yoga. Again, I lack enough room for even a proper *Downward Facing Dog*, so I improvise many of my standard *asanas*.

I run through fifteen postures, starting with *The King of Dance*, which means standing on one leg, holding the raised ankle behind my head—the fingers of my free hand near the steel wall in case of a sudden bounce. This time, it's not an issue. The railcar continues to rise and fall gently, rhythmically.

Next, I do low lunges and prayer squats, then drop down on one knee for *The Tiger*. I descend naturally out of that position onto my belly and raise my limbs into a bow posture—balancing on my abdomen with each hand grasping an ankle, pulling to my head. I draw in a deep breath and rock gently in the darkness, feeling the blood flow from my limbs into my body's core.

After about a minute, I exhale and relax. A few other prone poses before I finish with three supine ones: *The Plow*, *The Bridge*, and *The Wheel*.

Then, conveniently on my back, I lay still until I doze off.

* * *

I WAKE up totally disoriented.

The train is rolling, but *very* slowly, the clatters and clacks several seconds apart. I climb up to my viewing station for a peek, and after a few minutes see a white sign that reads MONCTON.

New Brunswick!

I've reached the East Coast.

Moncton is a relatively short stop, and a few hours later—when the train pulls into Halifax—I know the Canadian leg of my journey is all but over. With my nose to the hole, I can smell the familiar salty air—but from an ocean I have never seen. It smells somehow different from the one I know, perhaps caused by the curious adaptation in my olfactory receptors that has kindly rendered me unable to smell the dog food that once overwhelmed me.

I wonder if my container is about to be dropped into an airless cargo hold in the belly of a ship, where I'll spend weeks without even a pinprick of light to preserve my sanity.

I feel *so* sick.

* * *

THE TRAIN inches on by what can't be more than a car length or so, and stops.

Then it does it again.

And again.

And again.

And again...

They're unloading *everything* onto ships, since the train goes no farther than this, the biggest port on Canada's East Coast.

Outside the car, I hear a dog barking.

"Whattaya smell, bye?" says a male voice with a stout East Coast accent. The dog whimpers, and I hear a slurping sound at the bottom of the door. "There' sump'n in there, eh? Sump'n not right about this-here one, eh bye? Ee-ya. C'mon, bye. It's not a-goin'-to anywhere fast. Layt's go git the boss."

I hear the clatter of small rocks tumbling as the sniffer dog is dragged away, still whimpering.

All this for nothing.

I'm busted.

CHAPTER 56

HENDERSON SAT AT THE big oak desk in his study, struggling to think above the constant music, yipping, and frequent detonations of Saturday morning cartoons blaring from the home theatre system in the next room. He was inclined to go over there and tell the *wains* to turn it down, but presently felt too bloody weak.

Too sick, Too trapped. Too... too *fucked*.

He had set Kat Francis free, and probably doomed himself at the same time. A shakedown was imminent at GATSER.

He could feel it.

In the days since Kyösti Talo's disappearance, a hush had come over the facility. People had become more frightened than ever. The place was indeed bizarrely quiet, yet beneath the surface it was buzzing.

There was a rap on the door. "Dun-can," Mairi's gentle voice sang. "Sorry to bother you when you're working." She was by nature polite and considerate, but there was something unusual about her tone. "A man is here to see you. From work. He says it's important."

"Did he give his name?" Henderson whispered.

She lowered her voice to the level of his. "No. But he certainly *looks* like someone special."

"Crap," he muttered. "Thank you, Mairi. I'm not into anything here I can't resume later. Send him on in, please." He found himself scanning the documents on his desktop for anything incriminating, then realized how absurd this was. He had done nothing wrong *here*. He would never risk his family's safety in that way.

The door opened, and he again saw his wife's rounded cherubic cheeks and beautiful jade-coloured eyes. Though her face may have acquired a few lines and creases over fourteen years of marriage, the white strands gradually multiplying in her curly orange-brown hair, Mairi's eyes were still precisely as they were when Duncan first fell in love with her. He flashed a confident smile, but the uneasy look remained on Mairi's face.

She moved aside to make way for a man whose familiar large frame nearly filled the doorway. He had close-cropped steel wool hair, pale grey eyes, and the iron jaw of the retired five-star U.S. general he was. His thick neck was stuffed into a crisp white linen collar inside a tailored hunter-green suit. The breath was snuffed from Henderson's lungs at the sight of this man.

It was Charles Busby, the Director-General of GATSER. Henderson had seen him several times before, and the D-G had once stopped by the morgue for a tour, but they'd otherwise never had any direct dealings with one another. Henderson was far too insignificant in the grand scheme.

But now the D-G was here. In his private residence.

His *home.*

It was an invasion, possibly a threat to his family. Henderson forced himself to take in a deep breath, out of a genuine fear of fainting. He lifted himself out of his swivel chair with his hands on his thighs, discreetly using the opportunity to wipe the sweat from his right palm before offering it.

"Welcome, sir," he said.

Busby's grip was powerful, and cold enough to make Henderson wonder momentarily if the man was in fact an android. "I hope this isn't too much of an intrusion," the D-G said. "May we talk in private for a moment?"

"Of course," Henderson said. Mairi nodded, and drew in her lower lip. Henderson tried to give a reassuring look as the doorway swallowed her up.

The temperature in the room seemed to drop instantly by ten degrees, yet Henderson could feel droplets of sweat accumulating on the flesh of his back. "Please, have a seat," he said, rolling his own chair across the carpet. The D-G accepted it and lowered himself. Henderson dragged over a tall wooden stool brought here by Glenn, who used it occasionally to watch his father, and balanced atop it. He tented his fingers. "To what do I owe this honour," he asked, a reasonable question. Busby oversaw the entire GATSER operation, and his time was far too important to waste on hands-on work or house calls. Perhaps he had come here to kill Henderson personally, to make certain it was done right, and done right away. Whatever the reason, it had to be big.

"Straight to brass tacks, I see. I like that, Doctor. Never been one to beat around the bush myself."

Duncan nodded. "This is a most unexpected visit. Naturally, I'm concerned. Is something wrong?"

"That would be a ridiculous understatement. I seldom do this sort of thing, but we're into damage control of the highest order, Doctor. Your computer hard drive has been going like a table tennis ball between the Canadian Forces Information Operations Group, SIGINT and the NSA."

Henderson tried to laugh, but there was a malfunction inside him that created a convulsive cough instead. "They work quickly. I was using it no more than two hours ago."

"That was a *copy* of the original drive. The one you used before was removed nearly a week ago and shipped to the Communications Security Establishment's head office in Ottawa."

"The CSE has been digging through my files? Without my consent?" Henderson felt an inner seething of rage, and opted not to hide it.

Busby's steel eyes fixed on his. "*Nothing* on that computer is yours, Henderson. It all belongs to GATSER. And many of the things you had on there were absolutely none of your God-damned business."

"Fuck," Henderson said out loud. "You know bloody well Kyösti Talo put it all there. Why don't you ask *him* why?

Busby's lips twitched ever-so-slightly, confirming to Henderson that he'd caught the D-G at least somewhat off guard with this. "We intend to do that," Busby finally said. "*When* we find him. Everything of interest on your system was in fact duplicated on his, and our tech people have traced its path through the network. But what concerns us most of all is that it appears the data did not remain on your computer. Before it was deleted and overwritten, you made a copy, didn't you?"

"I most certainly did no such thing."

"The data in question was duplicated to an external storage device, and the Firewire adaptor used was found amidst garbage removed from the GATSER cafeteria, bunched up inside a small milk container. Chemical compounds unique to the unit were found on rubber gloves with your fingerprints on the inside."

"That can be faked. Talo…"

"For Christ's sake, Henderson! There isn't time to play that sort of game," he said, glancing to his watch as a reflex, probably too briefly to register anything. "There are more productive ways to squeeze the truth out of people.

I came here personally only because Director Weissmann tells me you're the finest neuropathologist alive and a vital member of our team. Frankly, he doesn't know who he'd replace you with. I want to give you the benefit of the doubt, maybe even set things straight. But you have to work with me, got it? Now what have you done with the God-damned data?"

Henderson set his jaw. "This conversation is over. I've told you all I've got to say. Please consider this my verbal resignation, which I will follow up in writing tonight. I would like to return with my family to Scotland as quickly as it can be arranged. The work here was gravely misrepresented when I was offered the position. Innocent people are going to die in great numbers."

The D-G raised his eyebrows. Henderson had let slip something big. "I won't contend that. But the number of innocents who are killed will be greater if our project fails. The Islamic world is a God-damned powderkeg, ready to blow the hell out of the way of life I've spent my life defending. We've got Osama bin-Fucking-Laden offering up a kilogram of gold for every American killed. Terrorists are crawling through the sewers of every nation like maggots under the hide of a rotting sheep. But these maggots are plotting against us all. I've read more than enough intelligence reports to be certain of it, and so have the heads of state who've approved our plan. These aren't just al-Qaeda or the few Palestinians who danced in the streets when the Twin Towers fell. It's legions of people who hate western governments and believe that anyone who disagrees is evil and needs to die. We're all in deep, *deep* shit."

"Can you hear yourself, man?" Henderson said, shaking his ruddy head, his eyes bulging from their sockets. "You've been brainwashed. My sister and her family are Muslims. They are *good* people."

"Among the few, then, I can assure you. Your naïveté when you signed on with our operation notwithstanding, you're plain stupid if you don't know by now that one does not simply *resign*. Especially given the knowledge that you've admittedly acquired, and the opposition you've expressed—even siding with the enemy, for Christ's sake. Just imagine the *quagmire* you could cause us. I won't hear of it."

Beads of perspiration appeared on Henderson's forehead. "Then have your underlings kill me. Like they did to Dr. Benson and Craig Butler and Lord knows how many others like them. Has everyone lost their fucking minds? This is a bloody genocide conspiracy, plain and simple."

"I was hoping it wasn't too late to save you, Duncan. My line of thinking was if you'd work with me, I'd do everything in my power to end your involvement as soon as possible and help you wash your hands. Renew my faith in your loyalty, and you have my commitment to work things out with everyone's best interests in mind."

"Bullshit."

A hint of gentleness appeared in the D-G's eyes. "If it weren't the truth, you'd be lying in one of your own refrigerated drawers by now. Think I've got nothing better to do than come here, Henderson? I'll even see what we can do for your sister. Naturally there is a master list of individuals to be spared, people like Imam Hassan who certifies our capsules. We have to run profiles on each member, but I may be able to have the whole family added if they prove benign."

Henderson didn't know how to feel. Even if Busby was sincere, it hardly seemed a victory to rescue a single family, even one dear to him. He reminded himself that the Nazis kept lists of "useful" Jews—skilled craftsmen, artisans and home manufacturers—but with no intention of letting these individuals outlive their usefulness.

As Henderson's mind reeled, the D-G continued his diatribe. "On the other hand—if you're *not* prepared to co-operate—the research scientists have expressed interest in seeing the effects of an especially virulent new prion strain on young children. I'm told this one has a short incubation period—symptoms expected within days—and a fairly agonising death shortly thereafter. I think a young boy and a girl would be the perfect test subjects." He tapped his fingers impatiently on the desk.

A trickle of sweat ran into the corner of Henderson's eye, and mixed with the tears welling there. "You *bastard*."

"Will we have the data, then?"

"It's not mine to give."

The D-G's cheeks and forehead suddenly flushed, and his brow descended in a frightening scowl. He hammered the desk with both fists, and stood. "What have you done with it? Tell me at once, or I guarantee you'll soon be performing some *extremely* unpleasant autopsies."

For a few moments, Henderson's body heaved as he sobbed. He composed himself and began by telling about the day he came across Talo in the morgue...

CHAPTER 57

WHILE I WAIT IN helpless agony, the train lurches, advancing only a small distance before stopping again. Along with my breathing and racing heartbeat, every sound seems amplified. I hear the high-pitched squawks of seagulls, the hisses of crane hydraulics, the deep, throaty whistles from ships and tugboats, and the reverberating rumbles and groans of very big things being moved around.

Finally, I hear the man's voice again: "Right over there," he says. "The red one, eh?"

The sniffer dog whines, and I hear him throwing gravel, eager to dutifully confirm the presence of a stowaway.

"Oopen 'er up, Sarge." I hear the door's locking mechanism rattle. There's a series of raps on the door. "Anyone in there?"

"Michel, tell me something. How long have you been doing this?"

"With K9 here? Since ninety-seven, I guess, when the Feds disbanded their port police and the Halifax regional force took over the contract. What fer d'ya ask?"

"Come back a couple of steps from where you are. What does the side of this container say?"

Michel reads the name out loud, pronouncing it Nut-Ray-Pet. "Premium nutrition for every life stage."

"What do you suppose is in that container?"

"A stoow-away, I'm guessin'. Or maybe drugs."

"What does Max here do when he smells drugs."

"Well, he goes nuts, Sarge. He's taught to do that, eh?"

"He *barks*, right? Is he *barking* now?" As if on cue, the dog whimpers again. "The poor pup is hungry. And that container... That container over there is full of premium fucking dog food. Why didn't you at least check the manifest from the targeting unit before you called me? What does this say?" There is a tapping sound, which I guess to be a pen on a clipboard.

"NutraPet Premium Adult dog food, thirty-six tonnes," he says.

"That's what has Max licking his goddam chops."

"Shouldn't we take a look-see, just to be sure?"

NO, I whisper audibly, and cover my own mouth.

An agonising lull, then the sergeant continues. "NutraPet has the minimum risk rating. Look, it's listed as a goddam crown corporation—owned by the bleeding Feds. I'd say you've eaten up enough of both our time. Get this thing moving again, constable. You're holding up a whole cargo ship. And feed your starving dog."

*　*　*

ALMOST TWO hours later, I see only part of a giant red-and-yellow crane as it hoists my container high above the harbour. I get glimpses of the skyscrapers of Halifax that appear to be built right out of the ocean itself, and by moving my head around a six-inch radius of the hole, can see every kind of ship from freighters and tankers to luxury liners. Stacks of colourful containers like the one I'm in are piled everywhere like a giant child's collection of Lego blocks. Perhaps more than anywhere else I've been on this strange trip, my interest in what's beyond these steel walls is piqued. I wish I could get out and take a look around this place, to find out what it has in common with my home at the other end of the continent. I am relieved when I continue to move upward, hopefully not to soon descend into the cargo hold, but be placed on the deck.

I say a little prayer, not sure if God involves himself in such things as container logistics, while the crane moves me along swiftly and smoothly. A series of impacts to the floor rattle the food bags, but I'm no longer afraid of them falling on top of me. They've held nicely after hundreds of worse bumps while hitching up to railcars all across the country.

From the height I'm at when the crane lets go, it looks like my prayer has been answered. I've been deposited on one of the uppermost levels, my tiny window looking off the side of the ship onto the harbour.

Thank you, Lord. Just one more thing. Please don't let me get seasick.

*　*　*

AFTER HOURS of listening to other containers being loaded, night falls. I look out at the lights of Halifax harbour, wondering where I'm bound from here.

*　*　*

A SCREAMING whistle rouses me. There is an augmenting rumble, and the ship begins to move. The city lights gradually grow distant, and little islands go by, blotches of black in pewter waves highlighted by an unseen moon. Now that the ship is moving, I know I'm on the starboard side, looking at the Atlantic ocean to the vessel's right. Probably south, though I can't be sure.

Nighttime at sea is even colder than on the prairies, I soon learn. I huddle in a crook between stacks of bagged food wondering if it would be wise to strip away some of the cellophane to wrap around myself. But I really don't want to destabilise the load, and possibly be crushed by it, for what would likely be a negligible amount of extra warmth. I decide to tough it out.

It's a long night, and it only gets colder. I peer outside regularly to see if the sun is coming up yet. The sky finally begins to glow, but despite the low, distant horizon, it seems an eternity before the sun comes up again.

The shivering has given me an appetite, and one chocolate PowerBar does not seem to be enough.

Hunger isn't the only peculiarity. For the first time since Duncan sealed the doors, I feel insanely claustrophobic. The panic continues to build inside of me, and I find myself thinking of ways to bust out of here. After brief deliberation, I decide I will use my drill to perforate a circle in the wall that I can kick away, then climb out and hide on various parts of the ship until it reaches land. Perhaps there is a kitchen somewhere, with *real* food. The thought makes me ravenous.

I take the drill, and press it against a randomly chosen spot near the base of the door. I squeeze the trigger, and the motor whines. Seconds later, the sound turns into a low groan, and it stops. Either Henderson failed to give it a full charge, or the battery has weakened over time. Perhaps I was lucky to have had enough power to make my one air hole. Could be it's just too damned cold for the motor.

I feel calmer now anyway, and set the drill down, then give it a kick.

* * *

OVER THE days that pass, I feel like a lookout in the crowsnest atop a medieval Spanish sailing ship's mast, watching constantly for land. I know it must still be days away, but I can't help myself.

The view never changes. I would be satisfied to see a bird or an airplane. It's hard to believe I was actually glad to arrive at the ocean. No wonder sailors have gone mad out here. There is absolutely nothing to look at. Waves, waves, and more stupid endless waves!

* * *

MY FOURTH day at sea, I'm startled when the ship's whistle blows in two short blasts. I scurry onto my bucket, nearly falling off in my excitement—and see nothing but the same damned water as always. Somewhere in the distance, I hear another whistle blast once. Minutes later, a freighter comes into view, surprisingly far away. It looks like another container ship. The whistle-blowing must be nautical etiquette.

More days pass, and I wonder more and more if I'm on a ship bound for nowhere. I seldom peer outside, no longer expecting to see anything, and sick of disappointment.

The morning of the ninth day at sea, I rejoice to see a pod of six bottlenose dolphins riding the ship's bow wake. I smile as they breach, jumping high into the air and landing on their backs. I think of the dolphins that nearly inadvertently helped Jean to kill me just weeks ago. Hopefully these are better talismans.

I wonder if their presence means I'm close to land. Of course, the ship could sail alongside a continent for many days before coming to a destination port. Maybe weeks, if Duncan was wrong and it's going to Africa—or through the Suez Canal to Asia. He was guessing, couldn't even tell me what port I'm bound for. I try not to entertain such depressing thoughts, but know I must also remain realistic. On the other hand, my food supply is dwindling...

* * *

I'M SOUND asleep when the whistle blasts again. This time I can't be bothered to look. Then I feel a bump—hardly more than a nudge, actually, but it's not a feeling I have had before. I climb onto my perch, still slightly vertiginous from my sleep. I wonder if I am dreaming, or hallucinating. It's nighttime, but lights are everywhere.

We've pulled into a harbour!

I allow myself a loud whoop, and don't give a rip if someone hears it. I'm on land. Somewhere.

Hours pass, and nothing at all happens. The sun appears, and rises, and I begin my exercises. I have been loyal to the routine throughout this journey. The very best thing about my workout is the time it consumes.

I pan with the flashlight, and count thirteen PowerBars scattered on the floor. Though I don't even know that this is *my* port, I oink out with a bountiful feast of two entire bars. My appetite has been suffering, but seems to be fully restored by this new development.

If nothing else, I have surely learned patience over the past two weeks. Even after several hours here, it seems almost too soon when my container begins to move. It drops so rapidly that I feel my stomach ascending my esophagus, and immediately question the sagacity of my biggie-sized meal.

The container gets locked into place, and I learn that I am not on a train, but on the trailer of another truck. It takes me through a series of quick turns, across bridges, and then roars along an expressway of some sort. Signs fly by, but they are all the incomprehensible "universal" type, or full of arrows and symbols that mean nothing to me. Then a wide blue one that's not in English appears:

R'dam-Pr. Jackander
Delft 10
Den Haag 15
A20

My European geography is not the best, but I am quite certain I'm in the Netherlands. The R'dam might then mean Rotterdam, and Den Haag The Hague.

The truck stays on the expressway for a few minutes, then pulls off into what looks like an industrial area. A few more turns and it comes to a stop, then backs up. My heart begins to pound. This may *really* be the end of my trip.

And the beginning of Lord-knows-what.

It's a short time—*especially* in relative terms—before there's a sound at the doors. I am nearly delirious with apprehension. This is when I find out if my workout routine is worth anything.

I intend to run my fucking ass off.

Hopefully I don't have to do it for very long, however, or the lack of a cardio component will be my undoing. I raise one foot to the door, and balance on the other leg.

With a snip, a rattle, and a squawk of hinges, I'm blinded by a widening band of white. Just as the door begins to open, I thrust against it hard with my foot. It swings fast, and makes a solid *konk!*—against someone's skull, from the sound of it. The thought is unpleasant, but I have certainly made good of the element of surprise. After a single quick step back, and without so much as a glance at my home of two weeks, I leap off the truck.

I land with a bit of trouble, but adrenaline and momentum keep me on my feet. I sprint alongside a red brick wall, probably that of the warehouse where the cargo was to be unloaded. My eyes fill with tears from the wind and brightness and joy. I ignore the voice calling out to me from behind, shouting my name.

My name!

"Kat! Wait up!"

Self-preservation won't allow me to stop running, but I manage to steal a dizzy glance back. I'm being pursued by a dark-haired woman.

Everything shifts into slow motion when I realize it's Jessica Bolduc.

CHAPTER 58

"WHAT ARE... YOU DOING... Here?" I gasp. Jessica wraps her arms around me, then stares into my eyes. She examines my face with what appears to be some form of awe. I must smell beyond horrible, yet she buries her face in my neck and clinches me hard. When she loosens her grip, I see she is bawling. A small trickle of blood runs from one nostril onto her lip.

"Oh, God. I'm *so* sorry about the door," I say. "Your nose is bleeding."

She wipes it away with the back of her hand and smiles. The bleeding seems to have stopped. "Dumb of me not to say something. Guess I just wanted to see your expression when you saw it was *me*. Should have known you wouldn't be expecting a friendly face. I'll explain everything right away, Kat. But we've got to get you the hell out of here. That truck driver is going to be some pissed when he sees there isn't really an old guy dying of a heart attack at the back of the warehouse."

"What?"

"Had to do something to get him away from the truck. Let's *go*."

She takes my hand and begins to run. I lose my grip, and labour to stay fairly close behind. We take a narrow lane between two buildings, hop a short brick fence, and come to a tiny red car. It looks like a sport-utility vehicle that has been shrunken to the point of absurdity. We get in. The small engine whirrs like a lawnmower on steroids, and we're off.

"Nice," I say. "How does it go so fast on such tiny wheels? I've eaten bigger donuts."

"And those were the mini ones, right? It's an Audi A2. You'll see even smaller, and when we need to buy gas, you'll understand why."

Jessica has adapted her police driving well to the small car and narrow roads. She flies around blind corners like a maniac, and squeezes past oncoming cars and trucks at breakneck speed—with mere inches of clearance. On a road built atop a water-flanked dyke, a tiny yellow convertible sees us coming and reverses to an intersection—its driver evidently aware there is not enough room for even two Lilliputian vehicles to pass one another.

"Where are you taking me?" I finally ask. I'm momentarily distracted by my first look at a real Dutch windmill. The blades of its rotors are enshrouded in something like black garbage bag plastic, and turn lazily in the breeze.

"Back to a little guest house where I've been staying the past few nights. You'll like it."

"Bet I will. I didn't think I'd ever *see* you again, Jessica. How did you ever find me?"

"Remember when I told you about Craig's female friend?"

"The date everyone gossiped about? Carol something."

"That's the one. I found out her name was Carol Benson, supposedly the business manager at NutraPet. A fake job title. Found out she was actually *Doctor* Carol Benson, a forensic pathologist with a medical degree from Duke U. A picture on an alumni Web page confirmed it. No one I talked to in town had seen her for months, which turned out to be because she'd moved away. Or *something*. The factory receptionist told me on the phone she'd been transferred to Kansas, but couldn't tell me where to look there. Total dead end. You can probably guess there was no trace of her in Kansas or anywhere else I tried. NutraPet owns the house she'd lived in, and now lends it to out-of-town visitors. I already knew the company was weird, but Carol Benson's disappearance right after that one known rendezvous with Craig made me smell a fish."

"You're right. I found a letter at Len's house that confirmed it. Len must've forgotten it existed. He passed out, and I was calling for help when I saw it on the wall by the telephone."

"Ted Kulchisky played me the nine-one-one tape. Slick of you to get Bonnyville to take him. Len was hanging in when I left, but he's a goner. Carbon copy of Craig's symptoms."

I take in a deep breath. This is anything but a surprise, but I'm nonetheless saddened by it.

Jessica grips my arm. "Looks like this Carol found out about Craig's investigations and arranged to hook up with him. She thought he could blow the lid off the operation without giving her away, but she made the mistake of being seen with an eligible bachelor in a small town. Word like that spreads fast."

"That's what I figured. Carol's superiors got wind and put two and two together. Then toasted her. Damn."

She gives a sullen nod. "Probably were concerned about Craig even before, but didn't think he was dangerous on his own. Then two days after I saw you last, Ted told me a car you rented had been spotted by a fisherman— underwater by the boat launch at Touchwood Lake."

"*Underwater?*" I'm stunned. "An old shed collapsed on top of it when the helicopter came to get me."

"Figures. Driver's-side window was open, and a dive team went in to search the water for your body. Touchwood drops off *fast* to about forty metres— deeper than any other lake in the area—so the dive team didn't have much hope of finding you. When I heard there was no body inside the car, I was pretty sure you wouldn't turn up in the water."

"So you guessed I hadn't committed suicide by driving into the drink? Isi Butler didn't kill herself either, by the way. Same guy who shot her was supposed to kill me. He told me all about it."

"But you were too smart for him, right? I'm glad. Guess I didn't know for *sure*. But Touchwood is hardly a place someone from out of province would pick to drown herself in, if she could even find her way there."

"I don't think I've ever heard of that lake."

"Bingo. There are hundreds of others with better access. The only in by car is a long gravel road not much wider than the one we're on now. My guess was that after you so inconveniently disappeared, they picked a lake where a body search would be quickly abandoned."

"The guy who killed Isi created that particular inconvenience. Plan was to question me, then drown me without any physical signs of a struggle. Maybe the car was already in the water, and they'd have dropped me in somewhere nearby from a helicopter. But I got to be a pain in the butt, and he lost his cool. Pistol-whipped me," I say, running my fingertips across the wound on my cheek. Nearly two weeks later, it remains somewhat sensitive to touch. "A deep facial wound from a couple of whacks with a handgun wouldn't have fit. Pretty ugly, aren't they?"

"Not at all. And it'll look better after we clean you up. Give it a month or two and you won't be able to tell where that was. I figured you could stand to look a little more rugged anyway." She smiles and touches a fist to my jaw, giving a playful nudge. I appreciate what she's trying to do, but don't buy it.

"You still haven't said how you knew to look for me here. So you had suspicions about NutraPet…"

"That's right. The factory staff comes and goes together in big black buses. Then there are a lot of other people with diplomatic licenses plates."

"People like Duncan Henderson?"

"He's one of them. Carol Benson might have been another, though I can't say I ever noticed. I'd pulled over Doc Henderson once before, and he was a perfect gentleman. Friendly eyes, and an honest way about him. You can always tell from the eyes. Yet his attitude hinted he wasn't happy at NutraPet. Said his was one of those jobs that looked a lot better on paper, that he just wanted to be back home. I took the chance that if I hit him with everything I knew, he might give in. When my shift ended, I took the squad car and went to his place. His wife said he was working late, so I staked out the road leaving the factory and waited for him to go home. I was ready to give up by the time his truck came along. Peppered him with everything I suspected from my own work, plus what you'd told me in the motel. He played totally dumb. Had me convinced he'd never heard of a prion or a Kat Francis, and wouldn't know one from the other. Then he said, 'I hope that satisfies your superiors.' I told him I was off-duty, that I'd get fired for what I was doing. He just gave me a look, like I was shitting him and he knew it. I was walking away, and thought *to hell with it*. So I turned and said, 'I'm in love with her, you fucking asshole,' then carried on."

I don't know what to say to this. Suddenly, the whole story about Duncan is of lesser significance. "But you left me in my room, never even said *goodybe*."

"I thought it would be easier. I'm lousy at farewells, and we were putting each other in serious danger. It was time to go. I told you I wanted to see you again."

I smile through my tears. "Well, thank you. For all you've done since then too. So you just left Dunc—Dr. Henderson—there?"

"I was ready to. I'd already closed the door to my cruiser, when he got out and ran to me, shouting. 'I think I saved her,' he said. We stood there, in the middle of the road, while he told me what happened. Some of it, anyway. He got as far as that you were in a container headed for Rotterdam, with food and water. Then we saw headlights, so I told him to get back in the truck. Good thing, it turns out. It was security from the compound, but they drove on when I waved. Next day, I reported to the station and told the chief I needed an immediate leave of absence for mental health reasons, and walked right out. Sort of expected him to chase me down and ask for my badge, but he didn't. Probably figured I'd be back in a few hours, but I stayed with my sister Tami in Edmonton for a couple nights and worked from library computers all over town to make sure I didn't leave a trail to her place. Booked a flight to Paris, then took a train here and waited for you. That part was the worst. I watched the container you were in get loaded on a truck, then followed it. Must have been a nightmare, locked in there all that time."

"All the comforts of home, if you're an Egyptian mummy. But Rotterdam isn't exactly a small port.

"Yeah. Henderson would have to pick the biggest one in the world to send you to. But I found out pretty well all the containers bound for Rotterdam go to the Maasvlakte, an artificial extension they built at the harbour's mouth. It's set up to handle the really deep-water ships. Some supertankers that dock there are too big for any other port in Europe."

"You just hung out and watched all the ships coming in?"

"That was the plan. But there were so goddam many of them, it would have been way too easy for you to slip by. I don't know if Henderson had any idea how many container ships there were, because he didn't tell me what terminal you were going to."

"I doubt he knew. The warehouse computer probably only listed Rotterdam as the destination."

She nods, and swerves around a young couple on bicycles. "Could be. Plus we ran out of time. Fortunately, at the harbour a nice stevedore named Jim approached me. Turned out his grandfather was a huge fan of Canadians for leading the liberation of Holland. The guy ran a computer search for me."

"Just because his grandpa said nice things about Canada, he looked up a private shipment for a total stranger?"

She smiles. "Well, maybe it helps if you fuss with your hair and swing your hips a little."

I shake my head. "You phony. I'll bet you broke the boy's heart. So by pure dumb luck he worked for the same company that operated the very terminal I was bound for?"

"His company, ECT, operates three of the four terminals on the Maasvlakte. So the odds weren't so bad. And only one container was scheduled to arrive this month from NutraPet. Since Jim's computer listed only the freight forwarding company that was to pick you up from there, and not a destination, I had to follow the truck until it made a stop. And that's where you came in. Or out, I guess."

"I'm surprised Jim gave you all that information, just for being sexy. You must have really worked it."

She smiles. "Well, I still had my badge, and sort of implied the RCMP sent me to follow a shipment after it landed here. All I needed him to do was point me to the right one."

"Back up a bit. *Implied?*"

Her cheeks redden. "I said there was an investigation being made into a Canadian organised crime group known to ship stolen luxury cars to Europe inside containers. That's a fact. I just didn't mention that the shipments usually go to ports in the Adriatic, en route to Russia."

I grin. "And you also neglected to say you didn't have any part in that investigation. Pretty praetorian, Jessica."

She rolls her eyes. "I did it for you. For *us.*"

"Well, thank you then. For a minute, I thought you might be loosening up a little. So lucky thing you hung onto that badge."

"I figured it might come in handy, even half a world out of my jurisdiction. Doubt I'll need it again, though."

"Not *here*, anyway. But back home, I hope."

"We can't go back, Kat."

"Sure we can. I've had a little time to think about it. We're taking this thing to the media."

"They won't believe us. Don't you realize how insane it would sound? We can't prove a damn thing. And the minute our names or faces turn up, our government would state that we're both mentally unstable, probably wanted on terrorism-related charges. Then we'd end up dying in some Syrian torture chamber."

"Will not. We'll work out a plan. We're smart and tenacious."

"That's us. Smart, tenacious, and banished for life." She flicks on her left turn indicator. "This is home."

CHAPTER 59

WE DRIVE ONTO A winding path, and the house that appears through a stand of trees looks like something out of a child's storybook, where Hansel and Gretel might have lived. The exterior is white stucco, and it has a thick rooftop of straw darkened to ebony over the ages. A wide brick chimney pokes out the top, above a row of three square windows.

"Quite a place," I say."

"It's *very* old. Those windows up there are our room. Helena and Drewes, the couple who own the place, hire it out only occasionally. Whenever some lost soul like me happens by asking if there's a bed and breakfast in the area. They've probably left by now to spend a few days in another house they own on the French Riviera. They invited me to stay on. I tell you, old people here just love Canadians. I let them know I'm expecting a friend."

"Of course you would."

"Pardon?"

I smile innocently, then lean over and peck her on the cheek.

Jessica leads me up the walk. She unlocks the front door, and waves me inside. "After you, m'dear."

The interior is rather dimly lit, and decorated with dark furniture and antiques. White-and-blue porcelain dishes hang in abundance on all the walls. The sweet scent of fresh baking is almost overpowering. Two big loaves of bread sit on the table. My voracious appetite warps my mind, giving me a bizarre urge to grab them both and run.

"Helena told me she might bake some of those for us," Jessica says. "You haven't had bread until you've tried the stuff she makes. God, you must be starved."

"You have no idea. For two weeks I've existed on nothing but PowerBars and water. It's all I can do not to pounce on them."

I pull out a wooden chair, and barely manage to restrain myself as Jessica brings two plates and table knives, followed by a dish of butter and a big bread saw. She rummages in a pantry and finds a few cardboard boxes of sprinkles and a jar of chocolate-hazelnut spread. I begin to hack the first loaf into slices, and add a fast smear of butter, then take a bite. Suddenly a gobbling automaton, I stuff the whole thing into my mouth, fighting not to inhale it while I saw off another. Jessica looks on, smiling in amazement. Is this truly the most heavenly bread and butter the world has ever known, or is my delight entirely the product of deprivation?

Jessica takes a slice, squishes a dollop of butter across it, and tops the whole thing with a snowstorm of white powder from one of the little boxes. The sweet anise scent brings me to conclude I'll try some of that next.

When we're done, only a heel from one of the loaves remains. Jessica wraps it in plastic, and motions for me to take the lead up a steep staircase. "I'll bet you'd enjoy a shower," she says. "Most of my clothes might be a little short for you, but I've got some big sweatpants and a T-shirt that should work."

The upstairs is mostly a single open space, with the walls inclining inward to a flat area across the middle of the ceiling, from which a modern-looking halogen light fixture is suspended. Even with the lights off, the three windows make it brighter here than downstairs. I immediately detect the subtle but unmistakable tang of a cat's litterbox. I spot it in one corner, next to a pair of stainless steel bowls of dry food and water. The cat is nowhere to be seen. A kitchenette is set up in an adjacent corner, comprised of a smaller oven than I ever thought possible, next to an equally dinky refrigerator and sink. The living space is elegantly furnished with a large, low-slung bed on four modern silver posts and matching night tables, plus a sitting area with a simple coffee table and a few inexpensive upholstered pieces. The bed and end tables are exactly the same as mine.

"The IKEA makes me feel at home," I say, running my fingers along the rim of a green ceramic vase that is identical to one Talo smashed in my house.

"Guess some things are universal," Jessica says. "If we find life on Mars, I bet they'll have those flower pots."

"They've got a cat?" I point to the litterbox.

"You could call it that," she says, and kneels at the bedside, bending to look underneath.

A giant of a tortoiseshell tabby tears out from under the opposite end and leaps onto a big blue chair that has had the upholstery on its back and arms clawed to tatters. It kneads the seat cushion with its paws and jumps onto an arm, then up to the top of the back. The cat's sand-coloured eyes study me while its claws tear restlessly at what remains of the fabric.

"Meet Liefje," Jessica says. "It means *sweetheart*, but that creature is anything but. Check out those nails, if you dare. She knows how to use them, so consider yourself forewarned."

"And that's *her* chair. Looks like she's spent some time sharpening them on it. I love cats," I say. I approach slowly and offer Liefje my hand.

"You're pretty brave for someone who doesn't like having scars," Jessica says. Liefje sniffs curiously, and gives my fingers a gritty lick. She begins to purr gently, augmenting to the decibel range of popping corn when I rub the glands in front of her ears. She jumps down onto the seat and rolls over to offer her belly, the ultimate gesture of submission for most animals, as it exposes the vital organs. I stroke her fur gently, and she closes her eyes and gives me a big kitty smile. I take a front paw and gently push the claws forward—and am taken aback.

"Yowzers," I say. "You weren't kidding, Jessica. Don't think I've ever seen talons like these on a *domestic* cat. I'll bet we can find something here to trim them with."

"Fucking amazing," Jessica says. "I've been here more than half a week and she hasn't let me near her." I smile and shrug, continuing to rub Liefje's flabby belly.

Jessica pulls open a drawer and takes out a packet of incense sticks. She drops one into a shiny metal holder and lights it. A soft, smoky scent fills the air. "Liefje doesn't bother me," she says, "but I can't stand the smell of her little turds. Helena said the box used to be downstairs, but she couldn't stop the cat from coming up here and pooping in that corner. Moving the litter there solved the problem."

"I'm fine with it. I'm in no position to complain about smells, am I?"

"If you were really that bad, I'd have taken you straight up here. Bathroom is right over there, whenever you're ready."

She gestures to a slightly open door, through which I see part of a toilet bowl and a pedestal sink. I smile and head straight to it. The toilet is a little strange, with a very small tank and shallow bowl, but I'm not feeling fussy. "You can't imagine what luxury this is to me," I say, flicking on the light.

"Take all the time you want. Towels on the wall are fresh, and the red toothbrush is new. I'll slip you the clean clothes. Enjoy."

She closes the door, and I undress and stand naked in front of the mirror. My face and even my limbs look tired, and my muscles just seem to hang there. I look very thin. The wounds on my face have indeed healed up surprisingly well, though some scarring is a certainty.

I take the toothbrush, and squeeze a generous smear of Crest across the bristles, then work up a great lather in my mouth. I enthusiastically scour away the residue from cases of energy bars, thankful that the brush is the ultrasoft kind. When I spit, streaks of red tell me it wasn't quite soft enough for my unaccustomed gums.

A tune starts to play, muted by the thick old walls. It takes me a second or two to recognise the voice, and I smile. *Ani DiFranco.*

I look at the shower stall, and wish I had a bathtub. Mere hours out of captivity, and already I'm wanting things I haven't got. At least today I've got my very own cop to watch out for me. I turn on the water, and step inside, savouring the sensation of its warmth raining over my skin. I close my eyes, tasting two weeks of salt being washed from my face before the water runs clean. I scrub myself thoroughly three times, not wanting a trace of the unwashed animal smell to remain.

I climb out of the shower and grab the larger and thicker of two terrycloth towels on the wall-mounted rack. It has wonderful floral scent from the laundry, and I enjoy the aromatherapy while rubbing myself down aggressively. The exfoliating friction is nearly as invigorating as the shower.

Jessica has left the clothes on the sink: a pair of simple black Calvin Klein panties with navy sweat pants and a white T-shirt. I put it all on. I can hear her banging around in the next room over Ani D's wailing as I transfer Duncan's watch into the pocket of my new pants and tie the drawstring waist.

Sort of a casual look for me, but that's fine.

I open the door, and fight to step back in mid-stride at the sight of Jean's grinning face.

CHAPTER 60

JESSICA IS PROPPED AGAINST the wall beneath one of the windows, her mouth covered with a wide strip of silver tape. Her hands are behind her back, and her ankles are bound with what must be nearly half a roll's worth of tape. Her eyes turn to me, their fine brows rising in an arch of apology or regret. On the dining table is a four-litre jug made of translucent plastic.

Jean takes a step towards me, his blond hair wild and his face still bent in a terrible grin. "How was your trip, Kat?" he says crisply.

"Sucked. What are *you* doing here?"

"I had to fly the national airline, if you think you had it bad. My kneecaps are permanently indented with the logo from the dining tray, and my baggage is still up there somewhere." He waves a hand to the sky, then laughs loudly. I glare at him, then look back to Jessica. Rage boils up inside of me.

Jean steps to one side and punches the power button on the little stereo. Ani's singing stops. "God*dam*, that shit's terrible," he says, shaking his head with a grimace before storming back into my face. I manage not to react, but see Jessica squirm. "Unlike me, you arrived ahead of schedule. By the time I got to the container terminal, you were gone. Then at the destination, I found the truck driver and a receiving clerk having a shouting match in Flemish or some fucking thing over a lot of missing dog food. Might have been screwed, except that your heroine here used her MasterCard twice in four days at the Shell station down the road. The attendant gives good directions. I think the boy likes you, constable. Little does he *know*." He winks at me. "Catching two fugitives in their love den: priceless."

Jean snatches my forearm and gives it a nasty jerk. He spins me around and pulls my hands together behind me. Forcefully, he wraps them with tape, and I hardly bother resisting. "What are you going to do?" I ask, thinking of the plastic jug on the table. "Burn the house down?"

"That's the general idea. Why? Think you can convince me you're safe to have extradited back to Canada?" He chuckles at the thought. "Maybe you can start by giving me what I came for."

"What the hell is *that*?" I ask, bewildered. "I don't have anything." Jessica shrugs at me and rolls her eyes.

"Don't fuck with me, Kat. I'm not your type," Jean says with a grin, glancing at Jessica to make sure his little funny is not lost. He wrenches my legs together, and gives four quick loops around my ankles before tearing the tape. "My colleague Duncan spilled the beans on you. Otherwise I don't think we'd have known you were alive until it was too late. Or bothered tracking down your cop friend."

"He *wouldn't* do that," I say defiantly. "I don't believe you."

"It's amazing what people will do if they believe it will spare their loved ones," he says. "What an ignoramus."

He grabs the jug from the table and holds it above Jessica. When he tips it, a clear liquid gurgles out. "Methylcarbinol," he says. "Good old grain alcohol. A lot harder for fire dogs or spectrometers to sniff out than petroleum-based accelerants, because it evaporates nice and clean. Not like I'm too worried about detection. I'll be home before dawn." He sets the jug on the table, and comes to me, reaching into his pocket to pull out a box of wooden matches. "So, Katherine. What have you got for your old friend Stompin' Tom?"

"Go to hell," I say.

"I suppose I will." He takes a match from the box and holds the head to the sandpaper on the side of the box. "I admire your bravado. But at whose expense?" His eyes slide to Jessica, who shoots him a stare of ice.

A wave of panic hits me hard at the thought of seeing my friend and rescuer burned to death. "I swear to God," I gasp, not knowing where my breath has gone. "I have no idea what you want from me. I just wanted to get away from your crazy organisation. Now that we're here, why the hell would we tell anyone? We're finally *safe*."

He sets down the matchbox with the single match on top of it and grabs me by the neck, sinking his thumbs into my throat. The room begins to blur as he lifts me from the floor and drives me backwards. I expect to hit the wall, but I land in the relative softness of an easychair.

Jean's face comes close to mine, so that our noses are almost touching. "*Where*," he growls, "is my goddam memory card?" He bellows the last two words at the top of his voice, and I can taste his minty breath. Jean follows this up with a searing backhand across my cheek and nose. A terrifying shriek comes from behind me, and then Liefje's mottled coat is suddenly in my face.

Jean steps back, but the cat appears to have embedded her famously long claws deep into his face and throat. Her hisses and yowls merge with his agonised screams, and it seems that the more violently he flails, the deeper Liefje sinks her talons. He falls backwards onto the dining table, and two of its legs snap away, sending chairs flying outward as his buttocks slam to the floor. The alcohol jug comes down beside him, and its contents quickly gurgle out. The puddle broadens rapidly, encircling him as he continues to do battle with the cat, rolling in the fluid and howling.

"Get this fucking thing off of me," he wails.

Liefje lets out a defiant *scree-owwl!* managing to remain on top in spite of Jean's efforts.

My attention is diverted by the sudden appearance at one end of the puddle of a bright blue orb of fire. *The incense stick!*

The fireball grows speedily, until it is almost fully wrapped around Jean and Liefje.

From the chair I'm in, I glance to Jessica and see her eyes have become as big as soup bowls, and she is trying to stand up. I raise my legs, so that my ankles are in front of my face, and wrestle my wrists under my buttocks, managing to loosen the tape just a little. There is a simultaneous and painful pop from each of my shoulders like the cracking of knuckles as I damn near dislocate the joints making enough clearance to get past my hips. It works, and I slide my wrists quickly upward against the backs of my thighs and calves.

I grab the loose end Jean left at my ankles and free them, then bolt to the bed and grab the duvet with my bound hands, and throw it over Jessica just as the flame climbs up her body. I fall against her bundled form, and roll overtop of her, trying to make sure the fire has been choked away.

I get my unified arms beneath Jessica, and she manages to sling an elbow back around my neck, locking herself on to me.

Jean is upright now, his long blond hair ablaze, the singed and wounded cat hanging on only by an opposing front and hind leg. Jean stumbles in our direction, but continues past—straight for the window.

He wants out.

The glass of the centre pane explodes, and Jean goes through headlong and tumbles out of sight. A trail of his burning clothing smoulders on the straw roof.

I head for the stairs, accidentally smacking Jessica's head against the doorway. "Sorry," I say, and she grunts out her nose in what could be either acceptance or exasperation.

Halfway down the stairs, there's an incredible *whoomf!* and I'm driven forward by a surge of heat as the vapour in the alcohol jug explodes.

CHAPTER 61

I SET JESSICA DOWN on the lawn, at what I hope to be a safe distance from the house. The thick grass is speckled with thousands of miniature daisies, and when I peel the tape from Jessica's mouth, she smiles at me, bedazzling with her dark hair fanned out against the white and green background.

"Thanks," she says, touching the pink skin around her lips. "That fucking guy came out of nowhere and slapped the tape over my mouth. I managed to make some noise, but I guess with the shower running…"

"I'm now a bath girl for life. Let's work on the rest of this tape."

"There's a knife in my pocket."

I squeeze my hand into the front pocket of her jeans and find a small black multitool—the kind with pliers, cutters and screwdivers, among other more mysterious appendages. I flip out a knife, and slice carefully through the tape on her wrists and ankles, then work at peeling it away while she cuts mine.

"Let's go," I say. She slaps at her pockets and gives me a look of shock.

"I don't have my car keys. They're up there." She looks over at the house, where orange flames consume the entire straw roof.

"Jean had to get here somehow," I say. Jessica follows me as I run around the side of the house, where a red Volvo S60 sedan is parked. I've never seen one in such a bright colour—it must be an only-in-Europe thing. I try the door, and it opens. A plastic key fob hangs from the ignition.

I give Jessica a thumbs-up, and she hurries to the other side and climbs in. I throw it in reverse.

"*Wait!*" she says, squeezing my wrist.

"What?"

"Look. There." I follow her pointing finger and see a small animal, limping in our direction. It's a second before I recognise it.

Liefje.

"We can't leave her here," I say. "Quick, I'll trade you spots." Out the door I go, and gingerly pick up the cat. She is purring the way cats tend to do when in extreme pain, and gives an anguished mew.

*　*　*

"HOW BAD is it?" Jessica asks once we're on a smooth road.

"Not good. In addition to the burns, she's got some nasty breaks. This leg worries me." I show her where the radius and ulna—bones that are elongated in felines—have splintered and project through the skin of her leg. Compound fractures. "They'll have to be pinned, and she's got third degree burns that need immediate treatment. We need to find a vet clinic right away."

"I'm heading for the Hook of Holland. There'll be one there."

"Something about Liefje scares me more than her injuries."

"What's that?"

"Her fur is soaking wet. Must have been water under the eaves."

"Oh, shit," she snaps. "There's a big stupid hot tub in the back. So that crazy asshole might still be *alive*! What the hell was he after, Kat?"

"A memory card, he said. But I don't have anything like that. Did Duncan Henderson say anything about it when you stopped him?"

"He was talking so fast, and kept getting more and more nervous. I don't think so. Just where he'd sent you, and that I was right about NutraPet. He rambled about killing the director of security, and something weird about your blood. Then I mentioned the headlights and he ran back to his truck."

"The only thing Duncan gave me was a watch." I pull out the old Scottish timepiece and show it to Jessica. "Does this look like a mem— Oh my God."

"What?"

"I just remembered what Duncan said when he gave it to me. *It holds a million memories.*"

"You think a memory card is in *there*? I don't know if that's even possible, Kat. There's no extra room inside a watch."

I flip it over and examine the back side. "Can I borrow that Leatherman I used to cut the tape again?" I gently lift the cat from my lap and lower her onto the middle of the back seat. Her agony is obvious, but she soon resumes licking at her wounds. Tough little lifesaver.

The smallest of the screwdrivers fits snugly into a notch in the rim of the watch's back cover. I twist, but it doesn't give. I try a little harder, and sense

I'm nearing the outer limit of the tool's strength.

With a *pl-ing*, the metal disc flies up at me, then drops back down on my lap. I pick it up and turn it over. In the middle, stuck on with clear adhesive tape, is a black plastic rectangle the size of my thumbnail and only slightly thicker.

"What is it?" Jessica asks.

"I think it's what we're looking for. It says *1.0 GB* on it.

"A gigabyte? That's a shitload of data for something so small. We need to find a way of accessing it."

"What does that mean? Guess we can't just stick it in a computer, can we?"

"No. We'll need some kind of adapter, which may not be easy to find. That must be one hell of a high-tech card to be so compact with a gig of storage inside. I can't believe Henderson didn't tell you the card was in there. That bit about the memories is a damned subtle clue to rely on you figuring out."

"No, it makes sense. There was a chance of me being caught before the truck got away from the loading dock. If I knew what was in that watch, they'd probably find a way to make me say so. Then Duncan is not only on the hook for helping me to escape, but he is guilty of a far greater betrayal. But I don't understand why he didn't tell *you*."

"Maybe he didn't trust me enough. He was already taking quite a leap. Could be we'll know when we see what's on the card. So we need to find a computer store. But first, a vet. We *owe* that cat."

Jessica stops the car, and points to a pay phone. I get out and immediately see the directory is missing. By the time I'm halfway back in, she's spotted another phone booth across the road, and is cranking the wheel for one of her crazy police U-turns when I yell, "*Stop!*"

She hits the brakes, and there's a clawing sound from the backseat as the injured cat fights to stay put on the slick leather.

"What?"

I point to a sign behind us that says DIERENZIEKENHUIS ANIMAL HOSPITAL in backlit burgundy letters.

* * *

THE VET is a tall, square-faced man named David Van Amstel who speaks decent but very accented English. Fortunately Liefje is in no mood to give him grief, and submits to an examination with only a few halfhearted offensives.

"You are American?" Van Amstel asks with a scowl while injecting the cat with a general anesthetic.

"No. We're from Canada."

Van Amstel nods, and begins to clean the worst of Liefje's burns. "What did you say happened to this poor cat?"

I swallow hard, and Jessica answers. "She saved both our asses in a house fire."

"A wall fell on her," I add.

"It's a wonder she survived then. Strange injuries for such a crushing impact as that."

"She ran onto the road in flames and got hit by a car," Jessica says. I can't help but smile, and turn my face away from the doctor. When I salvage my composure and look back, his brow remains furrowed as he struggles to reconcile Liefje's injuries with our story.

"We really have to leave her with you," I say. "There was someone else in the fire, and they took him in an ambulance."

Van Amstel stares at me strangely. "Oh, my. This is *terrible*. Which hospital is he at?"

"The big one," Jessica says, visibly uneasy. "By the way, is there a computer store around here?" I give her an elbow to the ribs, but it's too late.

"What do you need a computer store for?"

I can't think of a way out of this one, and when Jessica speaks again, I bite the inside of my cheek. "I have a Global Positioning System on my Palm Pilot, and I'm hoping to get a map database for Holland. Then I can find places like this and the hospital instead of driving around for hours, hoping to find someone who understands English."

"She's just like a man," I say. "Refuses to stop and ask for directions."

"There is a place not far from here that is very good, owned by two brothers. Brilliant boys. They speak English, as you'll find most young Dutch people do."

* * *

WE FOLLOW Van Amstel's hand-drawn map, and quickly arrive at the shopping centre, parking at the entrance he said is nearest the shop we need.

No one is in the store except a tall teenaged boy, who is enthralled by a video game that has him in the role of an amazingly well-rendered 3D gladiator. He cries out when his opponent—a freakishly muscled man with a horned skull for a head—strikes him a lethal blow. The blood pulses from individual, anatomically precise blood vessels. I grimace at Jessica, seeing fascination instead of revulsion.

The boy looks at us as if emerging from a nightmare.

"Are the owners here?" Jessica asks him.

He smiles. "I am one of them. My brother Hendrick is the other. Sorry to be distracted. I like to try all the new games at least once. Lucky thing I was born in peaceful times; I suck at bloodsports. My name is Johannes Van Etten. He shakes Jessica's hand, then mine. His skinny arm belies a firm grip.

I show him the memory card, and he barely glances at it. "This is a very new technology," he says with a frown. "Practically no compatible units on the market yet." His face brightens. "But it so happens we have just received one of the first consumer handheld units in all of Europe to support it. Hendrick has some pull with our supplier." He hustles over to a glass case, and uses a key to open a sliding door at the back. "May I?" he says, extending an open palm. I give him the card.

He slips it into one of three slots in the side of the little clamshell-style computer. To a happy chime, an icon appears on the screen. "You've already got data on it," he says.

I smile at Jessica. "That's good. What are you seeing?" He operates a wheel on the side opposite where he put the card, and scrolls through a number of files. "Spreadsheets, PDF files, a few MP3s, and some word processing documents. Should be able to read them all, but probably can't make changes."

Jessica grabs Johannes's hand and scans the files. "Open the one called *For Katherine.doc.*"

He clicks a button near the wheel, and a splash screen appears, then text. Jessica covers the LCD.

"It's okay," I say. "Let him read it. Maybe he can help us." Three heads huddle in front of the type:

Dear K–

I type in haste, as I prepare for my attempt to rescue you, with reasonable doubts you will ever read this.

For some time now, I have been searching for a means of escape from here, but with a family to worry about, it's not so easy.

The documents on this card were given to me. Not for my benefit, but in an attempt to have me purged from the operation as a consequence of having them in my possession. They contain, I am quite certain, enough condemning information about this organisation's activities to have its operations stopped.

A plot is underway to eliminate the world's entire Muslim contingent in order to stop a small number of extremists. The prions engineered with the help of my own findings have already become ingredients in two-piece capsules manufactured here, to be sold as a Muslim-friendly substitute to the forbidden gelatine ones that are the present standard. Millions of units will be distributed worldwide to manufacturers of pharmaceuticals, probably within days of your arrival in Europe. If this takes place, the consequences will be dreadful beyond anyone's imagination. Bottom line: within two years, a billion Muslims will be dead or dying.

I wish you luck,

D–

"Oh, *fuck*," I say. "My God. My best friend is Muslim. And I sent her to Afghanistan to be safe from those scumbags."

Jessica gives me a comforting smile. "I'm sure she's alright. She'd have to take one of those capsules to get infected."

"She's got a sinus infection," I say. I told her to get an antibiotic. Fuck, Jessica, I've *killed* her."

Johannes smiles, and clicks on one of the MP3 files. A voice comes from the computer's small internal speaker. It sounds a bit tinny, but I recognise it immediately—and feel nauseous.

"Sometimes we have to *make* time," The voice says.

"That's Kyösti Talo," I tell Jessica. "The guy who killed Isi."

After a pause, another voice comes on: "A capsule?"

"Henderson?" Jessica mouths. I nod.

"It only appears that way," Talo replies. "This little bomb will win the war against terrorism."

"Bomb? It looks like a little pill to me."

We listen to the entire recording in silence, then Jessica has Johannes play the other. "This is a joke, right?" he asks at the end.

"I'm afraid not," Jessica says, holding her badge up for him to examine.

"RCMP? You're trying to tell me *Canada* wants to destroy Islam?" he laughs and his eyes scan the upper corners of the room. "There is a hidden camera in here, perhaps? That is very silly."

"It's not a joke," I say. "The governments of Canada, the United States and Great Britain are all involved. You heard the tape. They believe it's the only way to stop terrorism."

"But you've got all the incriminating information right here. That is excellent."

I raise my shoulders. "We have no idea what to do with it."

"Now I *know* you are pulling my leg. We're fifteen minutes from Den Haag." He says the name of the place in a guttural way that sounds completely alien to me, the *Haag* part like he's trying to expel a big glob of phlegm from his throat. After a couple seconds of processing time, I get it. "The Hague?"

"Yes. *Vredespaleis*. The Peace Palace. Everyone in the world knows about it." This makes me wonder how ignorant I am. I don't think I've ever *heard* of such a locale.

Jessica's face lights up. "The UN International Court of Justice. Where war criminals like Slobodan Milosevic are tried."

"Of course," Johannes says with a big smile. "Now where is that camera?"

"There is none. We're dead serious. Please, Johannes. Someone may be after us right this minute. How do we get to the Peace Palace?"

"I will take you."

CHAPTER 62

JOHANNES DECLINES MY INVITATION to drive—saying he's never owned a drivers license—so Jessica is back behind the wheel, and I sit in the passenger seat with the handheld computer. Our guide takes Liefje's former spot in the middle of the backseat, the only one of us wearing a seatbelt. He guides us through narrow, tree-lined streets that neither of us could have ever found on our own, making me wonder more than once if he is just playing us. We tear along a dirt path, Jessica leaning side to side as she dodges bicycles and fluffy sheep like pilons—until we find ourselves entering an expressway.

"Take the next right," Johannes says a moment later. "That will get us to the *Vredespaleis.*" He slackens his shoulder harness and reaches between the front seats to turn on the stereo, selecting the FM band and surfing the frequencies. He stops on a station playing a U2 song from the eighties about Jesus and Martin Luther King. He begins to sing along, smiling and snapping his slender fingers.

"Is this a *game* for you, Johannes?" Jessica says. I see his grin disappear.

"Not really. But no matter how bad things are, singing cannot make them worse, can it? Come on, you two."

Jessica and I exchange a glance, and both of us join in.

* * *

WE PULL into a wide road, and Jessica and I look up in awe at the palatial structure. "It's intimidating," I say.

"They don't make them that way anymore," Jessica says. "Takes slave labour. Just look at this big old monster."

"It only *looks* old," Johannes says. "It was built at the turn of the last century."

"Where we're from, that's very old," I tell him.

He smiles mindfully, and leans to peer up at the building with us. "It was designed by a French architect who won a competition. Andrew Carnegie, the rich American, donated a pile of money to build it. The Dutch government gave the soil, and all the other UN members supplied the building materials and artwork. That clock up in the bell tower came from Switzerland."

"Not surprising," Jessica says. "A big ad for Swiss timepieces."

"Is she always such a cynic?" Johannes asks.

"She's particularly *buoyant* today," I say, winking at Jessica to be sure she knows I'm just teasing. "This whole complex is the Court of Justice?"

"No. It also houses the Permanent Court of Arbitration, the Academy of International Law and one of the biggest law libraries anywhere. But the Court of Justice is used to resolve legal problems between countries and to try war criminals. I think that's the place we need to go—"

I interrupt. "But I'm sure we can't walk in and hand this card to the judge."

"There are fifteen judges. And yes, I think that is precisely what we need to do. If we give one of the parties involved a moment's notice of our intentions, we're—what do you say?—screwed. There is a big trial going on right now, over the supposed use of illegal force in the bombing of Yugoslavia. The Netherlands and seven other NATO countries are implicated. I believe Canada is one of them. They're trying to turn it from a military attack into a Genocide Convention issue."

"That's good," Jessica says. "Everyone will be in the right frame of mind."

I nod at the grim probability. "There must be an application process you need to go through to bring something like this to the court's attention."

"Of course there is," Johannes says. "But if what's in these files is true, you don't have time for that. They may not appreciate the interruption at first, but this little card will not be ignored. I expect the court will be adjourned while they decide what to do with it. They'll probably turn it over to a number of Islamic countries, since only member states can file a dispute. Regardless, what you want is public awareness, right, and that's what this will get you."

"I still think we should just go to the media," I say, hoping Johannes will agree. "No one will take those capsules if it's on the front page of the world's newspapers tomorrow. We could just find an Associated Press office and hand it over to one of the reporters."

"If you want to, and then let AP spin it however they want." Johannes says. "That organisation is owned by more than a thousand American papers. I suggest you let all the media find out from one unbiased source, whether they're American, Chinese, or Palestinian. That way everyone is bound to be more objective. This is going to have a big effect on the way Western nations are perceived by the world. The last thing you want to do is give justification for a giant wave of terrorist attacks."

I wince at the possibilities that race though my mind. The terrible backlash generated by photos of American soldiers torturing Iraqi prisoners would be nothing compared to this. Even the most peace-loving Muslim leaders might be provoked to endorse a global call to *jihad*.

What the hell are we doing?

"He's right," Jessica says. "The place for this is the UN court. If it's already looking like the perpetrators are about to get slapped with some kind of cease-and-desist order when the news breaks, it might lessen the pandemonium. A single news agency could decide to just say an attack against all of Islam is at hand. Then it's bedlam. Probably war."

She stops the car at a security gate.

"What now?" I say.

"Let me handle it." Her window glides down. The man inside the gate smiles at us. Jessica holds her leather wallet out. "We've been called to speak on behalf of the Canadian defence team," she says in an orotund tone that betrays no uncertainty. "I understand they've got a chance to wrap it up soon, with what I've got to say and a little luck."

"You're with the Canadian police? All of you?"

"No, sir. This is my secretary and in the back is our expert in surveillance video enhancement technology."

"I'll need their IDs too."

I try to look flustered, which isn't very hard. "Oh, God. I left mine at the hotel. I'm so sorry." Johannes lifts his rump from the seat and reaches for his back pocket. Hiding behind Jessica, I open my eyes wide and run a finger across my throat.

"I don't have mine either," he says as he sits back down, a trace of his Dutch accent evident in spite of an exaggerated attempt to minimise it. The guard has a more pronounced one, so I'm hoping he doesn't notice.

"You two," Jessica scolds. "Do you realize what this *means*? You're going to cause another year's extension on the trial." She leans out the window. "I'm very sorry. They're both new at this."

"Just fill this out," the guard says, handing her a clipboard. "No terrorists would arrive so disorganised."

Jessica quickly scratches what might be random information into the fields, and the guard stamps it and hands back a copy. "See?" she says as we drive ahead. "A badge and a smile go a long way."

"Those doors," Johannes says.

"Let's leave the car here. I think this is as close as we get, and I doubt it's realistic to expect we'll be driving away from here on our own. Now hand me that memory card."

"Shouldn't we bring in the whole computer?" I ask.

Johannes speaks up. "No. It has a camera in it." He quickly removes the card and drops it into Jessica's waiting palm. She tucks it behind her belt buckle and smiles. "Hopefully they won't make me take the belt off when the metal detector beeps. They insist on it at airports now, but I'm hoping the security here is not as high. It isn't like the *Pope* is inside."

Johannes leads us through the magnificent entrance and across a vast mosaic-tiled floor. When we come to a man standing at a conveyor x-ray and walk-through metal detector, Jessica pulls out her badge and begins her spiel, producing the form she filled out at the gate.

"I am sorry," the man says coldly. "I cannot let you inside."

Jessica's tone becomes sharp. "You can't be serious. If we don't get in there, the trial will be delayed for a year or more. There's been a mistake."

"I'm sorry. I haven't been advised that you are expected. The judges are not hearing any new testimonies. I believe if there is any mistake, it is yours."

Johannes speaks to him in Dutch. The man's face takes on a puzzled look, and he shakes his head and utters a stern rebuttal. Johannes gives a nod, and speaks again. The man's expression changes. He smiles warmly at Jessica, then at me.

He pulls a plastic tray from a stack of others. "Please put your keys and coins inside." I set the Volvo key on the bottom, and Jessica tosses in her Leatherman. Johannes adds a small ring with four keys of his own. I walk through the metal detector first, without a sound. Jessica causes a chirp and the flash of a red light. The guard's wand gets a positive from her belt buckle. He continues scanning it in different directions—always to the same result—until Johannes walks through and a siren whoops. A different light goes on and stays lit.

The man's eyes open wide, and he takes another, bigger wand to Johannes. He looks at a screen. It responds when waved across his hands. *"Nitroglycerol?"* he says to Johannes.

The boy's mouth opens wide, then closes into a smile. He speaks in English for our benefit. "My father has heart troubles. *De angina.* He had an episode this morning, so I gave him a pill before I went in to work."

"That is all it takes," the guard says, and smiles at the reading on his computer display as he waves the wand across Johannes's fingers once again. "The machine is very sensitive. It will pick up just a few microscopic particles. You may go inside. Please take an empty seat towards the back. I will keep the knife tool for you." He looks me up and down and scowls. "You will notice we are not so informal in our courtrooms." I nod, and bow my head.

Jessica leads us to the first of two massive sets of wooden doors, and holds one open for Johannes and me. When we are enclosed in the space between these and the next set, she stops and looks to Johannes. "What the hell did you say?"

"I fibbed," he whispers. "I told him the *real* reason we wanted to go inside was that your grandfather was a Canadian paratrooper who died helping to free a number of people who hid in this chamber during the war. You fly home tomorrow morning, and were desperate to have a look at the place."

"That did it?"

"No," he says with a soft chuckle. "So I told him I was quite sure you would both spend the night with me if I got you in, and I would give him a hundred euros. That worked."

Jessica smiles at me.

The low drone of a voice inside the courtroom barely penetrates the heavy doors, but becomes much louder the instant I push one open. The speaker is standing at a podium beneath three enormous stained glass windows, where suited men sit in an inverted horseshoe around him. On either side, an enormous painting covers much of the wood-panelled walls.

The man speaking has a thick Eastern European accent. His eyes shift momentarily from the podium to look at the three new arrivals to the public gallery, and he pauses for a moment to find his place before proceeding: "These are not but fifty-five hundred soldiers or nameless pawns who were killed or seriously injured. Each of them loved life as do you and I, and each who died was mourned upon his or her passing and leaves a hole in many hearts. The three children killed by a cluster bomb in Doganovici village all had names. They were nine year old Endon Fisnik, thirteen year old Osman Burim and fourteen year old Vajdet Kosdan. In Velika Dobranja, a six-year-old named Artaa Lugic was killed and three other children seriously wounded. I wish I could tell you all the names and all the stories, or those of the three million children that the war and bombing left in grave danger. Or what will become of the hundreds of thousands of citizens who were exposed to poisonous gases and depleted uranium…"

I look at Jessica, and can see she is thinking the same thing I am. Should we interrupt this man, who appears to be presenting an important closing argument to the court?

"Let's let him finish," she whispers.

"I agree."

"Are you sure?" asks Johannes. "He's taking it to your countrymen."

I smile. "We're about to do them a lot worse."

People all around us are staring. I already felt hugely self conscious about the clothes I am wearing, and now here we are talking during a poignant statement. Everyone else is indeed well dressed, mostly in dark suits and dresses, and others in tidy sweaters with neckties or conservative blouses. As far as I can tell, I am the only one in sweat pants and a T-shirt with no bra.

Out of the corner of my eye, I see one of the big doors behind us open, and another person enters the room.

Good. Maybe we will be less conspicuous.

The newcomer sits directly behind us, and Jessica appears to study the painting to the left, then sweeps across the back of the room as if to compare it to the one on the facing side. Midway through, her eyes go big. She sucks in a sudden, quite audible breath.

I dare not look.

"Goddam it, it's *him*," she whispers, her face looking straight ahead and frozen in a look of horror. "The man from the fire."

I say nothing, but have little doubt my expression matches hers. Johannes looks at us both in bewilderment.

I sense Jean leaning forward. "Don't move," he says in a goose-like hiss, and Jessica and I both flinch. He continues: "I'm sporting a whack of plastic explosive. Just follow me out the door and everything will go just fine. If not, we're all going to make a helluva mess of these beautiful walls."

I swivel my torso a little, and turn my head to get a view of Jean. His hair is chopped quite short, so that all the blond streaks have been removed. His pale and strangely textured neck protrudes from a black button-up mandarin collar. His eyebrows look weird, and I realize it's because they have been filled in with eyeliner. That explains the uneven texture of his skin. He's covered in foundation to conceal the burns.

The speaker continues to eulogise at the front, his voice reverberating in my dizzied skull. It feels like I'm listening underwater. Jean's eyes stay glued to me, and he undoes the three knobby buttons that cross his sternum. The burns on his hands are too bad to hide with makeup, the skin having fallen off at the knuckles to show glistening crimson tissue and shocking white tendons. It's a few seconds before I see what he is showing me. It looks like a regular plastic bag, partly filled with light-coloured powder.

"This is a dirty bomb. Filthy, actually. Filled with very nasty prions. I'm wearing a suicide belt made of a plastic explosive called *detasheet*. Enough detonating velocity to kill a quarter of the people here, and everyone else will be dead in a month."

"He's lying," I say to Jessica. "The sniffer would have picked it up."

She grins wickedly. Her voice booms, echoing throughout the courtroom. "Excuse me, everyone. I have something very important to present to the court."

A dissonance of gasps and whispers flutters about the room.

I glance over to Jean. His lips work silently, and his eyes are like big circles. "Oh. Oh, fuck," he finally gasps. He begins to fumble with something within his shirt, then pulls free a small console strung inside on a wire. Johannes sees it too, but appears immobilised by fear.

"Order!" booms one of the judges. From each corner of the room, large men in dark suits move rapidly toward us.

"*BOMB!*" I yell, pointing at Jean, who grins perversely at me. "*He's wearing a BOMB!*" The burly men begin to sprint, the nearest two reaching him at almost the same instant and wrapping their bodies around him in the most selfless of embraces.

I dive for Jessica and hit her from behind, grabbing Johannes's sweater with one hand. This seems to pop him out of his trance, and he leaps forward with me, one hand on Jessica. As our tangle of bodies topples over the back of the heavy wooden bench, there is the most brilliant flash, coupled with a head-splitting *BA-ROOM!*

And that's all...

CHAPTER 63

One year later

"*AW, BILE ME HEID!*" Duncan Henderson mutters to himself, dropping to his knees on the seventeenth-century hardwood in search of a missing cufflink. Finding neither the bauble nor a cranny that might have swallowed it, he presumes the rental company messed up and supplied only one in the little accessory bag.

He takes his time buttoning his white cotton shirt and tying up the shiny black shoes. In spite of Mairi's multitude of wonderful attributes, it has always taken her *ages* to get ready for any outing.

Henderson looks through the rippled glass on the ancient art-deco window, down at the medieval square outside. He thinks about Glenn and Fiona. They both love his sister Fatimah—*Heather* before she converted—and are probably having a sensational time at her house in Glasgow.

A black Mercedes-Benz taxicab pulls up in front of the building, and the driver steps out.

"Mairi," he sings loudly, erring on the side of excessive pleasantness to mask the impatience that tosses his stomach and prickles his flesh. "Our chariot has arrived."

"I'm ready," she says, surprising him. He prepares to feign bedazzlement at her appearance, and is almost knocked off his pins by the real thing.

"Oh, *my*," he says, running his hands down the smooth skin of her arms, his fingertips barely making contact. "You truly look radiant." Mairi wears a bright cobalt-coloured dress, with small jewels stitched around the shoulders and encircling a large oval portal that reveals much of her ample cleavage. Her make-up is subtle, yet strikingly applied to call attention to her bright green eyes and reinstate the sculpted majesty of her cheekbones. *Mairi has used her artistry to magnificent effect. She is* gorgeous.

Henderson grabs his jacket, and opens the door for Mairi. They make their way along the elegantly patterned carpet runner to the elevator, and climb into the small chamber. Inside, Henderson checks the time and curses under his breath. He practically *tows* Mairi the rest of the way to the cab.

"How far is our destination?" Henderson asks the driver.

"About fifteen minutes."

"Double your fare if you get us there in ten."

With a squeal of tires, the taxi sets off, careening through cramped and congested streets at a speed that soon makes Henderson feel ill. *Canada has made me soft,* he thinks.

Nine-and-a-half minutes after it left the hotel, the taxi wheels up in front of a monstrous neo-classical red brick structure. Four granite pillars run way up to the top, dividing the face of the building into thirds—each with its own set of tall wooden doors. Henderson squeezes Mairi's knee, and she smiles warmly at him. "It will go well," she says, but a flutter in her voice gives her away.

He gets out and walks round the back of the vehicle to open Mairi's door, but the chauffeur beats him to it. Henderson takes her arm, and they walk briskly to the middle entrance. Inside, they are greeted by a tall young man with a small nose and short-cropped blond hair. One of his ears is mostly missing, yet he remains boyishly good-looking.

"Doctor and Mrs. Henderson," the young man says with a smile.

"Have we met?" Henderson asks.

"Not yet. But you were described to me."

"Bald, mustachioed, and *wickedly* handsome," Henderson says with a smile.

"Just the latter two, in fact. I am Johannes Van Etten. Mrs. Henderson, you have reserved seating at the front. Please follow me if you will. We are about to get underway. Dr. Henderson, you should stay here."

As soon as Mairi takes her seat, a tune begins to play on the organ. Henderson wipes his brow and turns.

Jessica Bolduc appears at the rear of the building in a scarlet Royal Canadian Mounted Police tunic, complete with canary-yellow-striped black trousers and brown leather riding boots with jack spurs. Her shoulders are adorned with the twin chevrons of a Corporal, and over her left breast pocket hangs a red cross, trimmed in gold. The Cross of Valour, Canada's highest honour for bravery. Rather than sport the traditional wide-brimmed felt Stetson,

Jessica has had her hair braided and pinned into a tall and elaborate updo. As she becomes visible, a multitude of delighted gasps and whispers flutter through the assemblage.

The young usher Johannes takes Jessica's arm, and begins to guide her to the front of the room.

Then Kat appears. She has on a form-fitting two-piece cream dress of silk, with fern leaves and tiny pearls embroidered on the front of the top. Her hair is at least an inch longer than the last time Henderson saw it and sculpted into neat curls across her forehead and temples.

A strikingly attractive woman with bold south-Asian features leads her by the arm. Kat smiles at him. "Duncan Henderson, I'd like you to meet my lifelong friend Zaina," Kat whispers. Henderson raises the offered hand to his lips and pecks Zaina's long, French-manicured fingers.

"I've been wanting to thank you, Dr. Henderson," Zaina says.

"Please," he replies. "The hardest thing I did was pull a lock of Kat's hair out. Isn't that a bonnie dress she's got on?"

Kat beams. "A mother's touch. Just needed a few finishing stitches."

Henderson gives a warm smile. "Ready?" he asks Kat. She nods. He takes her free arm and the three begin a slow walk to the front, where Jessica awaits.

Holland will be a good place for these two, Henderson thinks as he steadies himself. When she asked him over the telephone to do this, he was reluctant to accept, believing himself less than fit for such an honour. He had yet to overcome all the strife brought over his conscience by his disclosure of her escape. But Kat seemed to truly appreciate a man's need to protect his own family, and refused to relent. "It would make my day *perfect* to have a father figure give me away," she said.

That was all it took.

The Remonstrant Church, one of the oldest Dutch denominations, was among the first in the Netherlands to perform same-sex marriage ceremonies after Dutch law was amended to allow them in 2001—along with the upgrading of "registered partnerships" to full marital status. Canadian law was not far behind, with the province of Ontario allowing its first gay marriage two years later, backed up by a recent supreme court ruling to make such unions legal nationwide. Here in Holland, though, Kat and Jessica could do something not yet allowed at home: adopt a child. They were both fully smitten with a little boy in Batapola, Sri Lanka—his whole extended family wiped out by the Sumatra *tsunami*. The Dutch prime minister had fast-tracked the emigration process, and promised to certify the couple "eligible and suited" to adopt once wed. Sri Lanka had been among the first three nations to ratify the Hague Convention on Intercountry Adoption in May of 1995—and it couldn't hurt that Zaina was making most of the necessary calls to there, in her mother's Sinhalese. A former Dutch colony of a hundred and forty years, Sri Lanka would have the final say in the matter—when the couple travelled there for the court's decision. It looked promising, but there were no guarantees...

As for the Hendersons, they would continue living in Canada. When the perfect house had become available—on a West Coast island with a climate scarcely unlike that of Glasgow—they'd taken mere hours to make up their minds.

And Kat had given them a nice deal, thanks at least in part to Mairi's smooth negotiating.

Shortly after the prion scandal blew up, Henderson was cleared because of his role in rescuing Kat and arming her with the data—then enabling Jessica to get to her before Jean. Almost everyone at the helm of GATSER was arrested within days, except the Director-General and two of the U.S.-based regional directors. Henderson believed somebody had tipped the three off, and they were gone for good—living someplace tropical with new names and perhaps new faces.

The three implicated governments responded in differing ways. The British P.M. maintains he was misled by America, and continues to plead ignorance about the planned biological attack. The president of the United States and his secretary of defence are facing the scandal—christened *Capsulegate* by his country's press—with a stone wall of denial. They vehemently insist the prion gel-caps were to be distributed directly to terrorist cells and that measures were to be taken to prevent the infection of any *friendly* Muslims. Harmless versions of the capsules were to go to the vast majority of consumers, the president claims, vowing to locate the benign ones—which have gone missing.

Much like his counterpart in London, the Canadian prime minister is saying he was treated like a mushroom: kept in the dark and fed bullshit. He blames all Canadian involvement on former governments—despite his previous high-ranking postings which include that of defence minister.

Jessica's promotion and medal were clearly part of the attempt to broaden the optical distance between the current government and the scandal, though no one disputed that she was fully deserving of both. It matters little, Henderson thinks to himself. *She won't be going back.*

The only certainty is that it will take decades to work through all the criminal proceedings and appeals, and that it will be the guiltiest who go unpunished.

Henderson is pleased that Kat, Jessica, and young Johannes all remain clear of any symptoms of prion infection. The strains to which Kat might have been exposed at Craig Butler's house and those in the Peace Palace explosion were dissimilar in many respects, but had in common a short incubation period. The courtroom blast knocked Kat unconscious (and so she remained for three long days), but Jessica was quick to get back on her feet, and ordered everyone to breathe through their clothing and vacate the courtroom immediately.

Jean had been correct to believe that the *heat* produced by his explosive —*detasheet*, a new material that defied detection by the security sniffers— would not have been sufficient to destroy the prions he carried in with it. But he'd failed to consider *pressure*. A short burst of intense pressure—like that of the blast—when *combined* with heat, was one of the few effective means of disabling the pathogens.

As for the airborne prions in Craig's house, it might have helped that Kat consumed plenty of green tea to ward off the cancer in her family. The same polyphenol extract that prevented cancer cell growth had also been recently proven to block prion replication. It had been Henderson's pet theory for some time that the black tea loved by Brits—which contained a comparable amount of the preventative extracts—had thwarted a massive variant BSE epidemic there. Millions had eaten the meat and organs of Mad Cows, yet fewer than a hundred and fifty residents had officially contracted the human form. It could have—*should* have—been far, far worse.

* * *

THE CEREMONY is short but emotional.

Henderson takes it in with tear-filled eyes, seated between Mairi and the one other familiar face in the building—aside from those of the brides.

It's Pam, Kat's former animal health technician, who kindly assisted the Hendersons in their move and toured them around their new hometown. It looks as though he and Mairi may be losing her now, as a few hushed exchanges during the ceremony reveal she has clearly become enamoured with the Dutch capital—and is contemplating a job offer from an upstart animal hospital here.

Duncan Henderson smiles at the thought. Occasionally, things do work out quite nicely.

The vows, prepared by Kat and Jessica themselves, bring the biggest tears of the day. While Kat's words are lyrical and tender, Jessica pledges her commitment with fiery resolve—culminating in a burst of unbridled emotion. It's hard to say which of the two has the more profound impact.

This leads, of course, to the point at which the pastor asks if anyone knows of a reason for which the pair should not be wed. "Speak now, or forever hold your peace," he commands.

The church goes as quiet as a mortuary. "Phew," Kat says, tugging on the collar of her dress and triggering a welcome rumble of laughter.

"I've got something to say," declares a male voice from a remote pew. All heads turn.

A man in a double-breasted navy suit stands, wincing as he straightens himself. His pale face is lined with just enough wrinkles to look good, and his otherwise sable hair is streaked at the temples with white highlights. He appears, Henderson thinks, to be in his late thirties or early forties. He walks swiftly up the aisle with pain flashing in his eyes, biting repeatedly at his lower lip. Henderson looks to Kat, and sees she has blanched. Jessica's face takes on a protective scowl, and she moves forward. Zaina does the same, a half-step behind. The pastor lifts an open hand to halt the man.

"It's okay," Kat says. "Let him speak."

"Thank you," the man says to her with a nod, and turns to address the congregation. "For those of you who don't know me, my name is Jack Colman. I was married to Kat for more than six years."

A wave of murmurs, and one or two angry mutterings can be heard. Henderson looks to Kat, but finds her face impossible to read. She takes Jessica's hand and raises it slightly, getting a sympathetic smile in return.

"I couldn't stop myself from coming here today," Jack says, his voice shaky. "I'm sorry, all of you, but I have to do this."

He shuts his eyes tightly and raises a hand, which he plunges inside the lapel of his jacket. He grimaces as if in the worst kind of pain.

Several people gasp.

CHAPTER 64

JESSICA TAKES A HALF step forward, but Kat gets hold and pulls her back.

Jack Colman clears his throat, then whips a bundle of folded papers from an inside pocket and begins again. "You know, only a year ago, there's no way I'd have been bothered to fly halfway around the globe and show my ugly face here. But a lot has happened since then. Because of *that* woman, many things are different than they might have been." He points to his former wife with the papers and smiles, then unfolds them.

"This is what changed things for me. It's a copy of a letter Kat wrote a couple months ago to my big brother Sandy. I won't read it to you, because it's long and, quite frankly, too personal. So I'll summarise. For a long time, I believed Kat didn't care about me, didn't understand how I felt or why I did the things I did. But a lot of this was because I was too busy feeling sorry for myself. I took the care and support she gave me for granted, and chose not to believe her when she said it wasn't my fault she didn't love me the way she wished she did. Kat and I were the best two friends a lot of people ever saw, and I made the mistake of thinking that meant we should be married. Her mistake was in hoping if she went along with that, and then if she wished *real* hard to fall in love, she could somehow fool herself into becoming something she was never meant to be. In fact, it wasn't until I saw the way she looked at Jessica today that I could say I *completely* understood.

"I'll always love you, Kat. And if I know in my heart you are truly happy, I believe I might have a shot at finding some of the same for myself."

A few polite claps, then silence as Kat approaches Jack and embraces him. Jack offers his hand to Jessica, and she spreads her arms to invite him for a hug—which he accepts. More applause, and moist-eyed smiles all around.

The pastor steps back in. "So I take it you don't object to this union, Mr. Colman?" Jack cocks his head, and mouths an inaudible *no, I don't.*

"Then by the power vested in me, I pronounce you Wife One and Wife Two, in no particular order. You may kiss the bride." He spreads his arms and places one hand on Kat's shoulder and the other on Jessica's. "*Both* of you."

Kat and Jessica share a kiss, to a dead-silent room. Pam stands and gives a whoop, and the room bursts into a roar of cheers. The kiss continues.

When the pair finally unclinch, Kat speaks: "Now, to make darn sure this ceremony is followed by a wild all-night party, we've invited an extremely important Scottish couple. Mairi and Dr. Duncan Henderson, please rise."

The Hendersons stand, to generous applause. Duncan sits down, but Mairi remains standing. "Thank you, Katherine," she says. "My dear husband has been doing all the housework for the past few weeks so I could devote myself to a most special project. Duncan also conspired with Pastor Schmidt to have it received by the church in advance of this ceremony..."

The monstrous pipe organ begins a fanciful theme, and two boys emerge at the side of the altar dressed in white gowns. They are holding a large rectangular object, cloaked in a silky silver shroud. They stop at a point directly behind Kat and Jessica. Pastor Schmidt grabs at opposing corners of the drapery and, when the music reaches a crescendo, whips it dramatically away.

At a metre wide and nearly twice as high including the golden baroque frame, it is a beautiful rendition of the newlyweds. A composite Mairi painted from several photographic references furnished by Zaina and Jessica's sister Tami. Fabulously—miraculously—lifelike, Henderson considers it his wife's masterpiece.

Set on a North Sea beach beneath dramatic skies, Jessica stands in a form-fitting blue satin suit, arms folded around Kat, who wears a flowing emerald gown—its surreal crushed velvet texture detailed with a subtle rococo pattern. At Jessica's feet are two slinky felines, a calico and an enormous tortoiseshell. On closer examination, one might notice Kat is holding an object that, though once dutifully returned it to its owner, is today boxed and wrapped in tissue paper amidst a mountain of other gifts. An antique Scottish pocketwatch, the back only recently engraved:

To MEMORIES, OLD AND NEW.

POSTSCRIPT

It is by the kindness of my friend Duncan Henderson, in lending his perspective through many conversations via telephone and online, that you and I share a more complete picture of what precipitated these wild events.

Though I have in my selfish way stolen the final word, I think it most fitting to have begun and ended the narrative from his perspective. Without Duncan, there simply would be no story.

As to Jessica and me, there is much more.

… But not for telling here.

—Kat

AUTHOR'S NOTE

IN PREPARING TO WRITE this book, I visited a man who has investigated over a hundred mysterious animal mutilation incidents—more than anyone in Canada, possibly the world.

This man's name is Fernand Belzil. I drove out to meet him a skeptic, but after watching two carousels of his amazing slides, I had changed my mind. I still cannot claim to know who or what has caused more than ten thousand such incidents in the Americas since the first reported cattle mutilations in the fall of 1973. (Or why not a single person has ever been arrested or charged in relation to any of them.) But I can say I am certain they are not the work of predators or *ordinary* people.

Though I came up with the idea of the mutes being linked to covert prion disease surveillance while lying in bed one night, it turns out I wasn't the first—nor the last—to consider such a possibility. Seven years earlier, a former Alabama police officer named Ted Oliphant had posed a similar question after investigating more than thirty-five such incidents while on duty. He suspected the strange deaths were part of a publicly funded plan to track prion diseases, and even claimed to have followed unmarked black helicopters—the kind sometimes reported near mutilation sites—directly to a military installation.

Then after I began writing, the U.S.-based National Institute for Discovery Science (NIDS) released a persuasive white paper titled *Unexplained Cattle Deaths and the Emergence of a Transmissible Spongiform Encephalopathy (TSE) Epidemic in North America*. Credited in the report for furnishing previously unpublished research data was Fernand Belzil.

Not that any of this necessarily proves the existence of such a link—but I've enjoyed musing that whatever really is happening at night in those cold and lonely pastures, I am not alone in thinking it *could* be something like what you've read here.

THANKS

Tia, for reading, hearing, understanding, and believing;
Monique, for her eagle eye, sound advice, many hours—and *the music*;
Cori, for keeping the machine oiled and running smoothly while I fretted over words, plot, and sentence structure;
Carl, for his patience in answering my endless medical questions;
Blair, for the insider's perspective on being a real live Victoria vet;
Donna, for the spark...

And Fernand, for his kindness, and for being so different from what I expected. A link to Fernand Belzil's website is posted at BradSteel.com.

My heartfelt thanks to all who lent their time and expertise in making this story more accurate and true to life than I could have done on my own. For any mistakes in transferring that knowledge to these pages, I am solely responsible.

Please turn the page for a special preview of

CRUDE

the forthcoming novel by

BRAD STEEL

Coming soon from GRAPHOS Books

For more information, and to receive
Brad's free insider's newsletter, visit BradSteel.com

one

AFTER READING THE FINAL PAGE FOR THE FIFTH TIME THAT DAY, Blaine Ryley straightened it back into place and smoothed the crease at the stapled top corner with his thumb. He slid the document into a battered and stained cardboard dossier that contained another nine copies. His proposal covered everything. *It had better,* Ryley thought. *It's worth trillions.*

Each copy—aside from the one Ryley had prepared for himself—began with a thorough non-disclosure agreement, to be signed and notarised before anyone turned the page. He'd been emphatic that a Notary Public be on hand, and George Sanchez had assured him at least two were invariably on the premises during working hours. Blaine Ryley wasn't being too particular. Later, when the patents were secured and the licensing deals done, the whole world could know, but until that moment, confidentiality was *critical*.

He'd hand-picked each of the men who would be in the room. The two most important were Sanchez, senior research scientist at the Oil Sands Recovery Institute, and Philippe Prudhomme, the organisation's president. The other seven invitees were a Who's Who of respected petrochemical engineers and geophysicists—the most prominent members of the elite sixty-person team that worked together every day to come up with new and better ways of exploiting the world's largest petroleum resource: the Alberta oil sands.

Blaine had dangled the smallest carrot necessary to entice each essential individual to show up. Every one of them had confirmed, but none was aware the others would be there. And not even Sanchez, who had the most in-depth knowledge about the new process, had yet been told about the upgrading component—its greatest strength and the reason Ryley's new technology was destined to reshape the global energy landscape.

Although oil sands megaprojects in northern Alberta had produced nearly two billion barrels of high-grade synthetic crude in thirty-odd years of mining, and were currently shipping a million barrels each day, most of the world had only recently begun to take notice. OPEC was probably the biggest agent in perpetuating the dearth of credibility—having always refused to acknowledge oil sands when tallying up the world oil reserves. Not that the oil wasn't there—but very much the opposite.

There was far *too much* of it.

OPEC listed the world's total reserves at just over a trillion barrels, its eleven member nations—Algeria, Indonesia, Iran, Iraq, Kuwait, Libya, Nigeria, Qatar, Saudi Arabia, the United Arab Emirates, and Venezuela—possessing nearly eighty percent of this. To admit that the Canadian province of Alberta had *2.5 trillion barrels* of its own would officially diminish the cartel's share to less than a quarter of the world total. An instant fifty-five percent plunge.

It wasn't just OPEC. Even the United States had long refused to recognise oil sands reserves as *real* oil. But that was just politics. And it was changing. The U.S. Energy Information Administration, after ignoring the oil sands for decades, had recently added the bitumen that could be easily mined using existing technology to its assessment of available reserves. Just seven percent of what Canada held, but it bumped the global total up nearly a quarterfold.

There remained one genuine intrinsic hurdle the oil sands faced, and it was cost. Compared to drilling and pumping conventional crude, it was expensive to get the oil out of the sand. About two tonnes of material had to be open-pit mined, moved and processed—then replaced—to create a single barrel of tar-like bitumen. Bitumen was very heavy oil—a long-chain hydrocarbon—and still needed to be thermally cracked to turn it into market-ready oil.

Every step cost money. Price had always been the oil sands' albatross.

That would change very soon. Blaine Ryley had come across his breakthrough idea by accident in the laboratory he'd built outside his home. He had been feeding steam into oil sand contained within a large pressurised steel cylinder, an increasingly popular method of liquefying bitumen in deeper deposits. He'd installed a rectangular stainless steel combustion cell at the bottom of the simulated formation to abate condensation, and left it to do its work. When his absence from the laboratory had been unexpectedly prolonged by an extended trip to town, the water reservoir had run dry. Instead of steam, hot air was pumped into the oily sand. By the time Ryley returned and realized what had happened, the bitumen beneath the surface had been thoroughly aerated—and ignited.

His experiment was on fire!

An alarming discovery, but putting out the blaze was simple. He'd merely cut off the air supply, and when the oxygen was consumed, the fire choked.

He'd been furious with himself for his carelessness until he realized what the heat had done. It had cracked the bitumen underground, and the resulting product was high-quality synthetic crude.

Ryley had stumbled upon the key to the oil sands.

As long as air was injected at the right rate, the oil would continue to burn efficiently, and the heat necessary for liquifaction and thermal cracking would be generated indefinitely. Through subsequent experiments, Ryley found the addition of a refinery hydrotreating catalyst dramatically boosted the efficacy of the upgrading process. This could be injected with water to provide the hydrogen needed for stable cracking. Fortunately in the laboratory accident, there had been enough residual moisture in the upper sediment layers from the steam injection for hydrogenation. The unified separation and cracking process was relatively simple, and all that needed to be done next in the real world would be to drill a horizontal well at the bottom of the formation and pump the wonderful liquid oil out.

Ryley had worked day and night to complete a battery of experiments and analyses to validate his findings, test things like process control and sweep efficiency, then perfect his methodology to ensure it would consistently exceed the most rigid market tolerances.

His process, Horizontal Air Injection Combustion Upgrading, or HAICU, had worked beautifully under every condition he could simulate, including the deepest and most inaccessible known deposits. Compared to traditional oil sands recovery—which required first stripping off all the forest and from fifty to seventy-five metres of the muskeg, soil, peat moss and shale that sat atop the oil-rich sand—HAICU would leave a minuscule environmental footprint. And it emitted a fraction of the greenhouse gases released by current methods.

HAICU produced high-quality, light oil. Even very heavy bitumen with single-digit initial gravity and viscosity as high as 12,000 centipoise was lightened to the equivalent of refinery-ready crude. A further and unexpected benefit, the sulphur and heavy metal content were both reduced during the process by better than ninety percent. Within the reservoir, the heat from combustion could be used to generate electrical energy—enough to power upstream operations and surface facilities.

Even the breakthrough had breakthroughs.

Upgrading oil in its underground reservoir, before it was produced to the surface, would also eliminate a major bottleneck. It took longer to run bitumen through the massive coking units used for traditional thermal cracking than to mine it, so productivity was forfeited while the product sat in queue for upgrader space.

No longer.

Most important of all, synthetic crude produced by HAICU would be incredibly cheap. With virtually no exploration costs and all oil sands deposits situated practically right beneath the surface in relative terms, HAICU oil would be less expensive to produce than Saudi crude.

This had launched Ryley into an unbelievable neurochemical-induced euphoria, and he was more than overdue for it. Forever, it seemed, his life had been an agonising dance-of-the-dead. And the previous June, he'd been fired by Canadian Petroleum—the oil company to which he'd given fifteen solid years.

He had devoted himself wholly to his work throughout that time, the very model of a model employee. Work had become more than the most important thing to Ryley. It was the *only* thing. He'd been fully convinced that one day, his commitment and sacrifices would prove worthwhile. He would be rewarded.

Then he'd sneezed it away.

A consulting firm retained by Canadian Petroleum had identified a problem with internal misuses of company resources—and Blaine Ryley had fallen victim of the ensuing crackdown.

It was the product of a little bad planning and a whole lot of rotten luck. Blaine had promised to take his wife Sara Christmas shopping in Edmonton, then twice postponed the trip to get in extra work. The Friday before the last available weekend, he noticed his name on the schedule for the next two days. Weekend duty. A lot of the guys owed him, but they all had plans. He couldn't force someone else to compensate for his own screwup. But he *had* to take Sara to the city. For the first time in his career, he'd decided to call in sick when he was not. With all the overtime he put in over the years, it ought to have been nothing.

Right after making the call, Blaine had gone outside to start the car. He'd plugged in the block heater the night before, but at minus forty-two Celsius, the engine needed time to warm up. When he returned to it a quarter of an hour later, he recognised the sickly sweet odour of antifreeze. A rapidly growing puddle of green in the snow confirmed the radiator had popped. It would be impossible to get a new rad in Hilldale until after the weekend.

He could have borrowed another vehicle. Or asked for permission to take the company truck. His supervisor was a laid-back guy.

But Blaine Ryley had done neither.

He'd used a company truck for personal travel only *twice* before—and both times had managed to work in a business errand to legitimise the trips.

This one time, he'd taken a chance.

And got busted—the fleet number called in by an unnamed colleague who'd spotted the truck on an Edmonton freeway. Later that week, someone would blow the whistle on an engineer named Jerry Poitras. Jerry was ordered to open the trunk of his car, where a box of company computer accessories was found. Jerry the equipment pilferer and Blaine the hooky-playing truck abuser had been terminated immediately *with cause*—and without severance pay.

"Embezzlement is embezzlement, regardless of its ugly manifestation," CanPet president Wilf Porter had said in his office when dismissing the two men—then repeated many times to others. Ryley had robbed the company of a day's sick pay and the cost of wear and tear on the truck from six hundred kilometres of winter driving. His attempt to justify the pilfering through overtime forfeited in his contract—and presenting his personal credit card receipt for the gasoline bought to fuel his ill-begotten trip—took big chrome-plated balls, Porter said.

The firing made the company newsletter—and the front page of the local paper, providing grist for gossip mills around town and throughout the industry. Just like that, the problem of resource abuse at CanPet had evaporated, along with Blaine's career options.

After the dismissal, his relationship with Sara had deteriorated even further, to the point where they rarely had a normal conversation anymore. He'd designed and built his own lab outside their home and begun an independent research programme with lofty hopes. Over the years at CanPet, he had come up with numerous ideas and theories for improving oil extraction processes, and now was his chance to put them to the test. They all looked great on paper, but one after another, failed in the lab. Every setback hurt Blaine more than once. First, the crushing disappointment of the individual defeat. Then the aftershock—the realisation that his quest was one step nearer to a disgraceful ending.

Ryley was quickly exhausting the savings he and Sara had put aside over the course of his years with Canadian Petroleum. He'd applied for a dozen research and technology grants, but had been turned down for every one. His business plan was weak, they'd said. Or that working alone, he was gravely understaffed and vulnerable. No history of success as an independent researcher, and no proprietary technology or proof-of-concept to show. A *bad risk*.

It was beginning to look like they were right. And he had no Plan B.

Then—at the eleventh hour, fifty-ninth minute—things had turned right around. Ryley had only recently begun to contemplate how wealthy HAICU would make him. He hadn't gone into it for money, but almost purely for vindication. Partly to show everyone else a thing or two, but most of all to prove his worth to Blaine Ryley.

Blaine was not going to *sell* his new invention outright. What he had ownership of was technology—Intellectual Property—and he intended to license its many components in a way similar to that in which computer software is sold. The software buyer does not acquire ownership of IP, but a license to utilise the technology behind it under agreed-upon restrictions.

So it would be with HAICU. He'd be the Bill Gates of oil—only richer!

Everything was in the proposal. Ryley would require an initial investment of five hundred million U.S. from each oil sands operation, and he expected at least four of the seven major players to buy in immediately—the others paying a hundred-mill penalty when they followed suit soon thereafter. Chicken feed to operations like AllSands and CanPet. After that, each HAICU unit would be licensed at a million dollars per year—purely to use the proprietary technology of its design. Ryley would have to decide soon whether he would manufacture the devices himself or sell licenses to third-party manufacturers, depending on how complicated he wanted his life to become and how extreme a capitalist he would let himself turn into.

And *then,* the royalties.

In the long run, that would be the most lucrative part. Ryley had devised a sliding scale for oil produced by his technology, beginning at just over twenty cents per barrel and decreasing by about one-twenty-fifth of a penny with every hundred thousand barrels per day an operation put out. Ryley estimated HAICU would advance oil sands production by a factor of twenty in less than five years. At that point, even at fifteen cents per barrel—the lowest rate on the scale—Ryley's *annual* royalties would surpass a billion dollars.

It sounded incredible, but in the marketplace, these fees were far from prohibitive. Even the smallest existing operations had capital costs of several billion, and the cost-effectiveness of HAICU production made the royalty structure exceptionally modest. By comparison, the government of Alberta—as the *de facto* owner of all minerals within the province's borders—charged a twenty-five per cent net revenue royalty as soon as a project recovered its costs. Even if HAICU pushed world oil prices down dramatically, the government's take would be still be well upwards of a dollar per barrel. He was just asking for a few nickels.

Ryley was stoked. He couldn't wait to present the HAICU proposal to the researchers at the Institute. They would be blown away.

Ryley smiled as he contemplated his absolution, the instant renewal of credibility—*fame* even—and the complete satisfaction he was yet to feel from this great victory. His innovation would change the world.

Then an icy tentacle crept up his back. He recalled the threats. *The fire.*

Somehow, someone had learned about HAICU, and whomever it was had done an excellent job of putting a scare into Blaine and Sara Ryley. A few clues had led him to suspect the threats had come from PersOil, a company with interests in North Africa and throughout the Persian Gulf. Or, more specifically, someone *hired* by PersOil to bully Ryley into giving up his work. The latest threat, he knew, had been nothing more than a final desperate intimidation attempt. No one was going to *kill* him or Sara over this. Murder was farther over the top than an oil company would likely go. At least *in Canada...*

RYLEY HADN'T TRULY *ENTERED INTO* AN ADULTEROUS RELATIONSHIP. More precisely, he had rediscovered a forgotten love, quite possibly the very one he'd always been destined for. He'd dated Tessa Engler for a time in the twelfth grade, and then came graduation. Blaine went to college in Edmonton, and Tessa moved to Toronto. They pledged to stay in touch, and did in fact correspond for a year before the communication sputtered out and stopped. Blaine had never been much for letter-writing—and he'd met plenty of other nice girls. Over the years, though, he'd thought of Tessa often.

When they'd literally *run into* each other at the pool hall—billiards being the one indulgence Blaine allowed himself when he became desperate for a breather—it had been pure fortuity. Tessa had returned to Hilldale six months earlier to be near her failing father, now a widower. Her own marriage had been dead and buried for half a decade, and she'd not long ago been granted a transfer to a government office in the Hilldale Provincial Building. After work that particular day, she had agreed to stop in for a drink and game of pool with a female colleague concerned about her reclusive existence. Though a long-time refuge for Blaine, it was the first time Tessa had ever set foot in The Stick Club. He had left the place minutes earlier to put in another long night at the lab, then ran back in upon realising he'd forgotten his credit card. At the time of his second exit, Tessa was on her way in—and their worlds converged once more.

Recognition was instantaneous, as were the fireworks. They'd embraced, and she'd given him a kiss. Hardly more than a peck, but a delicious and magical one. How many years had it been since they'd last set eyes on each other? *Fifteen?* The sizzle of sensory electricity spread from Blaine's lips all through his body, gradually reducing to warm, persistent flutters in his chest. He realized all at once how much he'd been missing.

Sneaking around behind Sara's back was causing Blaine tremendous heartache, but it seemed necessary. After years of grim sacrifice and misfortune, the most important ingredients in his life were all coming together, and he could not forsake the incredible blessings suddenly bestowed on him.

Ryley had already been neglecting his wife for years in favour of his work. After the *reunion*, he became altogether withdrawn from Sara—denying her any contact more intimate and avoidable than a passing brush on the arm. The only time he spoke to her was when he needed help in the laboratory, and then he limited the discussion to the work at hand. Sara had picked up on this. She asked strings of questions directly related to the process or the industry. It was easy for Blaine to talk about those things. There might have been some risk in sharing the info, but she deserved to know what it was she was assisting with and its significance. Or was it just his ego that compelled him to tell her?

Sara's hurting was palpable, and though it tormented Blaine, he could not allow himself to be intimate with her—thus being untrue to *two* women. At least this way, he could feel somewhat faithful in his relationship with Tessa, absurd though it seemed in the context of his wedlock.

He had tried many times to provoke Sara into a quarrel that might give him justification to throw up his arms and storm out. But she could not be baited. In twelve years, not once could he recall seeing her behave irrationally, though he could hardly say the same for himself. He would never succeed in pinning the break-up on Sara. And she was proving too loyal to ever leave him, no matter how miserable her existence became—a cultural thing, perhaps.

There was only one way to end it.

He had to do it himself. And to tell the truth.

The duplicity was driving him mad, as were the charades on which it was dependent. Whenever he'd visited Tessa, he always brought his pool cue, so as not to leave it visible in his SUV in case Sara came by. She would not enter a pool hall, but she *might* check the vehicle. He grabbed it from the back seat—dismantled inside the black leather case to half its playing length. The repetitive act of parking near The Stick Club and walking with the cue made him nervous, and seemed to reinforce the deceitfulness of his affair. One day soon, he would park in front of Tessa's house and march up to the door—with nothing in his hands but a huge bouquet of flowers. And it would feel *right*.

He needed to find a suitable way to confess to Sara, causing her as little additional grief as possible. Tessa was sure to pressure him again today. But he needed her to hang in a little longer.

Ryley was waiting, and surely Tessa knew it. Not just for the opportunity to end his marriage, but for the deal. Although he may have no longer been *in love* with Sara, he did *love* her, and cared for her far more deeply than his behaviour showed. If he divorced her now, she might become destitute while he in all likelihood went on to be the wealthiest man in the world. He would sit Sara down and tell her *everything*, perhaps in a few days. Right after he secured the initial investments. The first wave of money—not extending to the royalties, which came later—would legally be half hers. Perhaps it would do little to blunt Sara's immediate pain, but knowing he was leaving her with a fortune would go a long way in easing Blaine's conscience. And perhaps it would pre-empt decades of legal wars.

As for Tessa?

No question she would forgive him.

He smiled as he opened the door of his sunset-orange Honda Element, then his eyes rested on the dossier full of proposal documents atop the passenger seat. Inconspicuous as the tattered brown folder looked, it was *far* too valuable to leave in plain view. He flipped open the glove compartment and plopped it inside. Then, just to be sure, he locked the compartment with his key.

WHEN RYLEY RETURNED TO THE VEHICLE, IT WAS NOT JUST the red wine that had him light on his feet. He was thoroughly, completely, *madly* in love. Tessa overwhelmed him with a kind of thrill he'd forgotten about many years ago, believing that sort of sexual arousal to require adolescent hormones. There was nothing immature about his feelings now. Tessa was a brilliant lady—experienced, worldly, and emotionally solid. Ryley enjoyed her uncommon intensity. She could be aggressive—*forceful*, even—yet when he felt a need to take charge, she intuitively knew, and made way for him to do so.

Now, just minutes after kissing the woman goodnight, he already hungered to be back in the house, undressing her all over again.

Imagine a lifetime together. To do anything we like, making love anywhere in the world we wish to. Paris, Buenos Aires, Manhattan, Singapore... No place too expensive, nor any luxury beyond our reach. That, dear Tessa, is our future.

He unlocked the Element, climbed in, and flipped the cue bag onto the back seat. No other vehicles remained in the lot, aside from one dreadful relic that had probably been abandoned. The old beater sat unmoved from the place where it'd been when Ryley had arrived earlier in the day. It was a dilapidated Monte Carlo, with most every body panel a unique colour, and encrusted in rust. He'd parked closer to the abomination than he might have liked in the then-full lot, but made sure to stay out of range of its super-long passenger door.

Ryley inserted his key into the lock and popped open the glove compartment to make sure the all-important documents were untouched. *Of course* they were, but his mind would be eased once it was verified.

He choked.

It felt as if mighty arms had encircled his chest and were now crushing his ribs, allowing no air back in.

The dossier was *gone*.

Ryley practically dove inside the glove box, grabbing at its contents with both hands and flinging everything out. Owners manual, insurance card, vehicle registration papers, a map, some two-dollar coins, and a red gel pen.

I must have put it somewhere else. I MUST have...

He reached underneath the passenger seat and slapped desperately at the urethane-covered utility floor, but his hand found nothing more than a plastic ventilation duct. He twisted his torso around and raked the floor to the rear of the seat with his fingers, then groped beneath his own seat. *Fuck. Fuck! FUCK!*

Who would have taken that stuff? Whoever it was didn't care about the six bucks in the glove box—and had *re-locked* the goddam door!

It could be nothing.

Yes, surely there was an explanation. Perhaps Sara had come by and rescued it. *She'll scold me for leaving such important papers unattended,* he thought as he turned the key, but his gut told him otherwise.

"Tessa—" he heard himself whisper, without the slightest inkling why.

Then, an instant of whiteness more brilliant than Blaine Ryley could have fathomed, and every experience he'd ever known—many of which he'd forgotten long ago—flickered before him.

And so it began....

ORDER FORM

To order additional copies of Brad Steel's *MUTE*, or to pre-order *CRUDE* at a special discounted price, please complete the form below and mail to:

GRAPHOS Books
Suite 200, 10310 Jasper Avenue
Edmonton, AB, CANADA
T5J 2W4

Ship to:

Name:_____ Apartment:_____

P.O. Box:_____ Street:_____ Province/State:____

Country:_____ Postal/Zip Code:_____

Please rush me the following:

_____ Copies of Brad Steel's *MUTE* at $24.95 (Cdn) or $18.95 (USD)

_____ Copies of Brad Steel's *CRUDE* at $19.95 (Cdn) or $14.95 (USD)
(To ship immediately upon publication)

Autograph inscription:_____
(Please print clearly)

_____ x _____ = $_____
copies   price   subtotal

_____ x _____ = $_____
copies   price   subtotal

_____ add 7 percent GST in Canada

_____ add $5.90 (CDN) or $4.90 (U.S.) Shipping

_____ TOTAL PAYMENT

Cheques or money orders only. Make payable to GRAPHOS Books in Canadian or U.S. funds. Do NOT send cash. *MUTE* will ship Priority Mail within 2 business days of receipt (orders paid by cheque will be made upon clearing the bank). *CRUDE* will ship immediately upon publication.

To buy **books or eBooks** securely online by credit card or with PayPal, and for the most up-to-date information about Brad Steel and his novels, visit

BradSteel.com